Dark Star Burning, Ash Falls White

燃星落烬

BOOKS BY AMÉLIE WEN ZHAO

Song of Silver, Flame Like Night
Dark Star Burning, Ash Falls White

THE BLOOD HEIR SERIES
Blood Heir
Red Tigress
Crimson Reign

This is a work of fiction. Names, characters, places, and incidents either are the product of the author's imagination or are used fictitiously. Any resemblance to actual persons, living or dead, events, or locales is entirely coincidental.

Text copyright © 2024 by Amélie Wen Zhao
Jacket art copyright © 2024 by Sija Hong
Map copyright © 2023 by Sveta Dorosheva

All rights reserved. Published in the United States by Delacorte Press, an imprint of Random House Children's Books, a division of Penguin Random House LLC, New York.

Delacorte Press is a registered trademark and the colophon is a trademark of Penguin Random House LLC.

Visit us on the Web! GetUnderlined.com
Educators and librarians, for a variety of teaching tools, visit us at RHTeachersLibrarians.com

Library of Congress Cataloging-in-Publication Data
Names: Zhao, Amélie Wen, author.
Title: Dark star burning, ash falls white / Amélie Wen Zhao.
Description: First edition. | New York: Delacorte Press, 2024. | Series: Song of the last kingdom; book 2 | Audience: Ages 14+ | Summary: Determined to finish her mother's mission, Lan seeks to destroy the legendary four Demon Gods, while Zen, who made a perilous pact with one of these demons, seeks to use their power to save his kingdom and the girl he loves.
Identifiers: LCCN 2023022651 (print) | LCCN 2023022652 (ebook) | ISBN 978-0-593-48754-9 (hardcover) | ISBN 978-0-593-48755-6 (library binding) | ISBN 978-0-593-48756-3 (ebook) | ISBN 978-0-593-80922-8 (international ed.)
Subjects: CYAC: Magic—Fiction. | Demonology—Fiction. | Government, Resistance to—Fiction. | Fantasy. | LCGFT: Fantasy fiction. | Novels.
Classification: LCC PZ7.1.Z5125 Dar 2024 (print) | LCC PZ7.1.Z5125 (ebook) | DDC [Fic]—dc23

Printed in the United States of America
10 9 8 7 6 5 4 3 2
First Edition

Random House Children's Books supports the First Amendment and celebrates the right to read.

Penguin Random House LLC supports copyright. Copyright fuels creativity, encourages diverse voices, promotes free speech, and creates a vibrant culture. Thank you for buying an authorized edition of this book and for complying with copyright laws by not reproducing, scanning, or distributing any part in any form without permission. You are supporting writers and allowing Penguin Random House to publish books for every reader.

To those history has left behind

CHRONOLOGY

Warring Clans Era
~500 CYCLES

The Ninety-Nine Clans fight one another to defend their lands. Several dominant clans survive (most notably the Mansorian clan of the Northern Steppes and the Sòng clan of the Southern Valleys) to become powerful hegemons that take on other clans as vassals.

First Kingdom
CYCLE 0 – 591

The hegemon clans establish powerful courts, their rulers taking on the title of "king" in an attempt to consolidate power. Territorial disputes arise, yet the hegemon clans remain in a gridlock for most of this era.

Near the end of this era, General Zhào Jùng of the powerful Central Hin Kingdom begins a war to absorb the other hegemons into what he envisions as a single, standardized kingdom of Hin. The Mansorian clan—along with its vassals—puts up a fierce fight but takes heavy losses. The Sòng clan surrenders, and members become advisors to the Emperor. General Zhào becomes the First Emperor Jīn.

Middle Kingdom
CYCLE 591–1344

The unification of the once-fragmented hegemon clans ushers in an era of stability, in which the First Emperor Jīn and his ancestors implement policies to instigate the economic development of the newly formed Middle Kingdom. Most notably, they outline the Way of Practitioning to standardize all practitioning activity within the Middle Kingdom and as a way to limit the power of the conquered clans. Throughout this era, skirmishes and uprisings by rebel clans are swiftly quelled by the Imperial Army.

At the end of this era, Emperor Yán'lóng—the Dragon Emperor—grows paranoid about a potential Mansorian uprising. He believes that Emperor Jīn's policy of allowing the Ninety-Nine Clans to retain their own lands, cultures, and identities ensures there will be rebellion. Weak, greedy, and afraid of a decline of power, he binds the Crimson Phoenix, the Demon God that has lain dormant in his family's control, and begins his military campaign of the Ninety-Nine Heads Massacre.

The Mansorian general Xan Tolürigin, aligned with the Demon God the Black Tortoise of the North, leads the counterattack and is joined by former clan allies. They lose, and in a fit of rage, Xan Tolürigin flees north, destroying Hin cities and massacring civilians along the way. To this day, it is unclear where his spirit rests—or whether it rests at all.

Last Kingdom
CYCLE 1344–1424

The Ninety-Nine Clans are almost eradicated or dispersed and forced to assimilate into the Hin identity. The Last Kingdom survives for only eighty cycles. Then, on the thirty-second cycle of the Qīng Dynasty under the rule of the Luminous Dragon Emperor, Shuò'lóng, the Elantians invade.

Elantian Age
YEAR 1 (CYCLE 1424) — PRESENT DAY

Dark Star Burning, Ash Falls White

燃星落烬

PROLOGUE

And when the first of mankind gazed upon
the Light of the Creator and his Angels, he felt
awakening in his blood the magic of metal:
power to be used to bring Light to a world
which saw only darkness.

—*The Holy Book of Creation,*
First Scripture, Verse Thirteen

Elantian Age, Cycle 12
Where the Rivers Flow and the Skies End

Snow fell over the temple in the mountains. It coated the white pines in the gray of ash and froze over the once-burbling rivers. Silken drapes hung still between open-fretwork eaves of a hall whose waterfall no longer streamed. In the quiet of a winter caught in rosewood and rock, sky and ice, came the sharp sounding of metal boots.

"High General Erascius. I bring news from our scouts."

Erascius set the Hin tome down next to the Elantian translation he'd been working on. The metal bands on his wrists gleamed in the gray sunlight as he lifted his head, hair the white of snow, skin the pale of milk, ridged with scars from a still-healing wound. "Speak," he commanded, the word a sharp puff of his breath in the cold.

The White Angel, a patrol assigned to the Elantian army at the new base on this mountain, bowed his helmed head. "Our scouts have searched the School of Guarded Fists and the periphery. There is no trace of a star map, a musical instrument, or the Azure Tiger."

Erascius found himself fixating on the irritating way the Angel's armor glinted as he delivered this. His breath came quicker as his anger licked up like white-hot flames.

One month. One entire *month* spent in search of the Azure Tiger—one of the Four Demon Gods that gave the Hin immense power—and nothing to show for it. They, the Elantians, had crossed the Sea of Heavenly Radiance to bring light to this fallen kingdom, to take it and its resources under the wing of the great Elantian Empire. They had toppled the Last Kingdom's emperor and eliminated most of the magic practitioners of this land—save for a handful. Most pressingly, during their attack on the last school of practitioning last month, they had let escape a boy and a girl, each of whom had bound to themself a Demon God: the Black Tortoise and the Silver Dragon.

The two had nearly singlehandedly taken down the entire Elantian army during the battle. And they might have, had they known how to fully use the Demon Gods' powers.

This had put the Elantians in a compromised position and driven Erascius to focus on finding one of the remaining Demon Gods for himself. They had traced the Azure Tiger to this School of the White Pines, but the Hin practitioning masters had set it free before the Elantians could capture it.

The deaths of all those Hin masters had been little consolation for the loss of the Tiger.

"No trace of the boy?" he drawled.

"None yet, High General."

"And the girl." His voice had become dangerously soft. "What of the girl?"

"Last spotted by a western base. They followed her until

she disappeared into the Emaran Desert with two companions."

"When was this?"

"Several days ago, High General."

The metal cuffs on his forearms flashed as Erascius pulled on his metal magic—magic that had once punctured the weak defenses of the Hin Imperial Army and qì practitioners like arrows through parchment. Magic that had expanded the Elantian Empire across this vast, resource-rich kingdom within a matter of weeks.

This was what differentiated the Elantian magicians from the vast majority of the Elantian army, and why they commanded while others obeyed. The Royal Magicians had been chosen by divine intervention to channel the power of their god. And there was no magician more powerful than Erascius. Through the different-colored cuffs on their wrists, the strongest of other Alloys might have wielded the magic of two or three metals. Erascius wielded that of thirteen.

With thirteen, Erascius held the power to secure the universe.

But not enough power by far to face two Demon Gods.

With a flick of his mind, he flung the White Angel into the air by the man's steel armor, and held him there. Slowly, he began to squeeze the armor like a tin can. As the patrol began to choke, eyes popping and mouth gaping, Erascius thought of the pet fish the governor of this kingdom kept in his cushy palace in the Heavenly Capital.

"Several *days*," Erascius said smoothly. "My top priority—a prize that could tip the perilous scales our rule rests upon—and you take several *days* to report to me? You, a White Angel, appointed as an elite member of the Elantian Empire?"

The Angel's legs kicked the air; his lips, turning blue, were moving as he tried to speak. ". . . The . . . governor . . ."

One more second and Erascius would have pulled the man's heart from his chest, summoning the metal present in the man's blood with his magic. But he paused at the soldier's rasps.

"The governor has a message for me?" he said, and with a slow, deliberate twirl of his finger, he sent the patrol crashing to the floor. The man's blood splattered the slate-gray stone, worn smooth by thousands of years of Hin feet.

Trembling, the Angel pushed himself onto one knee. His armor was dented, no doubt still crushing his ribs and squeezing his lungs—Erascius could feel the seeping blood and the broken bone from where he sat—but the man valiantly recited the message between gasps of air. "The governor . . . asks . . . for an update . . . on quashing the Hin . . . rebellion . . ."

By now, Erascius's irritation had reached a simmer. He held the governor in no more regard than he did this wriggling worm of a man before him, but the politician had been appointed by the Elantian king, across the Sea of Heavenly Radiance, who had been crowned by the Creator. Erascius was born unto this earth to serve the Creator through the king, and he had to believe the governor, too, held a role in that service.

Rebellion, the governor had called it, the word ringing in this hall of the conquered, amongst the Hin's tomes and histories and dynasties of practitioning knowledge. Erascius didn't like that word.

He waved a hand. "Tell the governor to continue his games of politics and economics. I will focus on winning this war for us. And send for Lieutenant Lishabeth. We make for the Emaran Desert by sunset. I want word out to every single base west of here to be on alert for the Hin girl. We find her, we find the star maps, and we find the remaining Demon Gods."

Erascius turned back to the Hin tome, barely noticing as

the messenger limped out, leaving a trail of blood. *Winter Annals*, he'd translated, the Elantian language striking left to right before him, straight and true like a sword as opposed to the messy waterfall spill of Hin characters. The book contained a history of the clans, banned across the Last Kingdom's bookhouses by the Imperial Court. There was a single page Erascius had focused on, and it had given him all the information he needed.

He leaned over, the gold on his fountain pen gleaming as he finished the chapter, then leaned back to survey his work.

The Binding of the Demon Gods. Half the key to this new universe he'd stepped in to conquer.

And the other half . . . Erascius lifted his gaze west, beyond the silk curtains and a colorless winter sky framed in the rosewood fretwork of the temple hall.

The other half lay with the girl. It was she who held the star maps, the maps that led to the Four Demon Gods. It was she they needed to find in order to conquer this land.

"Run, my little singer," he whispered, the wind snatching the words from his lips. "Run far and fast, for I am coming. . . ."

I will find you, Sòng Lián.

1

> Power is survival. Power is necessity. Those who seek power must first take it; where it does not exist, they must create it.
>
> —Unknown, *Classic of Gods and Demons*

Elantian Age, Cycle 12
The Northern Steppes

The ruins rose before him like a graveyard, blackened bones jutting from the ground and gaping at a storm-gray sky.

Xan Temurezen drew to a stop. The steady crunch of his sheepskin boots against snow fell away, and silence swept in, broken only by the distant keening of the wind and his own heartbeat. Around him: a landscape shrouded in white as far as the eye could see. The color of mourning. It was as though the earth itself grieved the day a people and a civilization had died, their last moments now buried beneath the passage of time, the turns of cycles.

Zen held his breath as he knelt by the remains of a charred stone wall. All the ancient tomes and scraps of maps he had studied had pointed to this place, where the great Mansorian clan's palace had once stood—and where he, Xan Temurezen, its heir, had come to reclaim it.

He brushed away a mound of snow, revealing an engraved stone plaque. He immediately recognized the swirly, linear writing as Mansorian, standing in sharp contrast to the neat, boxlike Hin characters. Some clans, like the Mansorians, had cultures so distinct that they had their own writing systems, different from the standardized Hin language the Imperial Court had forced all to adopt.

Zen's memory of the Mansorian script had faded, but he could read enough to understand.

Palace of Eternal Peace

His hand gave a tremor; his heart tumbled in his chest. This was it: the lost palace of his ancestors. The place from which Xan Tolürigin, the Nightslayer, had ruled until the end of his civilization. The starting point of Zen's revolution.

Zen had been born two generations after the fall of the once-mighty Mansorian clan, following the war waged by his great-grandfather Xan Tolürigin against the Imperial Army of the Middle Kingdom. Zen's grandfather, then a boy, had escaped with a small faction of Mansorians and retreated deep into the unforgiving plains of the Northern Steppes, where they'd built a nomadic life hidden from the iron rule of the Dragon Emperor, Yán'lóng. That was the life Zen had known until, thirteen cycles ago, the Imperial Army had slaughtered what was left of his clan . . . and then, twelve cycles ago, when the conqueror had been conquered and the Hin had fallen to the rule of the Elantians.

I have returned, he vowed silently to the unquiet souls who slumbered beneath the snow. *I will raise an army, and I will bring our clan back.*

The snow stirred and the night pressed a little closer. And then came a rattling whisper, like the scrape of a knife against the bone of his spine: *Army? You would call thirty or so half-fledged children an army?*

It was the voice he had come to dread: the voice of his Demon God, the being that made him powerful beyond all measure, and the creature that embodied his shame. In the world of practitioning, demonic practitioning was dangerous and forbidden; the masters at his school who had raised him had taught him why.

Zen had betrayed everything he knew and loved in order to gain the power of the Black Tortoise.

Pushing those thoughts away, Zen turned to the small caravan of people following him. They, too, had stopped and stood huddled together in the cold, their long, pale robes made for the temperate winters of the south, not for the harsh northern climate. These were disciples of what had once been the School of the White Pines, the last-standing ancient Hin school of practitioning, where Zen had grown up. Less than one moon ago, it had fallen in an all-out battle against the Elantian Army and its powerful Royal Magicians.

The school's disciples had evacuated first, escaping to safety over hidden mountain trails and through forests that led away from the east, where Elantian occupation held strong. It hadn't been difficult to track them down. That night, as Zen had been prepared to flee from Where the Rivers Flow and the Skies End once and for all, he'd picked up on their qì. He'd sensed their grief, their absolute terror at having lost their home and their entire way of life.

It had struck a chord, a memory buried deep.

A boy, not eleven cycles old, wading through the burnt feathergrasses of his homeland, weeping and alone.

When Zen had found the disciples, he'd made them an offer: pledge their allegiance and join his rebellion in exchange for his protection.

With all but two of their masters killed and their former

home destroyed, all the disciples, just children and teens, had agreed. Even two former masters—Nur of the Light Arts and the Nameless Master of Assassins—had followed.

Zen wasn't certain why he'd made the offer. It would have been foolish of him to believe that a group of so few practitioners, most only half-trained, would be the army to take down the Elantian Empire.

No, Zen thought, turning back to the ruins of the Palace of Eternal Peace: the army he sought lay buried somewhere deep inside, along with the bones and magic of his people.

Growing up, he'd heard whispers, among those of his clan who were left, of a fearsome army of riders Xan Tolürigin had led, who were powerful beyond imagination—and summoned by *magic*. It was said the Nightslayer had led these riders to defeat entire clans, to conquer whole territories and shape the Mansorians into one of the most powerful clans in history, second only to the imperial family. Zen remembered late nights curled up in wools inside his yurt, the firelight outside flickering against the walls and outlining the shadows of the adults who sat around the fire, whispering in half awe, half fear. The faithful riders of Xan Tolürigin still existed, they murmured, and could be awakened with a certain magic, one so dangerous and powerful that only Xan Tolürigin had been able to use it with the help of his Demon God.

Now Zen had inherited his great-grandfather's Demon God; he would find and raise this legendary army and declare war against the Elantians. And if there were any traces of the secrets and old magic Xan Tolürigin had used to summon his army, they would be found within the collective tomb of his people and his heritage.

Zen had thought it through: he would target the Royal Magicians first. The strategy was an old Mansorian war proverb: The viper is only as venomous as its fangs. The Elantians were only as powerful as their magicians. Take them out, and the entire army would be crippled.

Zen cast his gaze about the group of disciples, knowing that, no matter how many times he searched, he would not find the only face he sought. Pebble-bright eyes, curved in mischief; smile-tinged lips like flower petals; chin-length hair like black silk that shifted when she turned to gaze at him.

Pain cut across his chest, followed by the torrent of memories and crushing grief that came with any thought of her. The black-glass lake, swallowing the light of the stars. Lan, standing on the same shore yet a thousand lǐ away in that moment, betrayal filling her eyes when she learned of his bargain with the Black Tortoise.

Please, Zen, don't choose this.

And he'd uttered the words that cleaved their path in two, once and for all: *If you are not with me, then you are against me.*

Zen ground his nails into his palms, dragging himself back to the present. "Shàn'jūn." His voice cut through the whistling wind. At the front of the line, a disciple turned to him, a young man around the same age as Zen. His slim face, once smooth as river water, was now ragged with exhaustion, his long black hair unkempt where it had once fallen like a sheet of ink. His lips were chapped, the cleft on the upper lip crusted with dried blood. Shàn'jūn's gentle eyes had once gazed upon Zen with warmth; now the spark in them flickered and died as he lowered his head.

"Yes, Temurezen." His voice was calm. Cool, with a tight undercurrent of caution. He had taken to calling Zen by his full name in front of the others.

Zen and Shàn'jūn might have been friends once—but that was when Zen had only been Zen, practitioner and disciple at the School of the White Pines.

Now he was Xan Temurezen, sole surviving heir to the

Mansorian clan and great-grandson of former clan leader and rebel Xan Tolürigin.

He had no friends. Only allies.

"Stay here until I send word. The place is filled with yīn," Zen said brusquely, then turned and strode through the yawning gates.

Debris and remnants of stone foundations littered what must have once been a magnificent courtyard. As he did with most new places, he turned his focus to the qì flowing within. Qì—the energy in the makeup of all things in this world, both physical and metaphysical—was bifurcated into yáng, the energy of all life, light, and warmth, and yīn, the energy of death, darkness, and cold. Qì was also the basis of all practitioning—or *magic*, as the common folk liked to call it. It existed everywhere and in everyone; practitioners were merely those born with the ability to sense it all and weave different strands of it into Seals.

He could feel the thick layer of yīn clinging to the ruins. So much bloodshed, so much pain, and so much fear in its final days . . . yet before that . . . Zen closed his eyes and dug deeper. Before that . . . there had been light and *life,* which he now felt glimmering beneath the layers of yīn like the lost warmth of a cup of tea gone cold.

Hints of a life he should have had, one he had never known.

Ah. That inevitable voice came again, this time the rumble of distant thunder. The one he had come to dread in the hours after dark, once the fires died and the voices of his companions gave way to silence. *But I have known it.*

Overhead, the clouds darkened as a shadow stirred beyond them. It yawned to life, stretching across half the sky—a shadow only Zen could see, with a voice only he could hear. An existence he had bound to himself, one that continued to expand inside him until it threatened to drown him day after day.

Zen stiffened as the Black Tortoise flickered into clarity. Eyes the crimson of war and bloodshed burned as they turned to him; a claw shifted so that it appeared to grip the distant mountains as the Demon God lowered its head to him.

I remember your legacy. I can show you that which was stolen from you. That which you wish to rebuild.

That gave Zen pause. The Demon God had been in existence since long before the birth of this world. It had witnessed the tides and turns of history and all the triumphs and failures of humankind.

And it had been there with Zen's great-grandfather when he'd ridden into wars with his legendary army. What if the Black Tortoise could provide clues as to the ancient magic Xan Tolürigin had used with his army?

Since Zen had bound the Demon God to him at Black Pearl Lake nearly a moon ago, he had devoted every ounce of his energy to shutting it out. A demonic bargain was always one of exchange: surrendering an eye, an arm, a leg, or, in the most extreme cases, one's entire body in return for access to the demon's power. If Zen refrained from using the Demon God's power, he would need to yield nothing further of himself to the being.

The bargain he had sealed with it echoed in his mind, haunting him as it had for the past weeks.

With each time that you use my power, with each soul that you deliver, I take more of your body. Then your mind. Last, your soul.

No—he would pay no heed to the wicked temptations of this being. He had pledged his mind to the Demon God's control as part of their bargain, but he refused to lose it so swiftly to the creature. That meant he had to abstain from use of its power unless absolutely necessary, for Zen planned to unleash the power of his Demon God only in the final battle against the Elantians.

Zen kept walking, footsteps sounding quicker and sharper. Directly ahead was a great forsaken temple. Traditional Mansorian and Hin architecture bore resemblances in the upward-curving green roofs and red motifs—the two cultures had thousands of cycles of intersection and commingling, after all. Yet here and there, Zen could spot differences: the curved side domes, alluding to the yurts his people inhabited; the touches of gold and blue, representing the sun and the Eternal Sky his people worshiped.

There were no doors to the temple. The entryway yawned open between stone pillars. Zen paused with a foot on the first step, the hairs on his arms rising as a draft emerged from within, as though something there breathed.

Zen's focus tightened, homing in on the qì inside the temple. He hadn't given much thought to the stifling yīn earlier—attributing it to the horrors of war this place had seen—yet now, as he closed his eyes and parsed the layers, alarm began to grip him.

There *was* something inside, something roiling beneath the surface of yīn energies left behind from death, pain, and slaughter.

Nightfire—one of the few family heirlooms remaining to Zen, a longsword forged by the greatest blacksmith in the north and infused with the essence of fire—hissed as Zen unsheathed it. He brushed his fingers against the small black silk pouch at his waist. Embroidered with crimson flames, the sigil of the Mansorian clan, it was enchanted with a Seal that allowed it to fit much more than its size belied. Practitioners used such storage pouches to carry an assortment of magical weapons, and Zen's was no different; its belly was full of fú, Seals written on strips of bamboo paper, whose intended functions were activated with a spark of qì at a moment's notice.

Enough ammunition for whatever it was that awaited within.

Longsword flashing silver in the dim light, Zen stepped forward.

The earliest scholar-sages and practitioning masters had agreed on one defining principle: that qì was meant to be balanced. In a place with an excess of yīn, the energies could fester into something unnatural, something monstrous.

Something demonic.

Zen stepped into the ruins of the temple, and the temperature seemed to drop. His breath began to frost as he moved forward, Nightfire in one hand, the other reaching into the pouch at his waist. He withdrew three sticks of incense and a strip of yellow paper with a red symbol on it.

With a flick of his wrist and a jab of qì, Zen activated the flame Seal on the fú.

Light lanced through the cavernous hallway. Out of the corner of his eye, Zen thought he saw things scurrying off into the shadows. With the burning fú, he lit his incense sticks. Their tips flared red, throwing the remains of the temple into sharp relief.

Pillars led down into a corridor swallowed by darkness. There were traces of former finery: a portrait on the wall knocked askew; a jade horse cracked in half; jewels, pieces of silver, and shards of ceramics half buried beneath drifts of snow that had swept in through the entrance. The place bore marks of a fire: walls blackened with soot, charred birch and bark furniture rotting on the floors.

The smoke from Zen's incense began to drift, following the course of the cold draft pouring in from the open doorway. Zen watched this peculiar sight for a moment.

The common folk used joss sticks to pray to their gods—whichever of the pantheon they chose to worship—but the origin of incense had been lost to time. It was made with a concoction of herbs that detected strong yīn energies: yīn repelled the smoke.

Which meant whatever creature lurked in here lay in the direction opposite in which the smoke traveled.

Zen began to walk in the direction of the phantom wind.

What have you to fear, boy? The Black Tortoise's low chuckle rumbled across the building like thunder. *You are the most terrifying creature to stalk these ruins.*

The Demon God was right. What Zen feared most was not the demons that lay in wait in the shadows of this temple.

It was the demon that lay in wait inside him.

Silence, he commanded the Black Tortoise through the bridge of thought that connected them. Over the course of the past moon, Zen had learned that the only thoughts the Demon God could hear were those he spoke willingly to it; the rest of the time, so long as he kept that connection between them severed, it must remain a dormant, separate entity from him, unless his life was under threat.

For now.

He snapped down the mental wall between him and the Demon God, reminding himself—as he did more and more frequently—to keep it locked.

The incense smoke was billowing in earnest now, and the cold grew stronger.

A shape appeared in the darkness before him.

Zen raised his sword and his other hand, ready to trace a Seal, but the light from the tips of the incense sticks illuminated a statue. It took him a moment to realize what it was.

Taller than a bear, the obsidian tortoise statue gaped out at them from the end of the hallway. As Zen lifted his incense to it, smoke streamed away from it in a straight line. The red tips of the sticks gleamed in its pit-black eyes, and Zen had the strangest feeling that it was alive.

Watching.

There's a Seal on it, Zen thought. He touched a hand to the statue, tracing the faint paths of qì denoting the Seal. It had once been inscribed in blood, and while blood faded with the years, qì remained. The strokes, however, were more complicated than anything Zen had ever studied—and the syllabary was *different,* he realized. There were loops and curves written in this Seal that would never have appeared in the practitioning Zen had learned.

This was *Mansorian* Seal writing.

His pulse leapt in his throat, and a tremor of excitement went through him. This was a branch of practitioning that his own people had invented, had specialized in—an art of practitioning that had been wiped from the history books when Mansorian demonic practitioning was outlawed and the Imperial Army slaughtered his clan. The clan's last practitioners must have used Mansorian Seal writing as a last line of defense, gambling on the fact that Hin imperial practitioners had never studied it. Whatever secrets the Mansorian practitioners had been guarding had remained safe for nearly a hundred cycles—and could very well include Xan Tolürigin's army of riders.

Zen's elation crashed with a devastating thought: he had no way to decipher this Seal.

Ah, the Black Tortoise drawled, *but I can.*

Zen froze, hand on the belly of the obsidian tortoise. In his excitement, he'd forgotten to shield his thoughts from the Demon God. The Black Tortoise's every word reminded him of the bargain that hung like a sword over his neck.

He knew very well how these bargains ended; it was the fate that had infamously befallen his great-grandfather, the last Mansorian demonic practitioner. Once he had been a righteous general fighting for the freedom of his clan, but his ending had been writ in blood and tragedy when he'd lost the war to the Middle Kingdom's Dragon Emperor, and then his body, mind, and soul to the very Demon God now bound to Zen.

Xan Tolürigin's legacy was marked by his failure to control his Demon God, which had driven him to madness. His entire story had been overshadowed by his slaughter of thousands of innocent civilians in his final moments.

Zen swallowed. The qì of the Mansorian Seal seemed to pulse, calling out to him. His clan's long-lost legacy, literally at his fingertips. A way to achieve redemption, to rewrite the tragic history of his people. Was he to walk away from it all?

Just this once, he thought. It couldn't hurt to use an iota of the Demon God's power to unlock this one door.

Just this once.

He issued the command: *Open it.*

The wind around him seemed to stir with the Demon God's satisfaction. Then power surged through Zen. He felt that core of demonic qì inside him—the Black Tortoise's core, a concentration of qì that gave it power and vitality—expand briefly, energies pouring out and mingling with the qì in his own body. It rushed to his fingertips, and Zen watched in half horror, half fascination, as his hand began to move of its own accord, tracing a Seal from a memory he did not have. He could feel himself pulling on the thousands of strands of qì of which the world is composed—iron, stone, birch, air, gold, fire—and weaving them together in patterns far too difficult to follow. This was a level of practitioning that even the masters at the School of the White Pines had not attained.

This was the work of a god.

Within seconds, the Black Tortoise was guiding his finger to trace the circle enclosing the Seal. When the end joined the beginning, the Seal took effect.

Zen watched the patterns and strokes—incomprehensible

to him—flare dark red wreathed in black. And then the statue began to writhe, its belly settling until it was as smooth as a black-glass lake. Zen frowned, squinting. Inside, fog seemed to swirl, drawing together into shadows. . . .

A screech rent the air as a blur shot from the statue's belly. Zen reacted by instinct. Nightfire slashed; he felt the soft resistance of flesh, then sinew, then the crunch of bone. The creature shrieked and stumbled back, and Zen was already tracing with his other hand, drawing on the strands of yáng energies as he conjured the Seal for fire and light—he needed light—

His Seal exploded in a shower of gold sparks, illuminating the chamber and the creature.

It was a woman—or had once been. Its flesh had been gnawed by maggots and rats, leaving a face of gaping holes that opened to bone. Eyes, milky and half chewed through by worms, stared straight and unseeing through wisps of long black hair. Yet most unsettling was its thick brocade páo, a robe furred at the collar and patterned in small gold-and-black flames: the mark of a Mansorian clan practitioner.

Mó, thought Zen. A demon—the most terrifying of the four classes of supernatural beings. He'd met one like this before: a grandmaster who had bargained his soul to a demon and allowed it to inhabit his body after death as a last line of defense to protect his school of practitioning from the Elantians.

A mó was formed from a malevolent cesspool of yīn that had festered with hatred and wrath; to vanquish it, one had to counter its wrathful energies with those of fire, sunlight, warmth—and, most important, the intangible emotions constituting yáng: Peace. Joy. Love. All that made life worth living, and all that separated the living from the dead.

Summoning those now felt like trying to ignite a fire from ashes.

Zen funneled qì into his fingertips, tracing the strokes of a

Seal—this time, on the flat of his blade. He clenched his teeth and imbued his Seal with extra fire and heat before closing it off. It glowed briefly before the light rippled across the length of his sword.

As Zen raised his jiàn, however, he paused. His previous encounter with the grandmaster-turned-demon had been close, the creature wicked and cunning and able to manipulate qì to conjure Seals. Yet there was something off about this demon—something uncoordinated, clumsy, about its movements.

It turned to him now, face slack and mouth open in a snarl, and pounced. Zen sidestepped and brought his sword up. Resistance, then clean air, and the creature's head fell to the ground with a thud. He waited, expecting the corrupted corpse to return briefly to the original form of its soul's owner. To his horror, the head continued to snap its teeth, and its severed body continued to lumber toward him.

Zen raised Nightfire again, hesitating. Mutilating a body was taboo in Hin folk culture, as the commoners believed that the soul within it would not pass whole through the River of Forgotten Death into the next life. It was a superstition—Zen knew that souls were made of qì and most returned to the natural flow of the world after the death of the body.

It felt like sacrilege, though, to slash through the Mansorian practitioner's corpse again. Still, it did not die. Its darkened nails scrabbled against the stone floor.

Something at the creature's waist drew Zen's attention. He bent and snatched it before one of the creature's flailing hands could find him. Zen activated another fú for light and raised his find to its glow.

It was a small brocade pennant, patterned exquisitely with golden horses and tortoises. Embroidered upon it, the black threads emanating qì, was a Seal: a Mansorian Seal saturated with yáng. Yet at its center were strokes indicating a sort of one-way tunnel . . . a trap for yīn.

Yáng attracted yīn, yet instead of balancing out the energies, this flag seemed to channel and gather yīn into the body of its wearer. There was no demonic core tethered to this body; rather, it followed the principle of a yāo, a supernatural spirit formed out of a pool of yīn that had cultivated an awakening. In this case . . . the pennant had *created* this spirit by drawing yīn into the corpse.

Not mó. Zŏu shī, he thought. *Living corpse.*

Well done, came the Black Tortoise's voice, accompanied by what felt like a cunning smile. *Your ancestors favored creating living corpses as mindless, unseeing guards that did the bidding of their owners without question. Where zŏu shī were found would also lie their masters' darkest secrets.*

Zen's heart began to pound. So this was another lost art of Mansorian practitioning. Perhaps, he thought, staring at the writhing corpse on the ground, some arts should not be practiced.

And who, his Demon God said slyly, *decides which arts should be allowed and which should not?*

Zen pushed the being's voice away and turned his attention to where the living corpse had come from.

The belly of the obsidian tortoise yawned wide, the draft Zen had felt earlier pulling inward. It was a portal. The Seal he—his Demon God—had unlocked earlier had been some form of a Gate Seal: a Seal that opened to a different location. And inside . . . inside were more shadows walking with a slow, lumbering, aimless motion. Yīn rolled out like waves, cold and dark and engulfing.

There were more living corpses beyond the gate. Dozens, perhaps even hundreds, more.

Where zǒu shī were found would also lie their masters' darkest secrets.

His grip tightened on the pennant with the Mansorian Seal. Zen took a step forward.

Behind him, someone whispered his name.

He spun, Nightfire raised. He'd been so preoccupied with the gate that he hadn't even sensed anyone's approach. And suddenly, he realized the darkness around him had become a cloak, tight and suffocating, distorting his senses. His vision warped; the shadows twisted. There was a monster beyond, he knew; a pale thing slithering closer, ready to devour him—

"Zen? It's me."

He blinked. The shadows withdrew, yielding to the glimmer of a lantern. Why hadn't he seen the light just moments before? It illuminated the face of someone familiar.

Shàn'jūn came to a stop a good distance from him, hands held in a placating gesture. "Are you . . . are you all right?"

Zen lowered his sword. "I . . ." He pressed a finger to his temple. "Yes. Forgiveness. I am on guard."

"The yīn in this place is strong," Shàn'jūn said, suppressing a shudder as he glanced around. His eyes widened as they landed on the still-writhing corpse. "What—?"

Zen stepped forward, obscuring the zǒu shī from Shàn'jūn's view. "What are you doing here?" he demanded. "I told you to stay back until I gave word."

"We felt disruptions to the qì and worried for you," Shàn'jūn said, lowering his head. "So I came to check."

Worried for you. A quiet kind of ache pulsed through Zen's chest. It was Shàn'jūn's disarming kindness that threatened to crack the armor he'd built around himself.

He couldn't afford that.

"And they sent you, the only disciple without the ability to summon even the simplest Seal?" he said coldly. Shàn'jūn had been a disciple of Medicine: deft in the ability to detect and parse different strands of qì and trained in the arts of healing—but with no ability to manipulate qì like most practitioners.

Shàn'jūn's shoulders slumped slightly, but another voice spoke from behind him.

"He is not alone."

From the shadows stepped a second figure, seeming to peel from the darkness. Zen's grip tightened on his jiàn as the Nameless Master of Assassins came to Shàn'jūn's side, his footsteps velvet and his presence like wind. He had a face for forgetting, features so ordinarily Hin and nondescript that if Zen were to describe the man, he wouldn't be able to pick out a single defining characteristic. Only those eyes—black and as cold as night, watching with careful blankness.

Of all the masters at the school, this was the one who had inspired something like fear in Zen.

He doesn't know, he reminded himself. *He doesn't know.*

Most people didn't know he had killed Dé'zǐ, the beloved grandmaster of the School of the White Pines. Except for . . .

Zen's gaze slid to Shàn'jūn. Another seed of fear bloomed: What would the disciples do if Shàn'jūn told them Zen had murdered their grandmaster?

"Thank you," Zen said. How long had the Nameless Master been standing there watching? "Nothing of concern here. Please wait for me with the others. I will ensure that this place is safe to inhabit."

Zen waited until they were well out of sight before turning back to the gate. The door to the past of his ancestors and the secrets of his clan had been wedged open. The darkness awaited, beckoning him to step through.

And so Zen did.

2

> May the Eternal Sky take my soul.
> May the Great Earth take my body.
>
> —Mansorian funerary rite, First Verse

Zen found himself on a stairway that spiraled downward. He suppressed his desire to pull out a fú and light a flame. Fear of darkness was too human a flaw; Zen would embrace the shadows, the unknown. He could function well enough by reading the movement of qì in the place.

And movement there was . . . far down below.

He conjured up a barrier Seal at the obsidian tortoise's belly, one that would alert him if any qì passed through it. Then he began his descent.

The yīn grew stronger with every step, and it wasn't long before something else joined the mix: the sickly-sweet smell of rotting flesh.

It was a while before his feet hit the ground, and he sensed stone yielding to wood before him. Beyond that . . . the press of yīn, like floodwaters beyond a great dam.

Zen drew a fú from his pouch. With a sound like the strike of a match, it activated, light flaring golden and illuminating a set of red doors before him. Where the door handles or knockers should have been was the engraving of a Seal. It was dead—there was no qì flowing through it—and brown stains ran through the strokes in the wood. Zen could no more read it than he could the other Mansorian Seals, yet the realization of what he had to do hit him.

He lifted Nightfire and pressed the tips of his fingers to its blade. A sharp bite, and blood began to flow.

Zen pressed his hand to the engraving of the Seal. Qì flowed from him in the form of his blood. The Mansorian Seal began to glow—and there, on the surface of the paint, characters began to form. *Mansorian* characters, ones that had been wiped from existence by the Dragon Emperor and his Imperial Court. Ones that Zen had barely come to know before they'd been outlawed.

Anger wrought a sharp ache in his chest as he stared at the words he should have known like the lines in his own palm. It was anger that made him careless, anger that drove him to open his mind and summon that voice with the dry rattle of fallen leaves and dead things.

"Welcome, child of Mansoria," his Demon God read to him. *Your instincts are correct. This Seal is one that opens only with the blood of a Mansorian clan descendant.*

With a great *crack,* the doors before him scraped open.

The living corpses came all at once: a flurry of limbs and hair and peeling flesh, mouths open in broken shrieks from rotten vocal cords. Zen barely had time to raise Nightfire before he was slashing through tendon and bone. He flung a handful of fú, feeling their sparks of qì as they activated and exploded. Gut and sinew splattered the walls and his clothes. The cloying smell of decayed flesh was overwhelming, and his head was beginning to spin . . . he needed help, he needed—

He didn't feel the Demon God take over, only knew when it relinquished its hold. When Zen opened his eyes again, the chamber was still. Empty. A Seal burned before him, wreathed in fire and shadow, lending its red light to the scorched ashes that fell around him like snow. He could sense the lick of qì all around and knew that it had somehow come from him, from the other consciousness inside him.

"I did not ask for your help," he said to the silence.

And the silence answered: *No, but you needed it.*

Anger scorched his throat, but he redirected his thoughts. Layers of powerful Mansorian Seals locking this place away. Countless living corpses standing guard. This place had secrets.

That was when Zen noticed the graves.

There were about forty of them, caskets half entombed in the earth and lining the length of the rectangular chamber. They were made of stone and tightly sealed, which was unusual, as Zen's people believed that the Eternal Sky and the Great Earth accepted their souls and bodies after death. Drawing closer, he saw that each casket was engraved with an effigy of a person in classic Mansorian garb. Strangely, their eyes were portrayed as open instead of closed. Zen had the feeling he was being watched.

At the center of each effigy's abdomen was another Mansorian Seal.

Frustration burned inside him. There was something here, something so tightly protected by his ancestors that it had survived an entire century and a foreign invasion. And he, Xan Temurezen, descendant of Xan Tolürigin, could not reach it because he couldn't *read* the language.

He swallowed the heat of his anger and made a decision. "Perform the Counterseal," he said, and his Demon God did his bidding.

A low rumbling sounded across the chamber as the stone lid of the first casket grated off. Zen leaned over the edge of the casket and felt his body go ice-cold.

Within was a corpse—undoubtedly Mansorian, its owner once a high-ranking general, Zen surmised from the gold hilt of the saber clutched between its fingers, the finely woven silk tunic, and the samite sash looped over its waist. It was so perfectly preserved, Zen might have believed it to be a man asleep had it not been for the vortex of yīn surrounding it. The weave of its energies was far more complex than the cruder Seals that had driven the living corpses: mindless, weak things already falling apart from rot. No . . . this corpse was different.

Ah. His Demon God's voice came with a new, peculiar lilt. Of recognition. *The Forty-Four.*

"What is that?" Zen demanded, hating that the creature knew more of his ancestors' secrets than he.

A pause. And then: *I could show you.*

Zen gritted his teeth. "Show me."

The burial chamber flickered, and he had the sensation of plunging backward, watching as the walls stretched with time flowing in reverse. The frozen ground beneath his boots became grass, as green as emerald beneath a sapphire sky. An army numbering several dozen were mounted on long-haired Mansorian horses, and Zen's attention was instantly drawn to the man sitting astride a black stallion.

His great-grandfather wore his hair long and proud. His earthen skin was encased in armor glimmering black and red, spear in one hand and reins in the other.

Across the plateau was the shadow of another army: tenfold in size, all cavalry, though their horses were slender-legged, short-furred, and shivering, clearly unaccustomed to the frigid cold of the Northern Steppes. Zen nearly did a double take when he recognized the sigil—crossed sabers clutched in a falcon's claw—flown on their flag.

The Jorshen Steel clan—that of Yeshin Noro Ulara and Dilaya, from the School of the White Pines—was here. Fighting an ancient war against his clan . . . before the Imperial Army destroyed both.

The Yeshin Noro matriarch heading the army raised her double sabers and screamed an order. With a rumble that seemed to emanate from the earth itself, her army charged.

Xan Tolürigin was smiling. His smile grew and grew until he tipped his head back and roared with laughter. His riders joined in until their laughter turned to cries of war.

They charged.

They rode hard at first, their bodies flattened against their surefooted steeds. Beneath their feet, against the grasses whipping past, their shadows stretched and stretched. Zen could almost taste the yīn thickening in the air as the darkness grew around each Mansorian rider, rising from the ground and morphing into monsters.

As the first Mansorian rider plunged across enemy lines, his demon spread amorphous wings of shadow spanning ten men and swept over them. A swirl of darkness, and all that was left was empty saddles and screaming horses, blood slicking their fur as they skidded off-kilter without their riders.

Another sweep of a wing, a dozen more Jorshen warriors gone.

Fear was a powerful thing, and Zen watched, frozen half in terror and half in awe, as it spread across the ranks of the Jorshen army. They began to retreat as the other Mansorian riders and their demons set upon them—but by then, it was too late.

The scene pulled away, and Zen found himself back in the silent burial chamber, with the screams of the Jorshen army still ringing in his ears.

The Forty-Four, the Black Tortoise whispered. *Otherwise known in your stories as the Deathriders of Mansoria. Forty-four of the most powerful demonic practitioners loyal to Xan Tolürigin. They once swept the plateaus of the Northern Steppes, establishing the Mansorian clan's foothold as one of the central powers of the Last Kingdom.*

Zen's heart pounded. The Forty-Four were the magical army of his great-grandfather that Zen had been looking for. When he'd sought out the ruins of the Mansorian palace, he'd hoped only to unroot some clues as to their existence.

He hadn't expected to find the most powerful army in history entombed beneath these very ruins.

It was as though the ancient memory he'd experienced had imbued him with an instinct that tugged him like invisible threads toward the very back of the chamber. There, in the space between two caskets, sat a great birchwood chest. Zen lay a hand on it reverently. The passage of hundreds of cycles had layered it thick with dust. Beneath it, engravings glinted in the light of his fú. The paint had faded with time, but Zen could still make out the figures: palaces in the clouds, immortals twirling in long silken sashes amidst a pantheon of gods that the Ninety-Nine Clans had worshiped, the legacy of which had passed to the Hin.

And between them—a sight that drew a sharp inhale from him—were the unmistakable forms of the Four Demon Gods. They took up the four cardinal points: the Black Tortoise of the North, the Crimson Phoenix of the South, the Silver Dragon of the East, and the Azure Tiger of the West. Immortals danced around them; the other gods mingled with them.

Zen stared at the engravings. What were the four most malevolent beings of evil doing amidst the gods traditionally worshiped by the people? His ancestors had worshiped the Black Tortoise, but he'd never thought of the Demon Gods as *gods*. They'd always belonged to their own classification: demonic beings with godly powers.

His heart began a drumroll. He was certain that whatever answers he sought lay in this chest.

"Open it," he commanded his Demon God.

A flick of its qì and a Mansorian Seal scorched in the air before Zen. Symbols on the birchwood chest lit up like molten lava.

With a click, the chest unlocked.

Zen leaned forward. What he saw sent a sharp pang through him.

The chest was filled with Mansorian regalia. With shaking hands, he lifted out a brocade robe embroidered with the signature red and black flame motifs. Ornaments and headdresses made from lavish coral and turquoise beads; jade rings and other jewels; bronze bells and iron spears—rich parts of his heritage that he had never seen before. Zen had grown up wandering the steppes with what remained of his clan. His parents had dressed in coarse, practical clothing suited to hard labor, and sturdy sheepskin boots that guarded against the cold and had a sharp grip in case they needed to flee.

He held up a sparkling headdress. He tried to conjure his mother's face and how beautiful she might have looked in this, but he found that he could barely remember her features—just the ghost of her laugh, the depths of her gaze. An impression of her as faded as the snows with the turn of seasons.

Zen carefully set the headdress aside and reached back in. His finger scraped against something hard in the chest. As he lifted it out, he knew it was different from the other items.

The tome had been produced with care many dynasties past and was well preserved. Gold stitching lined its edges, and the title was inscribed with black silk intertwined with the feathers of a red-crowned crane. Zen traced the looping syllabary of the Mansorian scripture and found that he knew these characters.

Classic of Gods and Demons

A shiver ran up his spine. He'd never heard of this classic before. There were only four classics known to all schools of practitioning—known, that is, to living memory and the masters who had survived the turn of the Middle Kingdom into the Last Kingdom.

He held up his fú of light and swiped a finger along the pages of the book. He was about to crack it open when there was movement in the corners of his eyes.

Clutching the tome, Zen pivoted to face the open doors. In the darkness, he found a set of eyes glowing as they watched him. A warped face, a *demon's* face, teeth glinting and tongue lolling as it grinned at him from the shadows.

Zen did not hesitate. A Seal sparked to life at his fingers; he sent a blast of flame at the intruder.

The darkness before his eyes lifted as he swiped another fú, its light dancing over the doorway. Where he'd thought he'd seen the creature's face, there was nothing.

And yet . . . he looked up toward the spiraling stone steps. There was no mistaking it: the air there swirled, as though stirred by a cloak that had just whipped out of sight.

Someone—or something—*had* just been here. Could they have been powerful enough to slip past his barrier Seal undetected? He could think of but two people here who might have that skill in practitioning: the two former masters of the School of the White Pines, neither of whom possessed a demonic face.

A bead of sweat trickled down his temple. His knuckles were white against the black bindings of the tome.

Right now, only three things were certain.

One: his ancestors had Sealed an army of their most powerful demonic practitioners in this very chamber.

Two: he needed to find out how to summon them.

And three: someone else knew all this, too. There was a spy in this palace.

Carefully, Zen set the *Classic of Gods and Demons* back in the birchwood chest, along with the rest of the Mansorian treasures. He had a premonition that the secret to awakening the Deathriders lay within the tome's pages.

But he had already been gone too long from the others; he could not stay any longer without raising suspicion.

He would have to return later tonight.

As he reached the door, he cast one more look back at the chamber—the one that had Sealed the secrets of the Mansorian clan for a hundred cycles. Forty-four caskets; forty-four Mansorian demonic practitioners. A legendary army at his fingertips.

With them, he could raze the Elantian army. With them, he could reestablish the Last Kingdom and see the Mansorian clan rule once again. See his great-grandfather's honor reestablished as he took back the kingdom from the regime that had taken everything from him.

Forty-four Mansorian Deathriders, slumbering in an undead sleep for the past hundred cycles.

He would wake them all.

Zen extinguished the light of his fú and Sealed the doors. Beyond, the dead held still in their sleepless slumber.

Waiting.

When Zen stepped outside the ruins, the disciples were huddling together in the snow, seemingly in discussion with Shàn'jūn. The Nameless Master and Nur, the Master of Light Arts, spoke softly; they broke away from each other when Zen emerged.

As much as defeating the Elantian Empire would not hinge

on these practitioners, perhaps it was still better to have allies. Zen needed to gain their respect and earn their trust.

It started right here, right now.

He would use his Demon God's power one more time, then, to establish his base, his stake on this land that had once belonged to his ancestors.

Zen turned to the ruins of the Palace of Eternal Peace and reached for the bridge to the Demon God inside him: *I command you to return this place to its former glory. Unveil it from the snow and the rot and the damage. Restore what you can of its beauty.*

He sensed his Demon God's cunning crimson eyes watching him from everywhere and nowhere at once. *As you command,* it rumbled, and he felt its qì seep through his veins, taking control of his body.

Their Seal swept through the grounds, and it was like watching time run backward. Snow and ice peeled back to reveal green clay-tiled roofs lined with gold along the curving eaves. Rubble and debris from broken structures rearranged themselves to become whole again; emblems of flora and fauna and the Four Demon Gods shed the dust and mold that clung to them, regaining their bronze sheens. Cracks along the walls closed as colors seeped back into the stone: blue for the Eternal Sky and brown for the Great Earth, the elements the Mansorians believed balanced the world. Flames roared to life on torch sconces, filling the place with light.

When the Black Tortoise finished, Zen felt that he was looking through a window to the past. The land around him was desolate, whatever life and civilization that had existed here eradicated by the Hin Imperial Army and then by the relentless turn of time. Yet before him stood a magnificent palace, gleaming gold and blazing fire. It was far from perfect—he could see the fissures to the illusion in the parts that had been too damaged to fix, in the stone that was burnt beyond repair.

But it was something. A start.

Zen looked at the palace of his ancestors and felt a thrill and, simultaneously, the opening of an abyss of loneliness inside him. Once, this place would have been filled with life: the bay of horses and the bleat of sheep, the laughter of children and the beat of drums, the calls of guards and warriors striding through the long hallways. He could almost sense the ghosts of their souls weaving around him in the now-empty courtyard and felt as though if he reached out a hand and peeled back a curtain of time, he might see his great-grandfather sitting on his throne, his young grandfather bounding down the corridors with his hounds.

One day, he thought, *I will bring it back. One day soon. I vow it.*

If the spirits of his ancestors buried in the slumbering earth heard his vow, they gave no response.

Something wet and cold landed on his cheek. In surprise, he looked up.

It was snowing. Flakes fell from the sky. *As fat as goose feathers*, his father used to say.

A song came to him then, from a memory that haunted him through the long nights. One that threatened to destroy the fortress he had built around his heart. A bamboo forest, a girl with quick eyes and a mischievous smile, spinning before him in a páo that whirled white as snow.

Tell me your favorite song. Because I'm in such good spirits, I'll sing it for you. Her laughter rang in his ears like the chimes of a silver bell.

You would not know it, he'd said.

Which means you must teach me.

No. I'm terrible at singing.

I'll more than make up for it. A smile sweet as spun sugar.

You mock me.

The snow had wet his cheeks. Zen swept his fingers over

his face before turning to the group—his followers—standing beyond the palace gates. "Fellow disciples," he said, and then inclined his head to Nur and the Nameless Master. "Masters—shī'fù. Welcome to the Palace of Eternal Peace."

He paused. Most places Zen had been had a name for the building, and then a name for the place itself—the mountains and forests and rivers where it was located. The School of the White Pines had sat in the midst of Where the Rivers Flow and the Skies End.

He had no idea whether his ancestors had given a name to this cold, dark stretch of land, but he needed one now. One that would stitch together past, present, and future. One that belonged to him as much as it paid homage to his ancestors.

Overhead, in the expanse of deep night, a sudden streak of gold light trailed through the ink-black sky. A falling star, here and then gone, brightly burning for the brief moments it crossed the heavens. A near-impossibility, in a night of snow and storm clouds.

The shamans of old from his clan would have read it as a sign.

Zen thumbed the crimson flames woven onto his black silk pouch. The name came to him as naturally as if it were meant to be.

"Welcome to Where the Flame Rises and the Stars Fall." He summoned a smile. Felt nothing of it.

Xan Temurezen stepped forward into the last moments of golden light and the blaze of fire from the torches.

From here, he would begin to make the world anew.

> In the great Emaran Desert, when the sands
> sing, it is a song of death.
>
> —Unknown spice merchant, *Records of
> the Jade Trail,* Warring Clans Era

Elantian Age, Cycle 12
The Jade Trail, Southwest

The sands were singing again.

Sòng Lián paused to listen, adjusting her dǒu'lì on her head and pulling the bamboo hat's gauze veil tighter over her face.

The dunes of the Emaran Desert rolled in a glittering ocean of gold beneath the slant of the late afternoon sun. Silence rendered the sand an endless stretch of stillness, yet as night came on, the wind picked up and the desert sang. The Jade Trail merchants traveling in camel caravans and the locals inhabiting the sparse, dun-colored settlements in this part of the kingdom had dubbed the phenomenon shā'míng, or "sandsong."

Lan would liken it more to the howls of a dying dog.

For the past few weeks, she, Dilaya, and Tai had been following the trail westward toward the border of the Last Kingdom that ended where this desert began; beyond lay a no-man's-land that led to the kingdoms of Endhira and Masyria, the great Achaemman Empire . . . and the mythical city of Shaklahira. By now, Lan had come to dread the sandsong and what it meant. It was an indication of worsening weather, that a sandstorm was on the horizon. Yet superstition ran amongst the Jade Trail traders and the locals that a shā'míng storm was no ordinary storm, that it was one conjured by spirits and demons of the desert. Though magic and practitioning had long faded from the minds of the common folk, who believed them to be things of myth and legend, superstitions still ran deep in the Last Kingdom, as though its people remembered an echo of its true history in their bones.

Lan and her companions had spent their first night in the desert huddled within the rammed-earth walls of a ruin, listening to the skies shriek and watching the stars turn dark. Yet when she had tuned in to the qì mingled in the storm, she had found nothing supernatural in its midst. Nothing to indicate that yīn and yáng, the two components of all energies in this world, were out of balance.

Some superstitions were simply that—superstition.

Still, they needed to get to cover before the sandstorm started and made it difficult to breathe and to see.

Lan shielded her eyes as she squinted into the distance. Sand dunes. Sand dunes *everywhere*. She'd had enough sand for a lifetime. For multiple lifetimes.

"Time to call it a day."

Yeshin Noro Dilaya's shadow fell over Lan as the girl came to a stop by her side. A few days under the blistering sun had darkened her skin from a pale northern shade to sandy brown. She'd traded her initial gauze veil for a less transparent one that obscured her entire face—and for good reason. With her eye patch, Dilaya was too recognizable, since she'd been one of the three Hin practitioners to best a high-ranking Elantian Royal Magician and the entire Elantian army was likely searching for them.

Lan braced herself for the pain that inevitably came when

recalling the battle that had occurred at Skies' End. The wound was still fresh, the pain a lake of sorrow to drown in. Less than one moon past, the Elantian army had finally discovered the clandestine location of the last school of practitioning. Two masters had taken the disciples—children and adolescents, barely half trained in practitioning—and fled; their whereabouts were still unknown. The remaining eight masters, including the grandmaster, had stayed to fight.

It had been a massacre.

Lan blinked away the faces of ghosts.

It was during the fall of Skies' End and the School of the White Pines, in the grandmaster's final moments, that Lan learned that her mother, Sòng Méi, had once been part of an underground rebellion that sought to end the cycles of power struggles the Hin and the clans waged over the Four Demon Gods. After the fall of the Ninety-Nine Clans and the Elantian invasion, the Order of Ten Thousand Flowers had continued to operate in secrecy at the school, working to track down the locations of the lost Demon Gods . . . and the weapon that would return the cores of their essence back into the qì of the world.

The Godslayer, once meant to serve as a balance to the endless power the Four Demon Gods held, had been hidden away for dynasties by the imperial family as they sought to control all four. The imperial family had built a secret palace to store their most sacred possessions: Shaklahira, the Forgotten City of the West. Its location and form had been kept so secret throughout the ages that now it was believed to be nothing more than a myth.

Only one place in the Last Kingdom remained where all the myths and legends of these lands had been preserved: the City of Immortals, whose inhabitants had served as their guardians. Once ruled by the fabled Yuè clan, rumored to have cultivated the secrets to immortality, the city was said to house ancient tomes of history in a magical library that appeared once every full moon. If there was a map or record of Shaklahira to be found, it would be in the City of Immortals.

Most important, the city had withstood the trials of time, war, and regime shift. Today, it remained standing in the Emaran Desert as a trading post on the Jade Trail, known to the locals as Nakkar. And it was heavily guarded by Elantian forces.

Lan cast her gaze up the trail they followed. It was nearly empty at this hour, save for a few distant caravans, their shadows stretching long fingers across the unbroken dunes. Trudging along behind her, dressed in a purple turban and a black desert tunic they'd bartered from one of the Achaemman traders, was Chó Tài. Tai had learned of the Forgotten City from none other than the crown prince, as they had grown up together in the Imperial Palace. There, Tai had been raised to serve the emperor as their Spirit Summoner—for as a member of the Chó clan, Tai specialized in communing with ghosts and hearing whispers of the dead.

This was evidenced by the small silver bell that hung from his belt. It was no ordinary bell but a family heirloom from the clan of Spirit Summoners. Tai's bell chimed only in the presence of supernatural qì.

"Hurry up, Chó Tài," Lan called. "Why did your mother gift you with long legs if you're not going to use them?"

They'd made the decision to stick to the Jade Trail and take on the disguise of traveling merchants in order to blend in with the ebb and flow of traders from all corners of the east and west. Yet whereas trade caravans gladly stopped to rest and replenish supplies at the trade checkpoints, Lan, Dilaya, and Tai had avoided the checkpoint towns, going off-trail to sleep under the stars, huddled beneath the cloth pallets they carried. There was good reason for this: though the Elantian military presence rested heavily on the eastern coast of the Last Kingdom, soldiers guarded the gates of all towns along the Jade Trail to monitor the pulse of activities out west. Stopping at a checkpoint meant potentially attracting the attention of Elantian patrols—or worse, Royal Magicians.

Traveling along the Jade Trail also meant that they could not use the Light Arts to travel faster, for using any form of practitioning risked giving away their locations and identities to the Royal Magicians. Though Hin practitioners used a different branch of practitioning from Elantian metalwork, each had the ability to sense the presence of the other's magic, all of which used qì. This meant Lan had not been able to wield her two most precious possessions: a black clay ocarina inlaid with a mother-of-pearl lotus, and a small dagger that glinted like stars.

Lan's throat was scratchy with thirst as she watched Tai struggle up a dune.

"Did I"—the Spirit Summoner panted—"did I give you permission to call me by my truename?"

He then promptly collapsed onto the sand.

Lan crouched next to him. "Conceit's a little difficult for you to pull off, given your current circumstances." She plucked at his purple turban, which had been knocked askew. "Though I have to admit, this color suits your gold-gray eyes. Quite becoming on you."

"Becoming. I am becoming a sand spirit," mourned Tai.

Over the past few weeks, the Spirit Summoner's sarcasm had slowly returned, almost as though he were back to his former self. Yet there were moments when Lan caught him staring into the distance toward the east, and she knew whom he thought of: Shàn'jūn, the gentle Medicine disciple he loved.

An ache tightened Lan's chest at the thought of Shàn'jūn.

The last time she'd seen him, he'd been kneeling in the rain, attempting to revive their grandmaster.

Her father.

Whom Zen had murdered.

Zen.

Lan's breath hitched as a visceral pain seared her heart: torrential grief and burning fury. And beneath it all, a bitter self-loathing that she had once trusted him, loved him, and he had used that to betray her. He had made a bargain with the Black Tortoise, bartering his mind, body, and soul in exchange for its unfathomable power—a most dangerous, dark form of practitioning that had almost torn apart the Last Kingdom.

With it, he had killed the grandmaster, who had raised him.

In a memory that haunted her waking moments and made her nightmares, he stood before her, rain lashing them in a storm of demonic qì, his eyes utterly black and his face devoid of emotion. Beautiful—Zen had always been beautiful. Terrifying.

Demonic.

I have chosen my path. If you are not with me, then you are against me.

"We may not make it to the city tonight."

Lan's thoughts snapped back to the present. Dilaya had parted her veil: her remaining eye was the gray of sword metal, her mouth a slash of red across a long and angular face that bore a unique beauty in its fierceness. With her one hand, she shook out a parchment map.

"Ruins. More abandoned ruins," Tai moaned from the ground. "Sleeping on cold rocks. Once, I slept on silk sheets in a palace."

Lan scooted close to Dilaya, searching the map. According to their calculations, they would have arrived at Nakkar just past nightfall—but with dusk looming on the horizon and the sands beginning to sing, the prospect of a full meal and soft bed looked like a distant dream.

She traced a finger down the Jade Trail map, searching closer to their current location. They'd bartered the map from a Jade Trail merchant, who'd taught them the key: a camel represented a caravanserai stop (where one could fill up waterskins and buy a day or two's worth of dried foods), a house meant a town with shelter, and a crown with wings represented an Elantian trade checkpoint, a bustling town with plentiful supplies and resources specifically designed to welcome Jade Trail travelers.

"No trading posts in the periphery," Dilaya said. "I checked already." She looked up and sighed. The thought of another night sleeping on cold, hard ground weighed on them all.

Dilaya dug into her storage pouch, which, like each practitioner's, bore a stitching unique to her identity. Dilaya's was sheepskin with two crossed sabers clutched in a falcon's claw, whereas Tai's was gray silk stitched through with a white bell. Both bore the sigils of once-powerful clans that had been wiped out under the Dragon Emperor's brutal reign in the era of the Last Kingdom.

Dilaya withdrew her hand. Between her fingers winked a contraption that resembled two concentric rosewood boards, painted with obscure fēng'shuǐ symbols and rimmed in gold. A silver needle in the center spun gently with the motion. The luó'pán, or lodestone compass, was a geomancy tool and an utter mystery to Lan. Apparently, the oldest scholars of geomancy had designed it to track the stars in the sky and the movement of the ground in order to derive the precise direction of a place or object.

Lan thought it all a heap of useless turd if one couldn't even read the thing. "What do you need that for? We already have the map."

Dilaya placed the luó'pán flat on her palm and squinted down at it. The dial settled, shifting slightly as though to an invisible wind before growing still. "The luó'pán works on a combination of astrology and qì and can detect things that aren't on a map. I'm going to look for waves in the qì that suggest wooden or dirt structures. I just need to understand this symbol. . . . Chó Tài, do you remember what it means when the first trigram on the earthly plate crosses with the seventh trigram on the heavenly plate and the dial points to a flute and a horse?"

Lan could no longer resist. "A musical pile of horseshit?" she suggested.

Dilaya looked daggers at her, and Lan could practically see all of the Kontencian Analects working their way up the girl's throat. Their relationship had progressed from mutual dislike to a form of alliance and even respect, stemming from their common goal. Still, Lan couldn't resist needling Dilaya once in a while for fun, and the latter was only too glad to bite back.

"Hilarious," Dilaya snapped. "Perhaps you'd actually be able to *help* if you'd paid more attention in Master Fēng's classes—"

She stopped suddenly and drew a sharp breath. Lan's grin slipped from her face, and Tai sat up slowly, his gold-rimmed eyes reflecting the setting sun between his black curls. As the sandsong filled the silence with its mournful wails, Lan knew with certainty that they all shared a memory: Skies' End falling, the masters staying to protect the Azure Tiger, the Demon God they had kept hidden within the mountain for so long. The home they had lost to the Elantians in a night of rain and fire and blood. And, for Dilaya, the loss of her mother, Yeshin

Noro Ulara, the school's Master of Swords and the matriarch of the Jorshen Steel clan, a role that now fell to Dilaya.

The three of them bore an unspoken sentiment of guilt, the possibilities of *what if.* What if they had stayed behind with the masters to fight? What if they had been able to lure the Elantian army away from Skies' End?

What if Lan had been able to command the power of the Silver Dragon of the East, the Demon God her mother had bound inside Lan?

She could feel it within her now as her thoughts turned to it with a mixture of fear and disgust. Over the past few weeks, Lan had come to find that she could communicate with the Demon God when she willed it; when she didn't, it remained dormant within her, a silver core of unimaginable power she carried. Demonic practitioning bargains differed, yet the only bargain Lan had known of had been Zen's: a contract promising that with each use of the Black Tortoise's power, he gave more of his body, mind, then soul over to the god.

It was Lan's mother who had Sealed the Demon God within herself and, in her dying moments, in Lan in a desperate attempt to hide it from the Elantians twelve cycles ago. The price her mother had paid for the bargain was her soul.

It was a bargain Lan had replaced with her own: at the end of her contract with the Demon God, it would release Sòng Méi's soul—and take Lan's instead, for all eternity.

Lan touched the Seal imprinted on her wrist by the Silver Dragon. It contained the terms of their bargain. The sands had begun wailing louder now, an eerie phantom chorus that swept across a rapidly darkening sky.

"We should use the Light Arts," she said to Dilaya.

"And risk being discovered? I haven't walked in these godsdamned sands for *days* just to blow our cover—"

"There are no checkpoints nearby," Lan pointed out. "And at this point, with the sandstorm so close, any Elantian Royal Magicians *and* patrols would have returned to their checkpoint towns." Truthfully, anyone with some common sense would have found shelter somewhere indoors by now.

Dilaya hesitated. Lan could see the girl wavering as another gust of sand howled against them.

"Agree. *A-gree,*" Tai chimed in, sitting up, revived, with sand pouring from his tousled hair. His hand went to his spirit bell, which remained quiet as he carefully dusted it off. "Either we go or we die here in this sandstorm."

"Or get our souls sucked out by sand demons," Lan added. She mimicked the sound of slurping noodles and smacked her lips.

Dilaya looked as though she were considering murdering Lan. *"Fine,"* the Jorshen Steel matriarch growled. "But if we happen to run into any magicians, Sòng Lián and Chó Tài, I swear on your ancestors' graves I'll fish you both out from the River of Forgotten Death just so I can kill you again." She reached for her luó'pán.

And froze.

On the lodestone compass, which glinted gold beneath the sinking sun, the silver needle had begun to move. It jerked left, then right, then left again, and then began to spin. Faster and faster, until it became a blur.

Dilaya's lips parted. "What—"

But Lan was looking at something else.

Over the western horizon, an unnatural darkness had spread, obscuring the embers of sunset. Atop the cresting dunes, shadows had appeared, stretching long and distorted.

A caravan. Lan could make out the shapes of camels, a sight they'd come across not infrequently as they followed the Jade Trail. Yet something was wrong. The camels were approaching too fast—spread out and charging in their direction. As though fleeing something.

Lan opened her mouth to speak, but that was when they heard it: distant cries shattering the mournful rise of sandsong.

A gust of wind slammed into them, cold and biting to the core and suffused with a stench of energy that choked Lan. She'd encountered this type of qì only a handful of times before.

Demonic qì.

A deep rumbling echoed through the desert, like the roll of a great celestial drum.

And then Tai's spirit bell began to scream.

4

> Of all the Ninety-Nine Clans, perhaps the most mysterious is the Yuè, who have long perfected the secrets to cultivating immortality and whose roots may, in fact, not derive from mortals in the first place.
>
> —Various scholars, *Studies of the Ninety-Nine Clans*

Lan was already sliding her ocarina from the pouch on her belt, heart pounding in time to the shrill peals of Tai's bell. The sand beneath their feet was trembling, little pockmarks forming as though invisible raindrops splattered on the ground.

The sand dunes were rising into the sky, cresting higher and higher like waves. Pushing steadily toward them.

"Mó," Tai croaked. *Demon.*

Fear tightened Lan's throat, and with that, the other being inside her stirred to life. Eyes the blue of ice opening a crack. The shimmer of silver scales in the dark. A voice like a night wind rushed to fill her head.

Mó, the Silver Dragon of the East said softly. *I sense the wrath in the soul at its core.*

Lan gritted her teeth and broke the connection between them. The sole obligation of the Demon God was to protect her when her life was in danger; at all other times, she had been careful to keep a mental wall up between them, so it had no access to her thoughts.

As it retreated, noise of this world filtered back: the distant shrieks of the scattered caravan merchants, the howl of the sandsong, and the sand spirit that prowled forward, eclipsing half the sky.

Before her, Dilaya drew out Falcon's Claw. The curved dāo was an heirloom of the Jorshen Steel clan and her most prized possession, entrusted to her by her mother in the moments before death. From this angle, Lan could only see Dilaya's loose left sleeve billowing in the wind, her black eye patch, and the stubborn set of her chin as she glared up at the malevolent spirit.

"Dilaya. No. *No*," Tai called from behind. "You cannot defeat it. You cannot. The Elantian magicians. They will find us."

They had avoided practitioning for the past moon to remain undetected by the Royal Magicians. If they fought now, there was a chance the sand spirit's qì would mask theirs. Yet there was also a chance they would reveal their location.

Dilaya tilted her head. In the dim yellow light, her mouth was a crimson slash. "And what, Chó Tài? You would run and leave those merchants to the mercy of that mó?"

"Not," Tai mumbled. "Not what I meant."

Dilaya slashed the air with Falcon's Claw, its blade glinting in the last sliver of sunlight filtering through the smothered skies. "Did we survive Skies' End just so we could watch our people die? Did our masters train us to become practitioners just so we could cower before evil?" Her eye shone as she looked at her companions, and in her gaze, Lan knew, were the ghosts of all they had lost. Their masters. Dilaya's mother. Lan's parents. Shàn'jūn. Their home. "I am a disciple of the School of the White Pines. I am the matriarch of the Jorshen Steel clan. And I am a practitioner of the Last Kingdom. I will not stand by while my people die."

With that, she leapt, a powerful jet of qì she'd channeled through the soles of her feet propelling her high into the sky.

Lan's grip tightened on her ocarina, her thumb brushing over the familiar grooves of the mother-of-pearl lotus inlaid into the sleek black surface. This instrument was how she channeled the Art of Song, a long-lost magic that ran in her clan bloodline. Practitioners of the Art of Song wielded qì through their music, weaving Seals with combinations of notes and melodies that drew upon the infinite threads of energies in this world. Her mother had been the last practitioner to wield this art and had left the ocarina for Lan.

Within the instrument, Lan's mother had hidden the keys to finding the Demon Gods: four star maps, which only Lan could coax out through the Art of Song. The Black Tortoise was with Zen now and the Silver Dragon with her, leaving the remaining two Demon Gods, the Azure Tiger and the Crimson Phoenix, unaccounted for.

That was why every single Elantian Royal Magician was after her. The magician known as Erascius, who led the war against the Hin practitioners, had a personal vendetta against Lan: he had killed her mother twelve cycles past and was now intent on killing Lan and binding the Silver Dragon to himself, along with the rest of the Demon Gods. Then he would crush whatever remained of the Hin practitioners and any hopes of rebellion they harbored.

Lan looked to Dilaya, now a small red speck in the distance, charging headlong toward the great sand demon. To the caravanners disappearing beneath its roiling, suffocating claws. Her knuckles whitened on her ocarina. Fight, and they risked revealing their location to the Elantian army. Run, and they condemned dozens of innocents to die.

It had always come down to this: choices in a conquered land. And as she stood, frozen in indecision, a memory came to her: Zen, standing across from her by the black-glass lake, his face contorted in rage and grief. *Choices are for those with privilege, Lan. You said it yourself, that we're given shit choices and we have to make the best of them!*

Her throat closed; her vision blurred. There was a sudden ache in her chest, because these words from the boy she'd been regarding as an enemy and a traitor suddenly rang true.

Shit choices, Lan thought, squaring her shoulders. No matter what, she knew what she would always choose. Māma had told her that power was meant to be used to protect those without it.

Lan opened her senses, filling herself with qì, pushing it down, down to the soles of her feet.

She kicked off.

The sky was tinged a suffocating shade of yellow. The wind rose to a full scream, yīn energies rolling forth like great tidal waves, threatening to pull Lan under. She landed and staggered before falling to her knees, one hand raised to shield her face as the yīn pressed against her chest.

"Dilaya," she gasped. *"Dilaya—"*

The wind ripped her voice from her. Sand choked her nose and her throat. The stench of demonic qì threatened to suffocate her.

A shadow at the corner of her eye. The faint chime of a bell.

Tai knelt by her. Qì bloomed from his fingertips into a Seal, shimmering a ghostly shade of purple. She recognized the arrangement of scripture within it that conjured the Shield Seal, a barrier against the energies battering them as well as the sand and debris flying around.

As her vision cleared, there was movement before them.

Beneath the storm, a figure danced and weaved: a duet of sash and steel. Bursts of qì sparked from the tip of Dilaya's dāo, trailing crimson in the air as they formed Seals. Over the course of their travels, Lan had learned that the one-handed girl had worked with her mother, the Master of Swords, to devise a way to channel her qì through her blade, since it was impossible for her to spar with a weapon in one hand while conjuring Seals with the other, as most practitioners did.

Falcon's Claw slashed like an extension of Dilaya's body, slicing through a whirl of sand.

For a half breath, a gap formed in the sand, exposing the core of the demon: a shimmering being, a river of starlight, sand turned snow.

Lan saw it for just a moment before the sand closed over again. Dilaya, too, must have caught sight of it. Her movements stuttered as she turned to look back at where the being had appeared.

A mound of sand slammed into her midriff, knocking her into the air.

Lan cried out. Tai's face drained of color, his gaze confirming what she feared: they weren't getting out of this alive.

Not without a miracle.

Lan's hands shook as she grasped her ocarina. She had trained barely one moon at the School of the White Pines before the Elantians had invaded it, and much of the reason for her strong qì and innate practitioning abilities had been the Demon God her mother had Sealed within a scar in her wrist.

Without the Demon God bound to her, she was nothing. A barely trained disciple of practitioning. A street rat who'd survived by wits and luck in a colonized land.

Tai was gesturing, his qì stirring as he pulled it to his fingertips and began to form a Seal. It shimmered for a moment, sputtering against the gale of the sand demon before flickering out. As a Spirit Summoner, Tai was practiced in the art of seeking spiritual qì and hearing the voices of the dead. Seals and combat were not his strengths.

Lan looked at Dilaya's crumpled figure a dozen or so steps ahead, then at the vortex of sand that had opened overhead, a tunnel of darkness and demonic qì that howled with the grief and wrath of all the souls the demon had consumed.

It is the duty of those with power to protect those without.

Lan leapt forward. She heard Tai calling her name as she broke through the barriers of his Shield Seal. The tempest had risen to a climax, lightning cleaving the darkness, demonic qì threatening to drown her.

She slammed into the ground by Dilaya's side. The girl was unconscious, strands of hair loose from the two braided buns she wore in her signature hairstyle. Overhead loomed the sand demon's misshapen gullet, filled with the wails of a thousand thousand souls.

Curse the skies if I die saving the life of Yeshin Noro Dilaya, of all people, Lan thought. *She'll never hear the end of it from me in the next world.*

Just as Lan raised her ocarina to her lips, a hunk of hardened sand slammed into her stomach.

She barely registered the impact. All she knew was that one moment she knelt with her ocarina at her mouth; the next, she lay in the sand, winded and dizzy, a chasm of darkness and demonic energy closing in on her.

Death closed its teeth over her.

And something bit back.

The world turned a searing white as frost-colored flames ignited the swirling sand. The darkness drew back, and a pale light rose. Scales like snow, serpentine form glowing like the moon.

The Silver Dragon rose from Lan and towered over the sand demon. It gave one slow blink of its frigid blue eyes, almost lazily. Then it struck.

The sand demon's roar shook the ground beneath as it

collapsed under the might of a Demon God the way paper caved beneath steel. The Silver Dragon was silent as its body, long enough to coil across the entirety of the horizon, wrapped around the sand demon's form.

Squeezed.

Demonic qì exploded. Lan held on to Dilaya as the sand beneath them writhed and the world rocked like an ocean in a storm.

Slowly, all quieted.

Lan opened her eyes. Clear violet skies, rimmed by the corals of sunset. Clouds the blush color of magnolias, which rushed over the darkening skyline like a celestial river. The sandstorm was gone, the sandsong silent. Up ahead were specks between the dunes: the Jade Trail caravanners derailed by the demon, slowly stirring.

Alive.

Lan's head pounded. Dilaya lay still but for the rise and fall of her chest. Her qì was faint but steady. She would live—though she would need to see a healer, and soon.

Lan drew several long breaths before pushing herself up. She picked up her ocarina, which lay in the sand nearby, and slipped it into the pouch at her hip, feeling her breathing come more easily.

That was when she saw it.

A shimmering figure stood before her, long silken skirt and sashes billowing in an invisible breeze. A crescent-shaped sapphire glinted on her forehead, and the bangles on her wrists and brooches at her waist glittered gold.

Lan lifted her face and stopped breathing.

Hovering over the figure, as faint as a stream of coiled moonlight, was the form of the Silver Dragon. It faced the figure, utterly still but for its whiskers and mane, which rippled in the same invisible wind that rustled the figure's raiment.

Lan watched in trepidation as the Demon God bent its head to the figure's outstretched hand. They touched and, just like that, vanished. She sensed the Silver Dragon returning to where its core nestled inside her, dormant once again.

"Yuè."

Lan jumped. Tai had come to kneel by her side. The Spirit Summoner's brows were furrowed as he gazed at the spot where the figure had lingered.

"Did you see that?" she stammered.

"Yes. Yuè," Tai repeated. "She was Yuè. The soul at the sand demon's core." His spirit bell hung at his waist, silent, though he kept his hand on it as if in reassurance.

A demon's core was akin to a human's heart, and at its center was a soul: the original soul of the being it had been before becoming corrupted by malevolent qì and before it had begun consuming other souls to strengthen its power.

Lan stared at Tai. "You saw nothing else?"

"I heard. I heard." Tai looked solemn. "Such grief."

There was nothing to indicate that the Spirit Summoner had seen the strange sight of that Yuè soul touching the form of the Silver Dragon. Lan had come to realize that though she could see the Demon God bound to her, it remained invisible to all others around her. That was how she preferred it. Demonic practitioning was dangerous and forbidden for good reason: practitioners often lost control of their demons' power. It was a reviled form of practitioning across most clans, and the implicit agreement between Lan and her friends had been for her to never use her Demon God's power, knowing its dangers.

Lan did not want to imagine what Yeshin Noro Dilaya would say if she found out that the Silver Dragon's power had broken loose just now.

Her thoughts flitted back to the Yuè soul. Why would it

have greeted something as innately malevolent as a Demon God? There had seemed to be reverence in the soul's stance. Reverence, yet also melancholy, an ancient sadness lining her face. Lan wondered how someone so beautiful might have come to such a tragic pass, evolving into a wrathful demon and feeding on souls for thousands of cycles.

Lan did not have long to dwell on this.

Through the arid desert breeze came a new qì, one that pressed at Lan's throat and filled her lungs with the scent of copper. She would recognize that anywhere: the signature of those who haunted her nightmares.

Elantians. Nearby.

Lan drew her dagger, That Which Cuts Stars. It was small, and at first glance, appeared not to be of much use in hand-to-hand combat. But the blade's true value lay in its special ability to temporarily cut through demonic qì.

You aim for the demon's core of qì—the equivalent to our hearts. Then you pierce.

A voice like velvet midnight. A gaze like black steel aflame. She remembered the way Zen's fingers had felt, cool and steady, as they'd wrapped around hers. Guided the blade of the dagger to his heart.

Lan swallowed, furiously blinking away the memory. A shadow appeared over the edge of the horizon, less a silhouette than an absence of the stars that had begun to speckle the indigo sky. Lan froze as the figure seemed to turn; she thought she saw the gleam of an Elantian magician's metal bands and armor, thought she felt an icy gaze find her in the midst of that vast desert.

Erascius. The last time she'd seen him, they'd been plummeting to the ground from atop a cliff—a sure death for both of them, had Zen not come and saved her. Erascius should have died.

She shifted her grip on That Which Cuts Stars and stepped forward to confront that distant figure—

And then he was gone. Between one blink and the next, so suddenly that Lan wondered whether she had imagined it.

She stared at the dunes cresting the skyline for a few moments more, breathing fast, before a cough behind her drew her attention.

On the ground, Dilaya was stirring. She'd cracked open her eye, which was beginning to bruise. "Little fox spirit," she croaked.

Lan knelt by the other girl's side. "Horse-face," she said, relieved. "I never thought I'd say this, but I'm glad you're alive."

Dilaya looked blearily at Lan for a moment. Then her gaze hardened. "You used it."

There was no doubt what she referred to: the power of the Demon God within her. That which Lan had sworn not to use. And she hadn't; the Silver Dragon had unleashed its own power in order to protect her life.

But Lan understood the fear and reproach in Dilaya's eyes. They had all been there to witness Zen's downfall, how he had lost control over his Demon God. Had led the Elantians to Skies' End.

"The Demon God has the obligation to save my life. That and nothing more," Lan reassured Dilaya. "I have never called upon it willingly, and I will not easily do so. I remember what happened at Skies' End. You have my word."

Dilaya's eye darted from one of Lan's to the other, as though searching. Then she let loose a breath. She shifted her arm and cursed as she winced in pain. "Help me up."

Together, Lan and Tai pulled Dilaya to her feet. The girl swayed slightly, her face pale and shining with sweat. For a moment, she looked as though she might faint again, but she clenched her teeth and, perhaps through sheer stubbornness, remained standing.

"You need a healer," Lan said. "We have to get to Nakkar."

"Nakkar," Tai agreed. "We go."

Even Dilaya recognized the state of her wounds enough not to argue.

Lan hesitated. A few dozen steps away, the caravan traders who had survived the sand demon had begun to pick themselves up. "We should help them," she said.

"No," Dilaya said flatly. "We already have. We can't risk one of them recognizing us and turning us in for the pretty price the Elantians have put on our heads."

She was right, yet Lan couldn't help but feel that they had failed. A mother had begun wailing for her child; a man sobbed as he held his wife's prone body in his arms. In the dim light, none of them would see a small group of three stealing away.

Lan glanced at the skyline again. Nothing but a clear night of stars. She could have sworn she'd sensed that Elantian presence somewhere out there in the shadows of the dunes.

Perhaps one day, they would live in a land where they no longer needed to run.

The remainder of the journey to Nakkar might have taken only a bell or more, but time seemed to stretch as far as the unending desert before them. It was laborious work: the sand was soft and the night grew cold, and soon Dilaya's breathing became labored and her entire páo was soaked through with sweat. Just when Lan thought the girl might collapse, she spotted a change in the undulating landscape.

Nakkar.

Unlike those of other desert towns, Nakkar's walls were eggshell white and free of crenellations. The tops were crusted with blue jewels that glimmered like ocean waves in the moonlight. Beyond the walls rose rammed-earth houses, their roofs studded with gold and lapis lazuli. And towering in the distance were the shadows of snowcapped mountains that plunged into the clouds. A great waterfall cleaved them like a sheet of pale silk.

"Finally," Dilaya croaked, but Lan could tell she was impressed. "The City of Immortals."

Their awe was short-lived as they approached the city gates and the familiar press of metal weighed upon the qì—Elantian magic. They joined a throng of merchants and travelers from all along the Jade Trail awaiting entry. In the flickering torchlight that illuminated the gates, camels huffed, donkeys brayed, horses whickered, and their owners murmured to hush them.

"Veil down," Lan reminded Dilaya as they approached. "We should split up. I'll try to get in with one of the caravans. Tai, you take Dilaya as your wife. Tell them she suffers from a bout of sun sickness and the runs."

It was difficult to discern whether Dilaya or Tai was more disgusted at the prospect of being joined by marriage, but the disguise worked. The Royal Magicians might have Lan and her companions at the top of their Most Wanted list, but that served as low motivation to the foot soldiers stationed outside one of the largest trading cities, checking thousands of travelers entering and leaving through the gates each day. The patrol cast a cursory glance at Dilaya and Tai before quickly waving them in (covering his nose as he did so, as though afraid of catching whatever mysterious affliction Dilaya had).

And then it was Lan's turn. She squinted as a torch was shoved before her face, its light searingly bright after bells of darkness. There was a moment when she looked into the patrol's green eyes and thought of a different Elantian soldier from Haak'gong in a lifetime past—and she could have sworn this soldier would see the fear in her eyes, sense the way her body seized up.

But he only yawned and waved her through, the torchlight shifting away from her face to the next merchant.

Lan caught up to Dilaya and Tai where they awaited her, by the side of the road. The three had gotten into Nakkar, one of the busiest trading posts of the Jade Trail—and one of the most heavily patrolled in the west of the Last Kingdom. Now they had to locate the fabled library guarded by the Yuè clan and find out whether it would reveal the location of Shaklahira, the Forgotten City of the West.

5

> All things in this world have a point of birth and a point of destruction. That is the fundamental principle of the cycle of qì.
>
> —Dào'zĭ, *Book of the Way*
> *(Classic of Virtues)*, 2.7

Zen awoke suddenly sometime in the night. He'd dreamt of a city made of sand, a silver crescent moon, a dragon wreathed in shadows.

And he'd dreamt of Lan.

He straightened, rubbing a hand across his face. The tallow candle had burned to the end of its wick, and his inkwell had run dry; the burial chamber he'd made his base was steeped in silence and darkness. These were what the common folk called the "ghost hours," and the name had a deeper meaning than most knew: they were when the yīn of whatever worlds lay beyond this one filtered through most strongly. When one was most likely to glimpse spirits and souls.

Strewn on his makeshift desk was a horse-skin drum, a golden eagle feather, a palm-sized brass mirror, and the *Classic of Gods and Demons*.

He'd spent the past day in solitude, hunched over the tome he'd found in the birchwood chest, his eyes glazed over and shoulders aching from painstakingly translating the Mansorian syllabary—a language he *should have* grown up with, *should have* known as well as the lines of his own palm—into Hin scripture. He hadn't slept, hadn't eaten, and might not have drunk if not for the pot of pǔ'ěr tea Shàn'jūn had steeped for him, now long gone cold.

The shadow of the Black Tortoise pulled itself from the darkest corners of the chamber, hovering in the spaces candlelight did not touch. It had remained by his side over the past day as his tenacity yielded to frustration, and he hadn't bothered to break off their connection. He'd begun to rely on the Demon God to fill in the gaps when he became stuck.

And sometimes, he found, the line between his mind and the Demon God's began to blur. He would stumble across an unknown character, and the meaning would come to him, drawn from the ocean of knowledge that belonged to the Black Tortoise.

Zen stood. He lit a fresh candle and walked to the first tomb. He took in the sight of the Mansorian general, so eerily preserved that he might have been asleep in a bed of funerary silks. On impulse, Zen lifted his hand, drew qì into his fingertips, and began to conjure the half-deciphered Mansorian Seal he'd just learned.

He could sense its incompleteness from the moment it activated, the qì pulling unevenly like a quilt with holes. The combination of strokes and strands of qì sparked several times before sputtering out in a hiss of smoke, leaving him in the flickering light of his candle.

He wanted to throw something. So many times, in frustration and resentment of all that had been taken from him, he'd wanted to destroy this place in a tide of black fire.

He inhaled deeply, letting the flames of his anger cool.

Then he returned to his desk, picked up the *Classic of Gods and Demons*, and turned to the next page.

It was blank.

Zen stared, aghast, certain that his mind was playing tricks on him again. He flipped to the next page. And the next. Thumbed through the rest of the book.

All blank.

He returned to the last page that held scripture and ran his fingers down the first blank page again, studying it carefully. There was *something* on the page, steeped into the yellowing vellum, glimmering like Masyrian glass.

Zen touched a finger to it—and sucked in a breath.

His finger *burned*. The sensation rushed through his hand like wildfire, and his mind blanked at the pain. He stumbled away from the tome, knocking over the candle.

Flame swept through the chamber. It struck the burial tombs like lightning, and in a breath's span, impossibly, the entire dungeon was afire.

Zen summoned qì to him, whipping up a Seal that called upon the energies of water while channeling away all the air. It was one of the most basic principles he'd learned as a practitioner: in the great cycle of qì, air birthed fire and water destroyed fire. Summon the element of destruction and repel the element of birth, and the qì would be successfully vanquished.

The Vanquishing Seal swept across the room. Yet the water passed through the fire as though it weren't there; even when the air parted from the flames, they only blazed higher and brighter.

A tendril latched onto Zen's wrist in a flash of searing pain. Zen snapped a water fú at it; the water had no effect. It splashed against his skin without dousing the flames even as they continued to snake up his arm. His vision filled with red: a great bird with crimson plumage, turning to him with golden eyes. . . . The flames pierced his chest, and he couldn't breathe. . . .

Darkness wrapped around his mind and claimed the chamber. When he blinked again, he was kneeling on the ground, tome in hand. The candle had righted itself, lighting the place with a slow, steady flame. There was no trace of the fire or the crimson bird. The dungeon was as silent and still as ever, the walls now dripping gently with water from the Vanquishing Seal he had summoned in his panic.

Hands shaking, he swiped a lock of hair from his forehead. His fingers came away wet with perspiration. No burn marks or signs of injury—yet the pain, the flames, all of it had felt so *real*. He could sense the powerful energies of his Demon God relinquishing its hold on him, withdrawing once again to the places where light did not touch.

"What was that?" He hated that he sounded out of breath, his composure lost.

A Seal, came the response, slow and somewhat hesitant for the first time since he'd known the Demon God.

Zen picked up the tome again and flipped to where the blank pages started. There, in the center of the parchment, a Seal of indecipherable strokes now blazed out. He stared, mesmerized for a moment by the sheer complexity of it and how the qì within looked *alive*. Each stroke seemed to trail fire and blood, a well of unfathomable power unnoticed until one looked close.

This was mastery of the art that not even Master of Seals Gyasho or Grandmaster Dé'zǐ could have dreamt of achieving.

"Perform the Counterseal," he commanded his Demon God.

Another pause, and that new uncertainty he'd sensed. *I cannot.*

He growled. "Why not?"

This Seal bears the flames of one of the Four. That which is aligned with the sun, with the crimson of fire and blood and destruction. Attempting a Counterseal triggers the illusions of fire and pain you just experienced.

"The Crimson Phoenix." The bird with brilliant red plumage he'd seen. The Demon God known to have been in the possession of the imperial family for dynasties, unbeknownst to the world; the fourth and final Demon God, which Lan's ocarina and star maps had traced to an unfamiliar patch of sky and stars.

Yes. The other half of this book was locked and stolen by its binder.

Zen stared at the open tome, at the blank pages that came after the Seal. "You're saying that this Seal," he said slowly, "was conjured by the qì of the *Crimson Phoenix* at the command of the imperial family . . . and that the murderers of my clan hold the other half of this book?"

The shadows shifted as the Black Tortoise watched him. The answer was apparent in its silence.

Zen slammed his fists into the ground. With a resounding crack, it split. He sensed tremors rumbling into the earth deep below, into the stone walls all around, as the waves of his anger—manifesting in his qì—roiled through like a tide. For several moments, he couldn't see, couldn't *think*, from the fury that threatened to tear him apart.

The imperial family had stolen half of an ancient tome that belonged to his ancestors; the very tome that would allow him to call upon his great-grandfather's army of Deathriders.

Through the waves of his anger, he recalled something.

The Crimson Phoenix. It had been one of the two missing Demon Gods he and Lan had been able to locate through the star maps she'd conjured with her ocarina.

Star maps he'd *transcribed* weeks ago.

He fumbled in his storage pouch and found the pieces of parchment by touch, so often had he brushed his fingers against them to assure himself of their continued existence. Even without unfurling them and looking at the black dots representing stars in the night sky, he could see the scene as clearly as though it had happened yesterday. A girl playing the ocarina, four quadrants of the sky glittering above their heads. Red, blue, silver, black.

He unfurled the parchment and held it to the candlelight. The smattering of dots meant nothing to him here in this underground burial chamber, but he remembered distinctly that it hadn't matched any part of the night sky where they'd been in the Central Plains.

If he wanted to access the missing half of the *Classic of Gods and Demons*, he would need to find the Crimson Phoenix and have its Seal unlocked from his book.

But there was no telling whether the Crimson Phoenix had moved since they'd transcribed its location. And what could he offer a Demon God to persuade it to release the Seal?

It was another complication to his plan, another step between him and his goal.

Zen stood and made his way to the stairs that led up from the burial chamber. His head was pounding, whether from fatigue or suppressed fury he couldn't tell. The candlelight, the still air, the silence of the dead had all become asphyxiating. He needed air. He needed to see the stars.

The barrier Seal he'd placed on the obsidian tortoise's belly whispered to him as he passed through. A feeling of wrongness twisted in him as he looked around.

The open-air hallway of the ancient palace was pitch-black and cold. He could sense the winter breeze wafting in from the entrance—which should have remained open to the snow-capped mountains slumbering beneath an ink-black sky—but Zen felt as though a blindfold had slipped over his eyes.

He took two steps forward, then felt a shift in the air.

A voice behind him rasped his name: *"Temurezen..."*

Zen spun. That face again, in the darkness: flesh pale and dead, eye sockets empty, tongue lolling out, wisps of hair clinging to it. And in its hands—nails rotted and skin blue—it held a jar.

The monster he had glimpsed yesterday.

Zen drew Nightfire and slashed.

"Temurezen," the creature shrieked, lunging sideways. The jar exploded against the wall, and then the darkness was absolute. Only the echo of the creature's voice remained, with the faintly bitter stench of whatever it had carried in that jar. *"...murezen...rezen...Zen...Zen!"*

Zen blinked. His surroundings came into view as moonlight filtered into his vision, dusting the cracks in the palace walls and the rubble scattered on the ground. Before him stood a familiar figure, long hair tied in a simple ponytail, lips parted in shock as he beheld the shattered bowl of medicinal broth slicking the ground beneath his boots.

"Sh-Shàn'jūn?" Zen felt as though he'd just woken from a dream. A nightmare.

Shàn'jūn wrapped his arms around himself. "I... I couldn't sleep when I thought of you alone down there. I got up to deliver some hot broth to you, to replenish your yáng qì," he said, and Zen heard a tremor in his voice. "Forgiveness, Zen."

Zen sheathed his jiàn, trying to steady his breathing. He wanted to kneel at Shàn'jūn's feet and beg *him* for forgiveness, the one person left of his old life to stay with him and understand him. To return to the days when their biggest worries were whether the Master of Texts would punish them for failing to memorize ancient Hin verses.

"No, Shàn'jūn," Zen said. "It should be me asking for your forgiveness. All the yīn here . . . the history. . . ." He swallowed, uncertain how to go on to explain the monster he'd dreamt.

"I understand," Shàn'jūn said gently, and Zen looked away. He did not deserve sympathy. Not when he'd nearly hurt someone who had once been precious to him. "I will clean the tea."

"Leave it," Zen said, more sharply than he meant. He softened his tone. "Please. Go get some sleep. I will clean up."

Shàn'jūn hesitated. "The Elantians are gathering in the Emaran Desert," he blurted out, and Zen could tell this was what he'd waited up for. "The Nameless Master returned from a day of scouting. I overheard him tell Master Nur that he senses they are closing in on something—someone." His eyes shone with hope, and that struck Zen harder than any blade. "Do you think . . . would you think there is a possibility . . . ?"

Someone. There was no question as to whom Shàn'jūn referred; there was only one target besides Zen that might draw Elantians like a swarm of flies.

Sòng Lián.

Zen had begun running the palace as he would a camp, assigning duties to the disciples including procuring food and supplies. He'd asked the Nameless Master and a few older disciples to scout the area and bring him news of any Elantian troop movements. The Master of Assassins had a way of tracking qì over impossible distances, of hearing whispers in the way the winds turned and the trees swayed and the rivers shifted.

If the Nameless Master had declined to report the news to Zen at supper, it was likely a secret he'd meant to keep.

Zen had kept a few secrets of his own: That they weren't the only survivors from the School of the White Pines. That one of them was Chó Tài, the Spirit Summoner Shàn'jūn loved.

And that Zen had saved Lan that night.

Zen could not meet his friend's eyes. Instead, he looked out at the open-air doorway, at the stars winking in a sky of ink. "Why are you telling me this?" he intoned.

"Because . . . if Lan is alive . . ."—Shàn'jūn swallowed—"if she is alive, she might need help."

Zen shut his eyes briefly. How like the gentle-natured Medicine disciple to hope for this. "And if she were alive, would you leave me for her?"

Shàn'jūn's lips parted. He hesitated, but Zen already knew the answer.

Zen turned abruptly and made for the doors. He could sense his former friend's eyes on him, the silent answer to that question stretching taut between them—along with the plea Shàn'jūn had made.

She might need help.

Outside, stars reeled over his head, as bright as coins. He recalled a story his mother had told him, a myth of a realm beyond this one, beyond the River of Forgotten Death and the Nine Springs of Immortality, where the souls of the dead went to rest. The stars were the guardians of the veil between this world and the next, immortals who had given their cores of qì and their souls to the service of guarding the peace between worlds and lives.

Zen wondered what awaited him in the realm beyond this one.

He tipped his head to the moonlight spilling from the heavens and exhaled, his breath unfurling in a cloud.

The truth was, a plan had begun to form in his mind the moment Shàn'jūn told him the news. The remainder of the

Classic of Gods and Demons was locked by a Seal wrought with the power of the Crimson Phoenix—one so powerful, even the Black Tortoise could not conjure the Counterseal.

The star maps Zen had transcribed from Lan's ocarina music were wrinkled with wear. He averted his gaze from the quadrant holding the location of the Black Tortoise—seeing it never failed to provoke guilt as he recalled the betrayal on Lan's face when she'd found out his intentions to bind it—and focused on the quadrant that gave the location of the Phoenix.

To find the location a star map pointed to, one had to deduce which part of the world matched the view of the night sky presented in the map. In his time at the school, Zen had never put too much stock in the Art of Geomancy, which included astrology. The Crimson Phoenix, he'd surmised from the star map, was somewhere southwest of the palace.

Somewhere, if Zen's rough calculations were correct, in the Emaran Desert.

From the pillars of the entryway, the shadows stirred. They parted to reveal a man who might have been sculpted from them. It was impossible to say where he had come from, for there was nowhere in the chamber he might have hidden—but such was the talent of a Master of Assassins.

Zen's jaw tightened as the Nameless Master stepped out before him. His first instinct was to reach for his jiàn—but that was ridiculous, as the master was on his side. The master's hooded eyes, though, missed nothing. They darted to Zen's waist, to the slight twitch of his fingers. To the star maps Zen held in his hands, the tome tucked under his arm.

Zen wondered how much of his attack on Shàn'jūn the Nameless Master had seen. He had the paranoid suspicion that this man had the impossible ability to read minds.

Not so impossible, whispered the Black Tortoise. Its shadow lingered in a corner of Zen's mind. *Qì, as you know, is not limited* to the physical realm. *There remain few with the ability to sense the qì of emotions. Of thoughts. Of souls.*

Zen swallowed and inclined his head. "Shī'fù." No matter how far up in ranking and societal status one climbed in life, one's master of practitioning was forever his master . . . even if Zen now held the authority.

"The Medicine disciple informed you after all," the Master of Assassins said, his voice like wind on a starless night.

Not for the first time, Zen was uncertain how to respond. "Is there something I can help you with?" he replied, keeping his tone neutral.

"Dismiss your Demon God" was all the Nameless Master said.

"You do not give me orders."

"I have spent eleven cycles with you as your teacher. Were I inclined to harm you, you would hardly be standing here today." The Nameless Master's intonation was smooth; it was difficult to discern whether they were meant as a threat or a placation.

Zen gritted his teeth, but humored the master and severed his connection to the Black Tortoise.

The shadows seemed to retreat. The air seemed to lighten. And whatever wariness he had felt toward his master dissipated.

The Master of Assassins blinked. "You, too, feel it."

Zen kept his face blank. "I don't know what you mean."

"What did you see that drove you to attack Shàn'jūn?"

"I don't know what you mean," Zen repeated, a cord tightening in his chest. "He simply startled me."

"You do not see things that make you question what is illusion and what is reality? Perhaps a voice in the dark, a face in the shadows, a creature closing in on you?"

The hairs on Zen's neck pricked, and he thought of the

monstrous creature with the empty eye sockets and rotted skin. The feeling that something was always watching him, hidden to the eye, in the folds between the worlds of yáng and yīn, life and death.

The answer must have been apparent in his pause, for the master took a step forward. "I worked for the imperial palace. I know the effects of demonic possession. Specifically, the effects of so much yīn upon the balance of your core of qì. If you do not wish to lose your mind to the Demon God within you, then you must act now, before it is too late." Another step forward. "Your quest for the Phoenix brings you westward. I now impart to you another point of consideration.

"There was an ancient clan known to guard the truths of this world," he continued, his face turned to the dark corridor that led to the dungeons and all the secrets the Mansorians had buried within, all the histories lost to time. "It was said that the imperial family consulted them throughout the ages and grew powerful from the secrets they shared. With this clan's help, the imperial family was able to keep their sanity while being bound to their Demon God, enabling them to rule effectively for dynasties. And with this clan's help . . . they had access to secrets of the Demon Gods." At last, the master raised his eyes to meet Zen's. There was something like pity in them, and something like sympathy. "Your great-grandfather's mind was swallowed by the yīn energies of the Black Tortoise too soon. It is no small burden to carry, Xan Temurezen; there is a reason the forefathers of practitioning advocated for balance to be the Way. Too much yīn, and your qì will grow poisoned. Unstable."

Unstable. Zen thought of Xan Tolürigin's final act, the blood of the innocent he'd left in his wake that had stained his reputation. *Madness,* the village folk whispered. *Demonic possession.*

Pure evil.

Zen's grasp tightened on Nightfire's hilt. "How long did the imperial family have before they were consumed?" he asked.

"Do not misunderstand," the master replied. "The ending of a demonic bargain is always inevitable. But they were able to live a life in control of their own minds. That is what I have surmised from observing the imperial physician in my time at the palace."

But Zen had stopped listening. *Live a life.*

When he'd sworn his soul to the Black Tortoise, he'd cut off all remaining hope of having any semblance of a life, a future. He'd vowed to give all that was left of himself—body, mind, then soul—to take back this land from its colonizers and return it to the Ninety-Nine Clans, as it always should have remained.

And the Zen of one cycle ago—rigid, disciplined, and without a want for anything else in this world—would have harbored no regrets in carrying this out.

That was, until his path had become inextricably intertwined with a songgirl at a southern teahouse. When Zen dreamed, when Zen thought of the glimpses of joy he'd known in his life, his memories danced with her—with Lan. In that small village in the mountains, shielded from the world by mist and gentle rain, a new hope had taken root inside him.

Perhaps . . . just perhaps . . . there was a way for him to use the Black Tortoise's power without losing his mind—at least, for a while more. Perhaps he could take back this land *and* live to rule it, to see the clans reestablish themselves and practitioners once again walk the rivers and lakes of old.

And perhaps, just perhaps . . . he could do all of that with the girl he loved by his side.

Hope was a cruel thing. He'd done his best to douse those embers, yet with the Nameless Master's words, they began to spark again.

"Where is this clan?" he asked.

The Nameless Master looked unsurprised, as though his shrewd eyes had watched every thought in Zen's mind unfold. "In the Emaran Desert, near the edge of this kingdom, lies the City of Immortals. Nakkar, where the Yuè clan once resided."

Zen had read of the Yuè in sparse references that were seen as near-mythical in their world now. "The Yuè clan perished many dynasties ago," he said.

"Vanished," the Nameless Master corrected. "The Yuè clan knew the secrets to immortality, to the realms that may lie beyond our world. When mortals began to seek out those secrets in pursuit of their own ambitions, the burden became too much for them to bear. They simply vanished.

"Yet legends say that in the hours of night when the moon is full and the yīn is strong, the boundaries between our world and other realms—those of spirits, of ghosts, of souls—grow weak. Perhaps there are answers to be found in Nakkar."

Those sparks of hope caught flame. Nakkar. A real city. How would it feel to truly command the power of the Black Tortoise without fearing for his sanity, without feeling like his time was sand in a glass, slowly trickling to an inevitable end?

"Why are you helping me?" Zen croaked.

The Nameless Master blinked. "An understanding. You act as you see fit for the greater good. I was once the Master of Assassins for the Imperial Court and took lives for the benefit of the greater good. Yet what *is* the greater good? Who decides that? It is the one who holds power. I am powerless to stop you, yet I can provide my guidance and counsel in the hope that you find the best path forward. I would hope that, were you in any way Dé'zǐ's disciple, you would follow his lesson. That you would learn to make your choices out of love, rather than out of greed or hate."

It felt as though the Nameless Master had taken a hot blade

and cut Zen, so strong was the impact of those words, the memory they evoked: Dé'zǐ, lying in a pool of blood, gazing up at Zen. *I hope that your choices will be guided by love, not revenge. I hope you will remember what power can cost you.*

"Wait," he gasped, but the Nameless Master had vanished as he had come: without a stirring of wind or a single ripple of shadows. And Zen was left reeling beneath a sky of stars.

He had a long journey ahead of him to find the Crimson Phoenix and unlock the second half of the *Classic of Gods and Demons*. Even once he managed to do that, he would need his Demon God's power to summon the army of Deathriders and to lead the war against the Elantians.

He could not do it all while slowly losing his mind. The shattered teapot lay down the hall, and he felt Shàn'jūn's absence keenly. The tea lay spilled on the floor, now cold.

Zen lifted his gaze to the southwest. Would there be an answer to a seemingly unanswerable question in the ageless city once ruled by fabled immortals? Would he be able to use his Demon God's powers and retain his sanity?

And if so . . . could there be an *after* to it all, a life in which he might spend the rest of his days in a rain-misted mountain village with Lan?

He would find out in the City of Immortals.

He opened himself to the qì of his Demon God, feeling it surge through him. A Gate Seal opened before him: a desert city beneath a bright moon, wreathed in the black flame of his qì.

Without a backward glance, Zen stepped through.

6

> Few records exist of the Yuè save for a scattering of tales told by Hunters, practitioners who sought the secrets of immortality by dedicating their lifetimes to the search for an opening to another realm within the City of Immortals.
>
> —Various scholars, *Studies of the Ninety-Nine Clans*

The kè'zhàn was filled with the chatter of patrons, the scent of spices, and lit by a colorful profusion of brass lamps, ceiling chandeliers, and Hin lanterns. Lan slipped down the wooden stairs into the inn and chose a seat closest to the bar, between an Achaemman jeweler and an Endhiran spice trader who were haggling over the prices of lapis lazuli and cinnamon.

It was evening on their second day in Nakkar. The first night they'd spent in fear of being recognized by the Elantians, hastily stumbling into the first kè'zhàn that would open its doors in the midst of sandsong. All night long, Lan and Tai had crouched over Dilaya, Tai attempting all the healing Seals he'd learned from Shàn'jūn, Lan sweet-talking the cook into whipping up a hot ginseng chicken broth, then spooning it through Dilaya's parched lips. Thankfully, the Jorshen matriarch's injuries were less physical, more wounds to her qì from the sand mó's overwhelming demonic energies. By daybreak, color had returned to her cheeks. Exhausted, Lan and Tai had dropped onto a straw pallet and slept.

It was now nightfall. Earlier, the streets outside had been clogged with tarps of every color and pattern, merchants peddling silks and salts, perfumes and papers, ivory and dyes and every sort of goods imaginable. The scene had reminded Lan of Haak'gong, of its evemarket where she'd once hawked wares and visited an ailing old man who ran a rundown contraband store.

She ordered a bowl of beef broth with hand-pulled noodles. She'd left Dilaya upstairs in Tai's care; the girl was too noticeable with her eye patch and loose left sleeve. Besides, Lan was more used to "mingling in society," Dilaya had sniffed, and then with her signature haughty glare, she said, "Go use that sweet-talking mouth of yours for some good."

Rumors of the sand demon attack had spread like wildfire, though how the survivors had lived to tell the tale remained a mystery. It seemed there had been rising outcries over the Elantian regime and how they had driven Hin practitioners—who once traveled the Jade Trail fighting spirits and demons and monsters—to extinction. Now the Jade Trail and all of the Last Kingdom were left completely vulnerable, and traders from neighboring kingdoms were increasingly hesitant to come and risk their lives.

"It didn't used to be like this," the innkeeper said. He was a young polyglot, apparently fluent in all tongues spoken in the kè'zhàn, dark-haired and tanned from days spent under the sun. "Not back in the days when Hin practitioners walked the rivers and lakes. They protected us."

Lan glanced at the strips of gold paper stuck to the doors with rice glue. Inscriptions written in molten cinnabar cascaded down them, flickering in the lamplight. She'd seen these types of couplets before, in remote village homes, often stuck in discreet places to avoid detection: gold-leafed paper for those who could afford it, to mimic the yellow fú practitioners used, with characters written in red and enclosed in circles to mimic the Seals practitioners wrote in their blood. Of course, there was not an ounce of qì to these paper couplets, but superstitions had a way of blending in with what once had been real.

"Is this your family's establishment?" Lan asked the innkeeper, slurping down her noodles. The spicy beef noodles were delicious enough to make her want to cry. "A cup of tea, please."

The innkeeper brought her a glass of steaming black tea. It smelled faintly of cinnamon and roses. "My family's been running the Fragrant Sandcloud Tavern since before the era of the First Kingdom," he said proudly.

It was remarkable how history lived on in the common folk, who bore the changes of time with quiet resilience. If Lan sought a desert palace where the imperial family had attempted to bury their secrets, there was no better way to begin than by asking those whose families and homes had been here all along.

Lan widened her eyes and leaned forward, hands wrapped around her cup of tea. "Are the stories true, then?" she asked. "My aunt and uncle have spent their lives on the Jade Trail, but it's my first time here in Nakkar."

"Yah, what's your trade?" the innkeeper asked.

Lan grinned. "I'm a performer," she replied, and took out her ocarina. "Here, let me play you a song." She blew into her instrument, her fingers working fast and light to slip in strands of yáng qì: comfort, joy, and trust. Faint as to not be detected, but just enough to subtly improve her listener's mood and put him at ease.

By the time she finished, the innkeeper was smiling. "You're really good," he said. "Folks would pay a pretty coin to hear you perform. Got a gig yet?"

"Unfortunately, I do." She winked. "I'm in high demand."

She slipped her ocarina back into the pouch at her belt and leaned forward, cupping her chin in her hand. "So? Is this really the City of Immortals?"

"Sure. That's the direct Hin translation of 'Nakkar.'"

"And is there truly an ancient library here that the immortals kept?"

"Ah," the innkeeper said, nodding. "The Temple of Truths. Legend says it used to sit at the peak of the Öshangma Light Mountain, behind our city. Yah, they say its steeples grazed the clouds, and that it was the doorway to another realm."

Used to. Lan tipped her head. "We can visit the temple, right?"

A curious look crossed over the innkeeper's face. He was no longer smiling. "Well, no," he said slowly. "It's no longer there. The Temple of Truths—and all the monks of the Yuè clan who ran it—vanished hundreds of cycles ago."

It took Lan several moments to process his words. "Vanished?" she repeated, her heart sinking. "What do you mean? The entire temple's gone?"

"Exactly as it sounds, apparently," the innkeeper replied. "The story goes—so my grandmother tells me—that one day, worshipers made the trek up the Öshangma Light Mountain, and where the Temple of Truths had sat was nothing but earth and snow and pines. It was gone, as though it had never existed."

Lan uttered a curse that the innkeeper didn't hear, for at that moment, a call sliced through the hubbub of the Fragrant Sandcloud Tavern—in a language so harsh, it broke the harmony of all other tongues spoken in the place.

"*Curfew!*"

Too late, Lan became aware of the shift in the air, the cold and ominous press of metal qì that had slowly encroached upon the cheerful melee within the kè'zhàn. Two Elantian patrols stepped through the doorway, several feet behind where she sat at the table closest to the innkeeper's station.

"Not to worry," the innkeeper said softly. He seemed to have sensed Lan's unease. "They won't bother anyone. It wouldn't be good for trade relations if they terrified the merchants of the other kingdoms."

But Lan had gone very still for another reason. The two Elantian patrols held scrolls in their hands. They paused at each table, speaking in low tones to the clusters of merchants and pointing to the portrait of a girl inked on the scrolls. A portrait above which she spotted *her* truename—SÒNG LIÁN.

Her heart was racing like a rabbit's. Suddenly, it felt as though her Demon God, practitioning skills, and Art of Song were all gone and she was once again the helpless girl trapped in a Haak'gong teahouse, enduring the press of cruel fingers and the laughter of summer-green eyes.

Lan set down her chopsticks and slid a string of coins to the innkeeper. "Keep the change."

As she slipped away, the innkeeper called, "Yah, wait, miss!" The sound cut through the kè'zhàn, and Lan froze. Out of the corner of her eye, she saw the Elantian patrols glance up in their direction. "It's not safe out—especially tonight!"

Lan ducked her head and turned so her back faced the patrols. "Why not?" she asked, but she barely heard his response. She'd opened her senses to the qì around them and could feel the Elantians shift, their metal armor moving closer to her as they stopped by the next table.

Options raced through her head. Dilaya and Tai would be safe upstairs—safer than if the patrols discovered her here, at least. As the innkeeper had said, the Elantians would not terrorize foreign merchants and risk souring trade relations. The safest choice was for Lan to hide, or leave the kè'zhàn.

"It's a full moon tonight," the innkeeper was saying, and

something in his tone gave Lan pause. "Each full moon, people who are outside say they can hear things that . . . aren't truly there. It's different for everyone. Some customers have said they heard the wail of their long-dead lovers. Others, the sound of a clock chiming, a bell tolling, children singing in the dark . . . and so on." He dropped his voice. "You sought the City of Immortals. Well, some say that these occurrences are caused when the immortals of the Temple of Truths return as ghosts to haunt Nakkar . . . and that the City of Immortals resurfaces in our world."

The Elantian patrols had turned away, now bending over another table. Lan summoned a shaky smile for the innkeeper. "If I do meet the singing children, I shall join them," she said. "I've been looking for customers to perform my music for. See you soon!" And then she took off out the tavern door, leaving the innkeeper speechless at her quick exit.

The fear that had risen in her throat calmed slightly as soon as she slipped into the cloak of darkness outside, the night illuminated only by the eerie white glow of the moon from behind a cloud-covered sky. A cool desert wind had picked up, howling over the whitewashed walls. Gone from the now-empty streets were the colorful tarps of the daytime marketplaces; not a trace of the bright gems and bitter herbs and powdery spices remained. The kè'zhàns and winehouses had extinguished their lanterns and shut their doors, so that only their paper windows emitted faint flickering lights and the occasional trail of laughter or zither music.

She leaned against the tavern, its sand-smoothed walls digging into her scalp, gulping down breaths of air and calming the frantic beat of her heart. In the distance loomed the Öshangma Light Mountain, its snowy peak disappearing into the clouds.

"Hey! You!"

The words sizzled through her veins. Lan turned to see two more Elantian patrols, metal armor gleaming, making their way to her from across the street. Caution flared inside her. She'd seen a fair number of patrols last night, but only at the city gates and the walls. The streets of the city had remained clear.

She suddenly thought back to the figures she'd seen outlined against the sand dunes and the horizon. The feeling of a cold, wintry gaze raking her face. She had the feeling of a noose closing in around her neck. All those increased patrols. Those soldiers in the inn with the portrait of her.

The City of Immortals was not safe for her and her companions.

The silver of metal glinted at the edge of her vision. The Elantian patrols were making straight for her. "It's curfew," she heard them say. Her mind struggled to wrap around the Elantian words after having spent so long away from the language. "Why are you outside?"

Options flitted through her mind. Her hand was at her ocarina, her mind halfway toward the core of the Silver Dragon sleeping within her. But that would blow their cover. Even if she could use the power of her Demon God to get her, Tai, and Dilaya to safety, they would need to flee Nakkar . . . and lose their chance of finding anything related to Shaklahira here. Nakkar would be sent into a lockdown, its people interrogated. . . . She thought of Old Wei, the shopkeeper she'd befriended back in Haak'gong, killed at the hands of the Elantian White Angels simply because she'd given him a single silver spoon. . . .

Stay, and she had no idea what they might do to her. Would they recognize her, a lone girl fitting the description of one of the most wanted Hin practitioners in the kingdom? Or . . . her mind drifted to the Elantian general who had attempted to buy her one night at the teahouse in Haak'gong. His fingers wrapped around her throat, his casual laughter as she was choked by his hands.

Lan quickly glanced at her surroundings: a street of residential buildings, lanterns unlit, everything dim but for flickers of candlelight etched against fretwork paper windows.

She ran for it. She heard the Elantians' shouts above the *thud-thud-thud* of her boots and her racing heart. Sensed the metal qì of their armor following her; the strands of desert heat mixing with cold wind, traces of teas and fabrics and spices billowing this way and that . . . and then, in the midst of it all . . . one qì that seemed to wrap around her chin and force her to look its way.

One so familiar . . . it was impossible.

He stepped out from the shadows of an alleyway, shedding darkness as the night released him, hands catching her by her arms and pulling her after him as he ran.

She followed, half caught in the current of her shock and half by instinct. The shouts of the Elantian soldiers grew distant, the streets and houses peeling away until there was only him: his hand wrapped around hers, the familiar crook of his neck, that qì of shadow and flame she knew as well as her own heart.

Zen was here.

Zen was alive.

As the initial jolt of surprise faded, logic filtered back in, along with memories. A black-glass lake. Dead, cold gaze. Cruel, twisted mouth speaking cruel, twisted words.

They'd reached the other end of the alley. The doors of the multistory pagodas that served as teahouses were open, music and laughter spilling out into the evening air along with the light from their lanterns, which limned the sharp edges to his face.

The dream broke. Suddenly, she couldn't bear touching him. Couldn't bear the feeling of his fingers on her skin.

She wrenched her hand from his. In the same motion, she pulled That Which Cuts Stars from her waistband—the dagger he had gifted her—and held it to his neck. "Give me one reason not to use this," she breathed.

He was looking at her, lips parted, eyes as deep as the black waters of a bottomless lake. Whatever he had been about to say he swallowed at the sound of footsteps—another pair of patrols, approaching from the other direction.

Zen's eyes snapped up. "In there," he said, his throat bobbing against the edge of her blade.

She followed his line of sight. Across the street was a brightly lit pagoda. Pink lanterns hung from its curved terracotta roofs, and the sound of a zither and giggles spilled through its open doorways. HOUSE OF DRUNKEN ORCHIDS, the rosewood sign announced.

The footsteps grew louder, echoing through the alley. Closing in on them.

Lan turned away from Zen, slipped her knife into the folds of her sleeve, and made for the brothel. Magenta silks whirled in her face as she ducked through its entrance. The pungent scent of sandalwood incense mixed with perfumes concocted of various flowers enveloped her, along with the sight of tangled bodies on love seats. She skipped over an overturned wine jar and a translucent silk dress discarded on the floor, making for an empty corner.

Lan glanced behind her. Four Elantian patrols had entered the premises, their heavy metal armor discordant amidst the scene of soft silks and softer flesh. There was no mistaking it: she was being hunted.

It was too late to get out. The patrols blocked the way to the exit, prowling closer to her as they searched. Any minute now, they would spot her, a lone girl in travel clothes, who stuck out like a sore thumb.

A hand closed over her wrist; as she whirled, dagger raised, she was jerked behind a hanging silk that served to partially partition off this corner of the brothel. Lan stumbled, momentarily off balance. Her shoulder slammed into the wall; she righted herself, turning to drive her dagger down—

Zen froze, breathing hard, as her blade cut into the skin of his neck, a hairsbreadth from a major artery. He had pressed his palms to the walls on either side of her; at her look, he slowly lifted them in a gesture of surrender. They were so close that his páo pressed against hers, the movement brushing her knees.

She flicked a glance behind him. She understood what he was doing—mimicking what the other patrons had come to this brothel for—and only Zen could make such a gesture look gentle. Lan hated it, hated that he was still courteous and tender and patient and everything that had drawn her to him, even after what he had done.

She shifted the blade a degree, and he winced. Red dripped down his neck.

Impossibly, time had made him more beautiful, the unnatural pallor of his skin resembling cold porcelain, the dark sweep of his lashes and straight brows like brushstrokes of ink. Yet there were also cracks to the face she had known: the overly sharp cheekbones, the dark circles beneath his eyes. Something had kept him up, roughened the smooth exterior he'd always maintained.

Good, Lan thought viciously. In a low voice, she growled, "What are you doing here?"

His lips parted. "I—" he began, but then they both sensed a heavy scent of metal qì wafting in their direction. Zen paused.

His eyes darkened, and for a moment, she sensed a different qì rising from him. A demonic qì.

She understood the choice they faced. The power of their Demon Gods could easily destroy every single Elantian soldier in the area. Most likely, it would also take everyone else down with them: the Hin, the foreign merchants. The innocents.

Zen swallowed, likely coming to the same conclusion. He hesitated, eyes searching her expression. Slowly, he lowered his arms as though to wrap them around her, but he never touched her: one hand hovered over her neck, the other resting just above her waist. She could feel the brush of his fingers against her páo, the hitch to his breaths as they mingled with hers.

"You didn't answer my question," she whispered. She wondered if he could feel the beat of her heart. The press of the pendant he'd gifted her, still resting against her chest. She should have burned that thing a long time ago. "Why are you here, *Xan Temurezen?*"

He flinched, almost imperceptibly, at the bite she gave to his full name. She had never called him that before. "I came to Nakkar to find answers to a question," he replied. "Then I sensed you—the qì of your music."

The song she'd played for the Fragrant Sandcloud Tavern's innkeeper, she realized with a pang. He knew her qì so well that, in this big city filled with people, he had found her.

"So I came to you," he finished.

She assessed his face. He wasn't lying. The knowledge filled her with anger. *"Why?"*

His throat bobbed. "I need to find the Crimson Phoenix," Zen admitted on an exhale. "The star map we transcribed a few weeks ago . . . I need you to confirm whether the Phoenix remains where it was then."

Behind them, beyond the near-transparent silk that trapped them in this corner, a girl drunkenly slurred an insult at the prowling Elantian patrol; the merchant she was splayed against grunted a similarly inebriated insult. The patrol turned. His gaze met Lan's.

Terror slicked through her veins, burning and freezing. She recalled the scene in the Haak'gong pawn shop, the summer-green eyes of that soldier who had so casually, so cruelly, spoken of having his way with her. And as the patrol approached her, Lan made a choice.

Her hand went to the back of Zen's head, fingers threading through his hair. The other, she placed on his cheek as she pulled him toward her and kissed him in her best imitation of a passionate, drunken embrace. Zen made a surprised noise low in his throat, but he obliged.

From beneath her lashes, Lan saw the patrol's lips curl in disgust. She knew what the Hin in here likely resembled to him: trapped, lowly animals, fueled by fear and desperation and basic instinct.

She sensed Zen's exhale. His hands twined around her, one brushing against the nape of her neck with his fingers, the other cupping the small of her back. His eyes had fluttered shut, and he kissed her slow and soft, with yearning and in tender disbelief. There was something so vulnerable, so open, to the kiss that, for a brief moment, Lan believed it. His lips on hers were so familiar, so gentle, that she couldn't help but fall into a not-so-distant past when she had trusted him. Loved him.

Lan closed her eyes, the shell of anger she'd built over her heart cracking open to that dream she'd once known: the one of a village in the rain, drops sluicing off terracotta roofs beyond shutters that opened to misty mountains. There had been that boy who'd cupped her chin between his hands as though he held his entire world, and he'd tasted of snow and starless nights—and hope. The boy who had held her in her loneliest moments and promised to follow her in this life and the next.

She wound her fingers tighter through his hair. An ache built in the back of her throat. He had broken his promise to her, shattered the trust she'd placed in him. With the memory of that rainy village came, inevitably, the knowledge of what had come next. Of what he had been there to do. Of his betrayal in stealing the star maps from her in order to seek out and bind the Black Tortoise.

Perhaps, after all, Zen was the most skilled liar she had ever known. Perhaps he had never loved her, merely used her. And even now, she was falling for it all over again.

Lan's eyes flew open. The Elantians had gone.

She gripped Zen's shoulders and spun him around, pushing him against the wall. Faster than a blink, she pressed her dagger into his chest.

Zen hissed in a breath. The cut was skin-deep, the tip of the blade caught on the bone of his rib cage. One slip of her hand, though, a shift in pressure, and she could slide it between his ribs, into the soft, open flesh of his chest, straight into his heart. And she *should*, for what he had done.

Zen's eyes flicked down to the hilt of her dagger, then to her. Blood had begun to seep from the cut, winding down the length of her blade to her hand. He could have easily overpowered her, but he made no move. To anyone else watching, they were lovers leaning against the wall in an embrace.

Lan met his gaze. "So," she said slowly, "you want me to conjure the star maps leading to the Demon Gods? Just like the last time? So that you can—oh, let me guess—use them to bind another Demon God to you and betray me all over again?"

He lowered his gaze. "I do not plan to bind the Crimson Phoenix."

She frowned. "Then why do you need it?"

"To take down the Elantians."

"You already have the Black Tortoise. Use its power, raise the Ten Hells upon them. Wasn't that your plan all along?"

"It isn't enough," he replied. The implication behind his words, whether intended or not, was clear: She also held a Demon God within her. If they worked together, they might stand a chance against the Elantians.

Yet the last time they had unleashed the full power of their Demon Gods, they had nearly destroyed all that mattered to them. In attempting to protect Skies' End and the School of the White Pines against the Elantians, Lan had almost lost control of the Silver Dragon's power and razed everything in the vicinity. The Demon Gods were not merely sources of power, to be used and stopped at their binders' whims. They were sentient beings with their own goals, and once their power grew unfettered, they could overwhelm their binders' wills. History had taught them this.

Zen's great-grandfather had shown them this.

That was why she had to find the Godslayer, the weapon made to destroy the Four Demon Gods. That was the only way to protect her people.

She sobered, recalling the true ending to it all, the purpose of her journey to Shaklahira. There was no known way to separate a soul from a Demon God, once bound. And if Lan wanted to destroy all four, she would need to destroy herself and Zen along with them.

The thought softened her slightly. Lan plucked the tip of her blade from Zen's chest and held it to his neck again. He only watched her. A lock of his hair had fallen in his face; the fire in his eyes had dimmed.

"Then why?" she asked. "Why do you seek the Phoenix?"

He did not look away from her as he spoke, and she

despised how easily he surrendered his guard to her. "There is an army my great-grandfather once led—one preserved in magic that the Phoenix has stolen. I plan to take back this magic to call upon this army so that I may wage war upon the Elantians. And then I plan to reestablish the Ninety-Nine Clans upon this land, just as it was and just how it should be." His hand came up, his fingers touching her hand that held the knife. "We want the same thing. Am I wrong?"

She watched his blood continue to drip down his skin, stain the blade of her dagger red. Zen did not seem to care. His gaze trapped her, searing in its intensity, and she had the feeling he would let her cut his throat open if she wished.

"It does not matter what we want," Lan said. "It matters how we get there. I do not wish to defeat the Elantians only to find myself the victor in a path of blood. I will not use our Demon Gods' power to win this war if it means harming innocents along the way."

She had been one of those innocents—one of the common folk, one of the village girls, pawns in a game of chess. She would not risk any more lives for a quick victory.

"No war has been fought without bloodshed," Zen replied. "And no better life has been won without war."

"Is that what you would call the games of power the emperors played over the past eras? The Mansorian clan defeating other, smaller ones to gain power? Was that all for a better life?"

"A necessity. Without power, my clan would never have stood a chance in rising up against the Imperial Army." Zen tipped his head. The motion caused her blade to dig deeper into his skin. Blood trickled down to his collarbone. "Perhaps in this world, it is the way of things for those with power to devour those without."

The response sprang to her lips, the lantern in the darkness that had kept her foot firmly planted in the light. "And it is the duty of those with power to protect those without," Lan replied. They were her mother's words, and she recalled speaking them to him so long ago. She'd thought they shared this belief—and perhaps that was what pushed her forward. One last attempt to understand him. To know whether he was beyond saving. "Zen, do you think the Demon Gods should be destroyed?"

His lips parted. He hesitated, and that was all the response she needed.

Lan stepped back. Cold air rushed into the space between them as she lowered That Which Cuts Stars. "You'll have to kill me to get the location of the Crimson Phoenix," she said, sheathing her blade in a decisive stroke. "And next time, Xan Temurezen, I won't miss. Just as you taught me."

She left him there, feeling only the absence left in the wake of his qì. When she stepped outside, the night air stung, biting and refreshing compared to the suffocating incense of the House of Drunken Orchids. *This,* Lan reminded herself, was reality. Better any day to face the cold, hard truth than to deceive herself into believing dreams of smoke and illusion.

She blinked. A strange sound had filled the night. Beneath the mournful low of the desert wind, it rolled out, slow and rhythmic, permeating the streets of Nakkar: the curved-roof pagodas and rammed-earth houses, the back alleys and dirt roads. It drowned out the faint sounds of laughter emanating from the brothel. It rolled over the distant songs of zithers and lutes across winehouses until the air seemed to tremble with it.

It was the sonorous toll of a bell, growing with each chime.

Lan's hands came to rest on the ocarina and dagger hanging from her waist. The words of the innkeeper returned to her: *The sound of a clock chiming, a bell tolling, children singing in the dark* . . .

A gust of yīn energies swept across the city. At that moment, the moon grew brighter behind the clouds.

Goosebumps broke across Lan's arms.

At the top of the Öshangma Light Mountain, within the thick, roiling clouds, the shape of an ancient temple had appeared.

7

> And the immortals danced
> In a garden of blossoms on the clouds
> Beneath a palace of jade amidst the stars,
> Their shadows cast upon the earth only when
> the moon shone brightest.
>
> —"The Immortals," *Hin Village
> Folktales: A Collection*

Lan conjured a small Seal with her ocarina, one that pulled the qì of shadows toward her, just enough to let her blend in completely with the pockets of darkness offered by the silent streets. She slipped through the alleyways, past winehouses and taverns and sleepy residences, until suddenly, the roads and houses ended and she found herself at the bottom of the Öshangma Light Mountain.

The mountains on this side of the Last Kingdom were different from their lush, misty counterparts in the central regions. Here, the crags jutted sharp and unforgiving. The Öshangma Light Mountain rose at an impossibly steep angle; tall junipers shadowed any paths that might have wound up it, alternating with dry rock until they disappeared into the clouds.

Her heart slammed against her ribs. By some miracle, the innkeeper's tale had held truth; here, before her, was a chance at the answers she sought. A chance to find the path to Shaklahira.

Lan craned her neck. The mountain was unnervingly

steep, and she could see no viable way up without using the Light Arts.

The tolling sound, though, had shifted, and now Lan understood that it was qì presenting itself to her in the form of music, spilling from the top of the mountain and winding through the spruces and pines. Its tone was soft, hollow, and blended in with the wind. Lan knew this music was a Seal, a question awaiting an answer. A half circle awaiting completion.

Who are you?

Lan brought her ocarina to her lips, closed her eyes, and played her response, placing notes in the cracks between those of the ghostly song, meeting each note as if making a moon whole, a circle fully drawn.

I am Sòng Lián, survivor of the Sòng clan and heir to the Order of Ten Thousand Flowers. I will bring an end to the Four Demon Gods and the vicious cycle of power, war, and bloodshed they have wrought upon this land and its peoples.

Her song shifted, became a key to a lock. Before her, the surface of the mountain rippled. Rock became translucent, an essence that just caught the shimmer of moonlight.

A forgotten Boundary Seal.

Lan stepped forward. Each such Seal was different, depending on the intention of its practitioner and what kind of qì they wove into it. The one that had protected the School of the White Pines had assessed the qì within the soul of a person attempting to pass through it, in order to ensure that they meant no harm. This Boundary Seal felt slightly different; as Lan passed through, cool currents of qì brushed against her, as though invisible people stood just several steps from her, whispering.

When she emerged, she was in a cavern of sorts. A set of stone stairs led up and out, disappearing somewhere on the side of the mountain. It was brighter in here; moonlight poured in, illuminating murals on the walls and bestowing on them a patina of silver.

The pictures were of people draped in flowing silks and sashes, gliding on clouds. Interspersed with them were mythological creatures: the Demon Gods, a nine-tailed fox, a skull-headed wolf, a four-eyed bird. The legends of immortals had persisted among the Hin, yet as Lan studied the figures gliding among swirling stars and clouds, wonder and sadness arose equally inside her. Just how much of the beauty of life in this land had the humans destroyed over time?

Moving from one mural to the next, Lan marveled at the detail. She had read in one of the tomes in the school's bookhouse that the Yuè had once created enchanted murals that could move and flow, like paintings come to life. The ones here, however, lay cold and unmoving, etched in stone. Lost to time.

When she reached the end of the cavern, she began to climb the steps that wound up and out of sight. A laugh burbled up in her chest. *There are no shortcuts to the Way.*

She summoned qì, gathering it in the soles of her feet. Then she took off, propelling herself upward leap by long leap. In this manner, the ascent passed by relatively quickly, the wind whistling in her ears. Soon, the ground was sloping gently, the junipers and larches thinning out as the stony earth was covered in a blanket of snow. Fog began to creep through the trees, rendering everything in shadows. Up here, the air was near-frigid; Lan's breaths came in clouds.

Lan slowed on the snow-dusted steps. The mist had grown so thick that she could feel the wetness seeping into her clothes—she must be so high that she was amongst the clouds. So thorough was the silence that she felt she'd entered another world. There was something different to the qì up here . . . something she couldn't quite place.

In the fog, someone began to sing. The song was unlike anything Lan had heard before: a monotonous, rhythmic chanting. She followed it.

More stone steps appeared before her, ones she could swear had not been there before. Deep blue Yuè script gleamed on them like lapis lazuli.

Lan climbed up the steps, and the world shifted. The fog around her dispersed, and it was as though someone had pulled back silk curtains and opened a set of shutters into another realm. The moon had been shining as brightly as a silver coin; now daylight poured like molten honey onto a resplendent palace of jade and pale stone. Peach blossoms, orchids, and magnolia trees swayed in a gentle breeze, filling the air with their fragrance. The place appeared utterly empty.

In her short time at the School of the White Pines, Lan had heard of remarkable Gate Seals that did not just transport one to a different location but actually changed reality. This one was an enchantment the likes of which she had never come across. As she made for the palace doors, a bell chimed somewhere, its sound carrying in the silence. A wind rose, scattering the clouds to reveal two stone pillars on either side of the entryway, each with figures wrought in lapis, jade, rubies, and other precious stones—the same twirling figures she'd seen in the murals in the cavern. Above the entryway hung a sign of faded gold inlaid with jeweled Yuè characters. Lan crossed the threshold, passing the pillars, whose inlaid figures were now life-sized. Whether it was the fog or her imagination, Lan thought their eyes gleamed, following her.

She was in a long hallway that shimmered as though in a dream. As she walked forward, her surroundings settled, growing more and more solid. Alabaster walls lined with pillars, ceilings filled with those painted figures on clouds, a gold-threaded carpet that unfurled with each step that she took.

Mist still swirled around her, yet within it, shadows began to move. Silk-clad figures knelt, hands clasped, their whispers stirring the air. Whenever Lan tried to look directly at them, they vanished.

A woman appeared before her, dressed in cross-collar robes of deep cerulean, their gold stitching glittering like shards of sunlight on fresh river waters. Sashes trailed her, rippling in a whispering breeze. Her hair was gathered in an elaborate bun, ornaments gleaming with sapphires, jade, rubies, and gold. The most striking feature was her eyes: pure white, like starlight.

Immortal, Lan thought. Or the ghost of one, if the innkeeper's tale was to be trusted. Whatever this was—illusion, imagination, dream, or traces of history—clearly the fabled immortals of the Yuè clan had not disappeared entirely.

Lan inclined her head and brought her fist to her palm in a salute. "Venerable master," she said politely.

"*Our kind is not to be venerated, nor are we masters,*" came the reply, echoing gently through the hall. The woman's lips had not moved; she only continued to gaze down at Lan serenely, as though nothing in this world might perturb her. "*Rise, child.*"

Lan did as the immortal bade her. She took in her surroundings: the unearthly whispers, the billowing clouds, the banners shifting in that errant breeze. "Where am I?"

"*You have crossed a boundary of sorts,*" came the reply after a pause. "*A Boundary Seal woven of the qì of souls, which preserves all that was once our kingdom.*"

"The qì of souls?" Lan knew souls to have qì, for Tai could hear the imprints left behind by them. She herself had met ghosts drifting through this world and had even stepped into a scene from the past once before. But she had never heard of a Seal woven by the qì of souls.

"*The qì of souls, of ghosts, of all those who should have passed into the otherworld beyond the River of Forgotten Death. It is an ancient branch of practitioning forgotten since our disappearance. Yet there are ways for those who once tread this world to walk again, for secrets lost to be found. The souls of immortals remain after our physical bodies are gone, guarding all the truths of your world and the next. When the yīn of the moon is strongest, this realm of the past that is preserved within the boundary appears in your world.*"

All the truths of your world, Lan thought. "Is this the Temple of Truths?" she asked.

"*It once was.*" The immortal waited, watching Lan.

Lan dipped her head. "Then, please, help me find the path to Shaklahira."

The immortal said nothing. She seemed to be expecting more.

Lan swallowed. "I seek the Godslayer, to destroy the Demon Gods."

"*Destroy.*" The immortal closed her eyes, and she spoke her word with a slow flick of her tongue, as though tasting memories of ashes and war in it. "*Why?*"

Lan thought of all she had heard of the Demon Gods. Of the Order of Ten Thousand Flowers, her mother and father risking their lives for this cause and passing the duty to her with their dying breaths. Anger sparked in her. "The Demon Gods are the reason behind all the war and death and destruction my kingdom has seen," she said. "Since the first shaman practitioners bound them, countless battles have been fought over their power, and so much blood has been shed over them. So many innocent lives lost." The Elantian Central Outpost, Zen's blank, broken gaze in the aftermath. "They're dangerous. We, the practitioners, are the binders, but . . . they are really the ones in power."

The immortal watched her impassively. *"Are they the reason behind the war and bloodshed of this world?"*

"They corrupted the imperial family. They drove the Nightslayer—Xan Tolürigin—to madness, to slaying entire cities of innocents. Of course they're the reason."

The immortal was silent for a long time. When she spoke again, it was with resignation. *"Make northwest to the spring of a crescent moon. When the stars burn, you will see the path to the city carved in its waters."*

The path to Shaklahira.

Somewhere, a bell began to toll.

The temple filled with a great rushing sound like water. The carpet and marble floors beneath her turned to shimmering silver luminescence. The domed ceilings were disappearing, their jeweled flying figures—glittering just moments ago—fading into mist. A rising wind began to lift the immortal's robes, the sashes draped across her arms. It was impossible to read anything from her gaze as she said, *"The Godslayer will not work for you unless you understand the truth—the whole truth."*

"The truth?" Lan repeated. "What do you mean?"

"To wield any tool of qì, you must understand the intent behind it. Just as a Seal cannot be conjured without a strong will and a foundational understanding of its usage, the Godslayer, too, requires understanding of the truth of its purpose."

Lan knew the stories of monks and practitioners who spent entire lifetimes cultivating their power to unlock a single magical artifact or summon a single Seal. They dedicated their lives to reading philosophical scriptures of practitioning, to understanding the ways of this world.

A tool of qì, she thought. She had assumed the Godslayer to be a sword, a dagger, or any form of a weapon, but the immortal's phrasing was vague.

"What is the Godslayer, and where can I find the truth to it?" she asked, but her words were lost to the gust of qì that surged through this realm. The immortal's outline shimmered, and she began to dissipate like a cloud in sunlight.

"*The truth. Two sides to the coin. The yīn and yáng of this world. The duality of reality. The truth, child, to this tale of gods and demons, of demons and gods.*"

"Wait," Lan said, but then the temple was empty except for the fluttering silk banners and the pervading mist. The temple was being swept away, alabaster walls and lapis-wreathed pillars dripped like waterfalls, gathering into a roaring river of light.

Of qì.

Lan turned to run, but the front of the temple was gone. Night poured in, the moon shining eerily bright overhead. The river of light was too strong, wrapping around her and pulling her back. As the rest of the temple came tumbling down around her, the bell chimed to a crescendo; the currents of qì brightened to a blinding white.

Then it all vanished.

Lan lay atop the Öshangma Light Mountain. It was nearly pitch-black, the moon hidden behind clouds. A wind had picked up, whistling across the barren, snow-covered landscape. And the night was filled with the stench of metallic qì.

Lan tried to move, but something cold dug against her throat, her wrists, her ankles.

Metal.

She was anchored to the mountain, the metal jutting from the rocks in unnatural ribbons, digging into her skin.

A pale face appeared over her, a slice of a white smile she recognized all too well.

Erascius.

She tried to scream, but a metal strap pressed against her mouth.

"Hello, little singer," the Royal Magician crooned in the Elantian tongue. He knelt on the ground, leaning over her with that terrible grin etched into her nightmares. "Pity I can't hear your lovely music right now." He reached out and trailed a cold finger up the skin of her throat.

Terror welled in her chest, so overwhelming that her vision darkened and for a moment all she could see was his hand with her mother's red, beating heart clutched in it.

"I can let you go," Erascius said. "I ask only one thing." His gaze grew flat, his voice sharp and businesslike. "I want the star maps to the two unbound Demon Gods. Let us begin with that of the Azure Tiger."

Deep inside her, the power that lay coiled by her heart stirred. An icy eye opened, pupils ringed white like frost, as the Silver Dragon sensed her fear and the danger nearby. Scales of snow shimmered in her mind as it began to rise.

No, Lan thought. *I do not give you permission.* The Demon God was bound by its bargain to protect her life, and only that. She would not chance unleashing its power when there was an entire city at risk below these mountains.

Lan forced her breathing to steady. The panic cleared, and her mind began to work again.

When Erascius captured her and Zen at the Elantian Central Outpost, he had forced Lan to give him the star maps, intending to track down the Four Demon Gods and bind them to himself. Later on, when the Elantian army ambushed Skies' End, the masters of the school made the decision to free the Azure Tiger, which they'd kept trapped at the heart of the mountain.

Had the Phoenix moved since the last time she had

conjured the maps, or had Erascius simply failed to track it down? Whatever the case, he was now risking his life to find Lan and ascertain the whereabouts of both the Crimson Phoenix and the Azure Tiger.

But . . . where was his army? Lan reached out into the currents of qì around them, searching for traces of metal.

"I had my army remove their armor, if that's what you were searching for," Erascius said. He watched her with an almost clinical assessment. "To my understanding, you Hin practitioners are able to sense the different types of energies the elements in our world exude. *Qì,* no?" His fingers came to rest on the metal strap gagging her. With a tap, it began to shift against her skin, slithering up Erascius's wrist until it disappeared into one of the metal cuffs he wore.

"Why are you here?" Lan demanded. Her Elantian was clumsy, her tongue curling awkwardly over the syllables after not having to speak them for so long. "You know I could kill you. I have the Silver Dragon."

"Then use it."

She stilled.

Erascius smiled. "No? I was inclined to believe as much. Just like that boy. You Hin have access to such *power,* and yet you choose to turn away from it." He held his wrist up. The cuffs gleamed in the dim moonlight. The Royal Magician pointed to one of a brown-red color. Lan noticed it had an engraving on it, the Elantian letters running left to right, horizontally—something she still couldn't get used to after twelve cycles of conquest.

"Inclinations and deductions aside, I did, of course, come prepared. This cuff is made from a metal we call copper. Highly conductive of energy, which runs through the human body while we live. A type of qì." He paused, glancing at her to make sure she followed. "The engraving on the cuff is a spell I have cast, which connects it to copper plates my soldiers wear. Should I die, the spell will cease to exist; my army will know I am gone. And those soldiers and other magicians I have stationed throughout Nakkar in the past day will destroy every last life in the city. And they will not stop. We will burn this land to its roots until there is nothing left."

His words pierced Lan with cold. "You *monster*," she whispered.

"I suppose that is what all without power might think of those with," Erascius mused. "Your civilians, when they were slaughtered by what your people call 'the Nightslayer.' Your clans, when they were slain by your very own emperor. Your Imperial Army, when they were overtaken by us. It is the way of this world, Sòng Lián."

She despised the way he pronounced her name—so nearly accurate that she wanted to rip out his tongue. She despised the way he spoke as though there was a *reason* behind everything he and his people had done to her and hers. Most of all, she despised the way his words might have held a speck of truth.

Erascius's eyes gleamed as he leaned closer to her.

"Well, my little singer? Will you play a tune for me today?"

8

*He who makes decisions
in the heat of emotion loses the war.*

—General Haci Ulu Kercin of the
Jorshen Steel clan, *Classic of War*

Her scent of lilies remained with him long after she was gone. It had been easy to conjure a Seal over the cut in his chest. Lan had aimed at his rib cage, at bone, and had dampened his connection to the Black Tortoise with the dagger known to temporarily sever demonic qì. The blade had come in contact with his qì, yet it hadn't penetrated deeply enough to completely diminish it. Zen remembered training her with this very dagger, the feeling of her fingers in his as he'd brought the tip of it to his chest and told her not to miss.

She was the only one who didn't need a blade to pierce his heart.

He crouched beneath the wall of a house, gulping down mouthfuls of cold night air. Head cradled in hands.

She hated him. Of course she did. He'd seen it in her eyes: hurt, fierce and unforgiving. He had wished never to see her cry, let alone be the reason she did. And he had wished never to hurt her.

Zen clenched his teeth and inhaled through them. He'd

thought he had left everything behind, had thought he would be able to cut off his past and his emotions for the sake of the greater good—and gods, what even *was* that anymore? But seeing her had been like cutting a wound open, over and over and over again. Kissing her had been a breath of air for a drowning man. And now the waters were closing in over his head and he was sinking.

He should never have come. What had he expected, seeking her out to ask for the Phoenix? He had betrayed her, had accidentally led the enemy to the home she'd come to love. Had killed the father she'd only just found.

A shift in the qì caught his attention, but it wasn't the ominous press of metallic energies the Elantians gave off. No, it was a summoning. Someone was calling him, from the top of the Öshangma Light Mountain.

Zen stood. He could hear it, as faint as the whistle of wind: voices speaking his name.

Temurezen . . . Temurezen . . .

Gooseflesh pricked his skin. *Aba,* Zen thought. *Amu.*

Those were the voices of his parents. They spilled down with the faint moonlight that penetrated the clouds.

He followed the voices, pulled forward as though by an invisible line. Strange, how empty the streets had become in less than a half bell; the Elantian patrols were nowhere in sight, as though by some unseen command they had retreated for the night. There was also another strand of qì woven through the currents of the path he followed, like a weft in a tapestry. It was a qì all too familiar to him, one he'd sought to etch into his mind with the memories of a silver-bell laugh, a flash of silken black hair, a curve of bright eyes.

It wasn't until he was past the clump of spruces and came upon the glimmering remnants of a Boundary Seal that Zen realized something was wrong. The qì of the Seal lay strewn across the rocks like cobwebs. It had not been unlocked with the careful finesse of a practiced hand and a Counterseal—rather, it had been forced open and clumsily, violently torn apart where it would not yield.

That, and Zen now noticed another strand of qì cutting through the harmony of the night.

Metal.

No sooner had he identified it than energies exploded, cascading from the top of the mountain like an avalanche. In the eerie silence that had befallen Nakkar, Zen thought he heard someone screaming.

Lan.

He took off, air whistling past his ears, stars a blur overhead as he shot up the steps of the mountain. He could feel the qì coming to a crescendo; in that gale was a song, a familiar one that brought back memories. A village in the rain. A girl playing an ocarina, the light of stars reflecting in her eyes.

Zen crested the mountaintop. The sight nearly sent him to his knees.

By a cliff's edge was Lan. Metal shackles snaked up her ankles and wrists, chained into the rock of the mountain. She played her ocarina, the light of the star maps casting the terror and tears on her face into sharp relief.

For a moment—just a moment—Zen stared at the star maps of the Four Demon Gods hovering above them. At the quadrant glowing vermilion, shimmering like flames imprinted in the sky. The great sweep of wings and tail that was the Crimson Phoenix.

And he noticed that the stars overhead had begun to coalesce with the ones in the star map.

The maps flickered out, and that was when a shadow

behind Lan moved. Zen tore his gaze from the sky, the map to the Crimson Phoenix seared into his vision.

Erascius's teeth shone like the glint of moon on his blade as he looked at Zen. "Ah," he said softly. "We meet again. What will it be this time? Will you finally unleash the full potential of your Demon God to kill me, *Xan Temurezen?*"

Zen had spent cycles learning the Elantian tongue to use on the missions he had carried out for Dé'zǐ. It never failed to chill his blood, to conjure memories of a dungeon, of sharp scalpels and pale hands in the dark.

He pulled on his own qì. He was still a practitioner of the School of the White Pines. Even without the Black Tortoise, he could still fight.

"Zen, don't."

His head snapped to Lan, and in that moment, nothing else mattered. Erascius had pulled her against him; the metal shackles unwound from her limbs like serpents, disappearing into the metal cuffs Erascius wore at his wrists. He held Lan like a doll, a *prize,* his blade digging into the curve of her neck.

Zen's chest constricted; fury blazed in his veins. "Lan—"

"He has soldiers surrounding Nakkar." She spoke, detached and with clinical precision, as though the choice they debated had nothing to do with her life. As though one of their conquerors did not hold a knife to her throat. "Nakkar and other cities. If we strike back, innocent people die."

Let them die, whispered that faint voice of darkness and smoke in Zen's head. *War is not without cost. What is power to be used for if not to protect those you love?*

His stomach turned at the way his Demon God twisted words Lan had once used. No, he would not become Xan Tolürigin. He would not use his power senselessly, would not sacrifice without meaning.

"You Hin," Erascius sighed. "Always too noble. There is no power without sacrifice. There is no victory without death."

And with that, he rammed the hilt of his blade into Lan's temple and shoved her off the edge of the cliff.

Zen didn't think. Didn't blink. Just reacted.

Wind roared in his face as he leapt after Lan, a blur of shadows and shapes, tree branches and jutting rock. She tumbled before him, páo fluttering pale in the moonlight. He could sense demonic energies awakening within her: a silver glow began to emanate from her skin and all around her; the shape of a great, serpentine thing cocooned her.

Logically, he knew—*knew*—that the Demon God within her was bound to save her life. Yet Zen had always found it nearly impossible to act on logic when it came to Lan. There was no conceivable way he would simply stand and watch as the girl he loved plunged from a cliff.

In every life, whether this one or the next or ten thousand more, Zen would jump with her.

He pushed qì to his heels, propelling himself to fall faster, *faster*. . . . He could feel the qì of solid earth and trees rising to meet him. At this rate, she would hit the ground before he reached her.

He gritted his teeth and pushed himself forward again. Stretched out his hands. Wind shrieked in his ears. The ground loomed. His fingertips grazed the fabric of her sleeves . . . and then he caught her wrist and pulled her into his arms.

The ground yawned before them. He would not die, he knew that; the Demon God inside him was mandated to protect his life. But he had run out of space, out of time, before the Black Tortoise took over.

He twisted sharply, flinging out what he could of his qì to summon a Seal, expecting the power of his Demon God to take over.

It didn't.

With a *crack*, he slammed into the ground—and in the moment before his world went dark, felt the acute pain of every bone in his body splintering to pieces.

9

> Once formed, the Demon Gods are awakened beings, with wills and minds of their own.
>
> —Xan Tolürigin, Ruler of the Eternal Sky and the Great Earth, *Classic of Gods and Demons*

The world drew together, one piece at a time, behind the pounding pain in her skull. Stars crystallizing. Pines swaying. Mountains breathing. And underneath it all, a current of qì running as deep and dark as vicious waters.

Warmth trickled down her left temple. Lan touched a finger to it; her hand came away glistening. *Blood,* she thought, and the memories returned. Erascius, the threats, the star maps.

Her gaze snapped to the top of the Öshangma Light Mountain, yet she felt no more of the metallic qì signature of the magician. He was gone.

She had no recollection of how she'd gotten to the bottom of the mountain.

The currents of qì in the air intensified, washing over her in cold, wrathful waves. *Demonic* qì.

Lan spun. On the ground several paces from her lay Zen. In the faint light of a moon hidden behind clouds, she could make out the odd angles to his body, the blood pooling like ink beneath him, soaking into the ground.

Lan recalled the cliff's edge where Erascius had held her, the crack of pain as he'd rammed the hilt of his knife into her head. He must have pushed her off, in a cowardly bid to flee once he'd forced the star maps from her. Must have known that Zen would have had to choose between fighting him and going after her.

And Zen had chosen her.

She knelt by him. His chest was still, his body broken in a hundred places, yet his expression was peaceful. The dim moonlight rendered him in shades of black and white. He might have simply fallen asleep.

Her breath came in shards. She couldn't think of anything other than the fact that a lock of hair had fallen in his face, as it so often did, and how she'd always wished to brush it back for him. How she'd refrained in the past. Now her hand shook as she tucked it behind his ear. Her fingers rested against his smooth cheek, dotted with blood and growing cold.

That was how she felt the exact moment when he drew breath.

Lan started, her other hand flying to the hilt of her dagger. Zen's lips had parted, and the second breath he gasped in was violent, shuddering through his entire broken body. Blood welled from his mouth. His eyes flew open, and they were unfathomably, endlessly black, the whites swallowed by darkness. Demonic qì billowed from him as the presence of a Demon God stirred within. The qì intensified, pulling together until she could almost *see* it: a great eye the crimson of blood and war and death cracking open. A shadow looming over Zen's body.

"No." The word tumbled from her lips as she realized what the Black Tortoise meant to do. *"Stop!"*

Zen's body had begun to mend. Cuts smoothed over as flesh knitted over wounds; the parts of him that had been bent at odd angles jerked, righting themselves, as bone rejoined bone and tendons tied together. It was nauseating—*violating*.

Lan unsheathed That Which Cuts Stars. The qì shifted; she sensed the being's attention flick to her. In response, she reached out to her own Demon God.

Inside her, the Silver Dragon's icy-blue eye opened. It took in the scene with a semblance of detached curiosity. Lan flinched as its voice wound through her mind. *It would not do to interfere in this demonic bargain.*

Her grip tightened on her dagger. "He didn't agree to this," she choked out, her voice cracking.

So long as his heart beats, their bargain holds. Unless . . .

Lan inhaled sharply. "Unless what?"

But the Silver Dragon's cunning gaze turned away from her and vanished, leaving Lan alone in an ocean of demonic qì.

Their bargain. Each time Zen used the Black Tortoise's power, the Demon God gained more control over his body, then his mind, then his soul. The Black Tortoise could have used its power to prevent Zen from hitting the ground. Instead, it had chosen to leave Zen to the brink of death and then flood him with its qì to heal him. This required the heaviest use of its power and was thus the quickest path toward gaining complete command over Zen.

Lan pressed the tip of her blade to Zen's heart. If she severed the Demon God's qì right now, Zen would die.

Her hands trembled. Her dagger remained where it was until the last cut on Zen's face had healed. He lay in the moonlight, skin like porcelain against the dark pool of his own blood. Chest rising and falling against her knife.

When he opened his eyes, still completely black, Lan knew it was too late as she slid her dagger into the soft flesh of his side. He looked at her, blood trickling from his lips, and there was nothing of the Zen she'd known in that face. It was a

Demon God staring back at her, its vengeful fury tempered by an age-old cunning that curved Zen's eyes. The truth remained between them: the stars might burn and ash might rain from the skies, but Lan had not the strength to take, with her own hands, the life of the boy she had once loved.

And she hated herself for it.

The demonic qì stuttered. The black leached from Zen's eyes until it was him, truly him, gazing up at her through a mist of pain. His lips parted; he reached out to her.

She froze. Her mind told her to pull away, to run and never look back, but her heart commanded otherwise. As his fingers, sticky with blood, cupped her cheek, she shuddered and closed her eyes. Let herself lean into his touch, even as a litany of his crimes went through her mind: *Traitor. Murderer. Demonic practitioner.*

As if reminding herself of all the terrible things he was and had done could bring her to hate him as she should.

His palm was gentle and warm against her skin. She knew this touch, these hands—achingly familiar and tender—that would never hurt her. This was the boy she had fallen in love with, and as Lan clasped her own hand to his, her tears might have become the rain from a memory, a distant dream.

It was simple, really.

She had given her heart to a boy.

And he had given his soul to a demon.

He no longer existed.

Energy pulsed through the air. Zen hissed a breath. Something was wrong. The shadows and darkness were seeping back into the whites of his eyes. The demonic power that had been fading was now steadily returning. The familiarity of Zen's qì faded, drowned out as that of the Black Tortoise thrummed through his veins.

A cold, sick feeling slicked Lan's stomach. That Which Cuts

Stars was a dagger capable of severing demonic qì. So why hadn't the Black Tortoise gone, as it had the last time she'd cut Zen and cut herself? Why was his qì still overpowered by that of his Demon God?

Zen's back arched, his mouth open in a silent gasp. The last of the whites of his eyes were fading even as he looked at her with desperation. "Go," he rasped. "I—cannot—control—"

Lan slid the dagger from his side. Blood began to spill again, but Zen had no reaction. The blade of her knife was completely red.

What's happening? She directed this thought at the Silver Dragon. *I cut him with this blade. Why is the Black Tortoise's qì not severed?*

Their qì is beginning to fuse, came the response. *The being that you call the Black Tortoise exerted much power to bring him back from the brink of death. Its control over the boy grows. Their connection is no longer something so easily broken.*

Zen was going to lose control. The Black Tortoise's power would grow unfettered, dangerous, destroying everything in its path—as it almost had at Skies' End. It needed to be stopped.

Her hands shook as she lifted her dagger high above Zen's chest. Lan fought to steady the trembling in her hands.

No, came the warning from the Dragon. Its core stirred; she thought she glimpsed a shimmer of scales as it unwound behind her. *You cannot kill the boy. Not unless you wish to provoke the wrath of the Black Tortoise. Not unless you wish to war with one of the Four.*

Her breath shook. Slowly, she lowered her dagger and severed the connection between her and the Dragon. Her mind grew quiet.

There was no more helping him; even the power of That Which Cuts Stars was helpless against a Demon God that had begun to lay claim to its binder. No, the only way left to destroy the Black Tortoise and to release Zen was to find the Godslayer.

Summoning all the qì she could, Lan turned and kicked off with the Light Arts. The world blurred. Zen's gaze was seared into her mind.

We want the same thing, he'd said to her. *Am I wrong?*

No, she thought now, swiping a fist across her face. Her vision cleared. *You're not wrong, Zen. We want the same thing, but we've chosen different paths to it.* Walking the Wayward path—yielding to power and corruption rather than maintaining balance—in order to achieve the greater good did not justify one's actions. The end did not justify the means and the trail of suffering left behind.

Perhaps none of their choices even mattered. What awaited them after all this was the same ending to their stories, blazing in the star maps and in the legacies that had been left to them—a tale begun and a fate written long ago.

The Demon Gods had to be destroyed.

And with them, the souls of their binders.

10

> First thing upon rising, the emperor takes this broth, served in a porcelain bowl. Soon his qì steadies and his mind clears, allowing him to begin conducting state affairs.
>
> —Imperial Physician Rén Fǔ, *Records of the Physician's Visits to the Imperial Court,* Era of the Middle Kingdom

He was adrift in a lake of darkness. The currents were icy, the waters unfathomably black, bearing him along as though he were a leaf in a gale. He couldn't see, couldn't hear. He might have become a part of the water.

There were shapes. Smoke in the air, billowing before him to form silhouettes.

He saw her first: pale silken páo, chin-length hair like black silk, a smile turned to sorrow, the glimmer of tears. He reached for her, intending to wipe them away.

Under his touch, she broke like a reflection in water, fading into nothing.

In the darkness came other shapes. Voices, echoes. *Temurezen,* they called. *Temurezen . . .*

He recognized them as a part of his past, voices that had collected dust and faded to whispers in his mind. People who had turned to ghosts. Far above, so faint he might have missed it, a glint of light appeared. He began to swim toward it.

Aba, he tried to cry out, but this was one of those dreams where he had no voice. *Amu* . . .

His calls were swallowed by the waters, which had taken shape before him.

Xan Temurezen, came that familiar rumbling, borne by the currents. He could sense the Demon God's presence curling around him tighter, and suddenly the waters he swam in weren't waters at all but great waves of qì. The Black Tortoise was a lake, an ocean, and he merely a speck of sand struggling within it.

No, impossible. The present had begun to filter in, along with a piercing pain in his back. He remembered, between bouts of wakefulness and unconsciousness, that Lan had pierced him with That Which Cuts Stars, which should have severed the demonic energies inside him.

The Demon God shouldn't be here. His mind and his body should be his.

When Zen drew breath again, he was lying on cold, hard ground. It was still night, and he was freezing.

Something was wrong.

He couldn't move.

He tried to sit up. An invisible force bound him in place, coming from somewhere inside him. The will of the Black Tortoise rolled through his body, holding him still. He was no longer trapped in his mind but in his own body, the qì of his Demon God strong enough to command his flesh and bone even after the cut the dagger had inflicted.

He felt the Demon God's smile: cruel, cunning, calculated. *I used much of my power to bring you back from the brink of death. So much that our qì has begun to blend. Our connection is no longer something so easily or swiftly severed.*

"You can't do this," Zen choked out. "Let me go. *LET ME GO!*" His voice rose, sharp and uncontrolled in his panic.

The Black Tortoise's chortles scraped against his mind. *Very well,* it said, and he felt its claws begin to withdraw from his mind. As the Demon God's presence retreated, the being left him with a final, ominous comment: *I swore to protect your life for a price. No matter how much you resist, your end is inevitable.*

The world seemed to brighten, and he could breathe again. It was far past midnight—the ghost hours. While he'd been unconscious, clouds had come to choke the sky, smothering the moon so that only a pale light seeped through. The Black Tortoise had used its power to staunch the bleeding of the wound in his side, though not enough to stop the pain. Zen wondered if that had been intentional.

He pushed himself to his hands and knees and stayed there, steadying himself while his dizziness faded. His breaths came faster, grief turning to fury at his Demon God's deception.

Zen let out a yell and slammed his fists into rock. It cracked beneath the qì of his anger. Panting, he stared at the spiderweb fractures that radiated from his hands. Tears dripped down his cheeks, splashing onto his fingers, mingling with the blood and mud.

He held one of the greatest powers of this land, this kingdom, second to none . . . yet a power that he could not master, that threatened to drown him instead. He'd known of this inevitable end, yet he hadn't anticipated things spiraling out of his control at such a rapid pace.

He still had so much to do. He needed to find the Crimson Phoenix and unlock the rest of the *Classic of Gods and Demons,* to summon the army his great-grandfather had once led. He needed to take down the Elantian regime with that power, to reestablish the Ninety-Nine Clans and rebuild the legacy of his Mansorian clan. He had dared to imagine a life ahead, of a land reclaimed, of freedom for his people, of spending the cycles with the girl he loved by his side.

All his plans, everything he had dreamt, crumbled to ash before him.

As he stayed there, curled against himself, he recalled one person who had seen him close to such despair. Back in Where the Flame Rises and the Stars Fall, the Nameless Master had told him of the imperial family's ability to keep their sanity while being bound to their Demon God. They had been able to rule effectively for dynasties, with the help of the ancient clan of immortals in Nakkar.

Zen stood. Overhead, the moonlight brightened. It illuminated the snow atop the Öshangma Light Mountain. Clouds feathered the peak, rendered ghostly in the night, and between them Zen thought he saw moving shapes: trees and temples, the shadow of a great palace.

The Nameless Master's instructions came to him: *Legends say that in the hours of night when the moon is full and the yīn is strong, the boundaries between our world and other realms—those of spirits, of ghosts, of souls—grow weak.*

The wind picked up, and it brought those voices to him. *Temurezen . . . Temurezen . . .*

The ghosts of his parents called him from the top of that mountain, where an entire realm of immortals were said to have once lived in their palace of jade. An unnatural wind pulled him in that direction, and Zen had the feeling that the gods conspired to play with the fate of this world tonight.

He set off toward the mountaintop as though drawn by an invisible force, his steps quick with the Light Arts. The Boundary Seal, broken by Erascius's violent entry, remained open. The qì of metals lingered in the air, a bitter stench resulting from the Elantians' harsh, discordant magic. Erascius, though, was gone.

The mist at the peak rendered everything in gray when he arrived.

Zen paused. His footfalls, he'd noticed, made no sound. The qì had shifted into something he couldn't place, something amorphous and intangible and . . . new. The disembodied calls of his parents continued, drawing him forward into the fog.

The palace appeared between one footstep and the next, as though in a dream. Night had shifted back to sunset, corals blazing in the sky and limning blossoms and willows in streaks of fire. The color bled into the ground, turning the pale stone steps carnelian, as though Zen walked a path of blood.

He'd seen illustrations of the supposed immortals' palaces: sprawling, splendid things of jade and jewels, gardens of lush flowers abed foaming clouds. In the paintings preserved in the few tomes he'd seen at the school's bookhouse, these realms—lands hidden behind Boundary Seals, really—had been filled with life. Immortals of the Yuè clan twirling in their signature long sashes, deerlike qí'lín darting between cathayas, flower spirits crouched amidst the begonias.

The Yuè clan knew the secrets to immortality, to the realms that may lie beyond our world.

The palace now sat empty, devoid of life. Zen walked alone in the setting sun. The clouds continued to shift like a slow-moving ocean, and once or twice, he thought he saw movement out of the corner of his eye. Remnants of ghosts or spirits, perhaps, that still haunted whatever realm of the past he had walked into.

He paused at a pair of great doors that led into a long hallway. Sunlight poured in, staining the molten-gold carpet crimson. At the end of the carpet stood a figure, naught but a silhouette amidst the tangle of soft-blowing silks and swirling mists. His parents' ghostly calls had fallen silent.

Perhaps there are yet answers to be found in Nakkar, the City of Immortals.

Zen stepped through the open doors.

11

> The Goddess of Mercy once had a clear vial
> of the Water of Purity. One drop and a sweep
> of a willow branch will reveal hidden Seals
> to the wielder.
>
> —*The Way of the Practitioner,*
> Section Ten, "Artifacts"

Lan's breath feathered across the stars like smoke. One week's travel northwest, following the instructions from the immortal that Dilaya translated onto her luó'pán, had led to sharply plummeting temperatures and long nights. As they traveled, the needle of the fēng'shuǐ compass had wavered at first before finally settling and pointing steadfastly: a sign that they approached their destination. Lan had failed to fathom how pointing the eight trigrams at various symbols on the wooden board—a crescent moon, spring rain, a jade dragon, a red sparrow—yielded the precise direction to Shaklahira, but she wasn't going to question Dilaya again only to be lectured on the *Kontencian Analects* and geomancy.

Shaklahira, Dilaya had divined from that accursed luó'pán, lay near Crescent Spring, an oasis near the northwestern border of the Last Kingdom. *The spring of a crescent moon,* the immortal had told Lan.

It had been relatively smooth sailing across the sand dunes

of the Emaran Desert. The sandsong had remained silent each night, and this far north and west, towns and caravanserai grew sparse—meaning Elantian presence had also become a seemingly distant threat.

Lan knew, though, that they were never far away.

Erascius had seen the star maps; she'd made the choice to yield them rather than the lives of thousands of people—*her* people. She and the Royal Magician were in a bizarre stalemate: he could not harm her so long as she had a Demon God bound to her, and she refused to use the power of the Silver Dragon to kill him.

The race was on. In the end, even if he tracked down the Azure Tiger and the Crimson Phoenix, she would destroy them with the Godslayer.

Now, she simply had to find it. And she was getting closer.

Each step in the sand felt like time trickling out beneath her feet—not only on the Elantian front. Without much to keep her mind occupied besides trekking through the desert by means of the Light Arts, Lan's thoughts inevitably drifted to Zen.

She'd left him wounded and fighting the Demon God bound inside him for control of his life.

Kneeling over him with her dagger pointed at his chest, she had weighed her choices. Trying to kill him would have been futile with his life and soul guarded by a Demon God. Yet she'd wondered, as she contemplated sliding her blade into his heart, whether she could have done it even knowing he'd live.

Lan landed on the next sand dune, a stitch in her side and an ache deep in her throat. *I wish for you not to go anywhere without me. In this world and the next.*

She blinked back the sting of tears. "Liar," she whispered. Her breath misted before her, turning the clear sky and bright moon into a haze of cold silver. She swiped a hand across her face. The night came into focus again, and that was when she noticed something strange.

"Dilaya," Lan called to the blur that shot forward with stubborn persistence ahead of her. "Dilaya. Dilaya! *HORSE-FACE!*"

Several dunes away, the silhouette skidded to a halt and turned to face Lan with a raised eyebrow.

"We don't have time for another break, weak-lunged little fox spirit," Dilaya called. "If that Spirit Summoner who hovers between life and death each day can travel for leagues, then *you* can certainly keep going."

"I don't. I don't *hover*." Tai alighted on the dune next to Lan with a frown. "I *listen*. To the souls and spirits between life and—"

"It's just an expression, Ghost Boy," Dilaya interrupted, exasperated.

Lan pointed at the sky. "Look at the stars."

Dilaya rounded on Lan. "You are *dead meat* if you made us stop for some stargazing when we're only a few lǐ away from—"

"Same. They are the same," Tai breathed. "They are the same as . . . as a while ago."

"Dilaya," Lan said slowly. "For how long have we been 'a few lǐ away' from Crescent Spring?"

The Jorshen Steel clan matriarch's head tipped to the sky, her eye narrowed, as she made out the patterns in the constellations.

And then she swore and stamped her foot so hard, part of the sand dune she stood on collapsed.

Tai reached into his storage pouch, its white spirit bell flashing in the moonlight. From within, he withdrew a glass vial. It was filled with clear water. A single section of a willow branch drifted within it.

Lan eyed the vial with interest. In her time at the school,

she had read of the Water of Purity that was blessed by the Goddess of Mercy. Practitioners used it to reveal hidden Seals.

Tai unstoppered the bottle and poured a single drop onto the sand. It lingered for a moment, shimmering like a pearl, and then dissipated.

Smoke—or what resembled smoke—poured out of the spot where the droplet had vanished. It grew into ghostly willow branches, leaves unfurling and climbing into the air. Soon, there was a glimmering net of misty willow branches reaching into the sky.

Tai put a hand on his hip and shielded his eyes, gazing to the bright moon and translucent net that stretched as far as he could see. It seemed to encompass an area the size of a city. "A Seal," he muttered, tucking the vial back into his storage pouch. "All this time. We have been going in circles beneath an Illusion Seal."

A *thump* behind Lan: Dilaya had landed on her sand dune. "That's a huge area the Seal covers," she said, sounding doubtful. "It'll be difficult to conjure the Counterseal."

Lan waved a hand. "Can't we just walk through Tai's ghostly willow things?"

"No. *No*," Tai emphasized forcefully, frowning at her.

"Clearly someone didn't pay much attention in Seals class," Dilaya snorted, but she began to explain, not unkindly. "The purpose of an Illusion Seal is to beguile, and in this case, it worked. We've been walking in circles around it for the past bell or so without even realizing it. Some practitioners who walk into Illusion Seals never realize, and die lost and alone." She gnashed her teeth, glaring at the dunes as though they were to blame.

A very different thought struck Lan. "Whoever conjured this Seal clearly had a lot to hide," she said softly. "The area is massive—I'd say at least a few lǐ. Big enough for palace ruins."

"You know, you have your moments, little fox spirit," Dilaya said, which, coming from her, might have passed for fondness.

"Quiet. *Qui-et*," Tai said, holding his hand up. It was the first time Lan had seen him exercise authority over Dilaya. The Jorshen Steel matriarch clearly recognized how important this was and kept silent, her crimson lips pursed as she watched him.

From his storage pouch, Tai withdrew a bell: bronze, this time, its surface dotted with spikes. In his other hand, he clasped a wooden mallet. A golden inscription of his clan sigil ran along its length.

Dilaya grunted. "Míng'zhōng," she said gruffly, impressed.

"The 'clear bell'?" Lan asked.

"Yes. Companion to líng'zhōng, Tai's spirit bell. Míng'zhōng sounds only when facing a direction in which there are no Seals."

Tai stepped forward and struck the míng'zhōng with the wooden mallet.

Strangely, it made no sound. The night wind swept through the desert. The sands whispered. Clouds appeared in the sky.

And then, from an empty stretch of desert beyond the net of phantom willow leaves came a low, reverberating note.

"Follow" was all Tai said as he began to walk toward it, and the command brooked no argument. Dilaya was uncharacteristically pliant as she strode ahead of Lan.

By now, the willow branches conjured from the Water of Purity had nearly evanesced. As the three passed through the last of its wispy leaves, the desert around them began to warp, like a glass bending out of shape. The stars scattered. The crescent moon stretched. The dunes before them undulated as though in a heat haze.

They were in the heart of the illusion.

It was dizzying, watching the ground beneath their feet shift with every step they took. They started and stopped in response to each note of the míng'zhōng.

Lan wasn't sure how much time had passed when it happened. Between one step and another, a sand dune split into two, then four, then more, the effect disorienting. As the dunes separated, a flat stretch of land appeared, and *there*, between the dunes and the horizon, was an oasis silvered by the moonlight.

Dilaya made a noise in her throat. Tai stopped and tapped his mallet on the míng'zhōng again.

This time, the answering note came, clear and pure, in the direction of the oasis.

The moon seemed to grow brighter as they approached. At the center of the oasis was a spring in the shape of a crescent moon—just as the soul of the Yuè immortal had described. The water rippled gently in the breeze and glowed like it had captured the fluorescence spilling from the moon and stars. Duckweed dipped gently into the spring as though in slumber, the quiet rustle of the place filled with whispers of dreams.

They had reached Crescent Spring. But, looking at the sleepy oasis and the vast, empty desert around it, the question arose—

"So where is it?" Dilaya turned to Lan. "I don't see any palace or ruins."

" 'When the stars burn, you will see the path to the city carved in its waters.' " Lan spoke carefully, rolling each word on her tongue like a marble.

"Why must these ancient immortal souls speak in *riddles*?" Dilaya ground out, hands on hips. "It makes everything unnecessarily complicated. This is why, in the Jorshen Steel clan, we prefer to speak with our swords. I don't need to tell someone they displease me. I can simply—" She made a stabbing motion.

"Riddles," Tai mourned. "When the stars burn. When the stars. *Burn.*"

Lan stroked her ocarina absentmindedly as she stared at the reflection of the stars in the water. They glimmered like jewels, blues and silvers and purples—but they certainly weren't burning. How did one make stars burn?

The answer came to her.

"'Long ago, the Heavens split,'" she whispered, recalling the old ballad. "'Like teardrops, the fragments fell to the ground. A piece of the sun bloomed into the Crimson Phoenix.'"

She knew when she had seen the stars burn, recalled it vividly: when she'd sat in a rain-soaked village, the song of her ocarina wending skyward and conjuring four quadrants. The quadrant with the star map of the Phoenix, a constellation outlined in flaming red in the night sky, had been the closest thing to seeing stars burn.

It was a wild guess. Lan's fingers slid into place over the holes of the ocarina. She looked at the stars and began to play.

The melody unwound, spinning qì into the star maps. Black, silver, blue . . . and then red—the star maps hovered in the sky, then began to fade. Except for one.

The quadrant of the Crimson Phoenix seemed to grow. It settled like a stream of fire and mirrored exactly the constellations they saw overhead.

Then, without a sound, the stars began to fall like rain. Dilaya shouted and scrambled backward as the spring caught fire, but Lan remained where she was, her head spinning.

"A Seal," Tai said numbly. "The stars created a Seal."

The flames had swept across the surface of the water, coiling into indiscernible patterns. Lan could sense the qì burning hot within the fire, forming rippling waves. She traced it in her mind, racing to decipher the strokes—but before she could make sense of it, the fire drew a great ring, beginning to end, and the Seal snapped into place.

It was as if the world had shifted and the sky fractured, so strong was the whiplash of qì that cracked from it. A fierce wind rose, howling as it swirled over the center of the spring, where the Seal burned. And there, from the surface, emerged a thing of river water and fire, coiling into the shape of a winged serpent. Its screech pierced Lan with a wave of yīn.

A great blue eye snapped open inside Lan.

The sky at once darkened and began to burn as a colossal surge of water and fire smashed down toward her. The qì hit her first, bringing her to her knees. Then she felt flames so hot that she wondered if this might be her last sensation before her death.

Lan reached for her ocarina even as a tidal wave of water unfurled over her, enough to break her bones.

It never reached her.

Qì rushed from her to meet the great water demon in a burst of silver light. A cool wind billowed past, and she felt the earth tremble beneath her feet.

Lan opened her eyes to a spectacular sight.

Two great serpentine forms reared overhead. The Silver Dragon's qì was knitted like a net over Lan and her friends, protecting them from the fire that rained down from the river demon. Seeing the pale glow reflected on Dilaya and Tai's stunned faces, Lan realized that the qì from her Demon God was visible this time.

The Silver Dragon lunged, qì bursting in torrents of white

petals. The water demon screamed as the Dragon's claw scraped against its belly; burning drops of its scales splashed into the spring.

As the Silver Dragon reared back in preparation for another attack, something in the air shifted. The water demon froze, its head cocked as though listening to a voice on the wind. And then it bowed to the Demon God, water sluicing off it and flames extinguishing. It shrank, dissolving, until the waters swallowed it whole. Where it had once been, only embers of its fire remained, flickering faintly in a pattern. A Seal.

The crackle of qì in the air calmed as the Silver Dragon turned toward Lan. It towered above her, its head crowning the night sky. In that moment, facing the great being—the god—Lan had never felt smaller and more powerless.

The Silver Dragon gave a slow blink, and Lan realized she'd dug her nails into her palm so tightly that she'd drawn blood. Even if she hid her thoughts from it, it could sense echoes of her emotions.

If the Demon God felt Lan's overwhelming fear, it gave no indication. They watched each other until its outline flickered and disappeared, as though it had never been there at all.

"Lan..."

She jumped as a hand gripped her shoulder; looked up at Dilaya's sheet-white face and frightened gray eye. They gazed at each other a moment, and Lan knew the two of them shared the memory of Lan's promise not to call upon her Demon God's power.

She hadn't this time, for the Dragon was mandated to protect her life—but she wasn't sure if Dilaya would care. Either way, unleashing a Demon God was risky.

Lan tensed, prepared for Dilaya's anger.

It didn't come. Instead, the girl's mouth only tightened

slightly as she gave Lan's shoulder a squeeze. "You're fine," she said gruffly. "On your feet."

They were interrupted by a shout.

"Look. *Look.*" Tai pointed vigorously toward the center of the spring.

The embers of the water demon, still gently aglow, appeared to be sinking below the surface. There, they unfurled like a painting.

A painting of a palace.

It sat at the edge of a spring that seemed to extend from within this one, as though place and time split impossibly. An arched stone bridge led across it, on either side of which swept golden sands. Light spilled from red lanterns swaying gently in an evening breeze, gilding the curved rooftops and vermilion pillars of the palace and the jagged green pines lining its gardens.

Shaklahira.

"I don't believe it." Dilaya's voice was hushed with awe. The three companions stood at the edge of the Crescent Spring, staring at the reflection that wasn't a reflection within the water. At a palace they'd thought fallen to ruin, instead intact and resplendent.

Tai knelt at the water's edge, brows furrowed and jaw tight in concentration. "A Gate Seal," he muttered. "There is a Gate Seal on this *spring*. The likes of which I have never encountered."

As he spoke, the surface of Crescent Spring began to peel back, revealing an arched stone bridge at its bottom. Green moss slicked the sides of the bridge, and kelp draped over its handrails, which bore swirls of gold that hadn't faded with time or wear. The waters of the spring parted, and this bridge connected with one on the other side.

It was as though they were being welcomed into the Forgotten City.

"I thought the palace would be in ruins," Dilaya said, turning to Tai. Her tone was flat, but Lan knew it was the clan matriarch's way of suppressing her uncertainty. Perhaps even fear. "Why are there lights?"

Lan glanced at Tai. His gold-rimmed eyes flashed as they caught the light of the distant lanterns, the light of a city that seemed to fall upon them from another world. "Don't know," he muttered, half to himself. "Don't know. But . . . to find the Godslayer, that is where we must start."

Dilaya's mouth tightened. She and Lan were bound by the same oath to their mothers, both of whom had served in the Order of Ten Thousand Flowers: find the Godslayer, destroy the Demon Gods, and bring peace to the people of the Last Kingdom.

But Lan flicked a gaze up to the sky and voiced the thought that had gripped her since the stars had begun to burn. "The Godslayer is not all we will find in the Forgotten City," she said. "Did you both see the Crimson Phoenix's star map from earlier?"

They nodded, but only Tai's expression lit up with the shock of understanding. "It matched," he said hoarsely. "It *matched* the sky. The Crimson Phoenix . . ."

Dilaya's eye widened. No doubt she had studied star maps with the Master of Geomancy back at the School of the White Pines. When a star map matched the night sky overhead, it meant one stood at or close to the location delineated by the map itself.

Lan hitched the sash over her waist, placing one hand on That Which Cuts Stars and the other on her ocarina.

"If I'm not wrong," she said quietly, "it seems a Demon God lies in wait in the city we are about to enter."

The three of them gazed into the mirage of the golden palace in silence. There was no telling what other dangers awaited them across the bridge, on the other side of the spring.

Lan curled her fingers around the bulge of the amulet that rested beneath her páo. It had become a habit of sorts—a talisman, nearly. A way to remember the life she fought for: the first rays of sun threading through misty mountains, the chime of a school bell and the clear voices of disciples, the promises of a boy who'd loved her. Memories that had faded to ash, a past that she would never resurrect—but perhaps a future that she could build for what remained of her people by destroying the sources of chaos that had gripped their land throughout history.

Sòng Lián stepped onto the arched stone bridge and began to walk toward the light of Shaklahira, the Forgotten City.

12

> An imperial supper must be served in fifteen-part, to include the five flavors of sweet, sour, salty, spicy, and bitter, representing the harmony of the five elements. Balance must be sought by an even number of cold and hot dishes, of raw and cooked platters, of meats and vegetables and cereals. An example below.
>
> —*Records of Hin Imperial Cuisine,*
> Chapter Four, "On Suppers"

The waters on this side of the world reflected the same stars. The glow from the palace rendered the sky a crystalline shade of amethyst. As Lan walked, she noticed shapes beneath the surface of the spring: carp, their pale bellies flashing and scales gleaming like jewels as they darted away from her shadow.

The entire place was a scene plucked from the fingers of time—as though the events of the past twelve cycles had never happened and Lan walked through an imperial palace that still reigned over the Last Kingdom. The gardens were lush with flowers of all kinds: osmanthus, narcissus, begonias, and azaleas; well-tended pines were spaced evenly throughout. The palace was freshly painted in vibrant shades of vermilion patterned with deep greens and golds, gleaming beneath the lantern light.

"Something feels off." Dilaya's voice was low as she kept close behind Lan, her arm gripping the hilt of Falcon's Claw, her gray eye constantly searching for danger.

"People." Tai's deep tone was tight with urgency. "There are people."

Light gilded silhouettes standing at the other end of the bridge. As Lan drew closer, she could make them out: two people with shaved heads, dressed in sand-colored warrior's robes. One had a two-pronged spear, its tips curving in a crescent moon. The other had no apparent regalia but for a set of wooden prayer beads.

"Impossible," Dilaya muttered. "They resemble Táng monks. A clan of warrior monks," she added, catching Lan's confusion. "That clan vanished sometime in the late Middle Kingdom era."

Between the two figures was a diminutive girl. At first, Lan thought she was a ghostly apparition, for her shoulder-length hair fell in a cascade of pure white and her face was as smooth and colorless as pale jade. She had a delicate nose and cherry-blossom lips, but most intriguing was the cloth tied over her eyes, embroidered with the same designs as the páo she wore, a pale brocade in patterns of bronze and violet. She held a fan in her right hand, its twin in her left, though the night was cool.

Her lips parted as Lan and her companions drew closer, and Lan had the strange feeling that the girl could see them even with the blindfold on.

"You have traveled far." Her voice was faint and sweet. "Please, this way."

Lan was unsettled. There was an entire, functioning *palace* in the midst of the Emaran Desert. And there were people of a vanished clan here.

How was that possible?

She brushed her fingers against the pouch with her ocarina as she followed the blindfolded girl.

Lan and her companions were led up a set of steps carved

from a white stone that Lan recognized as marble: a most coveted material, traded at the Jade Trail markets and originating in a kingdom by a temperate sea in the distant west. The steps glittered as though they were encrusted with broken stars.

She'd thought the Rose Pavilion Teahouse back in Haak'gong was ostentatious—but Lan realized she had never seen true luxury until the great red gates of the palace lost to time swept open and she looked into its golden interior.

Jade, sapphire, lapis lazuli, and a hundred other gemstones dripped from the walls and ceilings. Gilded motifs of the Four Demon Gods, along with other gods of the Hin pantheon, gleamed in the cornices. Vermilion pillars plunged skyward like the fingers of titans.

At the end of the hall was a golden dais and a reclining throne carved from a beautiful yellow rosewood. On it sat a person.

Lan sensed Tai stiffen by her side, heard Dilaya draw a sharp intake of breath. They walked toward the dais, then stopped nine paces from it—nine, the number of emperors.

The young man on the throne rose, and Lan had the impression that she looked upon a god. Everything about him was steeped in a time long past, from the carnelian-colored hàn'fú he wore, with its great, billowing sleeves and long skirt, to the way his black hair fell, uncut. It parted at his forehead, revealing an eye painted in cinnabar. He was of average height and build, and though he was young—a few cycles their senior, perhaps—there was something ancient to his beauty, to the depths of his eyes. His cheeks were flushed as though with fever, his lips red as though painted.

The blindfolded girl leapt to the dais. Lan hadn't even seen her move; the cloth of her páo and blindfold rustled once, then fell still.

"Oh," the young man said, and his voice was a lofty tenor, melodious and smooth. "Well, *this* is unexpected."

"That should be my line," Lan replied, "especially after the water demon you sent to greet us." Her mind was spinning fast. The last thing they'd expected to find in Shaklahira was some semblance of the imperial palace that had been lost twelve cycles ago. Because if Shaklahira had been well maintained and kept secret from the outside world for all these cycles, then this young man must be . . .

He tipped his head back and laughed. The sound was long and rolling, echoing through the gilded halls. It lapsed into a fit of coughing. He hunched over, pressing a red silken handkerchief to his mouth. When he finished, he straightened, leaving a dark smear behind.

A memory found Lan: an old shopkeeper's rheumy cough, the whistle of his breath. She knew of consumption, a disease frequently found across poorer Hin villages. How had this young man, secluded in his palace of gold, caught it?

"By the Four," he exclaimed, descending the steps of his dais. He swept a long gaze over them. "How delightful."

"Who are you?" Dilaya seemed to finally have found her voice.

His eyes slid to her. But it wasn't he who answered the question.

It was Tai.

"Hóng'yì," he whispered.

The name jolted through Lan. Stirred memories of that winter twelve cycles ago, of that *world* that had—until this very moment—been lost. She recalled her courtyard house, the occasions when Māma had sat with her in the study and recounted stories of the Imperial Court, of the emperor and his one male heir, for the empress and concubines had been too weak to bear the emperor another son. Lan recalled the villages in the days after the Conquest, the whispers and tears shed for Emperor Shuò'lóng, the Luminous Dragon, and his only son, the lost heir of the Last Kingdom. Gone so soon, so young.

Hóng'yì, Hóng'yì, they'd cried. *The young heir, the Red Radiant Prince!*

The young man's expression turned thoughtful. "That name used to go after 'His Imperial Highness,'" he said. "Though I've lost every right to that title." He swept his arms open with a flourish of long red sleeves. "Well met. Zhào Hóng'yì, former crown prince and imperial heir to the fallen Last Kingdom. Ruler of Shaklahira and any and all subjects within this Boundary Seal. I hope Xuě'ér extended a warm welcome to you on my behalf."

Lan stood, frozen in shock. This was the imperial heir to the Last Kingdom, in flesh and blood. Son of the rulers who had persecuted Lan's clan, who had hunted down Zen's family.

"Well?" Prince Hóng'yì said. He studied them with open curiosity. "Will you not introduce your friends, Chó Tài? It has been too long."

Lan knew of the former emperors only by her mother's stories, and later Zen's. She had thought them dead, irrelevant to anything and everything. If the prince still lived, then what was he doing here, in a desert palace hidden to the world, with an entire staff at his disposal? Why hadn't he fought for the Last Kingdom or attempted to rally troops against the Elantians?

And then: did this mean he hid both the Godslayer and the Crimson Phoenix? Or was he, too, a victim of the imperial line's lies?

There was only one way to find out.

Lan curved her lips into a smile and dipped her head. "My name is Lán'ér," she said, shifting dialects to the southern tones she had picked up in Haak'gong. "I hail from Haak'gong, from a teahouse recently destroyed by the Elantians."

"Dí'ér," Dilaya said. Evidently, she had picked up on Lan's plan to mask their names and true identities. "My northern village was taken in the Conquest."

Prince Hóng'yì smiled faintly. There was still a trace of blood on his lip, but he either was used to it or did not seem to notice. "Where are my manners? You must be weary and hungry from your travels. Come, dine with me."

They were led to the gardens by the waters that Lan, Dilaya, and Tai had seen when they had crossed the arched bridge through the Boundary Seal. The air was cool and smelled of fresh pines as they sat at a beautiful round rosewood table that had been laid out for them. The two Táng monks retreated, but Xuě'ér remained at the prince's side like a pale shadow.

Servants rushed forward with trays laden with hot food. It was the richest spread Lan had seen in her entire life: roast quail with radishes garnished with osmanthus flowers, smoked duck with mushrooms and sweet beans, rice cakes with bowls of honey, and a steaming clay pot of mutton soup, all accompanied by an assortment of cold dishes.

"Please," the imperial heir said. A servant had set down a jade pot in front of him. When he lifted the lid, there was what resembled a single lotus seed on a small porcelain platter. It was perfectly round, as polished as a pearl, and glimmered gold as though made of liquid honey. "Medicine," he said, catching the three of them watching him. "For my cough. Please eat; no need to wait for me."

He popped the seed into his mouth and swallowed. Something inside him seemed to roil: a qì, Lan sensed, trembling like an earthquake. Hóng'yì's eyes were closed, brows furrowed.

It passed in a few breaths. When he opened his eyes again, his skin had lost the pallid shade from earlier, glowing a healthy gold. He picked up a piece of smoked duck with his chopsticks and laughed when he saw them all staring at him. "I told you, please eat. I'll not be so ill-mannered as to take my consumption medicine at the dining table next time."

Consumption. So she had guessed right. It was a slow-encroaching disease that resulted in death.

"Consumption," Tai said. "You did not have it. When we were children."

Hóng'yì shrugged. "Life is full of surprises. Some pleasant, some not."

Dilaya suddenly loudly slurped her soup. Lan bit into a piece of quail and, to change the subject, quipped, "Where did you get these? Not a lot of marketplaces around this neighborhood."

The heir leaned back in his chair, made of the same expensive yellow rosewood as his throne. He held a cup of tea in one hand and picked at the dried fruits on a small enameled plate with the other. "Tithes from the Jade Trail," he said. "My warriors are often hired by merchant groups to protect caravans from desert demons. We receive payment in the form of their goods."

"I did not expect this," Tai said. He was still staring at Hóng'yì as though he expected to awaken from a fever-dream at any second. "I did not expect to find you. *Alive.*"

"Indeed. So what *did* you expect?" Just like that, the prince's tone turned sharp, his question as quick as an arrow.

"An empty myth. Ruins."

"And now that you've found me? Am I—" The imperial heir

doubled over in another fit of coughing. He cast a shaky smile at them as he wiped his lips. "Am I not what you expected?" His voice rasped.

Lan set her chopsticks down. She suddenly felt nauseated from the richness of the food. "You've been here all this time," she said quietly. "Why? You are the crown prince, the imperial heir to the Last Kingdom. Where were you when your kingdom fell and your people needed you?"

The prince set down his tea. He would not meet Lan's eyes. "In hiding," he said quietly. "When the resistance to the Elantian invasion began to fail, Father planned to send me away. But before he could do so, he died, and along with him, the power of the imperial household . . . and the Last Kingdom. I fled. I was weak and sick, and it nearly killed me to reach the secret palace my ancestors had built in anticipation of a day like that."

Lan held her breath, listening carefully to Hóng'yì's every word. Dilaya and Tai had gone still, hooked by the imperial heir's narration.

"I spent cycles simply trying to survive, working out a supply route and keeping myself alive. There were others sheltering in this great desert who found their way to me . . . and slowly, I began to build an army. I didn't know if there was still a point to what I was doing—not when my kingdom had fallen so quickly and so thoroughly to the Elantians."

"So you bided your time." Lan couldn't help the tremble of frustration that had seeped into her tone. "You were able to conjure such a powerful water demon. You have guards; you have warriors taking down monsters in the desert, but you turn away from the real monsters that have our kingdom in their hold? From the people who have suffered for the past twelve cycles, waiting for a savior?" Her voice had risen; it broke on the last word.

She had been one of those people.

The prince bowed his head. "I was young and afraid. I was . . . I was a coward. I cannot ask for forgiveness, but perhaps I can make amends for my inaction over the past twelve cycles." Finally, his gaze found hers and held it. "You are practitioners, are you not? You have hidden from the Elantians, and you have survived to find me. Help me. Help me save this kingdom."

Lan's lips parted. Dilaya's jaw dropped. Tai blinked, watching the prince with an unreadable expression.

Hóng'yì cleared his throat. With a sweep of his long sleeves, his desperation vanished; in its place was the cheerful prince, hosting guests over a sumptuous feast. "I apologize. Hardly one bell of knowing one another and I already seek your alliance. Such heavy topics are meant for the morning."

"Some of us have not had the luxury of time," Dilaya said harshly. Lan kicked her friend under the table, but Dilaya ignored her. "I don't mince my words, so let me be plain and clear from the start. I am Yeshin Noro Dilaya of the Jorshen Steel clan. Ring a bell?"

Lan considered throttling Dilaya. The matriarch was not made for the art of negotiation and wordplay over fine dining and court silks; she had been built for the language of war and swords. In a single sentence, she had blown their cover.

Hóng'yì inclined his head. "Our ancestors were at war. Mine fought to eradicate yours." And then the imperial heir of the Last Kingdom did the unimaginable. He stood, then went down on bended knee. "My life was saved by members of the Ninety-Nine Clans. I cannot change the past, but perhaps I can atone for it by building a different future."

Lan's breathing eased. This could have gone in a very different, very unpleasant direction. Dilaya, too, looked momentarily shocked into silence. And then her gray eye narrowed.

"Good" was all she said, but Lan knew the prince had moved her with his confession. Yeshin Noro Dilaya giving any form of a positive response was akin to the sun rising in the west.

Hóng'yì stood. "I presume you will stay the night." He did not await a response. "My guards will escort you to the guest chambers. Please make yourself at home. It has been long since I've had company."

The three companions stood to follow them. Lan felt a hand on her shoulder, turned to see that it was the prince's.

"I'd like to walk you to your chambers if you would allow me," he said.

She let him lead her down his palace's corridors. The doors were thrown open to the cool desert air, and moonlight streamed through the paper windows. Gold silk curtains stirred in the gentle breezes that threaded the halls.

Hóng'yì paused before a set of sliding rosewood doors. "It wasn't always like this," he said. "When the Elantians invaded and Tiān'jīng, the Heavenly Capital, fell, I was powerless. I had only my squadron of guards and this luxurious, empty palace—a golden cage."

"And things are different now?" Lan asked.

He watched her through his long lashes. "Perhaps," he replied. "You asked me where I have been for the past twelve cycles while my people suffered. If I told you I was biding my time, gathering my resources and searching for a way to take this kingdom back, would you believe me?"

She was silent.

He drew closer. She had the impression that, beneath his perfumes and silks, he smelled of something bitter; of fire and things burning, smoke choking down her throat. It must be from the medicine he took for his consumption.

"I understand if you have secrets," the prince said quietly. "We all do. But I also know that it takes much more than an ordinary practitioner to beat that demon at my Gate Seal. And I hope we can learn to trust each other enough to confide in each other. I hope we can be allies, Lán'ér."

Secrets. Lan thought of the great dragon coiled within her. Of her map and how the Crimson Phoenix's quadrant had aligned with the stars in this part of the night sky, limning them in the color of blood.

Tai had said the imperial family held many secrets—one of which was their own Demon God. Something didn't make sense.

"You told us your father died along with the power of the imperial household," she said. "Did you mean the Crimson Phoenix?"

He blinked, those long lashes sweeping his cheeks. A haunted look came over his face. "Yes. Our power was decimated. That was how the Elantians won."

But my star map, Lan thought. *It tells me the Crimson Phoenix should be somewhere near here.*

That and the Godslayer. If Tai was right, clues to its existence lay here, in the imperial family's secret palace, where they hoarded all the treasures that lent them power.

She needed to win this fallen prince's trust. Perhaps then he would offer information that would lead to what she sought.

She hadn't garnered a reputation for a silver tongue back in Haak'gong for nothing. And perhaps, once she got to know more about this prince, she would find that their paths aligned.

Lan tipped her face up to him. Curled her lips in a smile and crinkled her eyes. "Then, Prince Hóng'yì, I hope we can become friends."

His smile came suddenly, replacing the look of grief. "I would like that," Hóng'yì said, then took her hands in his. She started at the touch, but there was a childlike innocence to it. His fingers were very warm, almost hot—which might explain the feverish flush to his cheeks. "It has been lonely here, Lán'ér. I am glad you came."

She wasn't sure what to say to that. Lan gently removed her hands from his. "Good night," she said, "Your Highness."

"Please, call me Hóng'yì."

The Hin put much stock in names and titles and how those reflected one's status in society. To use one's truename was an indication of intimacy. For a prince, an imperial heir, to ask to be called by his truename only was unthinkable.

Lan stepped inside the rosewood doors and slid them shut, her head swirling with thoughts.

13

> And from the celestial river arose a fearsome beast . . . a serpent the size of ten, with heads ninefold. Xiàng'liǔ: he who would bring flooding and destruction to the lands.
>
> —*Scripture of Mountains and Seas,*
> Book Three: *On Rivers*

It was the nights that stretched the longest, when the yīn of the world was amplified and the qì of the Black Tortoise was at its most powerful. Zen had begun to have long gaps in his memory, often coming to, when the first rays of sun appeared, in a place he didn't recognize. That was when the Demon God withdrew to its slumber.

Today, Zen awoke by the edge of a cliff, the rot of death and decay sharp in the air. He passed a hand over his face. In the distance, beyond the heavy clouds that smothered the sky, was a watery smudge of gray. Dawn was still far off, but even the sliver of light yielded enough relief to make him want to weep.

He clenched his teeth and staggered to his feet.

He was far north of the Emaran Desert, at the western edge of the Central Plains. Another few days and the terrain might change to steppeland. The Chó clan had traditionally occupied this territory, which came with its own myths and legends in Hin lore. Zen could see why.

An unnatural fog lay thick over the land, rendering everything in shades of gray: the barren rock of the mountains that clawed toward the sky, the red pines bearing the copper countenance of dried blood. Withered leaves crackled underfoot as he continued his trek along the mountain paths. He'd passed by the Chó clan's former stronghold once, on a mission from Dé'zǐ; and from the handful of tomes still existing about the Ninety-Nine Clans and the Hundred Schools of Practitioning, he knew that the School of the Peaceful Light resided near a river—the one after which the mythical River of Forgotten Death had been named.

The qì of water was strong here, yet he couldn't tell whether that was from the mist or he was approaching a body of water. He paused, the snap of a twig beneath his boots echoing into the silence. Ahead, he could sense a weave of qì that stood out from the natural currents around him.

A Seal. A faint one, perhaps nearly gone, but still, a vital clue.

He found the gate moments later: a pái'fāng with pillars of gray stone and black brick, a single arch wreathed in mist, and tiled roofs curving to the sky. On the other side of it was a cliff that plunged down to a bone-dry riverbed.

Zen studied the pái'fāng. The faded gold engravings on the pillars were unlike those of the Yuè temple or the imperial Hin structures, in that the Chó engravings revolved around bodies of water: rivers and oceans, waves curling with froth. At their centers...

Lotus flowers. They appeared to grow from the waters of a river, their stems curving upward. Nested within the petals, like pearls held in one's palm, were lotus seeds.

Hope twanged through Zen's stomach. He touched the image.

Atop the Öshangma Light Mountain, he had entered the

realm of what once had been the palace of the Yuè immortals, vanished dynasties past. Its appearance Zen could not explain. The Yuè, after all, had cultivated immortality, which preserved their cores of energy—their souls—long after their physical bodies had turned to dust in this world. The few mentions of them in tomes at the School of the White Pines bookhouse had described them as guardians of ancient truths, secrets of this world and whatever lay beyond it.

In the palace gardens, Zen had met the soul of an immortal beneath a red-leafed maple, its branches reaching to the sunset skies like a spiderweb. The immortal had been looking intently at a tangle of leaves, the veins on their surface golden and jagged.

I know what you are here for. Her voice had been the cool brush of river water. Shapes, swirls of qì that were souls, perhaps, eddied beyond them, skirting past the tree with faint whispers. *You wish for history not to repeat. You wish for the tragedy of your ancestors not to befall you.*

Zen had fallen to his knees and pressed his brow to the clouds that swirled on the ground. "Please," he'd croaked. "I want to do the right thing for this kingdom. I only need the strength."

I see it in your soul. You need not tell me. The immortal turned, her face at once youthful yet ancient and lined with lifetimes, eras, of knowledge. *Pass through the Ghost Gates and you shall see a river of death composed solely of yīn, balanced by flowers of life composed only of yáng.*

Zen looked again at the pái'fāng's illustration of lotuses growing from the silent river. In Hin culture, they were symbols of life and clarity. " 'Flowers of life,' " he whispered to himself, " 'composed only of yáng.' "

At their hearts, the immortal had whispered, *grow the Seeds of Clarity.*

The immortal had heard his deepest and most desperate desire that night: to protect his mind from his Demon God's influence. The imperial line had consulted the Four many dynasties past, and they had found a way: the Seeds of Clarity.

Zen hesitated, the immortal's last words—a warning—following like an unwanted shadow.

Yet beware, for the Seeds of Clarity are at once a cure and a curse . . . a double-edged sword, just like the power you hold.

But he was drained hollow from dancing at the knife's edge for the past weeks, always one step away from losing his mind. Zen did not think there could be anything that would stop him from taking a Seed of Clarity.

He walked through the gate.

Nothing. Mist curled around his ankles, but no mysterious realm opened, there was no Boundary Seal, and no lost ghouls attacked him. He merely stood on the other side, near the edge of the cliff above the dry riverbed.

Frowning, Zen circled the pái'fāng, examining every inch. The stone slate under the tiled roof—where the place name would usually have been inscribed—was blank, but Zen could sense the faint traces of the Seal he'd picked up earlier. It was as though the pái'fāng conspired to hide something.

It was broken, Zen realized with surprise when he focused his attention on it. He carefully parsed through the currents of qì woven together, so faint with time that it was like attempting to puzzle out a dusty fingerprint.

Zen knew better than to attempt to re-create a Seal he could not read. The Hin storybooks were full of practitioners who had wandered into traps by dabbling in unknown magic, out of greed or desperation. The stories had all seemed so illogical and far away when he'd read them growing up in the relative safety of the school.

None of those practitioners were losing their minds to a

Demon God. None of them had nearly hurt one of their own friends as a result.

Zen gritted his teeth and pulled on his own qì, flaring it as much as he could to drown out the other. Blinking away the black edges in his eyes, he focused on each stroke in the unknown Seal carved onto the pái'fāng. Several times, he thought he sensed the characters pulling together to summon something. And all the while, he thought of Lan and the possibility that he might never see her again.

His grief poured out in torrents, forming the final, circular stroke that completed the Seal.

Somewhere in the mountains, a ghostly bell sounded. The fog around him began to sift into the open arch of the pái'fāng, faster and faster as the chimes multiplied. The air shook with their notes, which grew so loud that Zen reached up to cover his ears. The fog that had gathered in the arch now rendered its opening completely opaque, blotting out the cliffs and sky on the other side.

Within the archway, a shadow moved.

Zen's right hand went to Nightfire's hilt, his other held before him in preparation for defensive Seals. The screaming of the bells was now all-encompassing, rattling the mountains around him and drilling through his skull.

All of a sudden, it stopped.

A demon exploded from the arch.

Zen cursed as he leapt into the air, propelling himself backward to avoid the lash of the demon's tail. Through the fog came more attacks: a flash of teeth above his head, a glint of scales beneath his feet—impossibly fast, as though more than one creature surrounded him.

Zen twisted into the air and flung a fú, which wrought daggers out of wind, cutting against teeth and scales. He landed on solid ground and stumbled back—only to feel a sharp pain in his shoulder as teeth punctured his tendons, lodging in bone.

His vision blanked. When he blinked again, he was kneeling on the mountain a dozen steps from the pái'fāng, blood slicking his hands and the stone beneath.

XAN TEMUREZEN. The Black Tortoise's voice sounded closer than it had ever been. More real, as though it were a part of him and ringing through the mountains at once. He imagined a dark glee in its tone. *DO NOT RESIST ME, SHOULD YOU VALUE YOUR MORTAL LIFE.*

Zen looked up, blinking pain from his eyes.

A serpent the size of a mountain towered over the pái'fāng. Its neck split into nine, and instead of heads, each ended in a skull that appeared a cross between snake and man. Fangs gleamed with what might have been poison, and the slivers of rotten tongues flicked out as all nine skulls beheld him.

This was no demon. This fell into the classification of supernatural spirits known as guài. A monster.

He had read something close to this creature's description in the *Scripture of Mountains and Seas*. Xiàng'liǔ, the beast in the *Scripture* was named: a nine-headed mythological serpent that held a deadly river in its belly.

A sudden inkling of what might await him took root in his stomach. The pái'fāng's gateway swirled, thick with fog—this time, supernatural. And the beast was positioned before it, tail wrapped around the pái'fāng like a serpent over its egg.

To get to the Seeds of Clarity, he needed to defeat this monster and get through the pái'fāng.

XAN TEMUREZEN, his Demon God boomed again. *Yield to me before the demon wounds you again.*

Zen blinked the shadows from his vision and tightened

his grip on the hilt of his sword as the nine-headed serpent screeched and sent a blistering gust of demonic energy at him. If he faced the beast again and lost, the Black Tortoise would take over. Another near-death situation would let the Demon God sink its claws into his body, mind, and soul nearly irrevocably. Zen did not know if he would recover from that.

But he'd be damned if he didn't put everything on the line to fight this creature on his own first.

He was Xan Temurezen, heir of the Mansorian clan leader and practitioner of the School of the White Pines.

I will live. I will take back this land. I will see Lan again.

With renewed strength, he snapped down the mental wall between him and the Black Tortoise, shutting it and its power out.

Zen drew Nightfire. His jiàn gleamed like an extension of his arm, an old friend and companion, as he raised it to face the monster.

Its nine mouths opened and it shrieked, lunging at him.

Zen dodged as one of the nine heads shot toward him; heard the snap of its jaw as it closed around air, and then the second was upon him, the third coming from below. Zen ran and leapt. His boot slammed against one of the necks, and he nearly slid but righted himself with a jet of qì from his opposing hand.

He bent his knees and sprang into the air, propelling himself into the mass of writhing necks and skeletal heads. When they came for him, he was ready.

He flung out fú in a sweeping arc. With the slightest flip of his finger, they activated.

Bright light and heat seared all around him as the fire Seals exploded. He heard screeches and through the smoke saw the heads rearing back as the monster stumbled.

Between its writhing heads came a flash of gold. An

inscription had appeared on the pái'fāng, engraved into the slate tab that hung between the two pillars:

鬼门
THE GHOST GATES

Pass through the Ghost Gates, the immortal had instructed him.

Zen took off and leapt, perhaps harder than he ever had before. Slashed as a serpent head came snapping at him, felt Nightfire cut through flesh and sinew. He tasted the thick tang of metal in his mouth, felt his heart straining as he pushed his body for more, more . . .

The pái'fāng loomed before him.

Ahead, the monster's tail curled before the open arch. With an easy pulse of qì—one of the earliest techniques of the Light Arts he'd learned at Skies' End—Zen somersaulted over the creature. And then the way to the gate was cleared and he was soaring toward it, the wind roaring in his ears and the thick, gray fog seeming to open to him.

Zen passed through, and the world fell silent.

14

> The greatest strategist is one
> who learns to love their enemy.
>
> —General Yeshin Noro Talara of the
> Jorshen Steel clan, *Classic of War*

Lan awoke to silk sheets, soft cushions, and sunlight streaming through patterned gauze curtains. She'd slept with That Which Cuts Stars and her ocarina in her arms out of habit. Someone had drawn open the fretwork windows and placed a steaming cup of tea and a bowl of dried fruits by her bed. The washbasin had been filled with clear, cool water, and a set of fresh páo the blue of spring water had been laid out by the bamboo basin.

Lan washed, dressed, and after a quick breakfast, stepped outside.

The palace was beautiful in the daytime. Sun poured like molten gold into its halls through the open shutters. A desert wind stirred the gauze curtains, which shaded her as she walked.

She passed by guards and servants who, for some reason, gave her a wide berth or would not meet her gaze. Despite the presence of a court, the place was disarmingly silent. Since she had no idea where Dilaya's and Tai's chambers were, Lan roamed along the hallways, her focus sharp as she took in the lay of the land.

Tai had told her the emperor kept his most precious possessions in this Forgotten City of the West. Lan had expected sealed-off chambers and secret passageways brimming with treasure—but she realized that Shaklahira was ostentatious in its decor yet almost ascetic in how few valuables it held. Each item here had been selected like a prized jewel, from the furniture of yellow rosewood to the woven-silk rugs patterned with blossoms.

Well, she doubted that the crown prince would have the Godslayer sitting on a cabinet with a neat placard underneath. The best way to start when one needed information, Lan had always found, was through conversation.

A serving girl in the gardens led her to a pavilion, where a flock of servants immediately offered up an array of teas and qi-remedying herbal soups and sesame cakes. Lan's cheerful attempts at making conversation went ignored.

"This is delicious," Lan said, flashing the servants her sweetest smile. "Have all of you been here for a while?"

They only bowed and shuffled back.

"They don't talk," came a voice, and Lan was relieved to see Dilaya striding through the rosebushes toward her, sabers at her hips. Without waiting for an invitation, she sat and reached for a platter of honeymelons. "Trust me, I've tried."

"Maybe that's because you're not very charming," Lan said.

Dilaya flicked a melon rind at Lan, who dodged it. Immediately, one of the servant girls scurried forward to pick it up.

"Let me," Lan said quickly. There was something uncomfortable about being waited on; she had spent too many cycles of her life on the other side of the screen, bowing and scraping for patrons at the teahouse. She reached for the melon rind, but her hand jabbed against the back of the girl's hand and pushed up the sleeve of her páo. On the girl's smooth skin, a pattern had been painted in cinnabar.

Lan's lips parted. Where had she seen this mark before?

The girl blinked and cast Lan a glance. She snatched her hand away and retreated, all but fleeing with the melon rind.

Lan straightened. She had the strangest feeling that she was looking at a painting that wasn't quite right, that was missing something. She glanced at a cluster of sand hibiscus, the blooms jarringly bright against the endless stretch of desert beyond. That was it: everything here was too beautiful, too perfect, from the neatly manicured gardens to the gilded palace.

None of it should have existed in the first place.

She leaned forward, speaking to Dilaya in an undertone and cutting straight to the point. "We need to spread out and search for the Godslayer—but first, we need to know what it is. Did your mother give you any clues?"

"I don't even think they knew," Dilaya replied.

"The immortal back in Nakkar told me it was a 'tool of qì.'" Lan blew a strand of her hair from her face. "That could be anything imbued with energies."

"Right." Dilaya's gray eye flashed. "Although we do have one point of leverage we should use to our advantage."

"And that is?"

Dilaya smiled wolfishly. "Haven't you noticed? Prince Hóng'yì has taken an interest in you. He could barely keep his eyes off you last night. I suggest you use your"—a lift of her eyebrows—"*charm* to try to squeeze some answers out of him, and to keep him distracted so that Tai and I can search this place."

Lan glanced around at the endless sands, the greenery and rosebushes that bloomed from arid land, the glittering spring that led to the other side of the Gate Seal. All was so tranquil, without any hint of demonic qì. So why had the star map of the Crimson Phoenix pointed here? And would Hóng'yì even know about the Godslayer? The imperial heir was an enigma of his own.

One thing was certain: beneath the idyllic oasis and languid dunes were buried secrets.

Waiting to be uncovered.

"We need to understand what he wants," she said. "He is the heir to the emperor of the former regime. A worthwhile ally, but I must first gain his trust."

Dilaya's jaw tightened. "Just be careful. That man's ancestors are responsible for slaughtering my clan."

Lan looked away. *People are not their ancestors,* she wanted to say to Dilaya, but then what of Zen, who had chosen precisely the same path of destruction that his great-grandfather had carved out in blood?

"I'll be careful," she said, and then switched topics. "Have you seen Tai?"

Dilaya scowled. "He always slept in till the hour of the snake, even back at Skies' End."

"The hour of the snake seems a good time to rise."

Dilaya opened her mouth as though to bicker, and Lan wished she would. Quarreling with Dilaya might bring some semblance of normalcy to this strange, silent place. But then the spark in the girl's eye died, and the shadow of their mission swept over her expression again, settling between them.

"I will find him, and we will see what we find in these golden halls," Dilaya said. "In the meantime, see what information you can glean from the prince."

Lan plucked a sand hibiscus from its bush and proffered it to Dilaya. "I never thought the day would come when you'd admit that my charm and wit have some use."

Dilaya smacked the flower to the ground and stomped on it. "Don't get used to it."

*　*　*

The imperial heir's study was at the very heart of the palace. Away from the shutters of the outer halls, it was dark, the only light that of flickering red lanterns. Several of the maids pointed Lan in the direction of the study, and she found herself standing before a set of elaborate rosewood sliding doors.

Lan could sense the Seals dripping from the intricate fretwork as she reached for the doors. So many, whispering with combinations of qì she could not yet hope to understand.

The doors slid open of their own accord, and she stepped into the prince's study.

The chamber was long, almost a hall of its own: dimly lit and perfumed by the scent of desert roses. Bookcases lined the walls, brimming with row upon row of gleaming tomes. At a dark cherrywood desk in the center of the room, a lantern burned, illuminating a seated figure.

Prince Hóng'yì wore a páo today, spilling in a loose tumble of red and gold, as opposed to the tighter, structured hàn'fú he'd worn last night. His hair was unbound, falling over a sliver of his bare chest. He looked up, the lantern casting their red glow into his eyes.

Lan inclined her head. "Your Highness."

"Lán'ér." He set down the horsetail brush he had been writing with and beamed at her. "I thought I was clear last night: you may call me Hóng'yì."

Lan returned his smile. "You are generous, Your Highness," she said as she took a seat across from him. It was only when his hair fell back as he angled his face to look at her that Lan recalled the cinnabar pattern she'd seen on the serving girl's wrist. It was the same one that the prince had on his forehead.

"Xuě'ér," the prince said, and Lan started as the figure of a girl moved in the shadows. Lan hadn't even sensed her qì. For some inexplicable reason, it took effort to focus on this girl's presence. "I will be fine alone with Lán'ér. Would you see to it that our guests Chó Tài and Yeshin Noro Dilaya have whatever they need throughout the day?"

Don't, Lan wanted to say, for if Xuě'ér went to tend to them, there was no way Dilaya and Tai could snoop around. She opened her mouth, searching for an excuse, but none came to mind that wouldn't be suspect.

Xuě'ér snapped one of the two fans she carried shut and inclined her head. Only her white hair—perhaps the source of her name, *xuě* meaning "snow"—rustled slightly, along with the silk of her blindfold. Then she was gone.

Lan made sure her smile was back when the prince's attention returned to her. "Interesting choice of wardrobe," she said lightly, gesturing to her eyes to indicate Xuě'ér's blindfold.

"She was given the blindfold when she was young, to help with her training," Hóng'yì replied, flipping absentmindedly through a scroll. "Now she seems to prefer it. Perhaps it reminds her of her mother."

"What sort of training would require a blindfold?"

Hóng'yì gave a noncommittal shrug and changed the subject. "You came to find me," he said, and leaned forward just so the lamplight limned his lashes. "Why are you here?"

She drew a sharp breath. There was something magnetic, almost hypnotic, about his gaze up close. Something that drew her to place her elbows on the table, just enough to close the distance between them. "I want to know more about you," Lan said, and it wasn't a complete lie. She wanted to know more about him to learn about the Godslayer. She wanted to know more about him to learn about *him*. The prince was an enigma; as with Shaklahira, she felt that there was something missing to the picture that she couldn't put her finger on just yet.

Hóng'yì's eyes were black pools, infinitely deep. "It seems we have a mutual interest," he murmured. "There is a way, Lán'ér, to open our minds to each other, completely and without lie."

"Is your plan to bribe me with plum wine and pork buns?" she asked, a teasing lilt to her tone.

His smile did not reach his eyes. She had a sudden, jarring memory of another boy who had beheld her, whose frown had melted as his lips curved and his eyes crinkled.

She drew back slightly. A familiar ache found her heart.

Hóng'yì did not seem to notice. "The Hin principles of practitioning focused on the different branches—the *Arts*—of specialization," he said. "But there is a school of thought, spearheaded by the former Yuè clan, that qì is segregated into three layers: qì of the flesh, qì of the soul, and qì of the mind. Practitioners mostly use the first layer, the qì of the flesh, to conjure physical Seals. Then there are those who converse with ghosts, with the echoes we leave behind after death, with the qì of our souls."

Lan listened, unblinking. She thought of Tai and his clan's ability to commune with ghosts and imprints of souls. The School of the White Pines had not categorized that ability, other than to bestow upon him the title of Spirit Summoner.

"Perhaps least common are those with the ability to manipulate the qì of the mind. This art is likely lost to the world of practitioning, for there was only one clan that possessed this ability." Hóng'yì smiled. "My clan."

Lan's lips parted. Not for the first time, her gaze darted to the cinnabar eye on his forehead and wondered whether that was related to his art. "And let me guess," she said, attempting to sound playful, "you hid away your art just as you hid away this beautiful palace."

"Indeed. But once in a lifetime, I am persuaded to be

generous." Hóng'yì held out his hand. "I could show you if you'd like. Reading and penetrating the qì of someone's mind, someone's thoughts, someone's emotions."

She looked at his outstretched hand. His fingers were slim, long, the skin soft and untouched by the hardships of life. She could not refuse this offer, not if she wished to find out more about this prince and the imperial family's secrets.

She placed her callused palm in his.

"To learn from me, you will need to discard everything you know about practitioning," Hóng'yì said to her. "Your masters at whichever school trained you taught you only the fundamentals. The *science* of formulating the different types of qì into Seals and using them for your purposes. But I will lead you toward the enlightenment the monks of old achieved; show you the layers of practitioning lost to time. Learn with me, Lán'ér, and you will see practitioning change from science . . . into *magic*."

Something in the air shifted, and when Lan looked into Prince Hóng'yì's gaze, she saw in their darkness the golden palace and bleeding roses, great feathered wings that burned. The pupils of his eyes seemed to expand, and she felt herself tip forward into them as they seized her whole.

The sensation was not physical; it resonated in her mind, yet seemed so searingly real that she felt as though a pair of hands had clamped over her cranium. There was a moment of pressure, and then her vision faltered as a foreign presence slipped inside her head.

Memories sifted past her in rushes of color and sound: a brightly lit teahouse, a girl in pale pink silks, a woman whose metal nails sliced, a dusty shop kept by an old man with a cough—

"The qì of the mind is fickle," came a voice. Hóng'yì stood across the river of memories, his red páo as bright as a flame.

"Find a memory and step within to stabilize the mind. The art, then, is to tease out information by rebuilding strands of the qì within, and coaxing your opponent to open more and more of their mind to you."

I am in my own mind, Lan thought.

Hóng'yì turned as a courtyard house appeared behind him, willows shifting in the slanted sunlight, and stepped into the memory.

When Lan blinked again, she sat in a study across a set of fretwork windows. They had been thrown open to a great courtyard outside. A warm summer breeze blew in, and the weeping willows whispered across fanstone paths. Sunlight gleamed across ponds, refracting on the arched stone bridge and pavilions that wound between eggshell-white walls. The entire thing felt like an image out of a dream.

Lan couldn't quite remember how she'd gotten here.

"You fell asleep copying sonnets again," came a songlike tenor voice behind her. She turned to see a young man seated on one of the lacquerwood chairs. He leaned over a tea table—she hadn't noticed the table—and loose parchments strewn on its surface fluttered in the breeze. Neat vertical rows of calligraphy spilled down their lengths, though upon closer examination, they seemed to blur.

"Is this . . . home?" she asked, and a pang of wistfulness hit her so strong that she thought she might weep. She couldn't fathom why.

"Of course," the young man replied.

She frowned and focused her gaze back on the young man. He, too, was familiar—beautiful, with a slim, chiseled face and hair that spilled down his shoulders like ink. There was something to his smile that was teasing as he shifted to watch her, his chin in his palm. His cheeks were flushed, his lips red as though they'd been painted, but as she looked at his forehead, she couldn't help but feel as though something was missing. Red... something red... why was she thinking of red?

"What are you hiding?" he asked her.

The question came out of nowhere. She startled, her thoughts reeling.

The star maps inside the ocarina—

On the tea table between them, her ocarina appeared, summoned by her thought.

Māma's Seal, which bound to me the Silver Dragon—

The air began to glow. Lan's heart started to race as her mother's Seal materialized before them. Within, a great serpentine form moved, as though trapped.

Something was wrong: all of her deepest secrets, ones she had never shared with anybody, were manifesting before this stranger.

Outside the window, the clouds were shifting; the color was leaching from the willows, glittering white snow sweeping over the grounds. No, this wasn't her courtyard house. This wasn't home.

Home no longer existed.

Winter crackled over the house, ice clamping over the green of the willows and freezing over the ponds. Pools of red bloomed across the snow, and the air grew heavy with the scent of metallic qì. Lan looked back at the young man sitting across from her. His face was blank, but surprise flickered in his eyes. She could sense them now, the strands of qì of her thoughts and memories he'd coaxed together, building into this memory.

Lan seized the qì and pushed it away.

The memory shattered.

Lan gasped and wrenched her eyes open. The scene—lacquerwood chairs, fretwork windows, weeping willows, and summer light—vanished like smoke. She sat on the floor in the prince's dim study, incense smoke from the altar table in the corner thick in the air. It smelled of desert roses, of something bitter and burning.

Across from her, Hóng'yì's eyes flew open. Beads of sweat had appeared at his temples, pearling over the cinnabar eye on his forehead. His lips parted, and for a brief moment, she imagined he looked annoyed. Then he puffed out his cheeks and blew and gave a shaky laugh, and the moment was gone. "Ah, I did not expect that. You did well for your first time."

She realized how low the lantern burned. It had felt like only several minutes. "I'm a quick study," she replied, picking up her tea to drink. She hoped he would not notice her hands trembling.

"The trick," Hóng'yì said, "is to convince your opponent that it's real. There are some who prefer quick attacks on their opponents: disarm them, lull them into a comfort, and then strike to penetrate their mental walls before they put shields up. That was my intent when I asked you for your secrets." His eyes crinkled. "If I tell you not to think of something, you'll find that you immediately will.

"But if you can learn to weave your own qì of thought into your opponent's mind, disguising it as *their* thoughts, their *will* . . . that is the true power of this art, Lán'ér."

"Have you used this art often, then?" She set down the teacup, keeping her tone light.

Hóng'yì blinked slowly. "Practitioning cannot be without the three layers of qì," he said, and she noticed he avoided her question. "Your qì comes from your core, your soul. You layer a Seal with will, intent, and emotions—which come from the mind. The last layer is the actual performance of the Seal, drawing upon our physical world. This is why certain monks and practitioners spend lifetimes cultivating their minds and souls, seeking out the sutras across various disciplines of practitioning to achieve enlightenment." The lantern flickered red against his cheekbones, his lashes, as he leaned forward. "I'd like you to learn this, Lán'ér, because I'd like us to be allies, at the very least. And I want you to be powerful."

She thought of what he had said last night: that he wished to be allies, that he wished to fight to take their kingdom back and change the future. There were still parts of the picture missing, but she would find them piece by piece.

Lan looked into the prince's eyes. "Again," she said.

A smile broke on his face, as though he had found something both surprising and delightful in her. Hóng'yì reached forward and tipped her face to his. This time, she sensed the exact moment his qì wove into her thoughts.

And she was still powerless to stop it.

A torrent of sounds and colors swept her away, but in their midst, a pair of hands found her. Crimson billowed in her vision, and Hóng'yì appeared again. He drew her toward him, and together, they fell backward into a source of light.

She stood on smooth pine floors. A gentle breeze drifted through the bamboo blinds between rosewood pillars, moonlight pouring in like a river. From outside came the sound of cicadas and a waterfall.

The Chamber of Waterfall Thoughts. She was at the School of the White Pines.

For some reason, Lan felt a surge of unimaginable grief.

"You're holding it too tightly."

Suddenly there was a young man sitting next to her. She realized she was clutching a horsetail brush in her hand, a pot of ground black ink shimmering before her. His fingers were curved over hers, and her heart skipped a beat before she even realized what was happening. They were so close that she could see the freckles on his skin, smell the scent of roses on his breath. Roses . . . and smoke.

The fragrance stirred something inside her.

"How did you best my water demon?" he asked.

The pot of ink swelled, and suddenly before them was a crescent-shaped spring the color of sapphire, reflecting the moon and stars. The reflections glowed brighter and brighter, the silver fluorescence gathering into a long, serpentine shape; the surface of the water began to ripple, qì surging from it—

The Silver Dragon burst from the spring, scales shimmering like snow. It reared to encompass the night sky, brighter than any moon or stars. As water sluiced off its body, demonic qì rolled from it in waves.

The young man's lips had parted. He had let her hand fall from his grasp as he gazed up at the Demon God—at Lan's greatest secret—with rapture on his face.

Wake up. The Silver Dragon turned its pale blue eyes to Lan. *WAKE UP.*

Its words jolted through her. She looked at the young man next to her—Hóng'yì, the imperial heir—just as the Dragon dove at them, its qì smashing through the illusion like a blade through paper. Hóng'yì was flung back, caught off guard—and Lan followed him.

This time, she grasped the strands of qì he had woven into her own thoughts—and she flung them back at him.

It was like being on the other side of the looking glass. As Lan fell into the qì of Hóng'yì's mind, his streams of consciousness swirled around her. She saw a palace in flames against the night, a tangle of desert roses dancing in fire without burning. In the acrid smoke and searing heat, there was a shadow in the shape of a young man cloaked in a crimson páo. Behind him, through her watering eyes, Lan saw great, fiery wings unfolding against a black night sky. A phoenix—the Crimson Phoenix—rising from ashes like a plume of heavenly fire, its qì so massive she could feel herself burning from the inside. It turned its gaze to her, and it was like looking into the sun. Its beak opened in a deafening screech—

—and just like that, it was over. She had fallen onto the floor and was staring at the legs of expensive yellow rosewood chairs. Her páo stuck to her body. She was gasping.

She had glimpsed the fourth and final Demon God, the Crimson Phoenix.

And Hóng'yì had seen the Silver Dragon hidden within her.

He was still in his seat, bent over his desk and gripping its edges so hard his knuckles had turned white. He, too, was panting, and as he lifted his gaze to meet hers, the truth sizzled between them like lightning.

Hóng'yì swiped a hand across his forehead. "I think I've been waiting for this moment my entire life," he said softly.

She stared at him, her head swimming. He had lied about almost everything. About how his father had died and the Crimson Phoenix—the power of the imperial household—had been lost that night. How he had fled the Elantian invasion, weakened and sick.

All along, the Crimson Phoenix had been bound to him.

Lan had assumed that those preceding Hóng'yì in the imperial family had been corrupted by the influence of the Phoenix, much as Xan Tolürigin had lost his mind to the Black Tortoise. Lan studied this prince's face in all its shadows and light. How much of him was truly him, and how much of his will had been taken over by his Demon God? She recalled, with an ache in her chest, how Zen had fought against the Black Tortoise's possession. How there had been moments of lucidity that were *him* . . . and stretches of time when she'd known the being looking back at her was inhuman.

In the lantern light, Hóng'yì's face had grown wan. His qì flickered; beneath that was the slow rumbling of another, greater power. Demonic qì.

The prince stumbled to a cabinet at the back of his study. He traced a burning Seal in the air to unlock it. Lan heard the clink of porcelain as he opened the lid to a small jar. She recognized it: a servant had brought it out to him the first night of their dinner.

Hóng'yì withdrew from it another golden lotus seed. Popped it in his mouth. Swallowed.

Lan stood, ensuring that the mental wall between her and the Silver Dragon was back up.

Something was happening to Hóng'yì. He was shuddering, and beneath the surface she sensed his qì roiling, crescendoing, so that the entire chamber seemed to tremble. When it faded, he placed the porcelain jar back into the cabinet—and Lan saw that the shelves were filled with row upon row of identical jars.

With a sigh, the imperial heir turned back to her. Color flushed his face, the ethereal golden tone having returned to his skin. His cheeks were pink again, his lips carnelian red and his eyes fever-bright. He approached her.

"I knew it," he murmured. "Since the night I felt your qì as you battled my water demon, I knew—I suspected."

She searched his face, unsettled by the unnatural vitality to his appearance. He had hidden away his family's greatest secret and source of power, had outright lied to her so fluidly and easily. A cord tightened in her chest.

If he had held on to the power of the Crimson Phoenix for twelve long cycles, her goal of finding the Godslayer might very well stand in direct conflict with him. Would Hóng'yì know about it, or had his family hidden it from him as well?

And if he had bound the Phoenix for so long, how much of him would it have corrupted?

She had wanted to be his ally, but the game had changed. And a game, indeed, it would become.

Lan tipped her head, pushing sincerity into her tone. "Why didn't you ask me?" she said softly.

"I was uncertain," Hóng'yì said slowly. "How would you have reacted if a stranger had asked you about your Demon God?"

She forced a small smile onto her face. "Not well."

"Precisely." He was breathing hard. "Who are you, really?"

The ruse was over. "My name is Sòng Lián," Lan said quietly. *My mother Sealed the Silver Dragon within her to hide it from your family. To destroy it.* She said none of this aloud but wondered whether the prince would remember her mother, one of their imperial advisors, who had fled the palace on the eve of the Elantian invasion. History had written their bloodlines as enemies, but it was possible to change the course. The question was on which side the crown prince would stand.

"Sòng Lián." Hóng'yì tasted the name on his lips, as though searching for a memory. "Of the Sòng clan?"

"Yes."

His gaze darkened with something like desire. "Well, Sòng Lián. Now we know each other's secret. A stalemate."

It was no stalemate yet, not until she found out what he knew of the Godslayer—if anything. And she had one last secret of her own that she held close to her chest: that she was here to destroy the Demon Gods.

She took a step closer to him. "What do you propose now?"

Hóng'yì took her hand, his skin hot to the touch. "I would've thought you'd have guessed by now," he said softly. "I want what all emperors want, and more. I want my kingdom back.

I want a home. And I want an empress who can fight by my side, and rule by my side, with *power*."

Her breath hitched. There it was again, that word, *power,* from the lips of the man who had been born into all the power in their land and who still craved more. The question was whether he sought power as a means to an end—or whether he sought it *as* an end.

"And what if I am unable to control that power?" Lan asked.

He tilted her chin to him. "Then I will teach you," Hóng'yì said gently. "I told you, Sòng Lián, that I would make you powerful." His finger caressed her cheek. "Be my empress."

She hadn't become Lan of the Rose Pavilion Teahouse for nothing. All those cycles of learning to please her patrons, to hide behind a mask of sweet smiles and fluttery silks, had taught her where her strengths lay. Both the directness and the speed of the proposal shocked her, yet she was careful not to let it show.

She lowered her lashes, blushing prettily as she stalled. "You honor me, Your Highness."

He caught her other hand. His fingers were hot against her wrists, and she forced herself not to flinch. "Forgive me for being so forthright," Hóng'yì said. He was so sincere, she might have believed it again—had he not sounded exactly the same when he'd lied last night about the Crimson Phoenix. "We could begin as allies, Sòng Lián, but we could become more—whatever you'd like. Perhaps you could learn to love me, just as we both love this kingdom."

Lan lifted her eyes to his. Looked into them and remembered the yellow rosewood doors cracking open to reveal fiery red wings that seemed to ensconce the world. Thought of the secrets still hidden within.

"Yes," she whispered. "Make me your empress."

15

> I walked beneath the pái'fāng and the world shimmered a moment. When I emerged, I knew I was not on the other side but in another world. Pockets of such boundary-realms exist, held together by unknowable rules I can only ascribe to magic.
>
> —*Scripture of Mountains and Seas,* Book Five: On Otherworlds

Zen stood at the same cliff's edge beneath a dark, colorless sky. In place of a bone-dry valley, a river had appeared, its waters as clear as glass and utterly silent. When he looked into its depths, he could see nothing of its bottom.

That was when Zen realized the water held no reflection. The mountains, the cliffs, his own face—they were all missing from the river's looking-glass surface.

Where was this? He hadn't sensed any semblance of a Gate Seal on the pái'fāng . . . no, the Seal craft had been different from anything he'd come across at the School of the White Pines. This didn't *feel* like a different location, for they were the same mountains and the same pái'fāng.

This felt like . . . a realm conjured by the type of old magic that had led him to the palace of immortals. A Boundary Seal woven of the qì of souls, of the otherworld.

His school had taught standard principles of Hin practitioning as dictated by the imperial decrees of the Middle Kingdom; so much more of this world and its secrets had been lost to time and conquest. Principles of practitioning that bordered on the mystical and magical, like the world of the immortals' souls he had entered on the Öshangma Light Mountain.

This place would be one of those secrets.

Lotuses grew from the river's surface, swaying gently in an unseen breeze. Their petals were as white as snow, wrapped around golden seeds that glowed like sunlight. Yáng energies emanated from them. These were the lotuses from the pái'fāng's illustration.

Zen knelt at the riverbank. *A river of death composed solely of yīn,* the immortal soul had said, *balanced by flowers of life composed only of yáng.*

There was no doubt the Seeds of Clarity grew on these lotuses. They were too far away for him to reach; he would have to swim to them.

He removed his boots and páo and, after some hesitation, Nightfire. His practitioner's storage pouch, however, he kept at his waist.

Feeling vulnerable, he drew a breath and waded into the water.

It was as cold as ice. He'd expected something to happen—another river demon to burst from the currents, perhaps, or an ancient Seal to trigger. But the water did not even ripple as he moved through it.

Zen approached the first lotus and reached out.

That was when the ghosts emerged. They appeared as shapes beneath the river's surface: skin pallid and hair drifting like seaweed. Their whispers overlapped. A mist had risen ahead over the water; within was a silhouette, growing steadily darker.

"What you see is not real."

Zen stumbled back. That voice—he would have recognized it anywhere. Its owner materialized from the mist. He wore the same white páo as always, same calm expression with a hint of a smile. His hair was the same black streaked with gray.

Dé'zǐ came to a stop across from Zen. It was clear from the way his edges shimmered and his robes dissolved into the water that he was an illusion, some conjuring of Zen's imagination. Still, Zen had the urge to prostrate himself at the grandmaster's feet and beg for forgiveness.

He remained rooted where he was, studying the grandmaster's form. "You are not my shī'fù." He couldn't help the slight crack to his voice on the last word.

"No," the spirit agreed. "*I am not. Your consciousness—the qì of your mind—has merely sculpted me in this form.*"

Zen could see the cracks in the apparition of Dé'zǐ. A small mole on the grandmaster's ear was missing; a scar on his hand was not quite in the right shape; the threads of his collar and samite belt looked roughly woven rather than fine.

As Zen noted these differences, they shifted to correct themselves in an uncanny fashion. Still, the apparition's expression and the way it moved and spoke were off.

"What are you, then?" Zen asked.

"*A guardian of this river.*"

Zen's gaze flicked to the golden lotus seeds gleaming just out of his reach. "I seek the Seeds of Clarity," he said.

The river guardian studied him. The wind rippled, and Zen thought he sensed the faint taste of yīn in the currents. "*Why?*"

"To strengthen my core of qì, so that I may command the power of the Demon God bound to me." He watched the river guardian's face carefully, but it yielded as little information as his former master's ever did. The spirit's long robes flowed like a waterfall.

"*The Seeds of Clarity will strengthen your core. But that comes at a great price.*"

The Yuè immortal's warning curled in Zen's mind: *The Seeds of Clarity are at once a cure and a curse . . . a double-edged sword, just like the power you hold.*

"Name it," Zen said.

The apparition blinked. *"What is it you live for, Xan Temurezen?"*

Zen did not ask how it knew his name.

What did he live for?

The answer was what tethered him to this world. He thought of his mother and father on the great plains of their homeland, waving at him under a brilliant blue sky. His young cousins rushing home from a day of herding to playfully fight over cold sweetened mare's milk one of their uncles made for them. He thought of the memory the Black Tortoise had shown him of his great-grandfather Xan Tolürigin, the greatest general and demonic practitioner of the Mansorian clan, kneeling before the Hin emperor. Begging for the lives of his clan to be spared.

He lived to right the wrongs of the past. He lived to bring the clans back to the Last Kingdom, to remake it as it should have been. He lived as the legacy of the great Mansorian clan, and he would give his life to see it rise again.

The flow of his thoughts shifted, and he was once again in a rain-filled mountain village, holding a girl with a scent of lilies in his arms. All the moments they'd gazed out the wooden fretwork windows at a land of lush pines and coiling mist and dreamt of a future here. Not one of grandeur, not one of power, but one of peace. One in which they could sit beneath the lambent light of a lantern surrounded by tomes and children and grow old together.

He swallowed against the ache building in his chest. Before him, the apparition's eyes seemed to flicker, as though it had witnessed every memory and every thought that had gone through Zen's mind.

"And what would you do for a chance at that life?" it asked.

"Anything." His voice scraped. "Everything."

"The Seeds of Clarity demand a price. They will ask for a sacrifice from your soul."

He had already given away his soul for a chance at his goals. Nothing frightened him anymore.

"Name your price," he said.

The apparition's gaze flickered. It bowed its head. *"You may choose a seed."*

Between them, the lotus swayed gently. The seeds continued to glow, as smooth and perfect as pearls, golden like the sun poured its light into them. When Zen stretched his hand forward, the petals seemed to yawn open beneath his fingers.

He hesitated, just for a breath, before he reached to the heart of the lotus and plucked out one of the golden seeds.

An icy wind surged through the realm as though it were letting out a breath. The stillness shattered; overhead, clouds twisted and distorted. There was movement in the river as the ghosts shifted, swirling with the currents and watching him with their sightless eyes. They gave the light of the lotus seed a wide berth, shying away from where its glow illuminated the murky depths of the river.

Except for one.

A ghost drifted forward, caught in the golden pulse of the seed's light. As it drew close, its features crystallized: this was the ghost—the soul—of a man. He bore kindly features, wore the coarse-cloth duàn'dǎ and conical bamboo dǒu'lì of the working class. The woven basket of grain on his back indicated he was a farmer; the lines on his face told of a hard life. He reached for the seed, which flared like a heartbeat. Zen felt a rush of qì between it and the ghost.

The seed's light grew to a blaze. The ghost's outline weakened, as though all the qì constituting it and enabling it to exist in this form were funneling into the seed. With a final sigh, the ghost of the man vanished.

The silence broke as, with a great roar, the river surged. Zen had only enough time to gasp a breath before the gray, unending sky arced over him and the waters pulled him under.

The world tilted, and he landed on the dust beneath the Ghost Gates.

Zen rolled over and retched, his body convulsing horribly as it fought to eject water and take air into his lungs again. Except, he realized, there was no water. His clothes were only a little damp from the thick fog and his sweat, but other than that, he was dry. When he looked over the cliff's edge, there was only a parched valley. No river, no water.

An illusion, he thought, only something had come back with him here, into this physical world. It dug into his palm. Zen uncurled his fingers.

The seed glimmered against his skin, sickeningly gold.

Zen dropped it as though it burned. He understood now. He understood the immortal's warning, understood the river guardian's riddles. *The Seeds of Clarity demand a price.*

These were not seeds.

They were *souls*. They were the souls of the spirits still trapped in that river, awaiting their release.

Zen began to shake violently.

What is it you live for, Xan Temurezen?

To right the wrongs: his family, his clan, unjustly and brutally wiped from this land. Reclaiming this kingdom and making it as it should have been. And a chance for a life with Lan.

And what would you do for a chance at that life?

The world blurred. Those shadows at the edges of his vision had returned; he could feel the looming form of the Black Tortoise, watching him. Could sense its qì mingling with his own, its awareness clinging to him, at all times—something he could no longer shake.

Xan Tolürigin had lost his mind to this being and killed thousands of innocent Hin. Kneeling at the cliff's edge, clutching his stomach as he retched, Zen finally understood something. When he had chosen the Black Tortoise, he had chosen unbridled power, and unbridled power was destruction. He would win the war, perhaps, but only by destroying everything around him, beginning with himself. His soul.

Then so be it. He had made his choice, set down this path. There was no turning back now.

Trembling, Zen dragged himself up and wiped his mouth against his sleeve. He picked up the seed from the ground. It pulsed beneath his touch, beating like a heart, like a thing *alive*.

He lifted it to his lips. His hand was shaking so hard, he thought he might miss.

Then he tipped his head back and swallowed.

It began with a burning sensation in his stomach. It spread through his veins, until he thought his bones would melt from the heat. And then that heat shifted, becoming a rush of what could only be described as vitality. His cuts and bruises glossed over, leaving alabaster-smooth skin; the scar on his abdomen from the wound Lan had inflicted shrank until there was nothing left but corded muscle. He felt it, too, in his mind and in his core: an intoxicating sense of strength, as though he'd been born anew.

The ominous presence that always lingered at the edges of his consciousness flared, the Black Tortoise's great eye settling on him.

It seems I underestimated you, Xan Temurezen, it said. The golden glow was beginning to eat away at the Demon God's shadow, too, like a piece of parchment burning to its end. *Of all the deeds my other binders have committed, this perhaps outranks them all. The question is: Will you submit to a lifetime of this? Will you reap more souls than you have bargained to me, for the sake of your own life?*

There was a low rumble of a laugh, and then the shadow vanished as Zen's core overpowered the Demon God's with his newfound golden vitality.

Zen breathed in deeply. His head was clearer than it had been in a long time, his body fully healed and strong, his qì replenished to the brim.

He was himself again.

And he hated every bit of it.

16

>If you strike the grass, you startle the snake.
>
>—Lady Nuru Ala Šuraya of the
>Jorshen Steel clan, *Classic of War*

Lan awoke early the next morning to a feeling she couldn't quite place. Darkness poured through the cracks of her wooden shutters, dawn still a bell or so away. In these ghost hours between night and day, the desert was so silent, it was almost stifling—no chirp of crickets, no song of birds, not even sandsong to break the stillness. There was something in the air that was deeply unsettling to her core.

A shadow by her bed moved. Lan had just grabbed her ocarina when a hand clapped over her mouth. It smelled familiar: sword steel. A gray eye flashed in the darkness, a curved crimson mouth.

"It's me," Dilaya hissed.

Lan rolled her eyes as her friend withdrew her hand. "Rather than descending upon me like an assassin in the night, did you think of knocking on the doors first?"

"No, but I think of knocking *you* out with every clever retort you give." Dilaya's tone turned urgent. "Where have you *been*?"

Quickly, Lan filled her friend in on how she had spent the day learning the practitioning art that allowed access to the mind and to thoughts. How this art had been passed down through Hóng'yī's bloodline. Dilaya's mouth grew slacker and slacker with disbelief until finally she let out an audible noise when Lan spoke of her betrothal to the imperial heir.

"This is an alliance we need," Lan said, and drove her point home: "He has the Crimson Phoenix, Dilaya."

Dilaya drew Falcon's Claw in a flash of steel. "That rabbit-whelped *bastard* of a coward! He's had a Demon God bound to him all along, and he chose to stay holed up in this delusional realm of comforts?"

"He's at the mercy of the Phoenix, Dilaya. He must be. We don't know how much control it already holds over him." Lan's fingers twisted on her silk bedsheets as she thought of Zen, of his great-grandfather the Nightslayer. "The Demon Gods corrupt their binders over time as the binders continue to call on the gods' power."

"*People* make those choices, Sòng Lián," Dilaya retorted, pointing her sword dramatically at Lan. "No matter how much you still love him, *Temurezen* made the choice to bind the Black Tortoise. He *chose* to betray and forsake you for power."

Lan inhaled sharply and looked away.

"I didn't mean it that way," Dilaya mumbled, as close to an apology as she would get. Awkwardly, she sheathed her sword. "By way of example, you have the Silver Dragon bound to you, but you are not in danger of losing yourself to it."

Lan made sure the Dragon's access to her thoughts was cut off before she responded. "My bargain with it is different," she said quietly. "The Dragon is sworn to my mother's soul. She made it promise to protect me." Lan made no mention of the new bargain she had made with the Dragon: that she had promised her own soul in exchange for freedom for her mother's. When Lan died—as all demonic bargains ended—the Dragon would consume her soul and let go of her mother's. "I've seen it, Dilaya. Zen made the choice he made, and I hate him for that, but . . . when I saw him again in Nakkar, he was fighting the Black Tortoise's grasp with every fiber of his being."

"Regardless, the people who bind these Demon Gods have a say in how much power they use from their bargains," Dilaya said stubbornly. "Not to mention, Hóng'yì lied to us when he spoke of his escape from the Elantian invasion twelve cycles ago. He's hiding something."

"That's why I agreed to the engagement," Lan said. "I need him to trust me. He is the living heir to the imperial line. Whatever secrets they carried, he is our last hope. I plan to get closer to him so I can find out what he knows."

Dilaya pursed her lips but gave no counterargument. She looked distracted. Worried. "Chó Tài's missing," she said, blinking, then turned her face to the fretwork shutters.

"What?" Cold gripped Lan. She hadn't seen either Dilaya or Tai since her shocking agreement to the imperial heir's proposal. "Weren't you with him yesterday, snooping around?"

"Yes. He and I were together the entire day, until he insisted he heard ghosts in the spring. I was going to entertain his truly bizarre notions and follow him to investigate, but that was when that little white fox spirit showed up."

It took Lan a moment to discern who "that little white fox spirit" was, as most people became little fox spirits to Dilaya when she was annoyed. "Xuě'ér?"

Dilaya's mouth tightened as she nodded. "Of course, it was pointless for us to snoop around with her tailing us, so we agreed to return to our chambers and wait for the palace to quiet down before meeting up again. When I went to find Chó Tài, he was gone." She moved to the shutters and soundlessly eased them open. "But I did find something. Come."

Through the floor-to-ceiling windows, a warm desert breeze carrying the sweet scent of roses rolled in. Lan found it another of those aspects of Shaklahira that should have been pleasant but felt off. Deserts were meant to be freezing at night and blistering during the day, yet the Boundary Seal and the many other Seals pulsing across this place kept it wrapped in a shroud of its own.

The sky was tinged with the faintest blue from the sprinkling of stars over their heads. The color lanced across Crescent Spring and the whispering silver grasses that surrounded it and illuminated footsteps leading to the water.

They were clearly Tai's—Lan had spent too long trekking in the desert after him not to recognize the print of his boots, the size of his feet. Dilaya cast Lan a look bordering on anxious.

Together, they traced the boot prints from the side doors leading out of Tai's room in the palace to the edge of the spring. The prints followed the shoreline to the other side, away from the palace gardens.

There, they simply disappeared. As though Tai had vanished into the water.

Lan stared at Crescent Spring, which reflected the night sky as perfectly as a looking glass. She recalled carp darting around when they'd first crossed the bridge into the secret realm of Shaklahira, yet the waters were perfectly still now.

There was something else, though, directly ahead of where Tai's footprints had ended. In the middle of the water was a cluster of lotuses, their pale petals catching the starlight. Curiously, the lotus seeds were golden, and as smooth as pearls.

The realization hit her: she'd seen them before.

"Hóng'yi takes these for his consumption," Lan murmured.

"Looks like Ghost Boy took a sudden interest in them," Dilaya said gruffly. "Damned flowers."

"There must have been a reason Tai tried to get to them," Lan mused, kicking off her straw sandals and hiking up the silks of her páo.

"What are you doing?" Dilaya, realizing Lan's intentions, grabbed her friend's arm. "Are you mad? There is a *water demon* in that spring!"

"Do you want to find Tai or not?" Lan retorted. Dilaya's scowl darkened, but she let go.

The water was freezing. Even in the warm desert morning, Lan began to shiver as she waded in deeper. The surface of the spring was as black as ink; as she put one foot in front of the other, she could not see past her ankles, where the water swallowed her feet. Cold seeped into her veins, taking root: its yīn energies seemed to thread over her core. A fog had begun to roll in, pressing in over the silver grasses until they were swallowed by gray. Only the lotuses kept their color, golden seeds full and shimmering like honey.

Lan reached out.

As soon as the tip of her finger touched the seed, qì rippled as though a great sigh had torn through Shaklahira and an invisible curtain had lifted. The surface of the water cleared, and Lan found herself staring into the face of a girl beneath the waves: pale, wearing an expression of terror.

Lan bit down on her tongue to stop herself from crying out. Around them, shapes were darting in the water: ghosts, their qì trailing, cold, behind them, their whispers filling the air with an eerie chittering.

The ghost of the girl reached out to Lan. The golden lotus seed brightened. *"Help me,"* the ghost said, her voice like the sigh of wind. *"Don't let him or his water demon consume my soul."*

The world tipped sharply out of balance. Lan's thoughts were frozen; she couldn't reconcile the reality of what she was seeing, hearing.

Far in the depths of the water, a great eye opened as the demon within Crescent Spring awakened and turned its attention to Lan. The ghosts underwater were streaming toward her, away from the demon, and she heard faint echoes of their distressed cries as they fled. Within her, the qì of the Silver Dragon stirred, sensing danger.

She palmed That Which Cuts Stars and her ocarina and braced herself, but the attack never came. Instead, the demon shifted, its attention caught by a strong wind gusting across the water from somewhere at the end of the bridge, where the Gate Seal to the outside world was.

It turned and plunged back into the depths of the spring. The last that Lan saw of it was the flick of its thick serpentine body, larger than a rowboat, as it vanished toward the other end of the bridge.

Lan craned her neck, trying to peer through the fog to see what had attracted the water demon's attention.

A hand snaked around her midriff. The next thing she knew, she was being dragged to shore. Sand and grass obscured her vision; when she blinked again, the fog was gone.

"What did you see?" Dilaya's eye was wide. Her hand went to the hilt of Falcon's Claw. "What was that?"

"Ghosts," Lan replied. She was soaked and shivering as her páo clung to her; she hadn't even realized how deep into the lake she'd gone. "Souls, Dilaya—the lotus seeds. He sacrifices souls and consumes them to replenish his own core. That's how he's kept his sanity while being bound to a Demon God." The image of the terrified ghost's face came back to her; the thin keens of the spirits as they'd raced away from the water demon.

Lan glanced back to the spring. The demon was nowhere to be seen. "Did you do something to distract the water demon?"

Dilaya shook her head, lips pale. Before she could speak, lantern light flared from the palace's windows. Her head snapped in that direction.

"He's coming," she said, and her knuckles whitened on the hilt of her dāo. "Sòng Lián, if we must fight—"

"No," Lan said quickly. "If we strike the grass, we startle the snake and lose everything. I can't lose Hóng'yì's trust, Dilaya."

Somewhere in the distance, a set of doors creaked open. The red light of a lantern spilled into a sky that was beginning to lighten into predawn gray; shadows shifted, approaching.

"Go," Lan said. "I'll be fine. I'll make up a lie—it's what I'm good at."

The twist of her friend's mouth showed her how much Dilaya disliked this plan. But she said nothing. Lan felt a ripple of qì, a thickening of the shadows, and then Dilaya was gone.

Not a second too soon.

The flame from the lantern warmed Lan's cool skin as the sand behind her hissed with footsteps. "Sòng Lián," came that familiar tenor, chilling her to the bone. "My betrothed. How surprising to find you out here at the hour of the tiger."

It took all of Lan's will to turn her head and face Hóng'yì. He had come alone, without a retinue of servants or even his faithful bodyguard. Somehow, this gave Lan a feeling of foreboding. She thought of the ghosts in the water, their fearful pleas.

"I went for a swim to clear my head," she whispered. The best lies were adjacent to the truth. She widened her gaze and gave her lips a false tremble. "I saw ghosts in the water."

The crown prince's face swirled with shadows, digging grooves into the corners of his mouth. The red of the lantern he held reflected in his eyes, lending him a haunted look. Even at this bell, he wore his court hàn'fú; the elaborate gold stitching on the crimson brocade glimmered in the lantern light.

Hóng'yì bent to her, tipping her face to his. His eyes searched hers, and she sensed the subtle brush of his qì against hers as he slipped into her mind. She let him, opening her thoughts to the memory of that girl, to the water demon slithering away from her.

She placed her hand in his palm; his fingers burned as they closed over hers and pulled her to her feet. She noticed the healthy golden sheen to his skin, the feverish flush to his cheeks and lips.

She schooled her features to show none of her anger. "Your spring is haunted," she said shakily, and made a cavalier stab at a smile. "You might have told me, since this is to be my home, too."

"That spring has always been haunted," Hóng'yì said. "But I will rid it of the ghosts if it displeases my betrothed. After all, you are correct: this is about to be your eternal home, too."

He traced a finger over her face, and she shivered under his caress. Zen had always touched her with restraint, with a gentle longing that made her feel safe, respected. The way Hóng'yì's fingers brushed her, though, made her feel like a trophy. "Good," Lan said, lifting her chin. "Escort me back to my chambers, so I can sleep a bit longer before the ceremony."

Hóng'yì hummed, as though considering. His lips had begun to curl. "I thought we could hold the ceremony now." His smile spread. "Right here."

She stiffened as his hand tightened over the small of her back. "Absolutely not," Lan said peevishly. "I'm soaked and I'm cold. I'm not even in a ceremonial gown."

"That can all be fixed," Hóng'yì replied. Qì flashed, a Seal appearing so fast that Lan barely glimpsed it.

Reds and golds bloomed on her nightdress, stitching into

an intricate pattern of roses and blossoms. The fabric had dried and turned hard, from silk to thick brocade. This was a level of practitioning that Lan couldn't even have dreamt of—one that might have impressed even the masters of the School of the White Pines.

"There," the prince said drily. He stepped back from her and splayed out his palm. On it appeared a thick white tome, its cover inscribed with a Seal unlike anything Lan had seen before. Its qì was so strong, Lan felt as though she were staring into the heart of a fire. When Hóng'yì flipped the book open to the first page, it was blank.

He began to trace a Counterseal, one with strokes so elaborate, Lan could not follow. Demonic energies began to stir. Smoke wound through the air, thick and acrid; the light of the lantern seemed to grow. Counterseal met Seal, melding into ash, and golden words appeared on the tome's leather binding.

Classic of Gods and Demons

Ink poured down the pages, looping into characters that were not Hin. They followed the vertical spill of Hin scripture yet bore circular loops and strokes more fluid than the steady, boxlike Hin calligraphy.

Hóng'yì looked up at her, his gaze burning. Behind him, against a sky that had turned coral with the dawn, great wings of flame seemed to unfold, a crown of feathers gilding the remaining darkness overhead. "Bound together, we will be more powerful than any god or demon that has walked this land," he said, closing the gap between them and drawing her against him. With his other hand, he held the tome. Demonic qì pulsed from it.

Bound together. Lan glanced at the tome, warning bells pealing in her mind. She thought of the souls in the water, the golden lotus seeds, the ghosts' screams trapped inside the spring.

It was now or never.

Lan took Hóng'yì's face between her palms, softening her gaze as she met his from beneath her lashes. Her heart pounded so hard in her chest, she was certain he would hear it. This was her one chance.

Disarm them, he had told her of the art of grasping the qì of one's mind; *lull them into a comfort. . . .*

She leaned forward and kissed Hóng'yì. His mouth parted in surprise at first, then very quickly came to crush hers, his hand tightening around her waist with greed. Her body was trembling, nausea gripping her stomach and quickening her breath. There it was again, that scent of smoke and things burning. The taste on his lips was metallic and hot—like blood.

. . . and then strike.

Lan pulled away gently. *Penetrate their mental walls before they put shields up.* She took Hóng'yì's chin in her hand and found his gaze.

If I tell you not to think of something, you'll find that you immediately will.

"Where is the Godslayer?" Lan breathed, and as his eyes widened in unguarded surprise, she flung her qì into his stream of thoughts.

Vivid bursts of colors, sights, and sounds swirled past her. She was tumbling headfirst into a bright light: A set of doors made of expensive yellow rosewood, a phoenix carved into it with molten gold, its wingspan stretching across both doors.

The doors cracked open just enough for her to peer in. To see the fire that engulfed the chamber beyond. To see the smoke of his subconscious arrange itself into the characters: *Godslayer.*

And then she was wrenched backward, the doors closing

before her. The qì of Hóng'yì's mind was distorting, lashing against the qì of her mind with pure fury.

The next moment, she was back on the shores of the spring, in Hóng'yì's tight grasp. A turbulent wind had picked up, creating waves that slapped at the banks. The sky was afire with demonic qì radiating from the imperial heir's silhouette like wings.

Hóng'yì flung Lan away from him. She slammed into the sand. When she looked up again, Hóng'yì was standing over her, his beautiful face contorted in an ugly expression. He held the tome—the *Classic of Gods and Demons*—to his chest.

"You wretched little *liar*," he snarled.

"Rich of you to say that." Lan gasped as his fingers wrapped around her neck. She scrabbled for her ocarina, but Hóng'yì's foot slammed down on her wrist.

"This Seal will bind you and the Silver Dragon to me," he said, lifting the *Classic of Gods and Demons*. "You will agree."

"Make me."

"If you ask." A corner of his mouth curled. The pressure on her throat and arm lifted as Hóng'yì stood back. He dusted off his crimson hàn'fú, then flicked his hand in the direction of the spring.

Its waters rippled. A shape appeared within and then broke the surface of the water.

A cry broke from Lan: "Tai!"

Tai was unconscious and miraculously dry, black curls hanging before his eyes as his head lolled. He hung beneath the control of whatever Seal Hóng'yì had put him under, swaying like a puppet.

"No doubt you've discovered the source of my pills," Hóng'yì said coldly. "The medicine for my, ah, *consumption*."

The realization struck her. "You never had consumption."

The imperial heir's grin was sharp. "A sickly, lonely prince searching for his cause, for allies to save his empire. And you thought you were the only one putting up a façade, Sòng Lián." His smile faded. "If you choose to disagree to a binding with me, Chó Tài's fate will join those of the water ghosts that languish in my spring, waiting for their souls to grow into the seeds that strengthen my core of qì."

Lan shuddered, imagining Tai as one of the helpless souls trapped beneath the water's surface. "Why are you doing this?" she choked.

His fingers shifted against her neck, their deadly grip loosening to a sliding caress. His expression softened into something nearly thoughtful, as he beheld her, perhaps imagining the Demon God she held within her. "Because I want power."

"You have power. You were *born* into power."

"I want more." His eyes glittered. "I want it all. My forefathers united this kingdom under our rule, but they left an opening—a vulnerability. Three vulnerabilities, in fact. Of the Four Demon Gods, we possessed only one. That was what allowed the Mansorian clan to nearly defeat us. That was what allowed the clan rebels to rise again. If I hold all the power in this world, I will ensure a stability to our reign never before seen."

"And you would sacrifice the souls of your subjects, of innocent Hin, to seize it."

"That is the nature of power, of this world, Sòng Lián. Those who cannot rule must serve, for the greater good. The flame that burns bright must feed on the common wood." He lifted his arms, hàn'fú scorching red, as he began to write the strokes of the binding Seal from the *Classic of Gods and Demons*. The air trembled; demonic qì rolled from him in waves as, finally, the Demon God within him began to take form. Feathers of fire trailed across the horizon; a crowned head blazing brighter than the sun, with eyes of molten gold as the Crimson Phoenix shimmered into this world.

Lan swallowed, her gaze darting to the imperial heir as she shifted her tone to be pleading—anything to get through to whatever shred of humanity was left in him. "The Phoenix is corrupting your mind," she said, for undoubtedly the Demon God within him already held influence over his mind, his body, and perhaps most of his soul. "You don't want to do this. We could be allies; we could take back the kingdom together—"

Hóng'yì's finger traced a blazing circle through the air. The binding Seal scorched between them, and Lan felt it tugging at the core of her qì and wrapping around the Silver Dragon nestled deep inside her.

A distant roar sounded from the direction of the spring.

Hóng'yì paused and they both cast their gazes to the water, which was roiling, a gargantuan shadow materializing within and rising to the surface.

Hóng'yì's eyes narrowed. "What—"

The water demon burst from the spring with an earsplitting shriek and plunged toward them, bringing a colossal swell of demonic energies that battered away Hóng'yì's binding Seal. Waves pounded into Lan, squeezing the air from her lungs; demonic energies surrounded her. She couldn't breathe, couldn't see, couldn't move.

Hands wrapped around her, gentle as they pulled her from the disorienting whorl. Lan expected to slam into the ground—but instead, the impact was soft. Cushioned. Wet fabric scratched her face, and beneath her, someone breathed.

Lan opened her eyes to a very familiar face.

Gone was the sickly pallor of Zen's skin, the rings under his eyes. He had a healthy glow; his cheeks and lips were tinted red; and his hair, soft as black silk, was full. But most changed,

Lan thought, were his eyes. Their gazes locked, and held, for a heartbeat. There was nothing of the frightening, unending black or the turbulence of a storm-tossed sea she had seen back when they'd stood on opposite sides of the cliffs at Skies' End and chosen their different paths. Instead, there was something calm and settled to his qì.

Zen reached up and brushed a thumb against her cheek, feather light. The moment stretched between them, and against her better judgment, Lan leaned into his touch. She opened her mouth to say something, but perhaps for the first time, she wasn't quick enough.

Zen rolled her over and pushed himself to his feet. He straightened, his dark páo and hair still dripping water as he turned to face Hóng'yì. In the eastern sky, the flames of dawn and the Crimson Phoenix seemed to dim slightly as the shadows of the western sky lengthened, the colossal energies of the Black Tortoise roaring to life to swallow even the stars.

17

> It is the duty of the ruler not to be loved but to be powerful and to be obeyed.
>
> —*Dissertations of the First Emperor, Jīn Dynasty,* era of the Middle Kingdom, Cycle 1

He had not used the full power of the Black Tortoise since he'd consumed the Seed of Clarity, yet in the morning light outside this palace built on the blood of the common people, Zen marveled at how easy it was to call upon the Demon God's qì. His own core was filled with power, and for the first time since binding the being, Zen felt fully in control.

He took in the scene before him: a man cloaked in a crimson hàn'fú, whose core, he could sense, brimmed with power and vitality—power and vitality he had stolen from hundreds, or thousands, or more of their people's souls.

"Zhào Hóng'yì," Zen said quietly, testing the name on his tongue.

The Crimson Phoenix unfurled its two colossal wings. Zen narrowed his eyes and those flames shifted: golden pennants bearing the Imperial Army's sigil against a bright blue sky. The smell of blood and screams of terror rent the air.

Yes, the imperial heir's name on Zen's lips did indeed taste of an ancient, bone-deep fury.

"Ah," Hóng'yì said, drawing the sound out. He had the tone of a man born into power and wealth, offered everything this world had to give. "Shall I hazard a guess? Xan Temurezen. Heir of the long-dead Mansorian clan." His mouth twisted in a grin as his eyes flicked to the Black Tortoise looming over Zen like a shadow in the night. "What an honor."

Zen's anger was a deep, yawning abyss within him, and if he allowed himself to fall into it, he would never climb back out. He could almost hear Dé'zǐ's voice: *Calm the storm of your emotions. A restless ocean is not one to sail upon.*

"No," Zen said slowly. "The honor is mine. The honor to put an end to you and the blood-painted path you and your family carved across this land."

Hóng'yì lifted an eyebrow. "I would not speak so casually of a 'blood-painted path' if I were you, great-grandson of the Nightslayer."

The embers of Zen's anger burned higher. He shifted his focus from the imperial heir's self-satisfied smirk to the tome he held in his arms. An ordinary leather-bound tome, with a familiar-looking Seal on its cover.

Here was the other half of the *Classic of Gods and Demons*.

After consuming the Seed of Clarity, Zen had tracked down the location of the Crimson Phoenix from the star map Lan had played for Erascius that night on top of the Öshangma Light Mountain. It had been difficult: the Boundary Seal Hóng'yì— and the Phoenix—had laid over Shaklahira ensured that no qì from within here could be detected, which was how this place had been kept secret from the world for the past twelve cycles and more.

It was seeing the lotuses in the spring that told him he had come to the right location. According to the Nameless Master, the imperial line had regularly consumed the Seeds of Clarity. Now Zen understood that they had somehow learned to grow them. Even the sight of the golden seeds had sent a wave of nausea pulsing through Zen. He thought of all the souls required to produce those seeds.

The imperial family had lived on the blood of the people they were meant to protect.

The demon in Crescent Spring had been distracted when Zen had slipped through, gifting him the element of surprise. From underwater, he had wrestled a Seal on the demon to gain control over it. He had watched Hóng'yì perform the Counterseal to unlock the missing half of the *Classic of Gods and Demons*.

Then the prince had begun to conjure the Seal that would bind the will and power of another soul to him—the Seal that Xan Tolürigin had used on his Deathriders. The key to all Zen had searched for: his great-grandfather's army of demonic practitioners, his one chance to overthrow the Elantians and take back this kingdom.

Now all that rested in the hands of the heir to the clan that had wiped out Zen's.

Zen drew Nightfire. The desert air crackled with frost as he drew upon the yīn energies of the Black Tortoise. The shadows behind him yawned, stretching wider and darker.

"Sòng Lián." He didn't have to look to know that she crouched behind him, watching. "Get back."

"No," came her voice, as bright as the ring of bells. The laughter that had once limned it, however, had faded. He heard her footfalls on the sand as she approached. "You don't get to tell me what to do. That bastard has something I want, too."

In the corner of his vision, he saw her draw up to his side. Her hand was on her right hip, where he knew the hilt of That Which Cuts Stars rested; her left hand she held before her defensively, and he knew she clutched her ocarina.

Neither, however, would be of much use against their mutual opponent.

Hóng'yì stood beneath the Phoenix as though at the heart of a flame, his back to his palace. His páo fluttered, a spill of crimson in the wind of energies that swept the sands. His hair was worn long, and on his forehead was a cinnabar mark in the shape of an eye.

Zen dug his heels into the sand, grounding himself into a fighting stance. "Sòng Lián," he said quietly. "If one of us must draw on the power of our Demon God to fight him, let it be me."

He, Xen Temurezen, born to the legacy of a clan tainted by the tragic downfall of the Nightslayer, who had traded his soul away long ago to walk the path of a demonic practitioner.

Lan gave no response, but he felt her eyes on his back, as keen as an arrow.

Across from them, the Crimson Phoenix let out a battle scream.

Zen allowed the power of the Black Tortoise to course through him. The world both expanded and shrank, became finite and infinite at the same time. He saw every star in the sky and every speck of sand, refracting the same light and same energies. This time, however, felt different. This time, he controlled everything.

And this rush of power was *intoxicating*.

The Black Tortoise's voice rumbled down the open bond between them. *The prowess of this lineage of emperors that has held control over this land for so long lies in the Art of the Mind. Be on your guard, Xan Temurezen, for I cannot defend your mind if you do not lend its control to me.*

Zen lashed out. An explosion ricocheted across the sky as the qì of the Phoenix rose to meet that of the Tortoise, crackling against the confines of the Boundary Seal that hid Shaklahira from the world. For an instant, their surroundings flickered as the Seal faltered, and Zen caught a glimpse of the true state of Shaklahira: a palace faded and weatherworn, half buried in the barren desert. He blinked and the Crimson Phoenix's Seals had recovered, along with the lush, vibrant illusion.

Sweat had broken out on his brow. Hóng'yì's smile, on the other hand, stretched wider. He'd had twelve cycles to practice channeling the Crimson Phoenix's power . . . and perhaps countless more of the Seeds of Clarity to bolster his own core, judging by those lotuses he grew at the other end of the spring.

Already, Zen could feel his own strength waning, his grasp on the flow of power beginning to slip here and there, patches of that familiar darkness and the Demon God's will clouding his mind. If this came down to a test of endurance, he would not win.

Lan had darted over to the shore of Crescent Spring where Chó Tài lay, unconscious. Whatever Seal the imperial heir had woven over him was gone now, relinquished as Hóng'yì turned his every ounce of energy to the duel. As another explosion shook the sky, Lan conjured a Shield Seal to protect them.

By the palace doors, people had appeared: Shaklahira's court, comprising guards and servants and cooks and maids. They clustered together in silence, the lightning and fire illuminating the fear on their faces.

From their midst, a familiar figure stepped out, decked in armor, one loose red sleeve fluttering behind her. Yeshin Noro Dilaya, matriarch of the Jorshen Steel clan, lifted her curved dāo and, with qì as sharp as the blade, began to trace a defensive Seal between them and the battle waging by the spring.

Zen returned his focus to the fight. "Hóng'yì," he called. "If we continue like this, we will destroy Shaklahira and the people within it. And once the Seal over Shaklahira breaks, the power of these Demon Gods will wipe out all the surrounding cities. Return the *Classic of Gods and Demons* to me, and I will walk away. The city of your ancestors' legacy will remain."

Hóng'yì tilted his head. "That is the difference between you and me, Xan Temurezen," he said, a new viciousness to his words. "If power is akin to fire, you are afraid of reaching too close for fear of being burned. But *I*"—he bellowed, and the wings of the Phoenix seared brighter, hotter—"I have embraced the fire. I have become it. If this world is fated to burn, then I will be the brightest flame of all."

This was madness—yet *this* was how the imperial family had managed to hold on to their reign for so long. In the history of the Last Kingdom and all previous eras, there had been challengers to the rule of this land, yet all had been quenched by the imperial line. The imperial line's end goal was not ruling this kingdom. *Power* was their end goal, and they would gladly burn down the kingdom for it.

"Even so, I agree," Hóng'yì continued. "It is, indeed, time to end this. On *my* terms."

The Crimson Phoenix rose higher, the tips of its wing feathers brushing the ground and leaving a trail of molten sand in its wake as it let out another battle scream.

A mountain of energies rammed into Zen. He barely had time to throw up a Defensive Seal—sand, air, heat, and all the threads that he could pull from the world around him, layers and layers that simply eroded to dust beneath the Crimson Phoenix's qì.

A thrum of alarm singed through his bond with the Black Tortoise. He heard the Demon God hiss, saw the sky shift as its great shadow turned to crouch over him—and then a searing pain sliced through his head, burning through it until only darkness was left.

Hóng'yì smiled, and somehow, Zen knew they were in his own *mind*.

Memories flitted past, rushes of sound and sight: white yurts on green grasses stained red, the acrid scent of smoke and blood in the air, the distant screams of livestock and people—

"No," Zen panted—

—Dé'zǐ, face slack and eyes blank, the last of his qì fading into nothingness as his lifeblood seeped out—

"No—"

—Xan Tolürigin in chains, kneeling on the stone at the emperor's feet, weeping and begging softly for his people to be spared—

Zen was on the ground, sobbing as reality and memory blended, as his mind was flayed open by the heir of his clan's murderer.

18

> The Heavens are high, and the emperor is far away. We have been abandoned.
>
> —Unknown, letters from the Heavenly Capital, era of the Last Kingdom, Cycle 1424

Lan sensed it the moment Hóng'yì struck with the Art of the Mind. She watched Zen recoil and his qì flicker out. His eyes snapped shut and his expression went taut, no doubt with whatever horrifying memory Hóng'yì had unleashed in his mind.

Her hands tightened against Tai, who lay nearly lifeless in her arms. His skin was clammy and cold, his face drained of color, but his chest rose and fell in shallow breaths.

An idea had come to her as she'd watched Zen and Hóng'yì spar. Despite the imperial heir's insouciance, there were brief moments when his smile slipped and an ugly expression twisted his mouth. He was expending more effort on this battle than he let on—and if he was so completely focused on defeating Zen, then he might not be so well guarded against other attacks.

This could be her chance.

Lan closed her eyes and pushed her senses beyond the Protective Seal that hovered over them. She combed through the flow of qì on the battlefield. Finding the qì of Hóng'yì's mind, thoughts, and emotions would be akin to finding a single thread in a grand tapestry. She cleaved past the tidal waves of cold, dark demonic energies from the Black Tortoise and felt the landscape shift into the heat and blinding light of the Crimson Phoenix's power.

And *there* . . . at last, she found the strand of Hóng'yì's twisted delight and triumph as he bore down upon Zen's mind, luxuriating in the cruelest and most terrible memories.

He was so distracted that he did not notice as Lan slipped inside his mind.

The scene shifted. The battlefield fell away as the streams of Hóng'yì's thoughts surged past her in pieces, memories like shards of a broken looking glass: a man swathed in gold bending over a cot where an infant cried, the shadow of fiery wings lighting the chamber; a toddler tugging at a set of heavy doors, wailing for his mother; a child seated upon a high chair with an entire hallway of servants kneeling before him. . . .

And there it was, the memory of the yellow rosewood doors with the engraving of the Crimson Phoenix.

Lan directed her qì toward it and fell into the memory. The doors opened without a sound.

She was in a grand chamber within the Imperial Palace in all its glory, ceilings painted with gold and cinnabar and lapis lazuli, walls encrusted with jade and other precious stones. In the midst of it was a boy.

Hóng'yì was older now than in the other memories, perhaps eleven or twelve, on the cusp of adolescence. He was dressed in a hàn'fú of pale green silk, the color reserved for imperial princes and heirs of the emperor. He crouched over something, and it was only when he drew back, shoulders shaking with sobs, that Lan realized what it was.

Lan had never seen the Luminous Dragon Emperor,

Shuò'lóng, the last emperor of the Last Kingdom, except in paintings. In all those, he'd had the look of someone born to power and riches, with the entire world in the palm of his hand. His hair had been as black as a pot of ink, his skin as unnaturally smooth as white jade. Less like a man and more like a god.

The man lying on the kàng bed swathed in golds and samites embroidered with the emblems of the Four Demon Gods looked more like a corpse than a living human. His skin clung to the bone, and he was frightfully pale, as though death had already cast its claws into him. Only his eyes, jutting out from his hollowed cheeks, showed a flicker of life as he looked at his son.

Those eyes were red, burning, bleeding.

"*Fù'wáng?* King Father?" Lan was startled by how young and vulnerable Hóng'yì's voice sounded. The boy shook his father by the shoulders. "*Please, get up, fù'wáng! Our capital city is under attack!*"

"*I am not your fù'wáng.*" The voice that spoke through the emperor's mouth belonged to a thing older than time, to one that owned a thousand, ten thousand voices. Each word reverberated with power, with a terrifying thrum of qì that threatened to tear the walls down. "*I am the being behind the throne. I am the one whose power he feeds off of like a puny river leech.*"

Shock rippled through Lan. It was just as she'd suspected: the Crimson Phoenix had controlled—at least, in part—the emperors of the Last Kingdom.

Hóng'yì's face was pale, his pupils wide with fear. "The Crimson Phoenix," he whispered, and then he lunged for a familiar porcelain jar by his father's bedside. "*Fù'wáng,*" he gasped, holding out the jar, within which rested a Seed of Clarity. "*You have not taken your medicine—*"

He broke off. The Demon God was laughing through the emperor's lips, a distorted, hissing sound that broke off in a burble of blood.

"*Your foul little trick seeds can no longer help him,*" the Phoenix said. "*Your fù'wáng's body and mind are already failing of their own accord. The end is nigh for him. He no longer has the strength to suppress my power, even with your golden seeds.*"

Hóng'yì stared at the thing that was not his father for a breath, as though at a loss for words. And then his expression twisted. "*You are my family's legacy! You serve us, and you serve our kingdom. I command you to take down those foreign invaders!*" His voice shook slightly as he spoke, but Lan recognized the steel-eyed glint of someone who had never been denied, who had never known fear or failure. Of someone who had never known the taste of powerlessness.

"*My power is constrained by this physical body and its ailing mind and soul, all of which have burned like a candle to the end of their wick. I am your family's legacy . . . and perhaps it is time for the legacy to pass on.*" A gleam of hunger shone on the emperor's face as it beheld Hóng'yì. "*Bind me. Together, there are no limits to what we could achieve. I sense within you power greater than that of any of your ancestors. Bind me, and we could take the skies and conquer the ends of this world and the next.*"

The Hóng'yì in the memory glanced behind him at some disturbance Lan couldn't see. The Elantians closing in, perhaps. When he turned back to the Demon God that spoke through his father, the naked fear in his gaze had shifted to greed.

"*I cannot,*" he said. "*I cannot make you a bargain while you are bound to another.*"

The emperor—the Demon God controlling him—gave a slow blink. His eyes burned. Then he said, "*It is possible.*"

Three little words that cracked Lan's world.

"The bargain may be ended and the binder's soul released," the Phoenix continued, *"so long as it is a mutual agreement."*

Lan stood in the memory, feeling as though her breathing had numbed and time had stopped. She had thought demonic bargains were irreversible: that once bound, a demon remained with the practitioner until death parted them. That would be when the practitioner's soul, instead of flowing into the River of Forgotten Death or dispersing into the world, would be consumed by the demon.

But I changed the Silver Dragon's bargain with Māma, she thought suddenly. *I wrote a new bargain with it, and it accepted.*

Hóng'yì was still speaking, in his memory. *"Then you will take fù'wáng's soul,"* the child version of the prince said, scowling.

"I will release it, in exchange for yours. Shuò'lóng has fed me tens of thousands of souls over our shared bargain; I no longer crave his, for his soul is weak. It will no longer sate me as yours would." A cunning curve of the emperor's chapped lips when the Demon God saw Hóng'yì's hesitation. *"Your father is dying. With war at your doorstep, he will agree to this, to transfer his power to his only son. The future of his lineage."*

Hóng'yì's lips parted, the uncertainty to his gaze hardening into greed.

The Demon God's smile widened on the emperor's face. *"Do you agree to this bargain with me, Crown Prince Zhào Hóng'yì of the Last Kingdom?"* it said softly. *"To hold command of my power, and in return, I will ask for you, all of you: body, mind, then soul."*

"Yes," Hóng'yì croaked. *"I take this bargain."*

Lan found herself rooted to where she was, unable to move and unable to cry out, unable to do anything but watch the events of history unfold before her. When the Last Kingdom had fallen at the hands of conquerors, she had always imagined a defiant emperor making his stand against the invaders and fighting to his last breath.

But the Last Kingdom had fallen by its own crown prince's hands. A prince who had stolen his family's power and hidden himself in a life of luxury while his kingdom suffered. A prince who reaped the souls of his own people in order to maintain his own.

The emperor's skin began to glow, as though a fire burned within him. Flames of qì leapt from his skin to Hóng'yī's, wreathing his body. The boy's mouth was open, his head thrown back in a scream that echoed across worlds; a scream that melded into the laughter of a being more ancient than time itself.

In the throes of his death, Emperor Shuò'lóng's eyes flew open—and this time, they were clear, black, rheumy. Unmistakably human, unmistakably his.

The dying emperor of the Last Kingdom looked at his son. He grasped Hóng'yī's face in his hands with surprising strength. With the last of his breath, he spoke a single word as he pressed his fingers to his son's forehead.

"*Godslayer.*"

The chamber was burning now, black plumes of acrid smoke billowing as fire licked up the gilded walls, melted the jade and lapis, and blackened the rosewood floors.

The cinnabar eye painted on the emperor's forehead had begun to glow. Qì bloomed from it, spilling upward into a series of indecipherable strokes within a single circle. Beginning to end. Within, Lan could feel thousands, tens of thousands, of layers of qì moving, as though each stroke held an entire world, multitudes of lifetimes.

A Seal.

The Godslayer was no sword, no arrow, no blade; it was a *Seal*. And unlike everything else here, she could feel energies pulsing from it because it was real, and it was here, conjured in this memory within the prince's mind. The emperors had stored the secrets to the Godslayer in their minds, passing it on from generation to generation and ensuring that it could never be found by those unpracticed in the Art of the Mind.

Lan reached forward and touched a finger to the Seal.

It was as though she'd plunged through a river of time. She was falling, falling through a night of stars, tumbling through space and time and drowning in qì. The stars swirled around her, and she was watching the first shaman practitioners of the Ninety-Nine Clans raise their hands to the skies as they prayed to the gods . . . saw the shape of a great tortoise move between clouds in the night . . . the moon weep light that reared into a silver dragon . . . shooting stars fall like ash and bloom into a blue tiger . . . and the fiery light of the sun spread wings and fly as a phoenix. . . . She saw fires and floods and earthquakes rage, heard the screams of the dying and the terror of the living . . . saw hundreds of practitioners gather, hands and bodies weaving in a dance . . . saw the Four Demon Gods bend their heads toward one shaman, and heard them heave great, rolling sighs of relief as their forms began to unravel. . . .

A blinding flash of light, and the scene collapsed as Hóng'yì's memory dissipated.

The world surged back in a rush of fire and darkness—only this time it was real: the flames singeing her face, scorching the earth, burning across the entire sky. Zen knelt in the midst of it all, under relentless assault of Hóng'yì's Art of the Mind; without his command, the Black Tortoise had retreated to a small sliver of darkness in the western sky.

Someone shouted Lan's name. A figure appeared before her, curved dāo flashing and red sleeve billowing in a dance of war. Yeshin Noro Dilaya conjured defensive Seals with the tip of Falcon's Claw, raising them to shield Lan and Tai from the unbearable demonic qì and flames rolling from Hóng'yì and the Crimson Phoenix as they bore down on Zen.

"Sòng-godsdamned-Lián!" Dilaya roared. "Get . . . up!"

Lan pushed herself onto her feet. The heat was suffocating as she gripped her ocarina and looked into the core of the Crimson Phoenix.

She had seen the Godslayer. That did not mean she could conjure it. The Seal was undoubtedly the most complicated she had come across in the short time she had spent learning practitioning. She had the feeling it was less of a Seal than something *alive*, a core of energies older than this world and more expansive than the sky. There was, somehow, *time* captured within, a story of centuries and dynasties held in the Seal's currents of qì.

I have to try.

In front of her, Dilaya screamed as a wall of flame slipped through her defenses. She stumbled back, eyes watering, sweat pouring down her face.

Farther out, Zen knelt, unmoving, his hands clapped over his temples. The Black Tortoise's darkness was becoming devoured by the Crimson Phoenix's flame.

Lan remembered the grandmaster's—her *father's*—words before his death, rain trickling down his bloodied cheeks and his eyes fluttering. *The Demon Gods were never meant to be wielded without a check to their power.*

"Dilaya!" she shouted. "Cover me, just a while longer!"

The girl's jaw tightened. She nodded.

Sòng Lián clenched her teeth and lifted her ocarina to her lips. She made sure the connection between her and the Silver Dragon was cut off, then dipped her mind back into the currents of the story she had seen in the Godslayer and began to spin it into song.

Time seemed to slow, the world rendered in crimson and

silver, blood and steel, fire and song. Embers rained from the sky, and light lanced across Hóng'yì's face as he looked in her direction, catching on to the tune of her Seal. There was shock and utter disbelief in his expression. The reaction of one who had thought himself invincible. Beyond power, beyond laws, beyond all constraints of this world.

Seals came to Lan naturally through music, through the Art of Song that ran in her bloodline. Whenever she played, she entered a trancelike state, whether it was the tunes she performed back at the Rose Pavilion Teahouse or the melodies she unspooled with her ocarina. It was akin to the meditation the masters at the School of the White Pines had encouraged: a state of interacting with the world that transcended the physical, as though she'd been untethered from her body and opened her mind to a world of song.

Now Lan searched for the same feeling as she attempted to summon the Godslayer, hearing the qì in the strokes of the Seal and transposing them into song with her instrument. Yet this time, she was attempting something far beyond her grasp. The notes came discordant and clumsy; slowly, shakily, the Seal started to form.

The Crimson Phoenix shrieked in fury as the Godslayer began to twine around it, cutting into its energies. Its glow dimmed as qì seeped from it like blood from a wound.

"What are you doing?"

Lan faltered; the qì to the beginnings of her Seal trembled as her focus began to split.

Hóng'yì had appeared before her. His expression was livid, his handsome face twisted into something beyond ugly.

Without warning, he lunged.

The ocarina was ripped from her lips as he slammed her into the sand, hard enough to rattle her teeth. Overhead, the half-composed Godslayer hung, wrought in her silver qì, like a liquid moon.

Tears salted her eyes, though not only from the pain. Before her was half of what her mother had searched for, her father and the masters at the School of the White Pines had given their lives for, and the peoples of this forsaken land needed to break the cycle of war, death, and destruction that greed for power had subjected them to.

I am so close.

Zhào Hóng'yì crouched over her. His hair was mussed, his face red and his eyes furious. "How dare you," he spat. "This is my family's birthright, my heritage. *My* Demon God and *my* source of power. I won't let you take it!"

Lan scrambled in the sand for her ocarina, but the crown prince slammed his elbow into her wrist, pinning her with his limbs. She clenched her teeth and met his gaze.

"All along," Lan said, "I thought it was the Crimson Phoenix that corrupted the hearts and minds of the emperors of this land, drove them to prioritize power above the well-being of their people. But I saw what you did to your father. I saw how you chose to flee rather than defend this kingdom. And how you'd step on your own people and take their lives to maintain your own. All along, it was *you*."

"Foolish girl," Hóng'yì snapped. "How could the Phoenix have forced my ancestors to make a bargain with it? From the very first step to the last, it is a *choice*. We may be required to sacrifice parts of ourselves, but . . . you've studied the classics of practitioning." His lips curled in a sneer as he began to recite. "'Practitioners of the Way engage in equivalent exchange, for there is no give without take. Borrowed power must be returned, and power itself requires payment.' We *chose* this, Sòng Lián, and we gladly paid for it."

She was numb, as though ice were spreading inside her, freezing her heart and bones and blood. The only thing Lan could think to say was "Why?"

"Why?" The prince grinned, his teeth slicked red with blood, as he lifted his arms to the sky. "Because I would rather burn down the Heavens than pass through this world without making a mark." Something went deadly still in his gaze. "Without power, we are nothing. And I refuse to be nothing."

She did not see the dagger that appeared in his hands until it was too late. It flashed, arcing through the light of the flames overhead as he plunged it toward her heart.

Metal whistled through the air. With a sharp *plink*, Hóng'yì's dagger fell to the sand. The imperial heir looked up. His expression twisted; with a burst of qì to his heels, he leapt back across the battlefield to the safety of his Demon God.

Qì cloaked Lan, bringing the relief of velvet midnight and snow across vast, vast plains. Blink, and he was there, fingers cool as he steadied her. Blink, and the world came back into focus: sand and sky and Zen. His lips were pressed together, ashen, with just a red trickle of blood from his nose as he lifted her into a sitting position.

Zen held out her ocarina to her. *Keep going,* he mouthed.

Her gaze flitted from her instrument to him. Zen had chosen a different path from her because he did not believe in using the Godslayer to destroy the Demon Gods; he wanted to use their power to fight for this kingdom. Yet now he was handing her the key to doing exactly what he opposed.

She palmed the ocarina and looked toward Hóng'yì, standing beneath the glow of his Demon God. The Phoenix writhed within the confines of Lan's half-formed Godslayer.

One more chance. Perhaps the last.

Lan raised the ocarina to her lips again. She closed her eyes and found the memory of the Godslayer that had been seared into her mind. Notes stumbled from her fingers. The remainder of the Seal formed, black qì twining around the shining white from earlier.

Yīn, yáng, she thought faintly, and then she was done, the last note of her song wrung from her cracked lips. Zen's face was tipped toward her Seal in a look of near-reverence, bifurcated by light and dark that poured from it. Together, they watched the final circular stroke close the Seal. Beginning to end. Start to finish.

The instant the two ends met, the world cracked.

Hóng'yì opened his mouth and screamed, and the air around them was filled with the sound, amplified ten thousand times by the silhouette of the Demon God that had reappeared behind him. The Godslayer's black and white qì had wrapped around the Crimson Phoenix and was beginning to tear it apart.

Beneath it, Sòng Lián and Xan Temurezen held on tightly to each other.

But something was wrong. The ribbons of the Godslayer that were wrapped around the Phoenix were beginning to fray. Pieces fluttered away like burning parchment, edges curling as they disintegrated.

"The Seal," Zen said. "It's not strong enough."

A shriek of triumph rent the air. A massive wave of demonic energies shook the world as the Crimson Phoenix spread its wings, breaking free from the fetters of the Seal. The Godslayer shattered, and Lan watched as its last, broken shards went up in smoke.

"No," she whispered. *"No—"*

The Godslayer was gone—but it had managed to inflict damage upon the Crimson Phoenix. The Demon God's light was dimming, its wings crumbling in rains of ash.

As the Phoenix's power waned for the first time in centuries, so, too, did the Seals it had spun around Shaklahira. The unnatural flowers in the gardens dissolved into sand. The bright colors of the palace faded. Overhead, the Boundary Seal flickered, while the Gate Seal at the Crescent Spring rolled back to reveal a broken stone bridge.

With a final cry, the Crimson Phoenix vanished, leaving behind a clear sky and a tremor in the air. The sands settled. The flames receded to darkness. The world grew quiet.

By Lan's side, Zen drew Nightfire. Sweat dotted his brow, and she could tell from the unsteady bursts of qì from him that he was exhausted, burning through his own Demon God's power now. "Do not let your guard down," he told Lan. "It will be back, sooner or later. It's merely wounded from the parts of the Godslayer you did manage to conjure."

In the desert, less than a dozen steps from them, a figure lay curled up between two sand dunes. The crimson hàn'fú he wore pooled around him, yet when he pushed himself up, his face had lost its unnatural beauty, the feverish flush to his cheeks and lips. He was pale, trembling. He looked . . . ordinary.

Hóng'yì lifted a hand. Qì began to gather around him, shimmering into what Lan recognized as a Gate Seal.

"No," Lan croaked. He must have heard her, for his eyes lifted, meeting hers from across the desert. There was pure, unfiltered hatred in his gaze. As the Seal spun around the prince in a whirl of sand, she saw his lips move, mouthing a message to her.

We are far from finished.

When the dust settled again, the imperial heir was gone, along with the Crimson Phoenix.

I've failed, Lan thought faintly. The world began to fade around the edges, and as the strength fled from her, she barely remembered her head hitting the sand.

19

> Táng monks are well-practiced in the Art of Double Swords. Originating in the northwestern mountains of the kingdom, they are devout worshipers of the Way and disciplined fighters.
>
> —Various scholars,
> *Studies of the Ninety-Nine Clans*

The crimson had drained from the sky, daylight leaving it a periwinkle blue over a horizon of cracked porcelain. Pale clouds reached spindly fingers from east to west. The sun's rays landed on the white leather tome before Zen, the traces of that blazing Seal scattering like windblown ash.

He reached into his storage pouch and retrieved the first half of the tome: his copy of the *Classic of Gods and Demons*, bound in black leather. He flipped it open to the page where he had discovered the Seal left behind by the Crimson Phoenix, the Seal that had stolen away the second half of the book... which he now held in his other hand, opened to the same page.

As he watched, the Seal in his black copy pulsed gently, mingling with the energies of the Counterseal Hóng'yì had unlocked on the white copy. Like magnets, the two halves came together, their pages blending, scripture flowing from one to the other.

When the process was complete, Zen found himself holding a single tome. One cover—*his* cover—was black with the title sewn in the feathers of a red-crowned crane. When he turned it over, the cover was white with the title stitched in gold.

All the answers to everything he sought—his great-grandfather's army, the key to taking back the Last Kingdom—now lay in his palms, two halves now forming a whole.

He exhaled slowly, feeling a weight lift from his shoulders. A breeze dried the sweat on his brows and tossed his hair from his face. There was so much more he needed to do. But all that could wait.

Zen turned to the girl by his side. She lay still in the sand, the red ceremonial gown Hóng'yì had conjured now reverted back to her simple white páo without the heir's Seal to hold it together.

Twice now, he and Lan had found each other against all odds. He had not expected to find her at Nakkar. And he had not expected to find her here.

Zen had not allowed himself to believe in the red threads of fate. But this moment, with the sun beginning to breathe light into the sky and the girl he loved beside him, felt like a making of destiny.

Please, he prayed, reaching for her. *Please be alive—*

That was when the world slowed and the darkness in the back of his mind unfurled. *You ought to be careful which gods you pray to,* came an ancient, rumbling voice.

Dread gripped him. It couldn't be. Already, the voice of his Demon God was back; already, its great shadow lingered at the edges of his mind, its claws beginning to sink back in. He had paid the price for the Seed of Clarity; it shouldn't have faded so fast.

But he had expended so much qì earlier fighting the Crimson Phoenix. He could feel the seed's strength waning, his own core of energies growing weak beneath the shadow of the Black Tortoise.

Not so soon.

The entire sky darkened, and then the Black Tortoise gazed down upon him, teeth glinting like stars.

I saw it, it said slowly, its voice rumbling through the desert dunes. *The Godslayer.*

Fear clawed through Zen. In those moments when Lan had conjured the Godslayer, he hadn't thought to keep his Demon God dormant, had forgotten to put up the mental wall between their minds.

It had seen everything.

"Leave," Zen commanded the Black Tortoise, but the Demon God just gave a low laugh.

You think those puny seeds can stop me, it mused. *You think the mortal girl you love can conjure the Godslayer—that which no mortal has managed in centuries. For dynasties.* It hissed, and it plunged to the earth before Zen in a plume of darkness, eyes like brimstone and a maw like a cavern. *I am a Demon God. It is futile to resist my control.*

But Zen gazed up at the being in the sky, and a realization came to him—one that he held tightly to himself, away from the bond that bridged their connection.

For the first time since he had bound it, the Black Tortoise was angry. Until now, it had watched Zen's vain, blundering attempts with an air of lazy indifference and mockery. But now fury pulsed from its qì.

It was finally beginning to take Zen seriously.

Which meant it was *afraid*.

Zen looked straight into the burning eyes of the Demon God. "You are powerful beyond possibility," he said, "yet do not forget who your binder is and who holds command."

The Black Tortoise's eyes narrowed, and Zen could swear its mouth curved in a wicked grin. *And how long do you think that will last, mortal boy? How long can you resist caving in to my power? With every drop of my qì you use, my command over you grows.*

"Get out of my mind."

What will you do with the girl now that she has looked upon the Godslayer, knows its tune? No doubt she plans to use it upon you as part of the mission her mother left her. Will you test whose love has the stronger hold over her: yours or her dead mother's?

"GET OUT!" Zen yelled, and slammed down the wall to his mind. Even then, he could hear the Demon God's distant rumble of laughter as it receded back into its core.

The horizon was clear. Desert dunes crested in every direction, sands sweeping over the landscape.

Lan lay crumpled before him, but another person was crouched over her. Yeshin Noro Dilaya's qì flared as she wove a healing Seal with surprising gentleness. Zen could sense vitality flowing from the Jorshen Steel clan matriarch into Lan.

He pushed himself to his feet. Dilaya's head snapped up. In an instant, Falcon's Claw was drawn and pointed at him. Dilaya stepped between him and Lan, planting her feet into the ground in a protective stance.

Zen put a hand on Falcon's Claw and gently pushed past, ignoring Dilaya's splutter of shock as he sidestepped her.

"If you think I'm going to let you get close to her—" she began, but Zen cut her off.

"Dilaya," he said wearily. "I just want to know that she's alive."

Something in his tone staved her off. Zen knelt by Lan's side. *Please,* he thought, pressing his fingers to the soft skin of her neck. *Please—*

A pulse. Faint, flickering, but there.

Alive.

The sharp press of Dilaya's blade was at his back again. Slowly, Zen rose, raising his hands in a placating motion. He allowed Dilaya to steer him away from Lan so that she stood between them again.

"You know now," Dilaya said quietly, her voice hard with fury. "It is not my duty or my destiny to end your life, Xan Temurezen—nor would I be able to even if I wished it." She drew herself up, clearly not used to being the underdog. "So I am asking you to leave."

"Dilaya," Zen said.

"Do not speak my name." Her lip trembled. An errant wind blew her loose left sleeve, as though to remind him of the crime he had committed so long ago. "You were a child when you bound your first demon and maimed me, Xan Temurezen. I hated you for it, and looking back, I know I was too harsh. But that hatred I felt was *nothing* compared to how I feel toward you now." She spat at his feet. "You *knew* of the dangers of binding a demon, and yet you chose to do it, regardless. You looked me in the face every day at the School of the White Pines, and you still chose the same path. No, demonic practitioner and binder of the Black Tortoise, do not expect me to tolerate your existence."

Zen lowered his gaze. Not a day had passed since the incident she spoke of that he didn't have nightmares about it, waking up in a cold sweat and imagining that demonic presence with blood-red eyes crouched over Dilaya on the floor.

I would not speak so casually of a 'blood-painted path' if I were you.

"I do not expect you to tolerate any part of me," Zen said. Perhaps it was his acquiescence that bought a moment of silence from Dilaya, a chance for him to keep speaking. Another gust of wind swept sand at their feet, stirring their clothing.

"I only ask that you allow me to wait until Sòng Lián wakes. I wish to speak to her."

Dilaya shot him a look of outrage. "Allow you to approach her while she is at her weakest? While you have the chance to destroy the only key left to the Godslayer, to our fulfilling our mission for the Order of Ten Thousand Flowers?"

"If I wished her any harm, I would not wait for her to wake. If I wished anybody here any harm, I would not have to—" He stopped, catching the way Dilaya flinched, the way a fleeting fear crossed her expression before she schooled it back to stubborn fury. Suddenly, he was disgusted with himself for even bringing up the prospect of harm, for reminding them that all it would take was a single thought for the Black Tortoise to waken.

"Go on." Dilaya's voice was dangerously low. "Tell me more about how you would harm us."

He loosed a breath. He'd lost his chance, and with it, all hope of seeing Lan one last time before he returned to Where the Flame Rises and the Stars Fall and began the final part of his plan.

"Dilaya," came a soft, feeble voice.

Zen's heart lifted. The world seemed to exhale.

Dilaya turned to Lan, her anger instantly forgotten. She swore, and the look on her face might be the most relieved Zen had ever seen her. "Curse you, little fox spirit! You had me worried for no reason."

Lan's eyes curved in the faintest smile, then lifted to meet Zen's. Any joy in them vanished. She swallowed and turned back to Dilaya. "I will speak to him," Lan said. "But first, I want some . . ."

"Water?" Dilaya supplied.

". . . pork buns."

★ ★ ★

Shaklahira had withered like a dead desert rose. Zen rather preferred its true countenance over the unnaturally lush gardens and radiant colors from earlier. He stepped through the piles of sand that its gardens had become, up the dusty steps, and through the front doors, their paint cracked and peeling.

The bones of the interior remained, yet its patina of splendor had been stripped. Gone was the luxurious decor: the lapis and porcelain vases, the glass trinkets from Masyria, the amulets from the Achaemman Empire. The once-gold dais was now faded stone, the gauze curtains billowing in the breeze moth-eaten and coated in dust.

Sand rose from the carpet beneath Zen's boots as he and Dilaya made their way toward the small throng of people gathered beneath the dais. Dilaya held Lan in her arm, refusing to let Zen touch her.

The group of people looked up at the sound of footsteps. Zen took them in carefully. Their countenances, their outfits . . . it was as though they'd walked straight out of an old tome about the Ninety-Nine Clans. There was a cluster of monks undoubtedly from the Táng clan, their heads shaven, their sand-colored robes made for the ease of combat. They held long-range weapons like spears, cudgels, and plows, a stark contrast to the wooden prayer beads around their necks. Two healers with hemp satchels knelt by Chó Tài, who was now awake and resting on a cloth pallet on the ground. With a pang, Zen thought of Shàn'jūn, of the boy's quiet heartbreak when Skies' End had fallen and he'd thought Chó Tài had not made it out alive.

One more situation to remedy, Zen thought.

"Listen up," Dilaya called, coming to a stop before the group. She set Lan on the ground with more gentleness than Zen would have thought the matriarch capable. "Zhào Hóng'yì and his Crimson Phoenix have been defeated for now, and you can thank this girl for it." She kept her arm wrapped around Lan's waist to support her. "If you stand with Hóng'yì, you are welcome to leave; I am not the type of person to duel a defenseless opponent, yet I would welcome the chance to meet you on the battlefield." Her teeth flashed. "But if you have ever wished to live a life free of imperial rule and free of conquest and you would fight for it, I would welcome you to our cause."

There was a momentary silence. Then, beneath the shadow of a pillar, a girl stepped out: small and slim, with hair the color of snow and a matching white blindfold over her eyes. She held a fan in each hand, stitched with the same patterns of bronze and violet as her páo.

Without a word, she knelt at Dilaya's feet.

"Yeshin Noro Dilaya," the girl said, her voice as soft as a breeze. "We are indebted to you and Sòng Lián. Zhào Hóng'yi has kept us here under the control of his mind, enforcing our loyalty. For most of us, it has been twelve cycles . . . yet the imperial family held me for much longer."

Zen's focus sharpened on this girl. She looked to be their age, and there was nothing about her to suggest anything out of the ordinary, but he had an inkling. . . .

"Xuě'ér," Dilaya said with surprising gentleness. "What is your truename?"

"Elanruya," the girl said quietly, "of the Yuè clan."

Dilaya's gray eye widened in wonder. "I don't believe this. I thought the Yuè clan vanished dynasties ago."

"We were nearly wiped out by the imperial family's ruthless hunters, who sought our secrets of immortality. My ancestors hid away our kingdom behind a Boundary Seal when their bodies expired. But the Zhào clan caught me and has kept me in their service ever since, enslaving my mind with their art and forcing me to harvest the Seeds of Clarity for them. I have brought shame to my people; please allow me a chance to remedy it." Elanruya held out her fans, splaying them before her, and touched her forehead to the ground. "Elanruya of the Yuè clan pledges her allegiance to you and your cause."

Behind her, the Táng monks, too, had knelt; the remaining residents of Shaklahira followed, heads bowed.

Dilaya looked around, her expression unchanged except for a new glint in her eye. "Good," she said, her voice echoing in the hall. "We will fight to take this kingdom back from the Elantians and to destroy the Demon Gods. We'll need all the swords we can get. Let's start with some healers for this little fox spirit, Sòng Lián. Cooks, we'll need a meal from whatever supplies are left in the kitchens. Then: Táng monks and whoever else knows a smidgeon of practitioning, you're with me to set up defenses around this place so we don't sit about like rabbits in open terrain. Ah, and . . ." Dilaya turned to Zen. "Take him down to the dungeons. So long as he remains here, he will do so as a prisoner."

He acquiesced with his silence, knowing this was the price he needed to pay in order to see Lan just one more time.

Dilaya gave him an assessing look and wrinkled her nose. "And draw him a bath."

Zen let the guards lead him through the palace, down to the dungeons, where they plonked a wooden bucket of water and bath powders on the ground.

The water was ice-cold, yet it felt good to bathe. In the darkness, his mind was clear—his strength was returning, and as it did, the Black Tortoise's presence in his mind began to fade.

He banished it back to its dormant state in its core.

When he finished bathing, he leaned back against the rough-hewn stone walls, reached into his storage pouch, and retrieved the *Classic of Gods and Demons*. In the faint light seeping into the dungeon, he cracked the tome open to the last page of *his* half—the first page of the portion Hóng'yì had stolen.

It was all there: the Seal to summon the Deathriders.

Zen traced a finger down the page, following the rich strokes of ink that made up the Mansorian Seal. As he did, he recalled the Seal he had watched Hóng'yì begin to perform on Lan on the shore of Crescent Spring.

Anger burned white-hot inside him. The crown prince had been performing the exact Seal that had bound the preserved bodies and souls of the Deathriders to their commander, only Hóng'yì had intended to bind a living, breathing person to him.

Lan.

Zen drew a long, ragged breath. He exhaled through his teeth, willing the fury pounding through his skull to cease so he could think.

Gradually, the throbbing calmed.

In the days since the Ghost Gates, he'd had plenty of time to reconsider the path of his life: one that had ostensibly been written in the stars he'd been born under, in the legacy he had inherited. Zen had simply misread it all along.

Or perhaps there had always been two sides to the story.

His great-grandfather had bound the Black Tortoise, wholeheartedly embraced its strength and given himself over to it. In the end, he had succumbed to a power that had become a trail of blood and destruction and tragedy. The Mansorian clan had become a stain upon history; the name of Xan Tolürigin had been spoken with fear even among the clan members Zen had grown up with. The surviving Mansorian fugitives, including Zen's own parents, had disdained the thought of demonic practitioning and had been left to flounder in the ashes of their fallen clan until the last of them had been swallowed whole by the imperial court.

Power, Zen reflected, leaning his head against the cool stone walls. He turned back to the tome, to the inscription on the first page.

Power is survival. Power is necessity, the classic began. This, Zen understood. Power was necessary; without it, peoples and clans and kingdoms were swallowed up by those with more power.

But the next line had stumped him.

Those who seek power must first take it; where it does not exist, they must create it.

This principle was in direct contrast with the first principle of the Way; Zen had spent the better part of his childhood reciting it at the School of the White Pines. " 'Power is always borrowed, never created,' " he muttered to himself.

Dào'zǐ had been right, in some sense. The power of the imperial family, including Hóng'yì, had been siphoned from the common people—they had literally taken the souls of their people, using it to fuel their cores of qì and control the Crimson Phoenix.

Power borrowed.

Yet now, Zen realized, staring at the page in the dim light, there was a new, third line of ink. It was darker and fresher than the rest of the book, as though written at a much later time. It must have been in the half of the book the imperial family had stolen, and had reappeared now that the two halves were made whole.

Zen's fingers trembled as he swept them over the new words.

Once power is created, one must know when to destroy it.
—Xan Tölürigín, Ruler of the Eternal Sky and the Great Earth

It was as though, with these words, the world clicked into place for Zen. All this time, he had searched for a truth but found only half. He had known his great-grandfather's story, of the necessity and dangers of power. But it had been a story unfinished.

The most basic principle of Seals, of practitioning, of the Way, was that everything had a yīn and a yáng, a beginning and an end, in a cycle of creation and destruction and rebirth.

The imperial family and Xan Tolürigin alike had realized the necessity of power. They had attained power in the form of the Demon Gods. But Xan Tolürigin alone had realized the need to destroy his power.

It had been too late; the power he'd taken had consumed him, leaving the cycle open. Creation without destruction. An endless, sorrowful spiral of four Demon Gods and the humans who fought to possess them—the "Ballad of the Last Kingdom."

Lan had realized this. Her mother, the grandmaster, and the Order of Ten Thousand Flowers had known—and they had sought to destroy power in the form of the Demon Gods.

Zen shut the pages of the tome, his thoughts racing.

It was time for him to finish this tale. To close the last chapter.

The doors to the dungeons clanged open. Light swirled in as one of the Táng monks guarding his cell entered. "She'll see you now."

20

> Change in people arises not as suddenly as storms or floods but slowly, over time, like the shift of a mountain or the drift of a river.
>
> —*Kontencian Analects (Classic of Society)*,
> 5:8

The palace of Shaklahira was filled with the easy, steady bustle of activity and a rare hum of emotion that might have bordered on relief and joy. Lan sat at one of the rosewood tables that had been brought in from the gardens—too warm and too sandy to dine in now that the Crimson Phoenix's Boundary Seal was gone, along with the Seals that had moderated the climate within Shaklahira. The former cooks of the palace had blessed her with a supper composed of a variety of dishes from their bountiful larders. Lan had learned that these had been kept full by the supplies Hóng'yì had received from merchants of the Jade Trail as tithes in exchange for his practitioners protecting them from sand demons. She tried not to think of this as she tore into the noodles with sesame sauce and the sweet glazed pork buns the cooks had brought to her with shy smiles.

The Seals of the red cinnabar eye had disappeared from the foreheads of the staff, and they moved around with renewed energy and purpose. Dilaya had covered the place in protective Seals, obscuring it from nearby travelers or less-than-friendly Elantians. The Jorshen Steel clan matriarch had already designated patrol shifts and drawn up several plans to defend against attacks.

Now, with the sun beginning to set and the sky darkening, Shaklahira was grinding to a stop.

Tai sat across from Lan, nursed into recovery by the talented healers here. He had finished his meal of cold noodles and now gazed into the distance. Someone who didn't know better might have taken his expression for one of apathy, but Lan could see the grief and longing in them.

He missed Shàn'jūn.

"Normal. It feels . . . almost normal."

She startled at his voice, and then at how much emotion there was to his words. Tai rarely, if ever, spoke voluntarily; much less so about his feelings. There was a hollow, haunted look to his eyes.

But Lan took in their surroundings again, at the former court members of Shaklahira sitting in clusters, the hum of their conversation lending a new and fragile peace to the moment. "I know what you mean," she said. "It feels a bit like home."

Home was Skies' End, its eggshell-white temples tucked into craggy mountains, the chiming of bells among waterfalls and pines. Home was gone, torn apart by the Elantians and buried with the bones of their masters.

Lan dragged her thoughts back to the present. The next steps weighed heavily on her mind. *Find the Four Demon Gods. Destroy them with the Godslayer.*

The last time she had seen Erascius was on the Öshangma Light Mountain, after she had chosen to give him the star maps to the Demon Gods rather than let him kill innocent civilians. Hóng'yì had escaped with the Crimson Phoenix, and she and

Zen were here with the Silver Dragon and the Black Tortoise. That left only the Azure Tiger for the Royal Magician to attempt to bind—if she didn't get to it first.

She did have the Seal of the Godslayer now, yet her attempts to conjure it had failed. She turned her ocarina over in her hands, recalling what the immortal at the Öshangma Light Mountain had told her. *The Godslayer will not work for you unless you understand the truth.*

Immortal. *Yuè.*

She was on her feet running before she knew it, toward the faded silk curtains that led to barren gardens. A lone figure stood in the hazy desert sunset.

Elanruya turned as Lan approached her. "You have come to ask me a question," she said, tipping her head as though to look at Lan through her blindfold. "I will answer if I can."

Lan came to a stop before the lone survivor of the Yuè clan. "I met one of your ancestors," she said, "atop the Öshangma Light Mountain."

Elanruya grew very still. A look of longing crossed her face. "I see," she said softly.

Lan probed inside herself, making sure the Silver Dragon was dormant, its core tucked away, before she spoke. "I asked her to guide me to the Godslayer, which she did. But she warned me that I would not be able to conjure it without understanding the truth to its intent." She drew a tight breath. "Do you know what she meant by 'the truth'?"

Elanruya's lips parted. "The truth," she said and, to Lan's astonishment, reached up and pulled on her blindfold. As it fell away, Lan understood why she had covered her eyes. They were the same white as those of the immortal Lan had met atop Öshangma Light Mountain. As she turned to Lan, she had the feeling the immortal saw right through her.

"I understand now," Elanruya murmured after a beat, and recited the exact words her ancestor had spoken to Lan. "*The truth. Two sides to the coin. The yīn and yáng of this world. The duality of reality. The truth, child, to this tale of gods and demons, of demons and gods.*"

"How did you know?" Lan whispered.

Elanruya tied her blindfold back on. "Our eyes see the truth to everything in this world," she replied. "With one look, I see your soul, your deepest desires, and all that you have experienced. It is overwhelming, which is why we have always used blindfolds." She paused. "As to your truth, you will find it in the *Classic of Gods and Demons*. Hóng'yì had stolen a portion of it, but it was returned to its rightful owner just this morning." She gave Lan a smile, and even through the blindfold, Lan had the feeling the girl saw right through her again. "Xan Temurezen."

Lan's jaw fell, but before she could respond, they were interrupted by the sharp clack of boots. Dilaya strode toward them from the palace. A few stray hairs had escaped the buns on her head, but she looked triumphant, her hand on her hip, Falcon's Claw strapped to her side. "Perimeters secured, protective Seals cast, so we are safe for the moment," she crowed, looking pleased. "I've been meeting with everybody. It's just as I thought: we're all clan descendants here."

"Hóng'yì's family collected us," Elanruya said tonelessly. A wind shuddered between them. "They wished to control us and collect our unique arts for their use."

"We need to get everybody somewhere safe," Dilaya said. "Hóng'yì isn't gone forever. Once the Phoenix heals, he may be back." Her eye snapped to Lan. "So what's next?"

Lan's hand went to her chest. Beneath the layers of her páo lay a silver amulet, nested by her heart. A reminder of a time long gone; a reminder that she had once known happiness.

It was time to put those memories to rest, once and for all.

Drawing a deep breath, she unclenched her fist and brought it to her side. "I'm going to see Xan Temurezen."

Evening had fallen over the Emaran Desert, a dusky violet coating the rolling dunes and cooling the air. Lan leaned against the doors to the chamber she occupied, taking in the sight of Crescent Spring. It glittered a lapis blue and was the only beautiful part of Shaklahira that had not been an illusion. Between the silver grasses, a figure in robes of purple knelt by the lotuses that grew in the water. Tai had gone to free the souls trapped within. The faintest chime of his spirit bell was carried on the breeze.

Lan sensed Zen's presence before he knocked. As she turned to greet him, he took in the sight of her just as she did of him, each assessing the minute changes in the other that, over the course of just two moons, had made them into entirely new people. She had left him in Nakkar, broken from a fall from the mountaintop, his qì increasingly smothered by his Demon God's as it sought to heal and possess his body and mind.

Now, standing in the frame of the sliding doors to her chamber, he looked as though he had stepped out of a painting. His skin was smooth and held a golden glow; his lips were flushed red. His eyes were a rich, midnight black, his qì steady again, and Lan thought back to the first time they had met, in that teahouse in Haak'gong; of how he'd taken her breath away with one look that had shifted the shape of her world.

She blinked and the memory vanished. The silence stretched between them. No, they were no longer the boy and girl who had found each other in the turmoil of a conquered land. They had changed irrevocably, past and present shaping their paths to be on opposite sides. It mattered not that she had once wished for their destinies to be bound and he had promised the same.

"Well," Lan said, "I don't suppose you stayed here for the delectable pork buns."

His mouth twitched in response. A sad echo to a joke they had once shared. "No," Zen said slowly. "So soon is the School of the White Pines Code of Conduct discarded. You forget I was raised on a diet of tofu stews, vegetables, and roots."

She exhaled sharply. This wasn't—shouldn't have been—possible. Demonic practitioning should have corroded him with time. He should have become colder, crueler. She should revile him as easily as she reviled Erascius and the Elantians. But here he was, seemingly identical to the Zen she had fallen in love with once a lifetime ago, once a world ago.

"What do you want, Zen?" she demanded, all decorum falling from her voice.

"To find a way to save this land," he replied, matching her tone. "That is all I have ever wanted. You know this."

"No," she cut him off fiercely. "I don't know anymore. When you choose fire, Zen, you risk burning down everything you once wished to save."

"Lan, we have both wanted the same outcome for our land and our people, from the very start. But we sought to approach it in different ways."

She raised her hand as though to slap him, but then curled it into a fist and brought it before her chest. "Don't compare us," Lan whispered. "You betrayed everything and everyone who loved you for power. Skies' End, the school, Dé'zǐ, me—" Her voice broke, but she pushed on: "And in the end, you chose power over us all."

Zen had gone very still. Only his eyes flickered, burning as though with a fire within. "I chose power because I needed it to *save* this kingdom—"

"—by destroying it first? You of all people should know what happens when practitioners make bargains with Demon Gods. You were willing to take that risk, to endanger all the people of this land—"

"How else are we meant to take down the Elantians?" he challenged, his voice rising. "Answer me that, Sòng Lián, and I'll gladly sever all ties with my Demon God."

She pressed her lips together.

"Answer me," Zen repeated. When she remained silent, he went on: "Do you think I've enjoyed fighting its influence every moment of every day? Do you think I wished to give my body, mind, and soul over to it—to sacrifice my life, the one I had planned to spend with you?"

His words were a hot knife to her heart. Lan clenched her teeth, fighting against her body's reaction as her throat closed and her breathing hitched. Through the haze of her tears, she fumbled for the red cord at her neck and tore it from her. The silver amulet flashed as she held it in her hands, crossed the room, and pressed it forcefully into his palm before quickly stepping back.

"Even after all you've done and how you've betrayed me, you expect me to believe you," Lan said quietly. "You disgust me."

Zen looked down at the amulet. He was silent for a few beats, his hair fallen into his face and obscuring his expression. Then his fingers closed over it and he nodded. "I once thought there wasn't anything I wouldn't do to become powerful, so that I could protect those in need and those I cared for. I threw away my sense of self-worth and everything I ever believed in. I turned myself into the worst kind of human." He swallowed and looked up. "But I've found there are things I've done to maintain this power that I cannot live with. Taking a Seed of Clarity was one."

Horror dawned on her as she took him in anew. The flush to his skin, the strength to his qì, the feverish red to his lips—those came from consuming the qì of another soul.

Lan took another step back from him. "You . . ."

"Yes," Zen said. "The guardian of those seeds warned me that power came at a cost. Back then, I thought there was no price I wouldn't pay. This . . . proved me wrong." His gaze sharpened. "That leaves me with a very short window of time to defeat the Elantians while I still have control over the Black Tortoise, Lan. And a very short window of time for you to learn to conjure the Godslayer to use on me afterward."

Time seemed to slow. The noises in the world—the susurrus of wind outside, the rustle of the silk curtains, the brush of sand against the paper shutters—faded, so that there was only Zen and the words he'd spoken, suspended in the air between them.

"What did you say?" Lan whispered.

Sometime during their conversation, the last strands of daylight had retreated from the sky. The waning moon had woken. Zen stepped forward into the square of silver light that poured into the room through the doors. "There is a very short window of time for you to learn to conjure the Godslayer to use on me," he repeated.

Her mind was stuck on those words. Their meaning would not filter through, as though he spoke in a different language. This had to be a trick, some other lie he had fabricated to use against her, to betray her again. "I don't understand."

"I do now." Zen's gaze was clear. "I understood the moment I set eyes on Hóng'yì, the moment I found out about the Seeds of Clarity he harvested from the spring outside. When the Black Tortoise began taking me over, I was angry and I was terrified. I wanted more time. I wanted . . . a life ahead of me.

"The soul of the immortal at the Ōshangma Light Mountain," he continued, "told me the Seeds of Clarity would strengthen my core of qì and help me maintain command over my Demon God's power. Little did I know . . ." That wry smile again, the flash of darkness to his expression. "Little did I know what it would cost. That I would be consuming another's soul to preserve my own. That is no life, Lan. That is no existence. I had taken the first step down a path that would bring me to the same destination as the imperial family I so reviled.

"And yet, my soul was tainted from the moment I killed shī'fù—no," Zen mused, "much earlier, throughout many moments in my life. Perhaps it was the moment I accepted a bargain with the Black Tortoise. Or the moment I betrayed you. Or the moment I annihilated that Elantian outpost, with the innocent Hin—"

"Zen—"

"—or when I hurt Dilaya all those cycles ago, or when I first sought out the demon He With Eyes of Blood. . . ." Zen's eyes had closed, his brows furrowed as though he were in pain. When he opened them again, they were only sad. "It began long before any of us knew about any of this, Lan. Hóng'yì was right. My path has always been one painted in blood. And if I must walk to the end, so be it—my soul is forfeit already, so let me give it in service of this land and its people." His voice was raw. "Use me. Let me unleash the Black Tortoise's power against the Elantian regime. And when the end comes, stop me from destroying anything more."

She inhaled deeply through her nose, fisting her hands. "Do you realize," she said, her voice low, "how dangerous the plan you propose is? To unleash the full power of your Demon God . . . what if I can't conjure the Godslayer? What if it doesn't work as it's intended? Innocents could die."

"Innocents *have* been dying. For the past twelve cycles, our kingdom has been suffering a slow death. The practitioners are nearly all gone. This is war, Lan, and people die during war. That doesn't mean we don't fight."

She chose her next words to be cruel, to cut. "Your entire life, you have feared following in the footsteps of your great-grandfather. Yet now you seek reason to walk down the same path."

His eyes had shuttered. "My great-grandfather did everything he could to protect my clan," Zen said. "What would you have chosen, Sòng Lián? Either way, death stared in the face of the Mansorian clan. Either way, we were doomed. My great-grandfather chose to fight, to use his power to try to change the course of history. Just as you said, his power burned down everything. His name, his legacy, his people—all gone." His jaw was tight, and his eyes glistened. "But you know what Xan Tolürigin wished but failed to do? He wanted to *destroy* the source of his power. Only the Demon God took him before he had the chance."

"That isn't possible," said Lan. "Xan Tolürigin went mad with the power of the Black Tortoise. He reveled in it, just like the imperial family. He never wished to destroy it."

"So the tale goes," Zen said quietly. "But I have a piece of the story we never heard. My great-grandfather wrote his desire in this book."

He reached into his storage pouch and drew out a tome: one side was bound in black leather, the other side in white. As he lifted it, Lan caught sight of the title.

She drew a sharp breath. "The *Classic of Gods and Demons*," she whispered. The book Elanruya had spoken of earlier.

The one that held the truth to the Godslayer.

If there were moments that felt like fate in the making, this was one of them.

Lan turned, tipping her head to the open skies visible through the doors of her chamber. The night was clear, stars glittering like diamonds scattered underwater. She was suddenly aware of how insignificant they were, two mortal lives in the great span of kingdoms and dynasties and eras, shooting stars in a great, unchanging desert. There, and then gone.

She drew a deep, shuddering breath. "You can't be serious," she said to the night.

Zen's steps were silent, that velvet tread he had perfected throughout his cycles as a practitioner, but she still felt his approach like a cord to her own chest drawing tighter. "I am always serious," he said.

Lan spun, and then he really was in front of her, just as she'd pictured, that lock of his hair fallen before his face and that courteous smile curving his lips. By the time it reached his eyes, it had turned to sorrow.

"Don't," she said, holding her hand up as though he'd threatened her. He had stopped moving, leaving a respectable five paces between them. She wished it were farther. She wished it were closer.

She drew a long, shuddering breath and glanced at him. "Is your Demon God listening?" she asked quietly.

Understanding flickered in his face. He shook his head. "I am still in control. We are safe."

She searched his eyes and nodded. This time, she did not pull her gaze away. "If I can complete the Godslayer," Lan said, "then I won't be long in this world, either." She tapped her ocarina. "You forget, the Demon Gods are tied to their binders' souls. Destroy them, and you destroy their binders as well. And I intend to destroy all Four."

His jaw tightened. "Not yours. Yours is tied to your mother's."

"I changed that. I made the Dragon switch the bargain.

When we reach the end of our bargain, it will release my mother's soul and take mine instead."

Zen's throat bobbed; for a few moments, he seemed at a loss for words. "The end of the bargain," he repeated softly. "I see."

They were silent, steeped in their own thoughts. Each stunned by revelations the other had yielded. Between them, the once-hazy realization began to take shape: that to end this cycle of power and destruction meant to end their own lives.

And it began with the Godslayer.

Lan cut Zen a glance. "Prove it, then."

"Prove what?"

"Prove that you tell the truth." She did not need to further press on the memory of his betrayal. "If you agree that the Demon Gods must be destroyed in the end, you must agree that I have to conjure the Godslayer. I failed today. Help me."

Zen studied her for several heartbeats. "Tell me how," he said, simply and readily, as though he had been prepared to offer this all along.

She pointed. "That book in your hands can guide me to conjure a full Godslayer. The Yuè immortal told me that I needed to understand the truth of it before I could wield it."

Zen's thumb brushed a caress over the *Classic of Gods and Demons*. Then he drew a breath and held it out to her. A tentative invitation. A fragile truce.

Lan stared at it. Once she would have approached him without a second thought. Now that trust, that certainty that he would never do anything to harm her, was gone. Broken in a single night, when it had taken so many nights to build.

But perhaps there was truth to what he'd said. Perhaps the act of taking a Seed of Clarity had shaken his faith in the path he had been so ardently pursuing at the expense of everything else in his life.

And perhaps...

How else are we meant to take down the Elantians?

The question she hadn't been able to answer had nagged at her throughout their conversation. If they held the only beings powerful enough to stand against the Elantian regime, could they truly throw all that away without trying? If there was a chance she could conjure the Godslayer, didn't that mean she could put an end to it all?

The first shamans gifted the Godslayer to a keeper, intending for them to use it as a last resort should the power of the Demon Gods ever spiral out of control, Dé'zĭ had once told her. *The Godslayer was a means to maintain balance in this world.*

She had been so adamant about pursuing the path that did not involve using the Demon Gods' power that she hadn't paused to consider whether there was something she had missed.

Yīn and yáng. Good and evil. Great and terrible. Two sides of the same coin, Lián'ér, and somewhere in the center of it all lies power. The solution is to find the balance between them.

She looked at Zen, the moonlight carving him into shadows and light. Her gaze flicked to the rosewood sliding doors. Beyond, Dilaya and the residents of Shaklahira would be cleaning up after dinner and taking turns patrolling the perimeters of the palace. She thought of Tai's declaration of how *normal* things had seemed. In a sense, Sòng Lián wanted nothing more than to run past Zen and bury herself in the *normalcy* of it all, in the dishes to be washed and the water to be changed and the sheets to be cleaned. And for a heartbeat, she wondered whether, given the choice, she would return to the teahouse in Haak'gong as an obscure songgirl dreaming of a freedom she could never have.

No. She was here *for* the common songgirls. For the ones who had died at the hands of the Elantians, the villagers whose homes had been destroyed, the masters at Skies' End who had died to protect a sliver of a chance at freedom, whose hopes and deaths she carried.

And what a heavy weight it was.

Lan exhaled and moved forward in the same beat, closing the distance between her and Zen. Setting her hand against his fingers, the book beneath both their palms, felt like touching fire and ice at the same time.

"All right," she said softly.

"This tome I discovered in the palace that once belonged to my ancestors," he said. "I confess, I have not yet read through its entirety, as half was in Hóng'yì's possession. But I would be willing to read it with you." Zen looked out the open floor-to-ceiling shutters. When his gaze returned to her, it was gentle. Hopeful.

"It's a beautiful night," he said. "Would you take a walk with me?"

It was a beautiful night, Lan had to agree. She wondered how many more nights like these they had left. "All right," she repeated.

The sand was soft beneath their boots, the desert air cooling. Constellations burned in the sky, so much more visible now that the palace lights were out and they were surrounded by nothing but vast dunes for miles and miles. As Lan fell into step by Zen's side, it was as though time flowed backward, their rift mending. Their sleeves brushed against each other, the silence comfortable, almost familiar. The breeze carried to her his familiar scent of night and flame, and she realized how much she had ached for it.

For the first time in a long time, Sòng Lián looked at Xan Temurezen and saw, in his silhouette, the boy she had fallen in love with once upon a misty mountain.

21

All endings are found in beginnings.

—Hin proverb

They made conversation as they walked together across the sand. Lan was quieter at first, hesitant to reveal anything more about her travels with the memory of his betrayal still at the front of her mind. So, for the first time since they had known each other, Zen talked more.

He talked about his childhood on the steppes, of how the cousins would steal each other's prized fermented mare's milk, of how they would sneak out of their yurts and read the constellations at night. She listened to the steady, low timbre of his voice, darting glances at him every so often. His profile was limned in moonlight, and his eyes seemed to dance with stars when he spoke of his homeland.

"I've never learned the constellations," Lan said. "I learned poems and sonnets—and arithmetic." She made a face.

Zen looked at her. "The stars are full of stories," he said. "Come, I'll teach you." To her astonishment, he flopped down where he stood, sinking into the soft white sand. He smiled up at her. "Lie down."

He still held the *Classic of Gods and Demons,* the book's presence like an inevitability that they were putting off for the moment. And that was exactly what this was: a small pocket of borrowed time.

She lay down next to him, feeling the sand sift against her hair and tickle her neck. They were close but not touching, and out of the corner of her eyes, she could see the rise and fall of his chest. When he spoke, his voice seemed to thrum from the ground and wrap wholly around her. He pointed out stars that told stories—the Orphan and the Bear, the Golden Arrow, the Hunter and the Stallion—and Lan realized these were unique to the Mansorian clan. It did not escape her that Zen was the only one in this world left who could tell such stories.

"Māma told me that the stars held the light of souls from our reincarnated lives," Lan said.

Zen was silent for a moment. "I'd like to believe that," he replied at last.

"Me, too." There was an ache in her heart, so she pushed on: "What do you think we would be doing in our other lives?" The stars winked above them, innumerable and filled with infinite possibilities.

"Hmm. You would still be smashing teacups into my face—"

"That was in self-defense!" she exclaimed.

"—and bathing in fountains of holy waters from the moon—"

She turned to give him a playful shove. "How was I supposed to know? It isn't as if they put up a sign that said 'Holy water from the tears of the moon here. Do not drink or bathe.'"

"—and stealing pork buns from the kitchens," he continued, relentless, a gleam to his eyes and a rising laugh to his voice. "Dancing in the snow and making fun of my singing, telling me that I'm always too serious and need to smile more. . . ." He trailed off and turned his head to her so that they were facing each other.

They were so close that she could count each of his lashes, see the individual specks of sand that had blown into his hair and clung there like pearl dust. And suddenly, looking into his eyes, Lan had the feeling that she was falling, that the world had reversed and they plunged together into the sky and the stars rose to catch them.

She dared herself not to look away.

He didn't, either.

"If we had another life," Zen said softly, "what would you wish for?"

The words were somehow intimate and sent a shiver through her. She knew the answer as deep as her bones, as surely as an arrow's path. Lan closed her eyes. "I would want my father to have remained with me and Māma instead of going into hiding," she murmured. "I would want my family to be happy together, eating mooncakes each autumn's solstice and celebrating the turn of each cycle with red lanterns. I would want a world without war." *And I would want to love you, without being forced to choose a different path.* But of course, she couldn't say that, so she finished, "What about you?" and opened her eyes again.

He was still looking straight at her. She could see herself reflected in the black of his irises, a girl in white illuminated by the moon. And in there, she thought she might have understood some of his answer.

Zen exhaled. "I would want the same."

Her heart was beating so fast, at any moment now, it would burst from her chest. "It's late," Lan whispered, "and we have an ancient tome to read."

"It feels almost as though we are back at the School of the

White Pines, rushing your reading last-minute," Zen said with a wistful smile. She did not miss the undercurrent of grief and longing to his words.

They sat up, shaking the sand from their hair. The night had fully fallen now, and the paper windows of Shaklahira had gone completely dark.

Zen set the *Classic of Gods and Demons* between them. It lay innocuously in the sand, its title seeming to gleam. He pressed his hand to the cover and looked at Lan. "Together?" he asked.

She leaned forward and placed her hand against his. "Together."

The tome had changed. Zen stared down at the opening page, certain his eyes played tricks on him. Instead of the dissertations on power and the Mansorian Seals of demonic practitioning he had painstakingly transcribed, the first page now held a title and a portrait, as though he had picked up a storybook.

Zen flipped back to the cover and let out a breath. He had opened it on the white side, to the half that Hóng'yì had stolen.

He was about to turn the book over when Lan stopped him. "Wait," she said. Her fingers were light and cool on his wrist, and he let her draw his hand back to reopen the book's pages.

Upon a closer look, he realized that beside each column of Mansorian script was fresher Hin text. Hóng'yì—or the member of the imperial family who had first stolen this book—had translated the Mansorian language into Hin.

Why would the imperial family waste their time translating a story? he wondered.

But Lan was staring at the words wide-eyed. "The Beginning and the Ending," she read aloud. Her hair fell over her face as she leaned forward to look at the picture, and Zen suddenly had the impression they sat together in a schoolhouse at Skies' End, studying. He hurriedly pulled his gaze down.

The first ink drawing was of a shaman in a páo, standing on a hill looking into the night sky. The pane was split into four parts, representing the four seasons: spring blooms and summer grasses yielding to autumn leaves, then winter white. All the while, the shaman stood in the center, watching the lands change and the currents of the world ebb and flow.

"'Our land is one of war and rebirth,'" Lan read aloud, tracing her fingers down the lines. She flipped to the next page, where the painting showed armies swarming the grasslands. Zen could almost hear the ground thundering with the beat of hooves, the clash of steel, and the screams of clans as they clashed.

"'It is one of life and death,'" he read, continuing. "'Of yīn and yáng, of power and vitality cycling through in the rises and falls of civilization. And at the center of it all is qì.'"

So the scripture began. They worked through the pages, taking turns reading, their voices and the paintings and the text blending together like a story being breathed to life.

"'A beam of sun fell like liquid embers,'" Lan whispered, wonder seeping into her voice. "'A shard of the moon like white jade, a drop of the stars like tears, and a swirl of the night like ink.'" She looked up in amazement. "Zen, this is just like the 'Ballad of the Last Kingdom.' Do you remember? The song my teahouse performed the night we met."

How could I forget? he wanted to say, but he only managed a nod. Did she remember every detail of that evening as he did? Was it carved into her heart as it was into his—the moment things seemed set in motion, the beginning of it all?

The Beginning and the Ending, he thought, recalling the name of the story in the book, and his chest tightened. So he read on. "'The shaman reached up, and the power of the gods entered his veins. At once, the winds gusted and the tides of a nearby ocean surged; the earth cracked open beneath his feet, and flames rose at his bidding. The gods had blessed the mortals with qì, with the power of the world and the energies from which they were made. They showed humans how to harness that qì, lending drops of themselves to the first shamans. Yet it was not enough.' "

On the next page, black smoke billowed across the plains as armies clashed, pennants waving in the wind before becoming splattered in blood. Bodies burned, children screamed, widows sobbed, and still, the four gods lingered in their corners of the skies, watching.

Lan read on: " 'So the first shamanic practitioners reached to the Heavens and proffered their souls to the gods' "—she inhaled sharply; she had not removed her hand from his wrist, and now he felt the squeeze of her fingers—" 'and from there, the shamanic practitioners created the Demon Gods.' "

Zen shifted his hand so their fingers became interlaced. He held on tightly to her, his heart in his throat. They were in this together, had been from the start. Here it was at last, the piece to the story that they had been missing all along.

The Demon Gods had once been *gods*.

And they had fallen to the earth and become bound by mortals seeking their power.

We created the Demon Gods, he thought, marveling at the simplicity of the truth.

Four shapes were drawn on the page in ink—four shapes that Zen knew all too well—emerging from the cosmos: The Crimson Phoenix, taking flight from the flames of the sun. The Silver Dragon, emerging from the light of the moon. The stars plummeting like rain to form the figure of the Azure Tiger. And when all that was left was night, the Black Tortoise taking shape from the shadows.

Practitioners danced beneath them, intertwining with the Demon Gods. War broke out, blood spilled, and the forms of the Four Demon Gods grew violent as they surged over the armies, absorbing the souls lost to war, the yīn energies that came with grief and wrath and death.

"Time in the mortal world corrupted the Demon Gods," the text continued. "Fettered by the greed of their binders and subjected to the wrath of the wars they fought, their power turned destructive."

Fires ravaged the earth; mudslides buried villages; and the Demon Gods surged in size, now sowing chaos throughout the mortal world.

Atop a snowcapped mountain, one of the very first shamanic practitioners appeared again. He thrust his hands into the skies, which began to glow with his qì.

Lan made a noise. "Dào'zǐ," she whispered, and Zen felt his heart quickening at the epiphany. The writer behind the *Book of the Way*, the philosopher behind so many principles of practitioning, one of the first shamanic practitioners known to this land.

Had Dào'zǐ written the first principle of practitioning—that power could not be created, only borrowed—*because* of the dangerous history of the Demon Gods?

"Zen," Lan said, and her tone caught his attention. She had turned the page, and now he saw why she was squeezing his hand so tightly.

The entire page had been inked black but for the Seal, hanging as brightly as a moon in a night sky.

"The Godslayer," Zen said. He recognized it from having seen her conjure it earlier that afternoon.

"Power is always borrowed," the scripture continued, "so long as it is returned. It may be used, so long as it may be destroyed."

Beneath the Godslayer crouched images of the Four Demon Gods. Their heads were bent to its light. And as Lan and Zen flipped to the next page of the classic, it was as if they watched the story reverse. The Crimson Phoenix shrank back into a droplet of the sun as the Silver Dragon returned to the crescent moon; the Azure Tiger dissolved into the stars, and the Black Tortoise faded into the night.

And on the final page of the story was the same painting as the first: that shaman in a páo, standing on a hill looking into the night sky. In the constellations, the shapes of four gods burned.

"The Ending and the Beginning," came the last words of the story, and that was that.

Zen blinked as though he had stepped out of a long dream. Around them, the dunes were silent, and when he looked up at the stars, he half expected to find four distinct shapes among them.

"*Gods,*" Lan exhaled, her breath coming out in a pale stream. Her face, too, was tilted to the skies.

They were quiet for many breaths, words alone inadequate to express the weight of what they had just learned.

As usual, Lan was first to speak. "It was us all along," she whispered. "It was the yīn energies of our human souls, the destruction and devastation of the wars of our world, that corrupted their cores. *We* turned the gods into . . . demons."

Zen was breathing hard. Lan was right: it had all been there, all along. Demons were beings formed of excess yīn energies comprising wrath, ruin, and a will unfinished in life. Those emotions belonged to humans.

"They needed to be returned to the qì of this world with the Godslayer," he said, "so that the yīn they accumulated in their cores was released, and so that no one lineage held on to that power for too long."

"But the imperial family hid the Godslayer," Lan continued. "That's why the cycle was broken and their power grew out of balance, turning destructive. That's why the Demon Gods remained in our world for so long, growing corrupted by the bloodshed and violence of endless wars. Their cores absorbed it all. Over thousands of cycles."

"They were never meant to," Zen supplied. "Dào'zǐ himself wrote it. In this classic as well as in the *Book of the Way*. Power can be created, so long as it is destroyed. We broke the cycle."

He noticed that her hands were still draped in his; she seemed to have forgotten, staring down at the last page of the story with that furrow in her brow.

Gently, Lan touched her fingers to the last painting, of the shaman gazing up to the quiet skies and the four gods looking down at the world below. "I understand now," she said. "The truth the immortals spoke of. The intent behind the Godslayer." She turned to him, her eyes bright with sorrow. "It is humans who bound the gods and turned them into demons. And the Godslayer . . . the Godslayer is not meant to destroy them but to release them."

22

> Destiny is an unfinished story of two souls
> linked by a red thread of fate. It spins across
> lives, times, and worlds, searching for an ending
> into eternity.
>
> —Unnamed scholars of the Yuè clan,
> *Theories on Reincarnation,* Chapter 1

The doors to Lan's chamber were open, as she had left them, the silk curtains stirring in a way that felt almost forlorn. Sand had blown in; their boots scuffed, Zen's and hers, as they pushed the sliding doors shut.

Everything and nothing had changed.

Lan took in the normalcy of the chamber, the soft cushions and blankets draped across her kàng bed, the elaborate yellow rosewood furniture carved with intricate fretwork. The sliding doors at the other end of the room led to the hallways of Shaklahira, which had quieted into slumber. Lan imagined Dilaya sprawled across her kàng, boots still on and Falcon's Claw cradled in her arm as a child might hold a doll. She thought of Chó Tài, who had the tendency to mumble in his sleep, perhaps in response to whatever ghosts he heard in his dreams. In a world without war, would their dreams come easier?

She wondered, then, what her and Zen's lives might have looked like in a world without war. Whether they would have had more time.

She remembered the feeling of his fingers clasped between hers, firm and warm and *right*.

Her head hurt; the revelation from the *Classic of Gods and Demons* was suddenly too much to bear.

Lan marched over to the chest at the foot of her bed. From within, she retrieved a jar of plum wine.

"What is that?" came the inevitable question from Zen. He had taken a seat at the other end of the room, shoulders slumped in exhaustion. He straightened slightly, and his tone shifted to incredulity as she unfastened the cord that held the cloth lid over the wine jar. "Are you *drinking*?"

"In case you hadn't realized, I don't have much time left in this world to enjoy a jar of plum wine," Lan retorted, and decisively tipped the mouth of the jar to her lips. The liquid was sweet and burned slightly as it went down, filling her with a satisfying warmth. She looked up to see Zen watching her with a slight frown.

She huffed. "If you're going to lecture me, Mister Practitioner—"

"I wasn't going to," he said lightly.

She closed her eyes, all the implications of what they had just discovered swirling in her brain. *The Demon Gods were never meant to be wielded without a check to their power*, Dé'zĭ had told her. She had held on to the first part of that sentence but never stopped to consider the reverse: if there was a check to their power, was the Demon Gods' power meant to be wielded for the greater good?

The fear of losing control, along with a lifetime of being taught that demonic practitioning was taboo, had led her to uphold an absolute: that the Demon Gods were meant to be destroyed, their power never to be touched. The path opposite from the one Zen had chosen.

But Dé'zĭ had taught her to seek the path of balance. *Two*

sides of the same coin, Lián'ér, and somewhere in the center of it all lies power.

"What will you do now?"

Her eyes snapped open at Zen's voice, the words coming as though he had heard her thoughts. Lan swirled the jar of plum wine. "Practice conjuring the Godslayer, then hunt down the Crimson Phoenix and the Azure Tiger. And then . . ." She trailed off, the unspoken end to their own lives hovering in the air between them. Somehow, it felt distant. Unreal.

"What will you do?" she asked.

"I told you, when we met in Nakkar, of the powerful army my great-grandfather once commanded, now preserved in an ancient magic. The Seal to summon them was partially in the half of the *Classic of Gods and Demons* that Hóng'yì's ancestors stole." His gaze settled on the rosewood cabinet by his side, where he had placed the tome. He withdrew it and opened it to a page he seemed to know by heart. Then he proffered it to her.

A gesture of trust. A message that this time, he would tell her everything.

Lan approached. Her every step was like a heartbeat between them. She set the wine down on the cabinet and took the book from him.

It was open to a page she could not read, of Seal syllabary that fell vertically down the parchment in elegant curves and loops. Lan flipped through the worn pages. She could sense Zen's gaze on her like a burning flame as she studied the art of his clan, of his people.

Lan shut the book and brushed a finger over its title, embroidered in gold interwoven with feathers of a red-crowned crane. "Zen," she asked quietly, "why would an army require a Seal from the *Classic of Gods and Demons* to be summoned?"

"Because they are demonic practitioners," Zen said, "and

I must bind their souls to mine to channel my will through them."

Her initial shock was followed swiftly by anger. Lan's nails dug into the tome. *"Demonic practitioners,"* she repeated with emphasis on each syllable.

He watched her unflinchingly, with that steeled gaze she knew all too well to mean he'd made up his mind.

"This is dangerous," she continued, her voice low. "You know that. To not only be bound to a Demon God but to also harness the power of undead demonic practitioners is madness."

"Not if I can control them. And when my Demon God is released, the cores of the Deathriders, too, will cease to exist."

"What if you lose control?"

"Then you will put an end to it," he said matter-of-factly.

"You speak as if it is an easy thing to conjure the Godslayer." Her voice trembled. *As if it is an easy thing for me to end your life.* "I won't agree to it."

"I will do it with or without you. I cannot afford to make the same mistake as I did back at Skies' End. Now that we have the Godslayer, I will do everything within my power to ensure that my strike falls true, that I have no risk of failure this time. I will root out the Elantian conquerors thoroughly and leave no means for them to return. And if that requires calling upon an army of demonic practitioners, then so be it." Zen paused, waiting for her to respond. When she didn't, he continued: "I would rather fight with you by my side, but I cannot wait for you to change your mind. With each passing day, the Black Tortoise's influence grows over me. I am running out of time."

Lan glared at him, breathing hard as though she'd just run. "You force my hand."

Zen gazed back at her. "Yes."

She picked up her plum wine and took a swig, wishing

she could smash the bottle on his head instead. He frowned at the violence of her motion but went on: "I will make for Tiān'jīng." He used the Hin name for the Heavenly Capital, which had been renamed to King Alessandertown by the Elantians. "That is where most of the Elantian leaders reside, along with most of their high-ranking Royal Magicians. The Elantians are only as powerful as their best magicians; they're the key reason the Hin lost twelve cycles ago. If I can wipe out the majority of their Royal Magicians, we can force the high governor to surrender and the Elantians to retreat."

Lan cast him a humorless glance. " 'Cut off the head of the serpent . . . ' "

" 'And the powerful body, too, is slain,' " Zen finished. It was an aphorism from the *Classic of War*. "You haven't forgotten everything."

"I told you once, I'm a quick study."

His smile faded. "I will work with you to hunt down the Tiger and the Phoenix. We destroy them first, and then we make for the Heavenly Capital to take out the Elantians and end their regime." He paused, his voice growing quiet. "Please agree to work with me. I cannot do this alone. While I fight the Royal Magicians and their army, I need you to march into the Heavenly Palace, where the high governor sits, and negotiate their surrender. Afterward . . . I am inclined to believe that the strength in my core would not last for much longer after this battle, so I will need you to end my life when I lose control."

A bitter pain had locked up her chest. Lan shoved the *Classic of Gods and Demons* back at him and took another gulp of her wine. The room was a little hazy now, and she liked it this way. Better than the dissonance she felt in the fact that what she had been taught to revile—using the power of demons and the Demon Gods—might now be the only chance for their people's freedom. Better than choosing the actions that would determine the fate of her kingdom.

"Lan," Zen began, but she cut him off.

"Why don't you tell Dilaya your masterful plan? I'm sure she would be thrilled to be working alongside you, the Black Tortoise, and your army of demonic practitioners."

"Lan," Zen said again, and something in his tone made her look at him this time. "You cannot tell them. Dilaya and Chó Tài . . . they will never accept me, nor the idea of a group of undead demonic practitioners fighting alongside them."

"Nor will I. I will not forgive you for this, Xan Temurezen. You leave me no choice."

He watched her, his eyes glinting in the dim light. "Yet should we succeed, the kingdom will be free, our people liberated, and the Demon Gods released. Is that not what you wanted, Sòng Lián?"

Lan stalked over to him, closing the last of the distance between them. She lifted her hand and slapped him full across the face.

The crack reverberated in the silence.

Zen pressed a hand to his cheek. He hadn't moved from the chair, but now he lifted his face to her. "You can take it out on me if it makes you feel better," he said. "I would deserve it all."

"I hate you," she whispered. Her eyes were beginning to sting, and there was nothing she could do to stop the way her breaths grew sharper and shorter.

He hesitated, then lowered his hand. "I know."

Angrily, she swiped at the traitorous tears that rolled down her cheeks. He stood for almost everything she was meant to stand against. Had broken every taboo of the Way, had killed and taken another's soul for his own and bound a Demon God and now proposed to call upon the power of demonic practitioners.

But all of that . . . might be the only way to save this kingdom.

She had once said to him that they were given shit choices. They had to make the best of them. Perhaps this *was* the only way.

What would Māma say? What would Dé'zǐ tell her? Lan closed her eyes. She would give so much for their guidance in this moment, to tell her whether she was making the right choice.

But Māma and Dé'zǐ, too, were gone.

"I never wanted this either," Zen said quietly. His head was bent and from this angle, she could see only the dark crescent moons his lashes carved against his cheeks. "Given another chance, I would not choose to walk this path." A flash of a humorless smile, and when he spoke, it was as though to himself. "In the worst moments, especially on nights when the influence of the Black Tortoise becomes unbearable, do you know what I hold on to? I think of the life I might have had, had there been no war, no conquest, no Demon Gods. I think of the life I would choose if I could relive this one, and it is a good life. A life devoted to the path of the Way, as a master of a school of practitioning. And in every iteration of my imagination, Sòng Lián, I am with you."

She knew they thought of the same memory, of that boy and that girl in a misty, rain-soaked mountain village, lying together in a barren room.

"Don't say that," she whispered, her voice breaking. "You have no right to say that to me."

They were knee-to-knee, her hand still raised from when she had slapped him. The faint moonlight that stole through the paper shutters coated his hair as though with pearl dust.

Lan leaned down and kissed him. He made a noise in the back of his throat, stiffening with surprise before he thawed, his hand coming to cup her face. His lips were salty, her tongue sweet with plum wine, and he kissed her back with barely restrained hunger so different from the courteous, distant Zen she had always known.

She loved him. She had loved him once, and then she had hated him, yet tonight as they'd lain beneath the stars and he'd spoken of his homeland and the family he'd lost with heartbreaking yearning, she had fallen in love with him all over again.

Perhaps that was what led her to pull away, voicing a thought that had formed in her mind a while back, one so selfish she hadn't even wished to admit it to herself.

"There is something I haven't told you about the Demon Gods," she whispered.

He blinked. Sometime during their kiss, his hands had found their way to her waist. "Tell me."

"I think there is a way to break a bargain." And Lan told him of the memory she had seen in the crown prince's mind. "The Phoenix said the bargain could be broken and the binders' souls released, so long as there was mutual agreement. If there is another binder . . . if our Demon Gods agree . . ." She swallowed.

Zen's eyes searched hers, and his face softened with understanding. His hand pressed against the small of her back, drawing her closer to him. The other went to her face again, caressing her hair. "We could break our bargains, let someone else take our places before casting the Godslayer?" he said gently. "If it were possible, could you live with yourself, with me, knowing the choice we made?"

Her eyes heated until he blurred; she knew the answer already.

She felt Zen's warm thumb against her cheek, wiping the wetness from her face. Then his breath against her hair as he pressed his lips to her skin, kissing away the tracks of tears. Just as he had once before, in that mountain village of mist and rain.

She was crying in earnest now. This small gesture was proof, proof that the boy she'd fallen in love with was still here, that it had all been real. And it only made everything hurt more.

"Please don't cry," Zen whispered. "If I have only this one night with you, Sòng Lián, it would still be better than a lifetime without you."

Lan met his lips with hers, thread her fingers through his hair. The world rocked slightly as she sought balance, placing one knee on the chair between his; he caught her shoulders to steady her. Then his hands traveled down her body to her hips, settling there as she slid onto his lap.

She felt his sharp intake of breath. They had been this close before, but not in a way this bold, yet as she caught his lips in hers, relishing the taste of him, she found that she no longer cared. They had spent so much time—time they didn't have—believing they were on opposite paths when, really, they had been reaching for the same goal. When they had been two sides of the same coin.

Zen made a sound low in his throat, then clasped her arms and pulled back from her. "Lan," he said, his voice ragged. "Do not tempt me into dishonor."

She swiped a hand at his sleeve, then held up the amulet with the red cord. Zen blinked; he had not even caught the moment she'd stolen it from him. "If you want a lifetime with me, Xan Temurezen," she said, "then make me a vow tonight that you will find me again in our next lives."

His eyes were dark moons as he shifted his hand to clasp

hers, covering the pendant he had once gifted her. It was the only token he'd had from his clan, meant to be given to the person he chose to spend his life with. The red cord represented the threads of fate that tied two souls together across worlds, across lives. So long as they were bound, they would find each other again, no matter how long it took.

Zen took the pendant from her and wound the cord over her hand. Then he slipped his fingers between the threads so that they were palm to palm, hands clasped, bound by the red thread. He tipped his face up to her. "I love you, Sòng Lián, more than anything else in this world. And I would wish to follow you into the next life and ten thousand more."

Lan looked at their hands, at the red thread of his pendant dangling from between their interlocked palms. They had no family, no masters, no elders to confer blessings upon them... no one but themselves in this moment, and that would be enough.

She reached out with her other hand and tugged on the cord, wrapping it fully around their hands until they were inextricably bound. "In this life and the next, and ten thousand more, I would choose you," Lan said, and spoke his name—his full name. "Xan Temurezen."

Gently, she swept a lock of his hair from his eyes and trailed a thumb down the length of his jaw. Tried to imagine, in a different time, a different world, the courteous young man dressed in sleek black whom she'd met in Haak'gong knocking on the doors of the courtyard house to call upon her. How they might have discussed philosophies and histories and music over a pot of steaming chrysanthemum tea, with teacups she would not have smashed into his face.

How they might have dressed in red before their families and friends and exchanged vows, hers as red cords and his as silver pendant earrings.

Lan held on to that image, in this barren little room of nothingness, and smiled as she pressed her lips to his again. He responded, his restraint falling away to pure desire as he pressed her closer against him and twined his other hand through her hair. His lips trailed down her jaw, placing kisses against her chin and then her neck in a way that made her shiver.

She clung to him with one arm, and with her heart in her throat, pulled loose the sash at her waist. Gooseflesh pricked her skin as her páo fell from her shoulders and the cold swept in. Zen's eyes widened at the sight of her bare skin. His lips parted in a rush of air as he looked at her.

Lan had heard stories from the older girls at the teahouse, had stolen their "court flower books" on lovemaking. For all the ways she had been taught to charm and flirt with customers, she had never known love. The notion had terrified her: girls being dragged upstairs against their will, then either disappearing forever or being cast out like used rags afterward. She had thought the feeling of a man's fingers on her would nauseate her.

Love, to Lan, had been an inevitable, nightmarish end to a songgirl's life at the teahouse, or an unattainable fairy tale like the stories Ying had always dreamt of.

This was different. This love was broken and remade, imperfect in the way their sharp, jagged edges had fit together, yet it was the deepest thing she had ever felt, and the most immutable truth she had known. Tonight, she wanted to know how it felt to be loved.

She met Zen's gaze, and he seemed to understand her unspoken permission. Holding her to him, he stood and walked them to the kàng. There, gently, so gently, he lowered her to the silk sheets, her páo pooling around her waist like a silver blossom. Her fingers worked the slips to his páo, the black samite giving way to the strong cords of his chest. She trailed her fingers over the hard, flat planes of his stomach, feeling the ridges of crisscrossing scars and knowing the pain they held.

Wishing that, for tonight, she could take that pain away.

He lowered himself over her, fingers still tangled in hers and the red cord of their promise, his weight suspended by his elbows.

"Tell me if you want to stop," Zen said softly.

"Don't." She tipped her head back and kissed him. He sighed against her, and she held on to him as he covered her body with his.

He didn't miss her sharp intake of breath, the way her muscles tightened. "Does it hurt?" he asked.

She shook her head, her heart beating fast. There were some things in life that hurt, Lan decided, but that were meant to be. Perhaps she and Zen were like that: for all the grief and pain and heartbreak she'd gone through, nothing had ever felt more right.

He moved tenderly against her, his gaze never leaving her face, searching for any signs of discomfort. She clung to him, curling her fingers against the nape of his neck and feeling the familiar silken softness of his hair. He dipped his head and grazed kisses against her neck, her jaw, her cheeks. Slow. Reassuring. Letting her take the lead.

She caught his mouth with hers, lips parting, their kisses growing longer and deeper. She closed her eyes and gave herself over to sensation, to his fingers on her skin, the heat of their bodies, the salt-and-sweat taste of him. The darkness became the night sky, she and Zen two destinies inextricably joined across worlds and fates. And she held on tightly to him as that night sky reeled into stars, their two souls bound in pain and pleasure, in grief and love.

They lay together, hands and bodies intertwined, fingers

joined by the red cord of her pendant. It was one of the first times in her life, Sòng Lián reflected as she gazed back at Xan Temurezen, that everything seemed to have fallen into place, if only just for a moment: that the winding, star-crossed fates that had led them together and then pulled them apart had finally found their true course.

23

> Blood draws more blood. Power desires more power. A vicious cycle cannot be broken.
> Unless it is destroyed.
>
> —Xan Alatüi, First Shaman of the
> Eternal Sky and the Great Earth,
> *Classic of Gods and Demons*

Xan Temurezen.
A whisper from the depths of an abyss. An abyss he stood at the edge of, an endless void of black that seemed to call to him.

Time runs out, Xan Temurezen. The end is near.

Zen awoke sometime in the night with a jolt, his heart in his throat. He could have sworn he'd heard a voice in the darkness, one that had pulled him from his dream—a most wonderful, impossible dream.

He looked down, and his heartbeat slowed. The panic, the frantic feeling, gave way to a calm satisfaction. There, nestled in his arms, was the girl who was the anchor to his world. Sòng Lián. Lan. The faint moonlight that seeped through the paper shutters and the cracks of the doors limned her in silver, so that he had the illusion she was dusted in a light layer of snow. She was warm and small against him.

Zen loosed a breath, closing his eyes and willing himself to sink back into that dream. Yet there was something in the air that felt off: an invisible static, a storm in the distance only he could feel. He frowned.

Against his chest, Lan stirred. Her eyes fluttered open, liquid as they caught the dim glow of moonlight. She blinked. "You're awake, too," she whispered.

Zen smiled, trying to quell the feeling of unease as he pressed a kiss to her forehead. "I am," he said, speaking against her temple. "I had the most wonderful dream."

She chuckled, a throaty sound laced with sleep. "Oh? I'm sure I was in it, then."

He trailed a thumb against her cheekbone. "You were."

She snuggled against him. "Tell me more."

"We were back at Skies' End," Zen said softly, closing his eyes and tasting the near-tangible joy of this moment. "Only . . . there were grasslands in the mountains, too. We rode horses beneath the sun and the blue sky, and we had children. Everyone was there . . . Dé'zǐ, your māma, my aba and amu, the disciples and the masters . . ."

"Even Dilaya?" she teased.

"Even Dilaya." He held her as tightly as he wished to hold on to that dream. It had been a good dream.

"I don't know how she'd react to being in your dream," Lan mused, playing with his hand. She pressed her palm to his, tipping her head to watch their fingers interlace. "But *I* am pleased." She flipped over and kissed him, speaking against his lips. "I command you to dream of me every day from now on."

He smiled into her kiss. "I promise."

The words had no sooner fallen from his lips than a colossal crack of qì rolled over the desert sky.

They flung on their páos and ran outside. A harsh wind

had picked up, howling through the dunes; within it came the threads of demonic qì. Not just any demonic qì—the energies of a Demon God. Hand in hand, Zen and Lan turned to face the eastern sky.

"It's coming from that way." Lan's voice was tight.

Zen gazed into the east. These energies did not feel like the burning qì of the Crimson Phoenix they had fought just yesterday. Which left only one Demon God to which this power could belong.

Dread crept up Zen's throat, and for a moment, he found himself unable to speak. *No, not yet,* he thought, and his grip tightened on Lan's hand.

The last time Lan had conjured the star maps, coerced by Erascius atop Öshangma Light Mountain, he had roughly derived the location of the Azure Tiger. It had been east: somewhere close to Skies' End, where the masters had chosen to set it free rather than to let it fall into the hands of the Elantians.

That night, Erascius had escaped, likely in pursuit of the Tiger.

"This qì . . . ," Lan whispered.

"The Azure Tiger," he said hoarsely.

They shared a look. There was only one reason a Demon God might suddenly erupt with such fierce demonic energies. He recognized the pattern in those energies from the night he had bound the Black Tortoise.

"Erascius found it," Lan said with dull finality.

Without another word, she took out her ocarina and began to play the familiar tune that would conjure the star maps. With the wind rattling the silver grasses and the demonic qì rolling over them, the four star maps began to appear in the sky: crimson and azure, black and silver. Phoenix and Tiger, Tortoise and Dragon.

Briefly, Zen studied the quadrant the Crimson Phoenix

occupied, hoping to glean some clues as to its whereabouts, but it was no use: like this, it was only a jumble of stars. Neither of them were well enough trained in the Art of Geomancy to read a star map on the spot.

When Zen looked at the Tiger's map, he noticed something. He placed a hand on Lan's shoulder and pointed. "The Tiger—it appears to be moving."

He couldn't pinpoint its exact location, but he could tell that it was moving eastward; the constellations behind its form spun, very slowly, in the opposite direction.

The music stopped.

"Keep playing," Zen said. "Please. We need to pinpoint its whereabouts."

"It'll take us days to read the star maps," she replied. "You remember the last time."

He couldn't think of that without his stomach sinking with guilt. "Yes."

"But we don't need to know exactly." Lan turned to him, her mouth a firm line. "Judging from the way the stars were rotating, the Tiger appears to be moving east. What is at the easternmost point of this kingdom? A place where, if you were a Royal Magician who had just achieved your lifetime goal of binding one of the most powerful beings in this land, you would immediately go?"

Zen exhaled sharply. "Tiān'jīng." The Heavenly Capital.

Lan gave a single nod. "Erascius has sought the Demon Gods for his entire duration here. You heard him, how he wants them so he can have complete power. How he envied us Hin for being connected to all branches of qì." She frowned, a shadow crossing her face. "If I know him at all . . . I think he is going to present the Tiger to the high governor in the Heavenly Palace, and that they're going to write to their king across the sea."

Zen nodded, his throat suddenly tight. They had considered this—Erascius binding the Azure Tiger—in their plans. They simply hadn't anticipated that it would happen so soon.

He was seized by a sudden desire to reach for Lan's hand. To wrap his fingers around hers and hold her by his side for as many more heartbeats as possible.

Instead, Zen swallowed and closed his fingers into a fist.

"Listen to me very carefully." He didn't know how he managed to speak in a moment like this, but he continued. If he thought of anything else, he might begin to regret his choice. "There is a group of disciples and masters—Master Nur and the Nameless Master—back at my base in the Northern Steppes. I will send them to you." She began to speak, but he cut her off. "Some of the older disciples may be able to fight, but many are young. They need somewhere safe to stay. Can you promise me to take care of them?"

She was looking at him in a way that might break his heart. Tears gathered in her eyes; she blinked, refusing to acknowledge them. Instead, Lan pressed her lips together and nodded. "We must leave, too. Hóng'yì will have felt this binding. He'll make his move not long after. It won't be safe here anymore."

"It won't," he agreed.

"I'll take them to the Sòng courtyard house," she said. "I've been thinking of a shelter, and I realized it was there in front of me all along. The Elantians would have long abandoned it." She swallowed. "It's where everything began, so it's fitting for me to return when everything is to end."

Her childhood home. He regretted that he would not see it with her. " 'The beginning and the ending,' " Zen murmured.

"I'll use some of the Silver Dragon's power to open a Gate Seal leading there," Lan continued, and then her fingers tightened on his wrists. "Come with us. Bring the older disciples there. We can form a battle plan together, and . . ." She trailed off at his look.

"I cannot," Zen said gently. "There is no time. My army lies in the Mansorian palace in the Northern Steppes. I will summon them and make for King Alessandertown before nightfall. Remember: I will aim to destroy the Royal Magicians and their army base, but I believe Erascius may show up with the Azure Tiger sooner. We must defeat him and release the Azure Tiger first. That will be the fatal blow to the Elantian government." His jaw clenched; he drew her hands into his and held them tightly. "Whatever you do, *do not* fight him. Leave that to me. I cannot have you lose yourself to your Demon God, Lan, when you hold the key to ending this all."

Her gaze had not shifted from his face. "I know what I must do."

Zen's gaze softened. From his sleeve, he retrieved the silver amulet with the red cord. He had thought of this long after she had fallen asleep by his side last night. "There is a Seal on this that recognizes my qì; it will warm whenever I am near." He lifted it over her head and fastened it. "In this way, I will be close to you. Always."

Instead of answering, Lan stepped forward and threw her arms around him. Zen's breath hissed out, and a sharp pain bloomed in his chest. He dropped his cheek to the top of her head and held her, feeling her heart beat against his.

The pulse of demonic qì was retreating from the sky, growing fainter and farther with each second that passed. They were out of time.

"You must find Hóng'yì after," he said softly into her hair, closing his eyes so he could remember the scent of her, the shape of her, the feeling of her in his arms at last. "Forgive me that I cannot be there by your side to finish it."

Her face was pressed to the crook of his neck. He felt her

nod against it, felt her shuddering breaths against his skin, the tickle of her hair against his chin, the warmth of tears soaking into the collar of his páo.

Gently, Zen stroked the back of her head. "I promised you we would meet after all this, in our next lifetime." He continued to speak, knowing that the moment he finished would be their last together. "There, we will have everything we didn't in this life. We will meet at a school bookhouse, perhaps—the courtyard outside a classroom, where you will be eating pork buns and I will be studying beneath a great cypress tree. We will wed, with a big ceremony full of family and friends and masters, and we will have children and teach them everything there is to know about this world. And there, I will love you every moment of every day that was owed to us in this life."

"You forgot one thing," she whispered against him. "When we meet, I will smash a teacup in your face."

He smiled against the sharp pain in his heart and spoke the words that came with every single memory of her. "How could I forget."

A breeze blew in, stirring their páos. It was time to go.

Zen drew back. He pressed his palms flat against her cheeks and held her tenderly as he kissed her one last time.

Then he turned and, without another glance back, stepped into the Gate Seal he had conjured.

His boot cracked against ice. A cold wind rammed into him, robbing him of breath as he struggled to adjust from the temperate desert climate. It should have tired him to draw the Gate Seal over such a long distance—no, it should have been nearly impossible, given the amount of qì it took—but Zen barely felt anything. Before, he might have berated himself for drawing upon the Black Tortoise's energies so liberally, but now he accepted it with resigned calm.

The end was near. He was a burning star across the night sky, his fire nearly gone.

Zen felt a thickening in the air as he passed the Boundary and Illusion Seals he had cast around Where the Flame Rises and the Stars Fall, and then he was back. Before him, the palace of his ancestors rose, frozen in winter's snow beneath the mourning moon.

He sensed the shadows shift before their owner stepped out in front of him.

"Something has changed" was all the Nameless Master of Assassins said. His face was as inscrutable as ever, but his eyes seemed to bore straight into Zen's thoughts.

"The Azure Tiger has been bound," Zen confirmed. "And the Godslayer is found. All will end soon."

The Nameless Master blinked once but gave no response.

Zen started up the steps to the palace gates. He felt, rather than heard, the master follow.

"It is no longer safe here," Zen continued as they entered. The hall was empty but for the flicker of Flame Seals draped over the sconces. Zen was glad the disciples had found a way to keep themselves warm in his absence. "Wake everyone. You must leave."

"Where to?"

Zen slowed. There was no point in hiding it anymore. He turned to face the master. "Sòng Lián, Yeshin Noro Dilaya, and Chó Tài are organizing a rebellion in the west. They will have safe shelter for the children."

The Nameless Master accepted all this without a change of expression. "What of you?"

"You ask too many questions." Zen kept his tone neutral, cold. The last thing he needed was for any more fuss, anything to delay him from what he had to do. "Wake everyone and gather them here. My Gate Seal will bring you to safety."

He turned just as Shàn'jūn emerged from one of the hallways leading to the kitchens. The boy held a clay bowl of broth in his hand. He froze as he spotted Zen, his eyes widening and his mouth dropping. "You have returned," the Medicine disciple said with a tentative smile.

Zen had wished to avoid this. He shot the Nameless Master a pointed look, and the man disappeared down the palace's halls to rouse the sleeping disciples. Shàn'jūn watched this exchange with open confusion.

"Is something happening?" he asked, and then glanced down at the broth in his hands. "Ah, I had made this to bring to the Nameless Master on his watch tonight, as I have heard him cough from the chill, but it seems he is gone." He brightened slightly. "There is more in the kitchen, I could get you a bowl—"

"Shàn'jūn." Zen's tone stopped him. The Medicine disciple's smile faded slightly. "The war is to begin, and I need you and the other disciples to be somewhere safe. That is why I have asked the Nameless Master to rouse everyone and gather them here."

Shàn'jūn's brows creased. Zen looked away. He could not stand the sympathy in his friend's gaze—not when he deserved none of it. "Zen'gē," he said, and Zen nearly flinched at the honorific. *Older brother.* Shàn'jūn had not called him that in so many cycles, not since Zen had lost control of his demon and hurt Dilaya. "I may be neither strong nor well-trained in combat practitioning, but . . . I am a disciple of Medicine. Let me go with you. Perhaps I can be of some use."

Zen exhaled long and looked at his friend. "I will not need it, but your skills will be of use at the place you are going."

"I do not understand. Are you not coming?"

"Shàn'jūn." How was he to explain an entire lifetime of regret? How was he to convey that he wished he had been kinder, that he had valued their friendship, so much so that he had been terrified of hurting Shàn'jūn as well and had thus begun to push him away?

He couldn't. Voices and footsteps were starting to sound in the hallways as the disciples began to wake.

"This is a war I must fight alone," Zen said instead, "and I do not know when we will meet again. Please know that if I have caused you any grief, I am so, so sorry. And that I wish you happiness always." There it was again, that pain locking up his chest and his throat, making it difficult to speak. Zen spoke through it. "I promise you will find happiness where you are going."

The hall was filling up now, former disciples of the School of the White Pines stumbling in, rubbing sleep from their eyes. Their drowsiness vanished when they caught sight of Zen.

"Zen'gē," Shàn'jūn said, but Zen was already turning away. "Zen'gē! Zen—"

Zen approached Master Nur of the Light Arts, who filed in with a throng of younger disciples. The Nameless Master followed closely behind.

"This is everyone?" Zen asked. When they confirmed, he nodded. "Follow."

The two masters seemed to have done well with consoling the disciples; they made no sounds of protest as they trailed after Zen into the freezing night. They had to leave the perimeters of his Boundary Seal in order for him to conjure a Gate Seal.

Once they were outside the Boundary Seal, Zen came to a stop. He turned to the disciples clustered together in the cold. "The war is to begin," he said, "and the place you are going will be safe." He dipped his head slightly. "It has been an honor."

The Gate Seal came to him easily once he opened his mind

and let the Black Tortoise in. *The Sòng courtyard house,* he stated, and the Demon God yielded the memory of the location. Zen paused for a moment as the image of Lan's childhood home drifted into his mind's eye: a traditional Hin courtyard house with gray terracotta roofs that curved to the skies over white walls. Round moon gates led to gardens and terraces; weeping willows dipped their branches into clear-glass ponds. No doubt this was an older memory and the courtyard house would have gone through the turmoil of the eras and Elantian invasion, but the location would remain the same.

He smiled as he traced out the Gate Seal, imagining a smaller Lan darting through the gardens chased by tutors. A swirl here, a dot there: departure, destination, a straight stroke to connect them, and then a circle to close the Seal. Black flame erupted, and in the midst of Where the Flame Rises and the Stars Fall, the courtyard house appeared through a bamboo forest beneath a coat of winter snow.

The ache in his heart resurfaced. Lan would be there, just within reach.

Zen swallowed and looked away, back to the disciples. "May the winds be smooth upon your path," he said.

Master Nur went first. He paused before the Seal, looked at Zen, and pressed his fist to his palm. A salute.

"Shī'fù," Zen said in quiet surprise.

"Walk well" was all Master Nur said. It was a shortened version of the saying *Walk well upon your Way,* a traditional parting greeting for practitioners. Zen watched him step through the Gate Seal.

Disciples followed, all familiar faces he had seen at Skies' End, some even classmates. Some dipped their heads in his direction while others only cast him frightened glances.

When it was Shàn'jūn's turn, the Medicine disciple paused. He reached out, clasping his hands over Zen's. "I left the broth for you on the table," he said quietly. "It will replenish your qì. When we meet again, I will make it for you fresh."

"Thank you," Zen said, and then his friend was gone, and there was only one person left.

The Nameless Master fixed an indecipherable gaze upon him. "If I predict correctly," he said, his tone like the whistle of wind through dry valleys, "then you have earned this greeting: 'Kingdom before life, honor into death.'"

It was the parting greeting the masters at the School of the White Pines had spoken, and Zen knew well its meaning: the honor of sacrifice, of giving one's life to protect their people. It was a farewell worthy only of the legendary heroes that had once walked the rivers and lakes of this kingdom.

He bowed his head. When he looked up again, the Nameless Master was gone.

Zen looked into his Gate Seal for a moment longer. Within, he glimpsed a courtyard house blanketed in snow, weeping willows bent over a frozen pond. He imagined Lan sitting at one of the fretwork windows, horsetail brush in hand as she bent over scrolls.

No—*pork buns* in hand.

A laugh welled up in his chest, replacing the sharp ache. The Gate Seal blurred before him, and with a wave of his hand, he closed it.

The image of the courtyard house vanished. A dozen or so paces away were frozen cliffs; beyond yawned darkness and a glittering landscape of ice and snow.

He made his way back to the Palace of Eternal Peace, empty now but for the ghosts of his ancestors long-gone . . . and the undead demonic practitioners that lay buried beneath its stone floors, waiting over a hundred cycles for the day they would rise again.

Today, their wait had come to an end.

24

> Snow camellias bloom only at winter's solstice and signify the union of lovers into death and beyond.
>
> —Medicine Master Zur'mkhar Rdo'rje,
> *Herbologist's Records of the Middle Kingdom*

Lan woke the Shaklahira court and told them of the plan. The night was still dark, morning a few bells off as they dressed and packed their meager belongings. When they gathered in the desert, none spared a backward glance at the ruins of the old imperial rule.

The Sòng courtyard house had been too far to reach with her own qì, so Lan called upon the Silver Dragon. Given her refusal thus far to summon its power, it had remained a dormant and disconnected presence in her mind, except when she had been in danger—as per their bargain.

When the Gate Seal completed, the ice-blue eye that had cracked open inside her closed again, and the Silver Dragon dissolved its qì with what felt like an ethereal sigh before retreating back into its core.

As Lan alighted upon the fanstone paths leading to the courtyard gates, she felt as though she'd stepped back into that day her world had ended. The air held the cold bite of a northern winter, and snow covered the ground. The entire place seemed trapped in an eternal winter, time frozen in a sheen of white.

As though it had been waiting for her ever since that day twelve cycles ago.

An ache bloomed in her throat. Time had not spared her home from its relentless claws. One foot in memory's door, Lan gazed at the reality. Gone were the white osmanthus trees under which the orange cat had once dozed. The walls, once kept pristine, were cracked and graying; the great red gates stood ajar, bearing the bite marks of swords. Looming over them was a sign covered in ice and faded with age.

Lan wove a Seal of yáng—fire and heat—and swept it across the surface. The ice melted and characters appeared.

宋大院
SÒNG MANOR

From behind her came sharp gasps as her friends and the former Shaklahira court members stepped through the Gate Seal.

"You—you lived . . . here?" Tai stammered, taking in the clear signs of faded splendor and looking at Lan.

Lived. The simple word hurt so much that, for a moment, she could not speak. She thought, instead, of a dream she had dreamt nearly every single waking second of her life in the nightmare of the *after*. What might have happened if Māma had ridden back that day with different news. If life had continued without the Elantians. The Sòng Lián of that reality would have grown up in this very courtyard house, studying chess, calligraphy, painting, mathematics, and music under a horde of tutors. Māma would have taught her practitioning, perhaps through the Art of Song, and Sòng Lián would have grown up to become a part of the imperial court. She would have kept her name; Lan would never have existed.

Even as she ran through the old dream again, Lan found snarls in its tapestry. Māma would have had to hide their practitioning abilities. They would have had to keep their clan heritage and the Art of Song secret or endure a punishment worse than death at the imperial court's hands. Perhaps Māma would have told Lan of the Order of Ten Thousand Flowers; perhaps she would still have died for their cause, and perhaps Lan would still have dedicated her life to the same mission.

No, her idyllic dream would never have existed, for the Last Kingdom had always been broken. It had only taken a foreign conquest to strip it to its rotten bones. For Lan to understand the reality of it.

"I did." In the winter's cold, her response unfurled from her lips in a feathery stream. "I once lived here."

She turned her attention to the currents of qì that flowed out from the courtyard.

"Empty," Dilaya said. "I checked already." Still, she did not release her grip from Falcon's Claw as she stared up at the courtyard gates.

"Not. Not empty." Tai's hand strayed to the silver bell at his waist. "I hear them. The ghosts."

"Ghosts don't count, you egg," Dilaya replied.

Lan brushed her fingers against the ocarina at her waist, drew a breath, and walked up the steps. The gates parted at her touch, and her home opened itself to her.

The Sòng courtyard was a place lost to time and bore the marks of violence and destruction at the hands of the Elantians. Where once weeping willows had swept over ponds filled with koi, lotuses blushing on the surface, the trees were now dead, snow-covered husks bending over frozen ponds. The white terracotta walls that separated the front of the courtyard from the back were streaked in mud; the circular moon gate stood overhung with frozen vines. Once filled with color and life, the Sòng courtyard was now cold and empty, illuminated by the colorless light of the moon.

"This place looks like it's been through the ghost's door," Dilaya sniffed. There was a crackle of qì and a spark, the scent of smoke as she snapped a fú for flame and held it up. The light only threw deeper shadows. "Well, since this is to be our base, might as well get to work. I'll set up Boundary Seals and basic defenses, and we'll rotate patrol shifts." She gave Lan a brisk nod.

Lan had, in part, told Dilaya, Tai, and the former Shaklahira court members of the plan: tonight they would launch their attack on King Alessandertown and she would face off against Erascius and the Azure Tiger. She had told them that Zen would be sending disciples of the School of the White Pines to join them.

As the others left with Dilaya, Lan continued through the courtyard house alone. The silence was the most discomfiting part of being back: she kept expecting to hear the laughter of maids as they hurried along the gardens with trays of tea and fruits, the soft-spoken instruction of her tutors mingling with chirps of cicadas beneath a summer sky, the strum of her mother's woodlute as it unspooled a melody beneath the moon.

Now all their bones lay deep in the ground.

The mesh screens had been slashed, chunks of doors ripped out by swords. Save for the heavy wooden furniture, the entire place had been looted, shelves upturned and fragments of smashed porcelain glittering on the rosewood floors. Whatever trinkets and smaller items the Elantians had not taken, desperate Hin had scavenged later.

When Lan returned to the main courtyard, the air was rippling with the qì of Seals. Dilaya's group had woven a strong Boundary Seal over the place, mixed with a variety of defensive Seals. The cooks had located the kitchens and started a fire, dusting off the clay pots and rooting through the supplies they had brought from Shaklahira to whip up a meal for everybody. Tables in the great dining room adjacent to the kitchens had been swept clean; someone had conjured Light Seals that drifted near the walls, bathing the place in a gentle glow. Soon, everyone was gratefully sipping on hot congee to warm their frozen fingers and toes while they waited for the sun to rise.

When the first light of day began to seep into the sky, there was a disturbance in the qì outside the gates of the courtyard. Lan pressed a hand to her chest, where Zen's silver amulet rested against her heart. It had grown warm.

Zen.

She stood and made for the courtyard gates, swiping a fú for a light as she ran. Behind her, she heard Dilaya unsheathe Falcon's Claw and Tai's heavy footsteps as he, too, followed. Lan knew it was impossible: Zen had told her he would send the disciples and masters to her through a Gate Seal. This wasn't him; the Seal on his amulet was only responding to the presence of his qì—

She burst through the front doors, lifting her fú high over her head. Light spilled across the snow-covered ground, reaching all the way to the forest of bamboo that had grown close around her house.

Nothing.

And then . . . movement. From here, she could make out silhouettes emerging from between the bamboo. Then someone familiar stepped into the light of her fú.

"Wow," said the disciple, his cheeks glowing red with cold. "You weren't lying when you told us you were a noble lady!"

"Chue?" Lan exclaimed. The kind-faced Archery disciple had been one of the first people to befriend her at the school.

Through the bamboo, she could see a group of people emerging. The dim lighting made it difficult to discern their faces, but that was before a familiar voice called out: "Lan'mèi! Lan'mèi!"

There was only one person she knew who still used martial titles to refer to their friends. Lan was about to respond when someone pushed past her.

It was the first time Lan had seen Tai sprint. The Spirit Summoner's sleepy scowl had been replaced by an expression of utter disbelief, followed by sheer joy, his wavy locks trailing behind him as he barreled down the stone steps toward Shàn'jūn. The Medicine disciple laughed as Tai scooped him into his arms, spun him several times, and kissed him.

Shàn'jūn's face, too, radiated happiness when they broke apart; his eyes glistened as he pressed a gentle hand to Tai's cheeks before turning to Lan.

Lan flung her arms around her friend. "We thought you were gone," she whispered to him, blinking back tears.

"Zen'gē saved me," he said. "He saved everybody here."

It was nearly surreal to see her friends and the other disciples from the School of the White Pines whole and hale and *alive*. Yet as Lan ushered them into the safety of her home and greeted her former classmates, she couldn't help but glance behind them. In the darkness that led into the forest and away from the light of the lanterns, there was the faintest ripple of qì where a seam to the Gate Seal had just closed. Zen's amulet grew cold against her skin.

Among the group were Master Nur of the Light Arts and the Nameless Master of Assassins. They were the only two masters who had survived the battle at Skies' End, for Dé'zǐ had tasked them with evacuating the disciples of the school through a back exit just before the Elantian invasion. As they made their way into the main courtyard, where the group from Shaklahira was gathered, Lan listened to them recount their journey.

The new additions to their party were introduced to the former Shaklahira court members, and very soon, the new arrivals were seated in the warmth of the dining room with bowls of congee and steaming dishes of tofu and salted cabbage soup. Tai and Shàn'jūn sat close together, their hands intertwined, murmuring to each other. It had been a long while since Lan had seen such easy contentment on the Spirit Summoner's countenance.

As dawn turned to day, they set about forming a battle plan. Dilaya had turned the living room and foyer into a war room: A map spilled over the long mahogany table where her mother's guests had once gathered. Weapons brought from Shaklahira had been piled in a corner cabinet where the household's brooms and mops had stood.

Lan played the star maps again for the two masters, who easily derived the location of the Azure Tiger: Erascius had returned to the Heavenly Capital already—perhaps by a Gate Seal easily conjured with his new powers.

They would move out at dusk, entering the city under cover of night. Lan would arrive first as a decoy, drawing the attention of Erascius and the Royal Magicians to her while teams led by Master Nur, the Nameless Master, and Dilaya infiltrated the Heavenly Palace and forced the surrender of the high governor.

"I will use the Godslayer against the Azure Tiger, to deal the greatest blow to the Elantian regime," Lan said. She had not told them of the part of the strategy that involved Zen, his Demon God, and the army of demonic practitioners. If all went according to the plan Zen had drawn up, she wouldn't have to;

the scene would come off as another Mansorian binder of a Demon God losing control, unleashing demonic practitioning upon the Heavenly Capital—and she, Sòng Lián, would conjure the Godslayer to end it all. The savior of the people.

So the stories would go.

"Erascius is one of their highest-ranking Royal Magicians," Lan continued. "The Elantians have been in a race against us to locate the Demon Gods. If we take down the one they have, we will force them to their knees and be in a position to force their surrender."

When Lan finished, Taub, the School of the White Pines' cook and Chue's mother, let out a muffled sob. Tears streamed down her face as she held a few of the youngest disciples to her, gathering them about her páo and the rough-spun apron that was a near-permanent fixture.

"A kingdom free of conquest," Taub whispered. "A land where my son and I may speak the tongue of our native clan and celebrate its customs without persecution."

Lan was aware of Tai watching her through the gleam of his gold-rimmed eyes, Shàn'jūn smiling gently by his side; her gaze sweeping farther out, she spotted Dilaya leaning against the trunk of a wilted willow, arm crossed over her chest and resting on the hilt of her sword. The matriarch of the Jorshen Steel clan gave Lan a nod of approval.

Sòng Lián looked to her peoples, the survivors of a brutal conquest who carried with them their individual heritages. So much had been lost in war, in the iron rule of the imperial family throughout the dynasties, and yet so much still existed today, before her eyes. She remembered, then, the words of a boy beneath a soft fall of rain that had carried her tears away long ago. *So long as we live on, we carry inside us all that they have destroyed. And that is our triumph; that is our rebellion. Do not let them win today.*

It was a shame that neither of them would live to see it.

"Yes," Lan said, recalling a phrase the masters at the School of the White Pines had used, a phrase to describe the multitudes of clans and cultures that bloomed in their kingdom. "The land of ten thousand flowers."

The rest of the day passed uneventfully, like the calm before a storm. They talked through the details of the plan, dividing up the disciples and the masters to form teams of equal ability.

Lan left the strategizing to Dilaya and the masters. She needed a quiet place to practice conjuring the Godslayer with the new knowledge of the intent behind the Seal. As she searched for an empty chamber, she found herself breathing in, relishing the way the cold pierced her lungs. She'd missed this, the northern cold. The winters that swept over the lands, ferocious and unforgiving, taking the old and dying of the past cycle and birthing it anew when spring bloomed.

Snow like goose feathers. The northerners had such a saying. She remembered Māma outlined against the fretwork windows of their study, opening them to the winter air. *Do not shy away, Lián'ér,* she'd said. *Breathe it in. This is the beauty and might of our kingdom, and we are children of this land. We must fight to protect it all.*

Lan wiped a hand against her cheek. Unknowingly, her feet had brought her to her mother's study. She stepped through the circular moon gate, remembering how her mother had ridden back that day on the tides of the end of the world. The snow had been falling thickly, and Lan had been in Māma's study memorizing poems.

The study bore signs of violence. Its fretwork doors had been slashed and broken—

—pale-faced soldiers clad in metal stomping past—

—the shelves and rosewood desk had been overturned; row upon row of scrolls and paper tomes had vanished, likely looted by the Elantians and taken away to study—

—swords flashing as the men bore down upon her mother, alone with naught but a woodlute—

—splatters of faded blood in the floorboards and against the walls—

—her mother's beating heart held in the hand of the Winter Magician. Blood, blooming as bright as poppies—

Lan cut off those memories. A gleam on the floor caught her eye. She knelt and picked up a piece of shattered porcelain. She recognized it intimately: the snow camellias glazed on the surface in blue, the inside still stained black after all these years. It was her mother's favorite inkpot, and Lan had spent bells every day staring at it as she sat with her tutors in the study. It would not have had much value to those searching the place for food, clothes, or treasures to pawn off.

When she flipped it over in her hand, her breath caught. Engraved on the bottom in neat Hin calligraphy was an inscription—a dedication:

> *For Sòng Méi: may our threads*
> *meet one day where the snow camellias bloom.*
> Shēn Tài'héng

She knew this calligraphy—had read books and essays written with it back at the school. Dé'zǐ had gifted this inkpot to her mother. And he had signed it with his truename, for "Dé'zǐ"—meaning "disciple of virtue"—was only a personal title. Once, it had been tradition for all Hin to take on personal titles when they crossed into adulthood.

"Tài'héng," she whispered. The name of a father she had barely known.

She tucked the piece of inkpot into her belt, perhaps as a token of good luck. Then she sat down at her mother's desk, marveling in the knowledge that her parents had once lived and loved in this house, that she had belonged to a family and had a home.

She closed her eyes and pulled the memory of the Godslayer Seal into the front of her mind. Going over each stroke felt like falling through dynasties and eras of time and history; now that she knew of the origins of the Demon Gods and the true intent of the Godslayer, the story of the Seal came to her slowly but fully.

It was late afternoon by the time she returned to the main courtyard. Taub and a few others were in the kitchens preparing supper; smoke wafted up into the twilit sky, and the courtyard was filled with the scent of tofu stew, steamed vegetables, and mántou dough buns. Lan sat with her friends and swapped stories of their childhoods, of their days at Skies' End, of what they would do and places they would visit and things they would eat after all this was over.

When the sun hung above the distant horizon like a swollen mandarin and the air began to cool, Lan stood. The fire had grown low in the furnace; a Seal had been conjured in the kitchens to capture its heat, and most of the younger disciples were gathered around the warmth, napping. Shàn'jūn had settled against a kitchen wall, leaning against Tai's shoulder. The Spirit Summoner's expression softened as he took the Medicine disciple's hand in his; his eyes glimmered gold as he watched the fire.

In an adjacent room, Dilaya and a group of Shaklahiran warriors were bent over the map, still discussing strategy with

Master Nur and the Nameless Master. They looked up when Lan approached and fell silent when they saw her expression.

"Well," she said, managing a smile to hide the sudden numbness in her chest. "It's time."

She was aware of when Shàn'jūn and Tai came in the room to join them. The Medicine disciple's face had paled. "Lan'mèi—"

"You know the plan," she said to Dilaya, cutting off whatever Shàn'jūn had meant to say. She dared not look at his face for fear that her heart might soften and she would grow afraid, or reluctant. "Infiltrate the Heavenly Palace, negotiate the Elantians' surrender. If all fails on my end"—she drew a shaky breath—"eliminate the leadership of the Elantian government."

"We will be right behind you, Sòng Lián," said the Master of the Light Arts. He forced a smile as he looked around the room. "The time has come to see which of these disciples paid attention in my classes for so many cycles."

"Better prepare yourself, old man," Chue said, grinning. Beneath it, though, Lan could see an undercurrent of fear. "I'm young and limber and ready to beat you to the capital."

"Lan, we are with you," Taub said. She held a young disciple in her arms; the child had fallen asleep against her shoulder, curled against the cold. "I'll have a pot of tofu stew warmed on the stove for you when you return."

"My blades are yours," Elanruya declared, stepping forward from the Shaklahiran group, the razor-sharp metal edges of her fans glinting in the moonlight. "It is time to undo what Hóng'yì did to us in that prison of a palace." Behind her, a murmur of agreement rose from the former Shaklahiran court members.

"Lan'mèi," Shàn'jūn said, and he flung his arms around her in an embrace. "I will forever be the healer behind you. I apologize in advance for all the caterpillar-fungus soup I will feed you after."

Lan held on to him tightly. "Thanks, Shàn'jūn," she whispered.

When she drew back, Tai was staring at her, his expression unreadable. His eyes gleamed beneath the wild tangles of his hair.

"Chó Tài," he said suddenly. "You can call me Chó Tài."

It might have been a bizarre parting sentence to any outsider watching, but Lan understood the significance. Tai was the monosyllabic Elantian version of Chó Tài's name, and he'd insisted Lan call him by it after catching her eavesdropping on him and Shàn'jūn back at the school bookhouse. Since then, he'd stubbornly refused to let her call him by his truename.

Lan cocked her head and flashed him a grin. "Honored," she said, and with that, she turned and began to walk away. Behind her, she heard the disciples and Shaklahiran practitioners stirring to action, longswords and broadswords and quivers clanking. She heard Taub's gentle murmurs as she guided the youngest disciples to the guest quarters within the courtyard manor.

"Sòng Lián!"

Lan glanced over her shoulder. Dilaya was striding toward her, away from the lantern light and the group of disciples. She stopped beneath the shadow of a broken willow, its branches slicing her face into black and white—and there, in the cut of the girl's stormy eye, crimson lips, and strong jaw, Lan thought she saw the ghost of Dilaya's mother, Ulara.

For several moments, Dilaya stood with her mouth agape, struggling to find the words to say. And in those moments, Lan wondered if she would witness a miracle: Yeshin Noro Dilaya being nice to her.

The matriarch of the Jorshen Steel clan seemed to read

Lan's thoughts. She clamped her lips shut and glared at Lan, then she loosed a breath. Her gaze flickered. "I learned the lesson from my mother that there is no telling what might happen in war," she said. "But I can tell you we will meet again. If not in this life, then in the next one." She paused. "And I will still beat you in every art of practitioning, little fox spirit."

Lan felt the corners of her mouth lift. A smile. She couldn't remember if she'd ever genuinely smiled at Dilaya.

Still, there had to be a good reason the Hin word for "goodbye" was not a farewell. It was zài'jiàn: "see you again."

"You too, Horse-face," Lan said. "See you again."

She strode through the moon gates where, once upon a life ago, she'd seen her mother enter for the last time. Lan brushed her hands against the instruments on her hips: a small dagger that cut the spaces between stars, and an ocarina that played the songs of ghosts.

She stepped outside the great vermilion front doors, patting the worn bronze lionhead doorknockers as she pushed the doors shut. She looked up at the place where she had known love and loss, the place that was the start of a tale that had now come full-circle. The beginning and the ending.

She summoned her Demon God's power, creating a portal to a city of bright lights and bustling streets and golden-roofed temples reaching for the heavens.

Sòng Lián stepped through the Gate Seal into the end of the world.

25

> And when Xan Tolürigin fell to madness beneath the weight of yīn from his own Demon God, the Last Kingdom was born: a golden era of light and justice. Darkness had been vanquished; turmoil had stabilized to peace.
>
> —Emperor Yán'lóng, *Imperial Records of History,* Era of the Last Kingdom

The tallow candles and incense sticks had burnt out and been replaced thrice by the time Zen finished drawing the Seals for the Deathriders—one set of Summoning Seals and one set of Binding Seals for every single rider. He leaned back against the wall as he drew breath after labored breath. His qì was an inkwell run dry: he'd traced out the Seals on the stone floor in his own blood, the strongest conductor of his qì and the surest way to inject his will into them. His hair and clothes were sticky with sweat.

The darkness and yīn pressed in on him; the chamber seemed to spin. Time flitted by unevenly with each blink; between one and another, it might have been a half bell, or it might have been several. The *Classic of Gods and Demons* lay before him, its pages spent; he shut it now, tucking it safely back in his practitioner's storage pouch.

Still shaking, he reached for the water jug.

It was empty.

The effects of the Seed of Clarity had worn off throughout

the day as he'd drawn upon more and more of the Black Tortoise's power. Now he sensed the Demon God's qì seeping back into his blood and his mind.

The Seals on the floor glimmered, waiting to be activated. It was time.

Zen stood unsteadily. He knelt by the nearest tomb, the first of the forty-four Deathriders. Her likeness was carved as an effigy in the stone, clad in glistening black lamellar armor. Like all the others, her eyes had been depicted as open, and Zen had the feeling he was the one being watched as he glanced around the chamber.

He looked at the name of the rider, engraved in Mansorian script: *Ker Saranejin*. The lineage name, followed by the individual's name—"Moon Flower." Zen had grown up hearing tales of famous heroes of times past: Rokun the Sun Archer, who had shot down the nine suns that scorched the earth to save humanity; Amun and Renghi, lovers who had partitioned the Eternal Sky and the Great Earth and breathed life into this world. But when those left in his clan had spoken of the Deathriders of Mansoria, it had been in tones of awe and fear. The Black Tortoise had shown him times when they had saved the Mansorian clan, riding against other clans into battle. Yet their names had not been revered in history, their deeds not sung by the bards nor written by the poets—because of who they were and the type of arts they practiced.

Demonic practitioning, the Wayward path.

If I must see darkness for our people to find light, he had once told Lan, *then I will make that same choice, over and over and over again.*

Zen reached into his storage pouch and withdrew four sticks of incense. He swiped a fú, and the tips of the incense flared, casting the burial chamber in a flash of blood-red.

Zen lifted the incense sticks to his forehead and bowed

one, two, three times. "May the Eternal Sky take my soul. May the Great Earth take my body."

It was one of the few phrases he remembered from Mansorian funerary rites. He recalled the great bonfires that stood taller than him, the flames licking up into the sky and the embers blending into the stars. For a Mansorian to be properly honored in death, they had to be burned: to release their soul from their fleshly prison into the Eternal Sky, and then for the ashes of their mortal body to fall into the embrace of the Great Earth.

To be encased in a stone tomb was to have one's body and soul trapped in a deathless death.

Zen straightened. "March with me into battle once more," he said to the chamber of the undead, "and I vow to honor you in true death, releasing you to the Eternal Sky and the Great Earth as it was meant to be."

He took out the *Classic of Gods and Demons* from his storage pouch and flipped it open. Zen drew a steadying breath, then yielded his mind and body to the Demon God that waited in the shadows.

As his qì flowed from his fingertips, buoyed by the power of the Black Tortoise, an unearthly gleam passed over the Seals he had painted on the stone floor.

The smoke from his incense was palpitating violently. The temperature in the chamber plunged fast, frost cracking across the walls and stealing into Zen's lungs. Black flames roared to life, ringing each stone casket. The Seals written on the carved effigy across the lid of each tomb had begun to glow: a deep red, spreading across like blood and fire. With hisses, they ate away at the stone until there was nothing left of the lid at all.

Yīn blasted across the chamber, a chorus of screams that nearly drove Zen to his knees. He stood by the strength of his Demon God, watching as, one by one, the preserved corpses of the Mansorian demonic practitioners rose. Behind them, outlined by the red light of their Seals, were shadows that did not belong to them. A wolf with elongated legs and jutting ribs; a hawk with wing feathers as sharp as knives; a horse with teeth like fangs; a fox with nine tails. Their once-human binders turned to him, eyes glowing, weapons at their hips, cores screaming with yīn. He could feel their souls connected to his in the same way he was connected to the Black Tortoise, ripples of their qì reaching him in a manner that was utterly intoxicating. Each Deathrider had the strength of an army of fully trained practitioners, if not more.

The Forty-Four stilled, as though waiting for his command.

Zen unfolded his left palm. At its center, puckered like scarred flesh, glowed a Mansorian Seal: the miniature version of the one he had drawn from the *Classic of Gods and Demons*. This was the Seal that bound the Forty-Four's wills to his and linked their demonic qì irrevocably to his core.

Together, they held the keys to liberating this kingdom—and to destroying it.

As the enormity of his task lifted from his shoulders, relief and exhaustion began to set in. Zen went to his hands and knees, shaking as sweat dripped down the side of his face. His energy was spent.

And something was wrong.

The floor was going in and out of focus. A strange buzzing had filled his ears, and his head pounded as though with a rush of blood. He could no longer feel the cold in his hands nor the stone ground beneath his feet. Zen sucked in deep breaths, blinking to clear his vision.

Zen, came that rumbling whisper in his mind, and the Black Tortoise's qì began to close over him, as massive as a mountain and as overwhelming as the night itself. *Oh, Zen. We are so close. So close to the end.*

No. Not now.

He gritted his teeth and pulled, replenishing the yīn energies flooding his veins with yáng and the strength of his own will. He would get through this. He would take down the Elantian army. And he would see Lan again, just one last time.

His story would *not* end like that of his great-grandfather.

Those thoughts pierced through the veil of yīn, light through dark waters. And Zen surfaced, gasping as the Black Tortoise's presence retreated from his mind. Sight and sound rushed back: the musty air of the dungeons, the cold stone beneath his palms and knees, the sweat drenching his hair and páo, the demonic practitioners he had summoned watching him with faces like stone. Their demons—the shadows on the walls—shifted, perhaps sensing the presence of a powerful Demon God amongst them.

Zen remained where he was a few moments more, waiting for his breath to steady and the world to settle again. When he felt strong enough, he pushed himself to his feet.

He managed to stagger up the dungeon steps. He gulped down lungfuls of fresh winter air when he emerged, the piercing wind that whistled into the hallway through the broken doors of these ruins a sharp relief to the suffocating stillness of the dungeons.

The sun was setting. It hung barely over the mountains in the west, staining their peaks orange and whipping fire into the snow clouds. Below, the rest of the world was steeped in shadow.

Zen watched the last of the sun sink beneath the horizon. Lan, and all the remaining practitioners of the Last Kingdom, would have moved out; their plan hinged on his being able to wipe out most of the Elantian army and their Royal Magicians in the capital. Without that, he was letting them walk into a trap in the city with the heaviest Elantian presence.

He closed his eyes and drew in a deep, steadying breath. Ran a thumb over his left palm, where the Seal pulsed, carrying his will and command to the Forty-Four demonic practitioners that waited at the other end.

"Deathriders of Mansoria," Xan Temurezen said, his voice carrying through the halls of his ancestors. "Heed my call."

26

> Sound east, strike west.
>
> —General Yeshin Noro Dorgun of the Jorshen Steel Clan, Sixth of the Thirty-Six Stratagems, *Classic of War*

The Heavenly Capital was nearly just as Lan remembered it from the times she'd visited with Māma in her childhood. Over the temples and pagodas and intricate rosewood fretwork of Hin buildings, the Elantians had hung their flags; here and there, they had erected their metal-and-stone structures.

At this bell, the streets were decently crowded, providing Lan cover as she wound through them. Walking felt laboriously slow, but using the Light Arts would have given her away immediately.

As she passed through streets ablaze with lantern light, Lan felt as though she had returned to a shadow of her old self—when the war had felt so distant and vast. Music and laughter drifted from the windows of winehouses that served as restaurants and entertainment hubs for the rich and the connected. Lan wondered which songgirl spun onstage tonight.

She turned to the roads that led directly to the Imperial Palace. She remembered it as a brightly lit building with multistory golden roofs that curved to the heavens themselves, vermilion pillars and walls encrusted with jade and lapis lazuli. Now a marble Elantian façade had been erected before it, its stone-and-metal pillars swallowing the original. Only the curving terracotta roofs still jutted out through the Elantian architecture, and those, too, had been cast entirely in silver.

A banner waved at her from one of the lampposts the Elantians had erected to lend their alchemical light to the city. Depicted on the banner, against a silver background, was a magnificent blue tiger intertwined with a white-armored, white-winged Elantian soldier. No, not a soldier, Lan realized, studying the figure's face more closely. The high governor had had the arrogance to have his own face painted onto the banners.

The star maps had not lied: the Azure Tiger was here, in this city.

She lifted her gaze to the columns of identical blue banners lining either side of the road to the palace square.

A shock coursed through her.

The vast square beneath the palace was crowded with Elantian soldiers, their metal armor catching the early evening light as they milled about, drinks and food in hand courtesy of the vendor stalls set up around the periphery. A large fountain glittered in their midst, the lotuses and yuān'yáng ducks and cranes it had once been filled with replaced by a marble statue of the Elantian king.

Looking more closely, Lan spotted figures wearing metal bands on their wrists weaving through the crowds.

Royal Magicians.

Lan touched the hilt of her dagger. She and Zen had been right: Erascius had bound the Azure Tiger and he had returned to the capital city. What they hadn't anticipated was that the high governor would host some form of festivities or a gathering tonight, of all nights. This was more forces than Lan and

Zen had prepared for: judging by the sheer number of people, it seemed as though all the Royal Magicians and soldiers stationed at nearby towns had been summoned to the capital city for tonight's celebration.

Lan touched a hand to her clavicle, where the amulet Zen had gifted her lay cold. It was too late to make any changes to the plan. All she could do was wait.

The sky was almost completely dark now; beyond the city, over the distant mountains that rimmed the capital like guardians, storm clouds brewed. The Elantians' alchemical lamps flicked on, casting a golden pool of light onto the square. At the very center, a path from the palace gates had been cleared.

By nightfall, Dilaya, Master Nur, the Nameless Master, and the disciples skilled enough to fight would have entered the city and likely be stationed somewhere in the vicinity, waiting for Lan to make the first move.

She touched her amulet again.

Zen was late.

Trumpets blared. In the square, a thunderous cheer arose as the palace gates drew open. Four lines of soldiers marched out, followed by a squadron of Royal Magicians suited in elaborate armor made of what Lan assumed to be the particular combination of metals each could wield.

Alloys, she thought. Magicians with the ability to control more than one metal—which rendered them exceptionally powerful.

Behind them, astride a magnificent black stallion, rode the high governor: a nondescript man of average height and build, his flesh made fair and soft with the luxuries that life had granted him. The jewels on his scepter flashed as he waved to the roaring crowd.

But Lan's gaze sharpened as she caught sight of the person riding behind him.

Erascius's blond-white hair had grown longer. A blue tiger's head had been engraved on the front of his armor. He, too, held a scepter, his decorated solely with sapphires. The high governor was showing him off, anointing the binder of the Azure Tiger as the crown jewel of their empire.

The high governor's parade had drawn to a stop; he was speaking. Metal plates around the square amplified his voice, and Lan caught snatches of Elantian words.

". . . Blue Tiger . . . Demon God . . . in our power. Royal Magician Erascius . . . demonstrate its might."

A show—they were going to put on a *show*.

Lan's hand went to her ocarina. Surely, Erascius knew the type of bargain he'd made and that frivolous use of the Demon God's power endangered everybody. Tonight, the Elantians tested the gods.

Hurry, Zen.

Erascius dismounted and stalked to the edge of the fountain. The crowd fell utterly silent. For a moment, there was nothing but the whistle of wind through the streets, the collective breaths held as the magician lifted his arms.

Demonic qì pulsed from him, shattering the stillness. There were a few cries from the crowd—even people without a connection to qì would feel something of the overwhelming yīn energies.

The water of the fountain was spiraling into the air, the streams unfurling toward the sky. Then they exploded into a hundred thousand droplets that shimmered like stars, gathering into the form of a great tiger the size of the entire palace. Its eyes glowed cerulean, and before the crowds who watched it with awe, it opened its maw and let out a roar that shook the entire city.

Lan's knuckles were white against her ocarina. Around her, the everyday working Hin—the street sweepers, the shopkeepers, the restaurant cooks and waiters—had all gathered outside to watch the show. Their gaunt faces reflected the Azure Tiger's eerie blue light, and their expressions broke something in Lan.

Awe. Fear. And resignation. The acceptance that their fate—to live under the Elantians—was sealed.

An ache squeezed Lan's throat. Her fingers trembled against her ocarina.

She could end this.

She *would* end this.

The Azure Tiger roared again—and that was when Lan's amulet warmed.

Gasps erupted around her and from the square. In the sky above the Heavenly Palace, a seam had opened: A Gate Seal, conjured from a place of snow-covered cliffs and blackened ruins.

From within, something speared down over the Heavenly Capital. It was the figure of a man, and as he landed on the highest palace rooftop, a shadow behind him eclipsed the sky.

Black robes and demonic qì billowed from Xan Temurezen as he straightened atop the roof of the palace that had held the conquerors first of his clan and then of his land.

On the ground, Erascius had gone deadly still as he watched this development. Slowly, he lifted a hand.

With a crook of his finger, the Azure Tiger turned to face the newcomers. Its snarl rumbled through the streets of the city as, with a flick of its tail, it pounced—and Zen's Black Tortoise, forming itself from cloud smoke, dove to meet it.

The ground shook with the first clash of the two Demon Gods. Shouts erupted in the square as the Elantian forces drew their weapons.

The Gate Seal in the sky remained open; more shadows were streaming from it, landing in the square and on surrounding buildings. A pagoda several streets down from Lan exploded when something struck its roof. As the dust cleared, Lan could make out a silhouette atop the ruins: a creature the size of a horse with fiery tails—nine of them, to be precise.

Mó, she thought, taking in the pure demonic power radiating from the creature. She had heard of the legendary fox demon with nine tails from Hin myths. But what drew Lan's attention was the woman who stood beneath the being. She was tall and strong, clad in thick boots and flowing robes fashioned slightly differently from the traditional Hin hàn'fú. Lan's gaze stopped when she noticed the red flame patterns sewn on the woman's black robes.

Mansorian.

The woman stepped forward, her movements sharp. Lan caught a glimpse of her face—utterly inhuman, like stone instead of flesh and blood, perfect and ageless and terrifying—and eyes that were completely black.

Demonic practitioner.

Another streak through the night, and down toward the residential districts, on the tallest roof, stood a man in the same billowing garb with the same ethereal, unmoving face. Behind him, in a swirl of silver, was a shadow with the likeness of a misshapen wolf: legs as long as a deer's and ribs jutting from its skin.

Another streak: a figure with a great golden hawk whose wing feathers looked sharp enough to cut. Another revealed a blood-colored horse with a snout and teeth like fangs. All around King Alessandertown, Mansorian demonic practitioners landed like dark shooting stars.

Seemingly as one, they turned toward the square where the Elantian soldiers were gathered. And then, by an unheard command, they took off in that direction with powerful blasts of yīn energies.

That was when the screams began.

The demonic practitioners attacked the Elantian soldiers like hawks diving for prey. Between the fountain and the palace, Zen and Erascius were engaged in combat as their Demon Gods clashed overhead. Amidst the cacophony, Lan spotted the high governor retreating into the palace. A group of Royal Magicians rushed after him, conjuring their spells of metal magic to pad the building with extra defenses.

Lan's fingers were slick against her ocarina. She could not begin casting the Godslayer until Zen took out enough of the Royal Magicians to allow Dilaya's forces a chance at penetrating the Heavenly Palace and negotiating surrender.

Yet as Lan watched, a palpable shift went through the Mansorian demonic practitioners. Their blank eyes latched onto the groups of unarmored, vulnerable Hin watching at the fringes of the square.

One of the Mansorians with a bearlike demon lunged first. Lan heard her own scream as the demonic practitioner bowled over a nearby Hin woman—easy, defenseless prey.

Quickly, the rest followed suit. Within seconds, the rhythm of battle was broken as the Mansorian Deathriders scattered, leaving their Elantian opponents free to retreat to the safety of the palace.

Horror squeezed Lan's throat. This wasn't supposed to happen. Zen was meant to direct his army to obliterate the Elantian troops. Together with his Demon God, they were meant to take down the Royal Magicians and clear the path for Dilaya's forces.

She needed to get to Zen—she needed to stop him. If he had already lost control to the Black Tortoise . . .

She didn't want to finish the thought.

With a burst of the Light Arts, Lan leapt onto the rooftop of the nearest pagoda. From here, there was nothing between her and the palace but the square and the stretch of residential houses bordering it.

Lan gazed up. High atop the palace, where the yīn energies and storm clouds gathered, was Zen. He was barely visible, but Lan had watched him practice martial arts, had sparred with him and knew the way he moved: with the fluidity of water, and sudden explosions like flame.

Now Zen stood unnaturally still even as demonic qì continued to billow from him. The Black Tortoise, made corporeal by dark smoke and shadows, clung to the palace, clashing with the Azure Tiger. Chunks of the walls were tearing off, tumbling down to the square and the streets below, smashing through houses.

I have to get to him, she thought.

Lan kicked off toward Zen in a burst of the Light Arts. The demonic qì grew too strong once she crossed the square; she landed on one of the lower palace rooftops, her fingers scraping against the terracotta bricks for purchase as a blow from the Tortoise shook the entire building.

Lan had just righted herself when, with a great cracking noise, the roof of a house directly below her collapsed. Lan heard screams; in the settling dust, she could make out the shapes of humans trapped in the debris. Songgirls and sweepers, vendors and families. *All Hin,* Lan realized with a sudden jolt of fear. *All vulnerable.*

The plan she and Zen had drawn up so carefully was unraveling before her eyes. He had lost control. This could end in bloodshed and tragedy, just like Xan Tolürigin's story.

I have to stop it.

She began to climb. Inside her, the core of the Silver Dragon had awoken. It watched her with those frost-white eyes, and she heard its voice echoing down the bond between them.

Unleash me.

No. Lan leapt onto the next roof and caught herself on the ledge. Swung herself up.

Her Demon God gave a slow blink. *It is only a matter of time before you do.*

Lan slammed down the mental wall separating their thoughts. She sensed the Dragon's retreat, its qì coiled over its core, its great eyes still watching her surroundings for danger.

Her muscles were cramping. Lan gauged the distance to the highest rooftop, where Zen was. With the last push of qì she could summon, she leapt and barely made it to the edge of the roof.

It was terrifying to be in the vortex. Lightning flashed in the clouds that had gathered over Zen, striking the ground every so often. Fires had started, embers and ash stirred up by the wind around them. And at the heart of the demonic qì was Zen, unmoving and unflinching as though he were carved of stone. His skin was the pale of porcelain, his eyes filled with black. Shadows seemed to slither beneath his flesh as he let the Black Tortoise's qì pour and pour and pour from him.

This was the tale all the history books had foretold; what their masters had warned them against; what the Order of Ten Thousand Flowers had sought to prevent.

It was also a scenario she and Zen had discussed.

What if you lose control? she'd asked him back in the chamber they'd shared in Shaklahira.

Then you will put an end to it. There had been no hesitation to his tone.

I can't, she thought now, glancing down at the square. There were still too many Royal Magicians; Dilaya and her forces would not stand a chance at infiltrating the palace. They would lose this war.

Demonic qì roared in her ears as she turned to the vortex. She took one step. Then another. Teeth gritted, eyes stinging, head pounding. He was right there, in front of her.

"ZEN!" Lan screamed. "ZEN, WAKE UP!"

He turned to her. His gaze met hers, but there was no recognition in them.

Too late, she saw a flick of the Black Tortoise's tail overhead; saw its qì rip up tiles from the rooftop beneath her. The world tilted, and the next thing she knew, she had slammed into the rooftop and hung over the edge by her waist, the ground a precipitous fall away. Lan spat out blood, then heaved herself back onto the roof.

Zen faced her, staring at her with those black-glass eyes. Slowly, he drew Nightfire from its sheath and raised it over her.

Lan did not move. Instead, she began to hum.

It was the song she had sung for him in that bamboo forest long ago, the song of his homeland. Of winter fallen upon the steppes, of the quiet earth slumbering beneath the silence of snow.

Something in Zen's expression flickered. A frown creased his brow; his lips parted, and somehow, in the cacophony of the battle, she knew he spoke her name.

"Lan."

The roof between them exploded in bright blue light. For a moment, she was falling, the world a kaleidoscope of sky and ground. Inside her, the Silver Dragon opened its eyes; its power surged, catching and righting her. She landed lightly on a lower section of the palace roofs.

The blue light faded to reveal a shadow in its midst.

Erascius stood across from her. He was drenched in the power and radiance of the Azure Tiger, his metal armor and winter-white hair glistening beneath the shifting radiance of lights and energies overhead. There, his Demon God faced the

Black Tortoise and the section of rooftop where Zen stood. It bared its teeth.

Erascius smiled at Lan.

They were driving her and Zen apart so that she could not call him back from the depths of the Black Tortoise's control.

Anger sparked in her. Before she could think, That Which Cuts Stars was in her palm, the familiar heft of its hilt an extension of her wrist as she hurled it at him.

Erascius lifted a hand, twisted, and the dagger vanished. Lan only felt it slice through the air toward her as she swiftly snapped a Defensive Seal, raising a wall of tiles to block. She heard a *plink!* as the dagger lodged into the wall; with a quick Counterseal, the tile wall crumbled and she caught her dagger in her palm.

The Winter Magician held out his hands, the multicolored metal bands on his wrists flashing. "Ah, my little singer," he called. "Time apart has already eroded your memory. You forget that Elantian magicians wield the properties of metal as our magic. A mere dagger could never hurt me. And now I hold the power of the Azure Tiger."

She struggled to keep up with his language, having been away from it for moons by now, then to form her own words: "All power has an end."

Overhead, the Tiger lunged at the Tortoise. The ground rumbled as they clashed, lightning searing the sky. It reflected in Erascius's eyes and illuminated his skin, rendering him something other than human. Something like a god.

"Oh, you Hin are such *fools*," he crooned, his voice amplified by the surge of qì all around them. "If you had leaned into the power of these demons, you would be the gods now."

We did, Lan thought. *And it tore us apart.*

Erascius's attack came out of nowhere. The world went bright blue, and then she was hurtling backward, the night reeling and the lanterns and gold-tiled roofs of the palace falling farther from her as she plummeted to the ground.

She spun, a fú already between her fingers. It activated in a snap of qì, and the air around her warped, thickening beneath her and rising in a gale to slow her fall. Even with another jet of qì to the soles of her feet to cushion it, the impact still hurt. A streak of pain shot up her right ankle.

Yet in the square, like a miracle, the tide of the battle had changed. Everywhere Lan looked, Zen's Mansorian Deathriders had turned back to battling the Royal Magicians, the air interwoven with the energies of demonic practitioning and Elantian metalwork spells.

"Zen." She whispered his name like a prayer, seeking out his silhouette at the top of the palace. Had he shaken the control of the Black Tortoise?

She needed to move. Get to a safe place so that she could conjure the Godslayer—

"I won't let you get away that easily this time, little singer."

Through watering eyes, she looked up. Erascius stood several steps away from her, watching her with that same cruel smile, with those cold blue eyes that told her this was all a game to him and he would savor it. Behind him, the Azure Tiger turned from its battle with the Black Tortoise, aligning itself with its binder.

As the Tiger lifted a great claw and smashed it down toward Lan, a wall of shadows rose to meet it.

Erascius's lips parted in surprise.

The sky above them had darkened; from the ground rose a hulking shape, head and shell, then claws, forming between Lan and Erascius. As the Black Tortoise materialized, Lan felt a familiar qì land by her side.

Zen was looking at her. His eyes were clear.

Gently, he reached out and touched a hand to her cheek.

His lips moved, the sound lost to the maelstrom around them, but Lan heard his words ring as clear and true as though he had spoken directly to her heart.

It's time to end this. I will find you again.

She touched her fingers to his. An unspoken response. *In the next life.*

Zen turned to face Erascius, who was no longer smiling.

And Lan ran.

Somehow, she made it through the battle in the square. Somehow, she managed to slip into the streets that led into the shadows of houses. Into safety.

When the sounds of battle were overtaken by the pounding of her own heart in her ears, she stopped, panting, next to a dilapidated temple. With a jet of qì to her heels, she propelled herself unsteadily onto its low roof and rolled onto her back.

Every muscle in her body ached. Her ankle burned, and she was soaked through with sweat.

Lan lifted her gaze to the skies above the palace, where two gargantuan figures circled each other above the curved roofs. The light of the Black Tortoise and the Azure Tiger's battle was reflected in the clouds.

No more hesitation, no more delaying it. Lan pushed herself into a sitting position, feeling every bone in her body protest. With trembling hands, she brought her ocarina to her lips and began to play.

The song came painfully slowly at first. She forced her mind back in time to when she and Zen had opened the *Classic of Gods and Demons* in the desert night, sand beneath their feet and stars above their heads. She thought of the story within the tome.

Stroke by stroke, the Godslayer started to form in the air above her like a silver river, streaming toward the two Demon Gods in the distance. There was a stutter in the qì of the Black

Tortoise and the Azure Tiger; they let out great roars as the Godslayer coiled around them.

Sweat dripped down Lan's chin; she was shivering, every fiber of her being wound taut to wring more qì from her.

She was so focused that she almost didn't catch the ripple of motion behind her.

A seam was opening in the tapestry of energies. And through it came a familiar qì that reached her with the scent of burnt roses and blood and smoke. The sky turned crimson.

Pain exploded in her back. The Godslayer faltered as she broke away from her ocarina. When Lan looked down, there was a sword protruding from her stomach, glistening with red. Her blood.

"I couldn't have you conjure *that*, my dear betrothed," Hóng'yì said in her ear. "Not before I joined the fun."

He twisted the sword in her, then ripped it out and shoved her.

She fell from the roof. Lan slammed into the ground shoulder-first; felt a sickening *crack* as her collarbone splintered. It was suddenly difficult to breathe; through the haze of pain, she realized the ground beneath her was rapidly darkening with her blood.

Hóng'yì stood over her, resplendent in his crimson hàn'fú. She caught the red curve of his smile as he spoke, but his voice was muffled, his outline growing blurred.

Inside her, something was breaking. A silver light blossomed from her wound, fractaling toward the skies. Lan felt dynasties of power pouring from her as, for the first time, the Silver Dragon's strength and will overcame her own.

A serpentine form lit up the sky, hoarfrost crackling to form its scales and ice gathering into claws and teeth. Lan felt as though she were being swallowed by that monstrous power. A frozen whiteness was settling over her mind, blanketing her world, erasing everything that she could see and hear and feel: Hóng'yì with the wings of the Phoenix unfurled behind him, laughing; the forms of the Black Tortoise and the Azure Tiger flickering, weakened by the part of the Godslayer she'd conjured... the palace with its curved golden roofs, the Heavenly Capital and everything in this world she'd been fighting for...

And as Sòng Lián began to die, the Silver Dragon reared back and let out an unfettered scream.

27

> Long ago, the Heavens split
> Like teardrops, its fragments fell to the ground
> A piece of the sun bloomed into the Crimson Phoenix
> A slice of the moon turned into the Silver Dragon
> A shard of the stars gathered into the Azure Tiger
> A splinter of the night became the Black Tortoise
>
> —Various composers,
> "Ballad of the Last Kingdom"

The Crimson Phoenix was here.

Zen had sensed its energies appearing somewhere in the vicinity of the Heavenly Palace: a spark at first, then a blaze. As the energies of the Black Tortoise and the Azure Tiger stuttered, held in place by a rapidly disintegrating Godslayer, he turned his attention to the streets behind him where Lan had disappeared. Across from him, Erascius, too, had paused in their battle; his face was pale, his mouth twisted, as he looked from the Godslayer to Zen.

"What is that?" he snarled in his language, but there was true fear in his eyes. *"What is she doing?"*

Zen ignored him. He sensed the other qì first: one of flame and bitter smoke. One that he had fought back in the desert and was intimately familiar with.

Hóng'yì.

He searched for Lan's qì with increased urgency. And . . . *there,* on the ground in a back alley, he found it—stuttering, weak, and fading.

Fear spread through his veins like ice.

The Silver Dragon rose into the night, higher than the surrounding mountains. Its crown grazed the snow clouds that had gathered as it tipped its head and let out an unearthly shriek. Across from it, the Crimson Phoenix unfurled its wings and responded with a battle scream.

For the first time, Zen and Erascius were united as they stood, frozen in disbelief at the turn of events. The Royal Magician stared at the Phoenix, his lips parted and his expression morphing into one of greed.

But Zen was focused on the Silver Dragon. He could sense a wrongness to its energies, the overwhelming power that could only mean it was fully unleashed. That it was no longer in Lan's control.

She hadn't been able to conjure the full Godslayer. The portion she had woven had only disrupted the qì of the Demon Gods temporarily. The power of the Black Tortoise was returning; the Azure Tiger's shape was flickering back to life. The sky had been split into four quadrants just like Lan's star maps: red, blue, black, and silver; phoenix, tiger, tortoise, and dragon.

All of the Four Demon Gods were present here tonight. Releasing them, to breaking this cycle of power, was more important than anything else in this world.

Zen turned and ran into the streets, down the path where Lan had disappeared. Out of the corner of his eye, he saw Erascius following behind him.

Zen put on a burst of speed with the Light Arts, unfurling his left palm as he did. The Seal binding him to the Forty-Four pulsed with qì; through it, he could feel the will of each of the Deathriders, could choose to dive into any one of their cores and take over should he wish.

His command reverberated down the connections that

bound them to him. *Take out all the Elantians. Do not touch any Hin.* He paused and conjured a few key memories in his mind: Yeshin Noro Dilaya, with her fierce gray eye and scowling red mouth, the dāo that had once belonged to her mother. Master Nur, the Nameless Master, the disciples of Skies' End.

Fight with them and protect them.

He sensed their agreement through the bond that connected them.

Zen put on another burst of the Light Arts, following the path of Lan's qì down the city's winding, empty streets. He was close, so close.

He saw Lan first. The sight of her crumpled on the ground in a pool of blood broke something in him.

Hóng'yì looked up only as the gust of wind from Zen's Seal slammed into him, forcing him back several steps. Leveraging this moment of surprise, Zen bent to the ground and scooped Lan up. He slipped her ocarina into his storage pouch. Then he began tracing another Seal.

Flames erupted overhead as the Phoenix let out a furious cry. Zen held Lan against him, gritting his teeth as he shielded her from the searing heat. Through the strokes of the Seal he was conjuring, he saw that Hóng'yì had reoriented himself. The heir wore an ugly look on his face as he lifted his hand, beckoning his Demon God.

Zen traced the last stroke of his Seal. Overhead, a blue light illuminated the sky, moving their way; he looked up to see Erascius emerging from one of the streets, the Azure Tiger following overhead. As the Royal Magician's pale gaze latched onto Zen holding Lan, his expression darkened, and he slashed his arm down toward them.

Zen's Gate Seal opened. The last he saw of the battle was the Azure Tiger and the Crimson Phoenix clashing in a maelstrom of fire and water before he tumbled into the cold, clear night.

Zen alighted on a mountaintop. It was silent here with only boulders and pines, everything frozen beneath a thick coat of snow. He knew this as the mountain separating the Northern Steppes, which the Mansorians had once held, from the rest of the Last Kingdom. To the north lay his homeland, the great plains of ice that thawed to summer grasses beneath the sun each cycle. To the south, beyond the cliffs, was a stretch of forest that ended at the Heavenly Capital. He could see it from here: the glow of lanterns and Elantian alchemical lamps, now drenched beneath the flickering blues and reds of the two remaining Demon Gods.

His father had brought him here before, so long ago. He'd told Zen this was the highest summit in all the lands and that it was here that the skies had opened and the Mansorian clan had reached up and touched a god, which had granted them their powers. The Skies' Opening, his people had called it.

The Hin had a name for it, too: Heaven's Gate.

Zen knelt in the snow with Lan in his arms. Gently, he cradled her head on one arm. Her skin was cold to the touch. Red soaked her midriff and was beginning to stain the snow. He could feel her life qì seeping out with her blood. The Silver Dragon's energy wrapped over her, sustaining her life, but just barely—so it could retain control and use her as a vessel, a puppet.

Just as the Black Tortoise had used him.

He could sense both of the Demon Gods watching them, their forms barely visible: one whose qì stirred the snows on the ground and in the pines around them, and another whose qì roiled in the clouds overhead.

Zen ignored them. He pressed a hand to Lan's midriff. Closed his eyes.

His qì began to flow into hers, knitting over the embers of her core and weaving together flesh and veins and muscle. Shàn'jūn had been the one with more finesse, with the patience and love it took to make a good Medicine disciple; Zen had performed only passably in Master Nóng's Medicine classes, just enough to learn the basics.

Allow your qì to take root, Master Nóng had told them in class. *You must replenish your patients' cores with yours. In a way, your qì will always remain with them—both literally and symbolically—for having saved their lives. Poetic, is it not?*

And take root it did. Lan's core opened like a flower, drinking from the qì he gave her, and Zen gave and gave and gave. Sweat formed along his temples; his body temperature was dropping and his breathing growing rapid at his exertion. He rested his chin on her head, leaning against her, and that was how he felt her stir.

He looked down. The world had grown a little hazy, but everything cleared when her eyes opened again.

Her lips parted. "Zen," she whispered, and he might have given the world to hear her speak his name again. "What have you done?"

He was tired, but he did not wish to see her shiver from the cold. Zen cast a Seal for warmth and wrapped it around them. He closed his eyes briefly, letting himself hold her for a moment longer. Remembering her faint scent of lilies, the tickle of her hair.

Then he drew back. Reached into his storage pouch and pressed her ocarina into her hands. "We haven't much time," he said softly.

"Zen. . . ." She pushed herself into a sitting position and looked back toward the Heavenly City, from where demonic energies rolled out in heavy waves. "What happened? Hóng'yì—Erascius—"

"They are fighting." He could sense the clashes of their energies.

"And Dilaya, the masters, the disciples—"

"—will be safe. My Forty-Four will protect them." Zen took Lan's hand. Her head snapped back to him, her eyes wide.

"All Four Demon Gods are here tonight," she said. Her thumb gave an involuntary stroke of her ocarina as she gazed back to the city, her face outlined in the red and blue glow of the Demon Gods as they clashed.

"Yes," Zen said steadily. "Sòng Lián." Perhaps it was the way he spoke her name that made her look at him again. "I have one more favor to ask you."

Lan searched his face. "What is it?" she asked, a small crease between her brows.

"Make sure your Demon God is not listening," he said.

Her frown deepened, but she pressed her lips together and gave a small nod.

He had thought this through a hundred times; there was no fault to his plan. "A demonic bargain can be broken upon mutual agreement between the binder and the demon," Zen began carefully. "You found this out through Hóng'yì's memory: his father and the Phoenix broke the bargain by mutual agreement, knowing the emperor's health was frail and the Phoenix could move on to a stronger soul. And the Phoenix relinquished the emperor's soul." He paused a beat, then made his demand. "Give me the Silver Dragon."

"You're mad," she said.

"The Dragon's bargain is formed with the soul of your mother. Not yours."

"I changed the terms of the bargain—"

"When you reach the end of your bargain, it will release

your mother's soul and take yours instead," he said, and her eyes flashed. "You told me this in Shaklahira."

"That's right. It will take *my* soul."

"But you will never reach the end of your bargain," Zen replied. "With the Godslayer, you will *break* the bargain. Don't you see, Lan?" He brushed back a lock of her hair that had fallen in her face. "Your soul was never the one the Dragon would take with it when the Godslayer released it. Your mother's soul is the one still bound to it—until the end of your bargain."

Her eyes grew wide as his meaning began to sink in. "I could end it now," Lan said quietly. "*I say when it ends; I tell the Dragon when I am done, when I am ready to give up my soul. Those were the conditions.*"

"End it and jeopardize conjuring the Godslayer?" He kept his voice soft. "All for what?"

Her throat bobbed. "Zen—"

He leaned forward. "Relinquish the Silver Dragon, and let me bind it instead to take down Hóng'yì and the remaining Elantian army. Once I am done, conjure the Godslayer and release the Four. Their cores—along with all the souls they have consumed—will become one with the qì of this world again."

She stared at him, the implications of his offer clear. She would live; he would die. She would become known as the Ruin of Gods, the one who vanquished their conquerors and defeated another Mansorian demonic practitioner who had nearly destroyed the world.

"Why are you doing this?" Lan whispered.

"Because this is how it was always meant to be." He had seen it, so clearly, like all the pieces of a puzzle fitting together. Everything they had been taught in their life, from the principles of practitioning to the lore of the Demon Gods—all of it pointed to this. "Creation and destruction, birth and death—everything in this world is a cycle, Lan. Two parts of a whole. And we are a part of it as well. If I am the creation of power, you must be its destruction. If I must use the power of the Demon Gods, you must end it." His throat grew tight at his next words. "You are meant to live, Lan, and I am meant to die. Let me finish in the shadows so that you may continue in the light."

Her eyes were liquid, her breath coming rapidly. Lan shook her head, a tear spilling down her cheek as she reached for him. "No, no I won't—"

Demonic qì exploded from the capital. Against the night sky, an arc of blue cut across the black, streaking toward them like a shooting star. In a blink, Zen had drawn Lan to him and leapt back a dozen steps, toward the pines that grew on this mountaintop.

Erascius crashed onto the cliffs in a maelstrom of demonic and metallic energies. The Azure Tiger's outline flickered overhead, like stars winking. Both were badly wounded.

Erascius looked up, wearing a very ugly expression beneath the glow of his Demon God. His eyes found them, and it was the first time Zen had seen the magician look wildly out of control. Desperate.

Erascius pointed a finger at them. "The Dragon first," he panted. "Get the Dragon first—"

A second burst of qì cut off his words. It was as though a seam had split in the sky and the fires of the Ten Hells themselves poured upon the earth. Erascius looked up and screamed as flames consumed him, flames so powerful that even his Demon God could not defend against them.

Zen and Lan knelt in the snow, hidden amongst the pines. They held each other tightly, hearts beating in the same rhythm. But she did not tear her gaze from the Elantian magician. And Zen, too, gazed upon the man who had carved scars across his body, and whose regime was responsible for brutalizing all the peoples of this land.

A golden glow had appeared from somewhere behind Erascius. A blood-red whip radiating fire extended from it, slashing through the air and coiling around the magician's neck.

His eyes widened and he opened his mouth, perhaps in genuine disbelief that he could have been bested in such a manner. His surprise lasted a split second before a gust of otherworldly qì rammed through him.

Within a blink, he was gone, no more than an empty shell of metal-plated armor and a few embers curling in upon themselves as they drifted through the air.

The Tiger's form wavered, its qì flickering as its bargain shriveled in the face of its binder's death. Its form broke, scattering into a thousand, thousand crystals that hung suspended in the night like stars.

Then, slowly, the crystals coalesced into a single, glowing blue pearl.

From the Gate Seal overhead, a figure descended. His crimson hàn'fú rippled as though his body were enshrouded in flames. The glow of the Azure Tiger's core undulated against Hóng'yì like water as he touched his finger to it.

Zen shouted, but it was too late. A storm of qì swept through the mountains around them as the binding began. The Tiger's core exploded, tendrils wrapping around Hóng'yì's body and settling into his skin, his flesh, his bones.

Hóng'yì breathed in deeply and lifted his hands. The skies themselves seemed to light up in red and blue, from horizon to horizon, as both the Crimson Phoenix and the Azure Tiger reared up behind him.

The prince was laughing as he turned to Zen and Lan.

"Behold," he boomed, an unearthly wind gusting behind him. "The most powerful emperor to have ever set foot on this land. The Last Kingdom is mine now. And I will rule it with the power of all Four Demon Gods."

Zen gave a command to the Black Tortoise: *Shield us*. He sensed its energies spill from him as his Demon God turned to the two other ancient beings across the mountain range. Sensed its willpower begin to twine around his mind, fighting to claim what was left of him.

He gritted his teeth and turned to Lan. "The Dragon," Zen choked. "There is no other way. Sòng Lián—"

She looked at him then, and he forgot whatever he meant to say next. She had always worn her emotions on her face, and her expression told him everything he needed to know.

Lan flung her arms around him. Her body was wound so tightly around his that he could feel her shaking. Yet with her in his arms, the chaos in his mind calmed and the shadows that always pressed so close seemed to yield to light.

Gently, Zen let his arms fall to her lower back. Turned his face to hers so that he could breathe her in. Spoke against her temple, her hair tickling his cheeks.

"Say yes, Lan," he murmured. "One word. You usually have so many."

Her face was pressed to his neck, and it was wet. But that was how he felt her lips move.

"Yes."

Behind them, wind stirred the snows of the mountain. A bright beam of moonlight cut through the clouds, and within, a great serpentine form rose. It turned its head toward Zen.

Back at the school, Geomancy Master Fēng had read in his oracle bones the circumstances of Zen's birth: how the stars and the red sands had blown and the words carved into the bones of the wild horse chosen for him had written his destiny. And the world had whispered of the tragic history of his people, and how the last Mansorian heir was cursed to follow.

Here he stood, nearly one hundred cycles after his great-grandfather: the very finale to Xan Tolürigin's tragic tale that Zen had fought to escape for his entire life.

Yet his would end differently. And if Zen could close his eyes and pick the single point in time when his story had begun to diverge from his chosen path . . . it would be the moment in the crowded Haak'gong teahouse when he'd set eyes upon the girl with the silver-bells voice and a páo like snow. He'd felt his gaze drawn to her as though a force greater than he could understand had encircled them, spinning them toward each other like opposite ends of a centrifuge. And when she'd looked up and, of the entire audience gathered that night, met his eyes, he'd felt something click into place. Yīn into yáng, their threads ensnaring to come together into a fully woven story.

Life, death. Creation, destruction. Power, weakness.

At the center of it all: balance.

Tonight, they would restore it to this land and its people.

Xan Temurezen lifted his face to the light of the Silver Dragon.

"Silver Dragon of the East," he said. "I have a bargain for you."

28

> Capture the general and win the war.
>
> —General Nuru Ala Šuzhan of the
> Jorshen Steel clan, *Classic of War*

They descended upon the Heavenly Palace like wraiths in the night, taking advantage of the chaos in the square.

Yeshin Noro Dilaya had always preferred the language of steel to the language of shadows, and she would much rather have been out in the square, soaking in the heat of battle and feeling the thrill of wielding her dāo as an extension of her body. A deadly dance, her mother had called it.

Her hand tightened on the hilt of Falcon's Claw, stroking the thumb ring on its hilt and thinking of the woman who had worn it before her.

Watch over me, È'niáng.

The palace faced south, with all its noisy fountains and the grand walkway that extended into the city, inviting people to gather like sheep to celebrate the bloodsucking monarchs within its walls. So Dilaya and the others approached from the north. The lights here were dimmer, it was quieter, and there wouldn't be the risk of running across one of those demonic practitioners set loose by Xan Temurezen.

She tried not to dwell on the fact that they fought on the same side—after all, they shared a greater common enemy at this moment. Worse was that Sòng Lián had not told her about this alliance with Xan Temurezen. But as much as Dilaya hated to admit any of these factors, everything had worked out to their advantage.

The square was now a graveyard of Elantian soldiers, thanks to the Mansorian demonic practitioners; even better, they had taken down most of the Elantian forces within the city, including a large number of Royal Magicians. Dilaya also didn't think it was just luck that the demonic practitioners hadn't come after her or any of her forces.

Too much thinking, she scolded herself angrily, and cleared her mind to focus on the mission at hand.

She landed on the parapets of the palace. As much as she had despised the building and all that it stood for before, the sight of the Elantian symbol over it now turned her stomach.

No matter. It would soon be gone.

She glanced up at the skies. It seemed Lan had decided to take the fight elsewhere. Over the mountains rimming the city in the north, unearthly lights flickered against the snow clouds: red, blue, silver, and black. Currents of demonic energies rolled through the city, so strong that she could barely sense anything else.

"Stay safe, little fox spirit," Dilaya muttered to the wind.

Someone bumped into her elbow. Dilaya's hand shot out to grab Chó Tài before he plunged off the walls.

"Try to be competent, will you?" she hissed. Unfortunately, Chó Tài was the only one who knew the layout of the palace, which was why she'd been paired with him. Her task was to protect him until they were inside, and then they would join with the rest of their army and take the palace.

He glared back at her but swallowed whatever retort he'd

been about to give when someone appeared by his side. A flutter of white, a flash of fans, and Elanruya was there, landing with the ease and grace of a cat.

Dilaya bit back any further immature bickering and straightened slightly. On the rooftops of other temples and the sections of the parapets closest, she caught flashes of shadows and the smallest sparks of flames.

Their army was in position.

Dilaya peered down at the palace courtyard. It was eerily deserted, the main doors at the back locked. She could feel the energies of Elantian metalwork spells radiating into the air with a slightly bitter smell. So there *were* some of them still alive, and they had chosen to barricade themselves within the palace walls. They must have bolstered the defenses and doors.

Cowards.

"I'm going to blow down those doors," Dilaya muttered to Elanruya and Chó Tài. "But I need a cleaner aim. You two stay here until it's safe. Elanruya, make sure Chó Tài doesn't fall off the parapets."

His protests fell to the wind as, with a jet of qì through her heels and a well-placed kick, Dilaya took off.

She landed on the lowest section of the curved terracotta roof, which offered a straight view to the doors. She had remembered them as red with great golden knockers carved in the likeness of the Four Demon Gods. Now the doors were blue and the knockers had changed to silver lions.

Dilaya drew a Destructive Seal against the door and, with a burst of her qì, activated it.

Wood splintered; the doors creaked but didn't budge.

Irritated, she lifted her hand to draw another Seal when two figures materialized by her side.

The Nameless Master of Assassins had arrived so quietly

that Dilaya hadn't sensed his qì, even when he used the Light Arts. He held up a hand, gesturing at her to stop; she obeyed.

"Your way is one of steel, Yeshin Noro Dilaya," he said, his voice like wind between pines, and she sensed him beginning to channel qì toward the door: a thin, steady stream, softer than her explosive Seal, curling into the cracks between the wood and the metal. "Sometimes, it is necessary to apply the way of shadows I teach in my art."

If a peer had told her this, Dilaya might have retorted: *That's cow dung, and I'll do it my way if I like.* But this was one of her masters, and she had the teachings and Code of Conduct of the school engraved deep within her. She bowed her head. "Yes, shī'fù."

He cast her an unreadable glance, as though he might have heard her thoughts. Then his pinky twitched—and, impossibly, the doors clicked. They began to swing open.

"Duck," he said.

"What—?" Dilaya began, but he'd disappeared from her side. She heard the whistle of an arrow; reflexively, she raised Falcon's Claw and swung at it. The force of the block knocked the arrow off course and sent Falcon's Claw spinning from her hands. The arrow stuck into the roof, and Dilaya saw that it was no normal arrow but one made completely of metal, head, shaft, and fletching. A dozen steps back, Falcon's Claw clanged to the ground below.

Dilaya began to draw her other dāo, Wolf's Fang, but a second arrow was already on its way. She moved—too slowly—but a pale silhouette appeared before her. Elanruya spun, catching the second arrow in the metal ribs of one of her fans.

Dilaya leapt down from the roof and picked up Falcon's Claw. "I owe you one," she called.

Shouts rent the air; the palace doors had opened, and

Elantian guards were now shooting arrows at them. Elanruya barreled toward them, fans whirling and páo spinning as though she were dancing. The Nameless Master stepped out from a Gate Seal, his dagger arcing across a guard's throat. Master Nur followed close behind, steel-edged whips lashing out. Then Chue appeared, firing arrow after arrow with speed that Master Cáo, the former Master of Archery, would have been proud of.

As the disciples of the School of the White Pines emerged from the night, fighting their way into the palace, Dilaya felt emotions rise thick in her throat. She joined them, Falcon's Claw flashing, and perhaps it was the elation of the moment, the hope that *they could actually win,* tonight, but Yeshin Noro Dilaya felt her hand guided by more than instinct.

This is for you, È'niáng, she thought as she danced. *This is for you, masters.*

This was for her people who had suffered, whether at the hands of the Elantian conquest or under the cruel imperial regime before that.

Within minutes, the main hall of the palace was theirs.

The practitioners straightened, looking around in disbelief.

The palace was a thing of splendor, Dilaya had to admit. Splendor built on the lives and sacrifices of this land and its peoples by both ruling bodies that had presided over it: the emperors and the Elantians. Gold and jade and lapis lazuli dripped from the walls. Polychrome paintings of flora and fauna, gods and immortals, filled every bit of the ceiling, which was topped with filigreed cornices covered with intricate carvings.

Vermilion pillars engraved with gilded Hin characters and patterns ran the length of the hall, though here, too, the Elantians had made their mark. Silver had been inlaid in the pillars, and in the walls and furniture as well, and the blue-and-white banners fluttered between the pillars. Hin signs had been removed, replaced by the strange, sharp horizontal lettering of the Elantians.

"It is quiet," Master Nur remarked, his hands tightening on his whips. "Do you sense anything? The demonic qì is so strong, I can barely feel anything else."

By his side, Elanruya was silent, her blindfold fluttering as she cocked her head, perhaps attempting to sift through the currents of qì, just as everyone else was.

Chó Tài pointed. "The throne room is that way."

"There are still Elantians in this building," the Nameless Master said. "I sense them."

A few of the disciples held their weapons higher.

"If we find nothing, we split up," Dilaya said. "Paint this place red with their blood."

Behind them, one of the Elantian banners rippled.

Elanruya whipped around and flung out a fan. One of its steel spikes shot out, piercing the fabric.

There was a faint *plink* as it pinged off metal.

"Magician. *Magician*," Chó Tài said, and that was when an arrow whistled toward him.

Dilaya leapt, Falcon's Claw in her hand. A swing of her mighty blade and the arrow clattered to the floor. As she turned in the direction it had come from, one of the banners shifted and an Elantian Royal Magician stepped out.

Recognition was cold ice seeping through her veins. She had seen this magician at the invasion of Skies' End, at the right hand of the white-haired magician who had killed Ulara. *Lishabeth*, they had called her.

Lishabeth's lips twisted grimly. She held up two fingers and gestured.

From all around, other Royal Magicians emerged.

Dilaya tightened her grip on Falcon's Claw. Tonight, she would avenge her mother.

"In formation!" Lishabeth roared, and her army drew into a tight circle, back to back, weapons out.

The magicians raised their arms, metal cuffs at their wrists gleaming.

"Surrender," Dilaya said in the Elantian tongue. She had not studied it as carefully as Zen had back at the school, but she knew enough. She pointed her dāo at Lishabeth, then toward the square. "All are dead. You will not win. *Surrender.*"

Lishabeth's sneer of disdain was one Dilaya would never forget or forgive. "Never," came the response, and all hells broke loose.

Dilaya had never engaged in close combat with Elantian magicians, for the battle of Skies' End had been fought by the masters. She could see, now, how the Elantians had taken the Last Kingdom in the span of weeks.

The Táng warrior next to her went down with a gurgle. When Dilaya looked at him, she realized with horror that a drop of metal had latched onto his chest and was growing *inside him*. His mouth gaped open, and liquid silver filled his throat, then his eyes, then his ears. With a solid *thunk,* he fell onto the cherrywood floor by her side.

"DEFENSE!" Dilaya bellowed, backing away and weaving a Seal. "DEFENSE—"

But it was no use. Another Shaklahiran practitioner crumpled before her, and when Dilaya sought out the culprit, she saw Lishabeth standing several paces away. A fresh heart dripped blood from her hands, steam rising from it into the cold.

The battle around Dilaya blurred. Here was more Hin blood—more *clan* blood—spilling under her command. So many practitioners had died fighting the initial Elantian invasion. How many more of their precious lives was she willing to wager?

Would there be a people left for them to rebuild after—*if*—they took back this land?

That was when she noticed Lishabeth turning, those emotionless gray eyes focusing on Dilaya. Saw the magician's hand begin to curl, felt the singe of metal energies in the air at the beginning of a spell.

I'm next.

She knew nearly nothing of Elantian magic, of how exactly the magicians wielded metal in such precise, scientific ways. She knew no Seals with which to defend herself against a spell that plucked live, beating hearts from humans.

Dilaya hurled a fú, which began to smoke at its edges. Lishabeth flung out a hand, and a metallic net closed around the fú, extinguishing it before it could even explode. All the while, the Royal Magician's other hand formed a metalwork spell, and Dilaya felt a tugging sensation in her chest as the spell latched onto the metal in her blood.

É'niáng, protect me.

Lishabeth raised her fist—and that was when the night itself seemed to sweep through the entrance and swallow her. The magician shrieked as the formless shadow barreled her over, pinning her beneath great claws.

Dilaya could only gape as the rest of the creature materialized: a flicker of orange, like fire, coalescing into a snout, ears, claws, and nine tails.

"Nine-tailed fox," she whispered, and in her mind, thought: *Demon.*

A woman had stepped out from the demon's swirl of shadows, too: a woman who seemed to glide rather than walk, whose eyes glittered like obsidian. Her long black hair swirled beneath a beaded helmet; the patterns of red flames against her black páo were all too familiar.

Mansorian. The woman was clad in Mansorian clan garb.

The nine-tailed fox demon bared its teeth in a growl that rumbled through the hall. Lishabeth was pinned beneath it, her face a mask of terror. She opened her mouth in a scream—

The Mansorian woman blinked, and the nine-tailed fox bore down upon Lishabeth in a blur of white fangs and orange smoke. When it lifted its head and stepped forward, all that was left on the floor was a dried-out husk of a corpse.

Dilaya heard screaming behind her, but her mind was frozen on one thought: This was a Mansorian demonic practitioner. This was the *power* of a true Mansorian demonic practitioner.

The woman turned unseeing black eyes on Dilaya, and Dilaya suppressed a shiver. She'd fought demons before, of course—too many lingered in remote corners of the Last Kingdom where cesspools of yīn energies gathered—but though she had learned to hate them and fear them, never in her life had she fought against a fully trained Mansorian demonic practitioner, historically the sworn enemy of her clan.

Dilaya drew her sword and gathered qì, ready to weave into Seals.

But the woman merely walked past her as though she weren't there.

As though sensing a greater enemy, the Royal Magicians were turning to face the woman and her demon. One lifted his hand and flung a dagger at her.

Blade met flesh; the hilt protruded from the Mansorian's chest, but she continued her slow, steady march forward. With each step, the dagger in her chest began to disintegrate. The metal burned like parchment, its ashes fluttering away and dissolving until there was nothing, not even a scar, left.

The woman gave another slow blink, and her nine-tailed fox demon set upon the Royal Magician who had thrown the knife. His shriek cut off abruptly.

Behind her, more shapes were emerging from the night: a golden hawk with razor-sharp wing feathers, a skeletal gray wolf with hooves, a horse with canine features and fangs. They came in with gusts of demonic qì, the demonic practitioners with unmoving faces like the dead, and began to fight the Elantian Royal Magicians.

Not a single one of them touched Dilaya's army.

Dilaya's suspicion turned to certainty, followed by a strange feeling of dissonance. Indeed, it *hadn't* been mere coincidence that she and her group had gotten through the city unscathed.

The demonic practitioners had been ordered not to harm them.

She lifted her gaze in the direction of the mountains. "Xan Temurezen," she muttered, her grip tightening on Falcon's Claw. The bastard. If he thought doing this was the right thing, if he thought this might buy Dilaya's forgiveness, he was wrong.

She would never forgive him.

But . . . perhaps she could understand him. Just a little better.

Dilaya turned to her own army. "Well, what are you waiting for?" she roared. "Scour this palace and round up the remaining guards! Root out the high governor and court officials, and either they surrender or they *burn*."

With a rallying cry, her army set out, led by Chó Tài. The palace was like a maze, but with insider knowledge, they made quick work of it. They found the high governor, court officials, and another handful of Royal Magicians barricaded in the great throne room. The demons swept through the chamber, incapacitating the magicians.

Dilaya stepped forward. The great throne of the Hin emperors had once sat here, its gold threaded through with red: the imperial colors of the Last Kingdom. The Elantians had painted it silver and woven blue into its patterns, but it was really one and the same: encrusted with jewels and corrupted with the stench of power.

Dilaya had many times attempted to picture the kind of man who might govern their kingdom under the direct command of an Elantian king from a distant land across the Sea of Heavenly Radiance.

The man staring at her from the seat of the throne, shielded by several of his non-magic-wielding officials, was nothing like the god she'd once imagined. He was a pale, wrinkled man of average height and build, sweating like a pig.

Falcon's Claw trembled in her hand as she stared down at him. Here was the man who had fed on the suffering of the people, who had drained her land of resources, and who had attempted to wipe out the Hin as though they were vermin. Here was the man whose magicians and army had marched upon her home, slaughtered her masters . . . and killed Ė'niáng.

Grief and fury surged in her. She lifted her dāo.

And hesitated.

This man was no more guilty than the emperors who had sat upon the throne before him throughout the eras this land had seen. He was no worse than the Royal Magicians who spilled Hin blood without batting an eye. He, and men like him, waged wars like playing games while the common folk of her land suffered.

No more.

It was time for power to return to the people, at last.

The land of ten thousand flowers. She could almost hear her mother's voice, see that rare, stern smile that had always meant the world to Dilaya.

Yeshin Noro Ulara's final words, spoken beneath the thick fall of rain, came to her. *You will one day lead a clan, a people....*

Dilaya lowered her dāo. Stepped forward. And pointed the tip of the blade at the high governor's neck.

Capture the general and win the war.

"My name is Yeshin Noro Dilaya," she said in the Elantian tongue, lifting her chin. "Matriarch of the Jorshen Steel clan. I am here to negotiate the surrender of the Elantian Empire to the people of the Last Kingdom."

29

And the goddess of the moon drifted back into her celestial palace of ice and snow, to gaze upon her lover from the light of another world.

—"Goddess of the Moon," *Hin Village Folktales: A Collection*

When Lan came to, it was cold, the stone beneath her hard and digging into her back. She gazed at the sky for a moment, taking in the gray, roiling clouds and the white specks that drifted from them. They fell on her cheeks in pinpricks of momentary cold.

It was snowing.

She sat up, marveling at the lightness of her being, at the silence of the world. The wound in her abdomen was closed, and touching her hand over it, she felt qì like a handprint of night and flame, weaving a Seal to staunch her bleeding and heal the flesh beneath.

Zen.

Lan snapped her left wrist up. Her breath caught as memories flooded back.

A boy, his black páo draped in moonlight, reaching up to touch the night.

A beam of light unwinding, curving into a long, serpentine shape with glittering scales.

A horned head, eyes like the ice of northern mountaintops, bending to his will.

A flash of white light, and then darkness. Just like the day Māma had seared the Silver Dragon into that Seal on her wrist and everything had been set in motion.

It hadn't been a dream: the mark of the Dragon's bargain was gone from her arm, the skin there unblemished, as though it had never existed at all.

Say yes, Lan. One word. You usually have so many.

He had promised the Silver Dragon so many more souls— souls of the Elantian army, souls of his demonic practitioners. In the end, Lan knew the terms of the bargain would not matter, for the Godslayer would unwind all that had been made in the demonic bargain. The souls consumed. The power accumulated. The gods corrupted.

All would be released back into the natural qì of this world—as was meant to be.

An explosion of demonic qì caught her attention. On the other end of the mountaintop, the sky was aglow in flashes of light. Even from here, their glow refracted on the snow clouds: red and blue, silver and black, dividing the world into four quadrants. The gods, come down to dance with mortals.

And she was tasked to return them to the skies.

She could see two figures beneath the light of the Demon Gods. Hóng'yì, as bright as a flame in his blood-red hàn'fú. He was laughing as he twirled his fingers, commanding attacks with an insouciance bordering on delight. And opposite him, like night incarnate: Zen, in a whirl of black and silver, the shapes of the Tortoise and Dragon weaving and lunging over him as he fought.

Another burst of demonic qì tore across the sky and raised tremors in the ground. In the clouds, the red and blue glow was rapidly gaining ground, the black and silver seeming to retreat.

Zen dug his heels into the snow, shaking with the effort of holding his ground. Of defending her.

She recalled his voice as she'd reeled from the pain of breaking the bargain. *I will buy you time, but you must use the Godslayer. You will have one chance to end it all.*

Lan pushed herself into a sitting position. Without the strength of the Silver Dragon, she was suddenly aware of how vulnerable she, a human, was in the face of these gods. Her hands shook as she fumbled for her ocarina.

Hóng'yì struck out, and a flaming wingtip of the Phoenix sliced through the Black Tortoise's qì. Thunder cracked through the heavens as the Tortoise reared back.

Zen staggered. With a wave of his hand, he directed the Dragon, which surged forward in a shell of glittering ice and writhing water. The energies of the Tiger met it, and the two intertwined in flashes of white and blue.

Hóng'yì laughed. His eyes were the color of blood, his entire being drenched in the light of his Demon God. "Despicable Mansorian," he shouted. "Our ancestors fought like this at the end of the last era. You already know how the story ends."

Zen said nothing. His body was rigid with exertion, and as he dipped his chin, Lan caught sight of his eyes: the black had nearly swallowed the white.

He was losing control to his Demon Gods. There was no telling how long he had before the Black Tortoise—and now the Silver Dragon, too—took complete command of his body, mind, and soul.

It was now or never.

You will have one chance to end it all.

Zen yielded a step, and the Dragon hissed a scream as the

Azure Tiger bit into its neck. The Black Tortoise roared as the fire from the Phoenix closed in on it.

Use the Godslayer.

Lan lifted her ocarina to her lips. Closed her eyes.

And began.

Time flowed past her as though she were a stone in a river, watching the tides of her kingdom pass by. This land as it had been without humans at first: endless stretches of yellow grasses and ice-capped mountains to the north, lush pine forests interspersed with hills and rivers at the center, bamboo oceans and mist-shrouded lakes in the south, and glittering golden deserts and basins of aquamarine blue as though carved from the skies in the west. She saw the sun and the sky, the moon and the stars, the forces that shifted through them to sculpt this earth.

The gods, she realized, had existed long before this world. They had laid down their bones to form this land, the earth and mountains and deserts; they had blown a breath across and given it wind; they had shed tears and gifted it rivers and lakes. And then they had spilled a few drops of their blood to gift to humans, to the shamans who had come to know how to wield the qì of this world.

The Godslayer was a story, and now Sòng Lián knew its beginning and its ending.

She coaxed the song from her ocarina and, in her mind's eye, watched her land's history unfurl. The first shaman practitioners who had reached to the heavens and made their pacts with the gods. The sons, daughters, and children of their lineages who received the blessings of power and grew greedy, casting aside the truth of the origins of the Demon Gods generation after generation as humans warred for power . . . until one day, the truth was forgotten.

The era of bloodshed during the Warring Clans Era . . .

the unification of the First Kingdom, the rise and fall of dynasty after dynasty thereafter . . . the eradication of the clans descended from the first shaman practitioners. . . . Familiar faces and stories emerging in the great gray river: The Dragon Emperor Yán'lóng, binder of the Crimson Phoenix, facing off against Mansorian High General Xan Tolürigin, binder of the Black Tortoise. The generations of imperial heirs who grew up within the Heavenly Capital in an empire held by the iron fist of their regime and the power they held. The birth of a squabbling infant on the most auspicious summer's day, soothsayers exclaiming over a destiny that stretched toward the future like samite. Another spoke in the wheel of power and inheritance that continued to churn, churn, churn.

And then: a baby born to a sky of snow that fell like goose feathers in the ghost bells of the morning with only the embers of a dying fire to light his way. A dark fate, one made to walk in the shadows, the clan's last fortune-teller had predicted as he read the alignment of stars overhead and listened to the rattle of the wild horse's bones.

Another twelve moons and four seasons, into the spring when a second babe wailed in the kàng bed of a great courtyard manor, the willows sweeping over a stained-glass lake where lotuses bloomed brightly. A mother leaning over her to play a familiar melody with a woodlute, whispering that one day she would grow up to serve her land and her people, not the throne. . . .

Lan watched the prince grow up just as the oracles had foretold: a filigreed life made for monarchs and kings within the walls of palaces, protected by the source of power his family had jealously guarded over the cycles. Seated on a throne of blood and gold, guarded by a great phoenix even as its flames burned down the kingdom.

In the plains of the north, the Mansorian boy knew a

peaceful life of sun and sky and grass, of herding sheep and riding wild horses with what remained of his clan. And the girl—Lan knew exactly how her story went in the sheltered courtyard manor.

She followed the tale of the Mansorian boy and the Sòng girl, knowing how they would each come to lose everything they loved, how they would spend cycles apart beneath the hand of another ruling monarch, yearning for that blue sky and freedom again. Watched their paths speed toward each other, two stars fated to an inevitable collision: the boy now a young man clad in black and the girl as a young woman in a páo of white gauze, their gazes clashing across a crowded teahouse. Yīn and yáng, coming together, at last.

Power is always borrowed, Dào'zǐ had written. *It exists to be used—so long as we remember to return it. It may be created, so long as we know to destroy it.*

The balance, Dé'zǐ had told her with his dying breath. *Yīn and yáng. Good and evil. Great and terrible. Two sides of the same coin, Lián'ér, and somewhere in the center of it all lies* power. *The solution is to find the balance between them. Do you understand?*

She hadn't then, but she did now. *They* were the balance: she and Zen, one made to create and one made to ruin, one to wield power and one to destroy it.

Lan's song shifted, and the tides of the river of her land began to flow backward. Through the dynasties that rose and fell like the ever-shifting dunes of the Emaran Desert; through the wars and bloodshed and death . . . all the way back to that clear night of stars and grasses, until she thought she might have stood at the first shaman's side.

The Godslayer bloomed from her fingertips. She closed her eyes, pouring the story she had learned into its qì, weaving the truth of what was meant to be: balance. Creation and destruction. A cycle of power, approaching its end.

In the distance, something screamed.

When she opened her eyes, the Godslayer shone brightly in the sky beneath the snow clouds. It reached its tendrils of qì toward the Crimson Phoenix.

The Demon God shrieked again, its flames sputtering. Beneath it, Hóng'yì looked up. His eyes found Lan. Understanding lit them, shifting to hatred. He flung out an arm toward her.

Hóng'yì's qì faltered. He staggered and fell to his knees, undoubtedly feeling the impact of the Godslayer, so inextricably was his qì now tied to the Crimson Phoenix's core.

She continued to play, guiding the Godslayer forward. Its qì found the Azure Tiger, then wrapped over the Black Tortoise, dimming its thunderous energies; last, it found the Silver Dragon. The demonic energies stabilized as the Godslayer fettered their cores.

Beneath them, Zen staggered. He managed to right himself, swaying slightly as he straightened.

Lan approached them. She faced Hóng'yì, who thrashed as the Godslayer closed over his two Demon Gods.

"*You fool!*" the imperial heir screamed. "Relinquish me! Do you not remember the bargain we made? I could make you the most powerful empress this nation has ever seen; we could be immortal; we could rule this land, this *world,* into eternity—" He fell to his knees, holding one hand to his heart as the Godslayer began to take effect.

Lan lowered the ocarina from her lips. The Godslayer remained, its unyielding grasp fettering the Four Demon Gods. Waiting for the end of her song, her final command.

"I have seen era after era and dynasty after dynasty of powerful rulers," Sòng Lián said quietly. "All they have sought is more power. All they have served is themselves. It is time power served the people of this land."

She turned away from him, toward the other end of the cliffs. Something inside her had numbed, the last flame of a candle gone out. She felt cold, as though she'd set one foot in the River of Forgotten Death. As though she were buried beneath the snows of an eternal winter.

Across from her, Zen met her gaze. He had fallen down and now lay in the snow, his chest rising and falling faintly. The darkness had faded from his eyes as the Black Tortoise's control over him had been broken by the Godslayer. The light of the Four Demon Gods reflected on his face, red and blue, black and silver.

He smiled, soft with sadness and knowing.

It was snowing heavily now, the flakes gray like ashes, melting on her cheeks as she closed the gap between her and Zen and knelt by his side. Gently, she drew him into her arms. Breathed in the scent of him, of night and smoke and mountain wind, committed the shape of his body to memory, the way his fit so perfectly against hers. Felt the silky locks of his hair brush her cheeks, his lips graze her ears as he whispered, "Finish the story."

She leaned against him as she unspooled the last notes to the song of the Godslayer. The Seal grew bright, its fetters tightening and expanding over the Crimson Phoenix, cocooning it in water. The Demon God's flames began to sizzle out, embers turning to ash, fire to smoke. A maelstrom of qì howled around it, unleashed into the atmosphere to rejoin the clouds, the wind, the water, and the earth.

There came a last flare of light, and all that was left of the Crimson Phoenix was a fleck of light the size of a pearl, so bright and golden, it was as though the sun itself shone from within. Then that, too, exploded. A gale swept over the earth like the sigh of a being put to rest.

The Azure Tiger went next, and its core seemed to shimmer every shade of blue as it unwound.

The energies stilled. There was nothing left of either Hóng'yì or the two Demon Gods on the other side of the peak but for a patch of rock untouched by snowfall.

And then the Seal turned toward them.

She heard Zen speak to her, looked into his face, carved in black and white by the shadow and light of the two remaining Demon Gods. He was so beautiful, just like the first time she'd caught sight of him across a crowded teahouse.

"Smile, Sòng Lián," he said, and pressed his two fingers to the corners of her mouth, just as she had once done to him. She held on to his hand, pressing it against her cheek as her tears fell. "With you by my side, I have already known a lifetime of joy." The dark crescent of his lashes swept across his cheeks. "Thank you."

Gently, Zen leaned forward and pressed his lips to her face, kissing away her tears just as he had once a world ago, in the forsaken village of rain and mist. She felt his hand scrape against her collarbone, felt him lift the amulet she'd carried with her.

The Godslayer twined over the Silver Dragon. Its scales began to disintegrate, falling like ash and dissipating into the night. It dipped its great head, one icy blue eye turning to glance at Lan, and she was suddenly reminded of the sight she had seen in the Emaran Desert: the immortal soul released from the sand demon, reaching up and touching the Dragon with reverence. As though facing a god.

Lan gazed up at the Silver Dragon. She could not have hoped to read the ancient, vast emotions on its face, but she thought there was something like peace in the way it exhaled and gave her a slow blink.

Lan inclined her head at the being. It gave no acknowledgment but to close its eyes, and with the next gust of wind it was gone, snow and moonlight stirring the mountaintop where it had stood.

In her arms, Zen shuddered. "Lan," he whispered. "Will you tell me a story?"

So she did. Sòng Lián lay down next to him and held him in the snow as she told him, once again, the story they had dreamt of back in Shaklahira: of another life, another world, one free of war and conquest, when a boy and a girl would meet in a school courtyard. He would catch her breaking the Code of Conduct, and she would smash a teacup in his face, and there would be something familiar to both of them in that moment, as though they might have encountered this in a past life—though that would be impossible. She would tease him relentlessly, and slowly, he would warm to her, each drawn to the other like sun to moon, flame to darkness, as though a predestined path brought them together. They would fall in love, wholly and irrevocably. They would don red wedding outfits and gather with a great group of their families and friends to exchange vows and bind that red thread of fate between them, the one that, unbeknownst to them, had tied them together through past lifetimes and guided them to each other in this one.

Lan spoke to him softly, keeping her gaze on his face as, at last, the Black Tortoise's form faded into night. She kept talking even as the energies around them stilled, as the light dimmed in Zen's eyes and the cold crept into her arms, until the mountaintop was empty and the earth silent but for the hush of snow falling.

30

Age of Ten Thousand Flowers, Cycle 13
Where the Rivers Flow and the Skies End

The snow camellias had bloomed and spring had arrived at the School of the White Pines. Up and down the zigzagging mountain, disciples in white páos ducked beneath sprigs of plum blossoms whose petals dusted the stone steps of Skies' End with pale blushes of pink. Sunlight spilled like honey upon winding creeks, and a warm breeze threaded through the gentle wisps of mist coiled through the pines.

"You little turtle-egged ratfart—*get back here!*"

Sòng Lián strode through the doors of the Chamber of Waterfall Thoughts, nearly giving heart attacks to the meditating disciples. The Master of Seals, seated at the very far end of the hall, gave no indication she had noticed anything. She sat as still as stone in her meditation, not even the ends of her white silk blindfold fluttering.

"Elanruya," Lan said, hands on her hips. "Where is he? I swear he came this way—" She faltered as the other woman put a finger to her lips. "Ah." Lan glanced around the hall of startled disciples staring at her. She put her hands together and, clearing her throat, switched to a tone more suitable for a master of the school. "Forgiveness for disturbing the peace of your meditation, disciples."

She heard a few giggles and winked at several of the young girls as she backed out of the chamber. She wore her hair in two long braids now, just as people in her late husband's clan had worn it. Creases lined her eyes where she often crinkled them in laughter, and the planes of her face had hardened with age. Her gaze, though, held a spark of that same mischief and playfulness—which her son had inherited.

Nearby, bushes rustled. A small shape streaked out of them, making for the steps that led uphill.

"Xan Tsomurejin," Lan called, hurrying after him. "I'm warning you!"

She glimpsed him again as he ran over the wooden bridge toward the Chamber of a Hundred Healings. In the pond, carp scattered beneath his shadow. At the other end, two figures crouched over the water, speaking in hushed voices.

"Tài'shū!" Tsomurejin called as the taller of the two men looked up. "Uncle Tài! Hide me!"

Chó Tài said nothing, but it spoke volumes that he let the boy duck behind his wide purple páo without a word. He turned to the entrance almost defensively, his gold-rimmed eyes flashing as he raised his eyebrows at Lan. By his side, the other man straightened, too. A smile broke over his face as he took in the scene.

"Jin'ér," Shàn'jūn said, leaning behind Chó Tài to grin at the child. "What have you done now?"

At twelve cycles of age, Tsomurejin was beginning to grow with the speed of a bamboo shoot. He possessed strong black brows and high cheekbones that rendered him the spitting image of his father and garnered him praise from the aunties in the capital city. Even Clan Councilwoman Yeshin Noro

Dilaya begrudgingly showed him affection in her own way, gifting him a Jorshen Steel sword when he became old enough to take classes in the Art of Swords.

Tsomurejin's spirited playfulness, though, he had inherited from his mother. He had her quick smile and sharp tongue and was capable of being charming even as he planned mischief.

"Shàn'jūn'shū," he laughed. "Māma likes you most—won't you beg her to spare me?"

"That little rabbit-whelped heathen stole my ocarina," Lan said, striding onto the bridge. "I need it—I'm teaching a class on the Art of Song at the People's Capital, and we were meant to leave a half bell ago. Yeshin Noro Dilaya will wring my neck if I'm late again."

"You shouldn't call me a rabbit-whelped heathen, Māma," Tsomurejin said slyly. "You said that was disrespectful to Bàba."

Lan frowned at him. "Your father would call you the same thing. Chó Tài, give him to me. I'm going to teach him how I was disciplined when I was a child."

Chó Tài scratched his beard and then reached behind him and awkwardly nudged the boy. "You," he said. "You go."

Tsomurejin caught hold of Shàn'jūn's sleeve. The Master of Medicine patted the boy affectionately on his head. "Come, now, Jin'ér," he said gently. "Hand the ocarina to Māma. You have an important journey ahead of you."

Tsomurejin pressed his lips together. "Can't you come with me, shū'shu?"

"Shàn'jūn'shū must stay to teach," the Master of Medicine said gently. "There are so many other disciples here. We mustn't be unfair to them, right? Besides, there is much for you to learn on this journey—about the history of our land. It wasn't always like this, you know. Besides, didn't Dilaya promise to raise you as a disciple of Swords?"

"Pah—she *dreams!*" Lan exclaimed indignantly. "Jin'ér will take after me in the Art of Song."

Still, the reminder touched her. Where Lan had thought Yeshin Noro Dilaya might spurn the heir of the Mansorian clan, the Jorshen Steel clan matriarch had treated Xan Tsomurejin with nothing but stern kindness and, arguably, some gruff fondness. The clan councilwoman had even taken steps to rectify the records of history, honoring Xan Temurezen's lead in helping defeat the Elantians thirteen cycles ago—and his sacrifice thereafter.

The Mansorian clan name was a noble one to bear in this age.

"All right." Tsomurejin stepped out from behind Shàn'jūn and went over to Lan. He dipped his head and proffered the ocarina from within the sleeves of his páo. "Forgiveness, Māma. Here is your ocarina."

Lan took the instrument from him and slipped it into the silk storage pouch at her hip. "Forgiven, little ratfart devil," she said, pinching his nose. She lifted a hand at her friends. "See you in a moon. Don't miss me too much."

"We won't," Chó Tài groused. "We *won't.*"

"I will have medicinal stew brewed for you by the time you return," Shàn'jūn called cheerfully.

"Please don't," Lan muttered.

"Lots and *lots* of healing caterpillar-fungus soup. May the winds be smooth on your journey!"

Tsomurejin was silent as they walked downhill. At the bottom of the mountain, beyond the Boundary Seal, a horse and carriage from the capital city awaited them. The carriage was engraved with intertwining flowers: plum blossoms and yellow chrysanthemums and pink peonies and blush lotuses—and at Lan's personal request, snow camellias.

"Māma," Tsomurejin said quietly. He had grown somber,

with a small crease between his brows that reminded Lan, achingly, of someone else. "Each time I visit the capital and the city of Where the Flame Rises and the Stars Fall, people talk to me about Bàba. What if I can't be as good as Bàba when I grow up?"

Lan slowed and bent slightly so that she was at eye level with her son. He wore his hair short, in the style that some Hin men had kept even after the Elantians had withdrawn their forces across the Sea of Heavenly Radiance. A lock had fallen over his face.

She gently tucked it behind his ear. "Is that what you're worried about?"

Tsomurejin lowered his gaze, his eyelashes carving black crescents across his cheeks.

Lan pressed a hand to her son's cheek. "Xan Tsomurejin," she said. "Today, I will tell you the words your father once spoke to me. You must remember them."

Tsomurejin's eyes flitted up. He nodded, always eager to know more of the father he had never met.

Lan drew a steadying breath. Thought of the rainy bamboo forest where she had once lost everything and everyone she'd loved, where a boy had taken her by the hand and given her the will to live again. "He said, 'You do not only live for yourself. You live for those you have lost. You carry their legacies inside you.'"

Thirteen cycles, and the pain had become a familiar one that she carried from day to day. It was a good pain: a reminder that she had once loved deeply, one that made the golden moments in this life seem sweeter.

"Your father gave his life for this kingdom," Lan said, "so that we could choose to live as we would wish. He and I were born into a land where we had little choice." She waved a hand around, at the schoolhouses nestled in the lush mountains, at the quiet sounds of meditation and lecture drifting from within. "Once, all this was banned."

"Tài'shū taught us in History," Tsomurejin said, but his eyes were wide and as curious as a bird's.

"There was also a time," she continued, "when our history could not be taught. When you would have grown up with a different name, and you would never have known of Bàba's and Māma's clans." She touched her fingers to his chest. "So long as we live on, we carry inside us all that they destroyed. That is our triumph."

Tsomurejin looked down at her hand. A deeply pensive expression had crossed his face, and that was how Lan knew his father's words had taken root.

Gently, Tsomurejin took his mother's hands and cradled them between his own. His lips curved in a grin, but Lan could see thoughts still swirling in his dark eyes as he turned and began to continue down the stone path. "That sounds horrible. I don't know that I'd be able to endure a life without riding horses on the steppes."

Tsomurejin adored the long-haired horses on the Northern Steppes. The summers he spent there at Stars' Fall and the Palace of Eternal Peace were amongst his favorite times.

"No horses," Lan confirmed. "No sweetened fermented milk, no weaving Seals from your flute."

"Dogfart." He sighed.

"No dirty words," Lan chided, but she gave him a conspiratorial grin. "Bàba would disapprove. Now come. Let us visit the People's Capital, and then we'll be off to the Northern Steppes."

Her son brightened at this. Together, they made for the nine hundred ninety-nine steps that led down the mountain. Before them stood the age-old boulder that denoted: WHERE THE RIVERS FLOW AND THE SKIES END.

A sudden brush of wind touched her cheeks. Lan had the strange sense that someone gazed at her from behind. When she turned around, there was no one: an empty courtyard strewn with plum blossom petals. The Chamber of Waterfall Thoughts had been vacated, Seals class dismissed for the day. Yet as Lan gazed into it, another breeze swept through the mountain, stirring the pines and the flowering trees that hung low over the schoolhouse. In a corner of the chamber, one of the gauze curtains rippled, shifting shadows and sunlight. And for a moment—just a moment—Lan thought two figures appeared in the shade, bent over inkpots and scrolls and tomes. The girl shifted, horsetail brush in hand, as the boy's gentle fingers came to wrap around hers, guiding her strokes.

She blinked, and they were gone. The gauze curtains and lotus lamps flickered in the wind. A trick of the light, then.

Sòng Lián smiled. *In the next life, Zen,* she thought and, taking their son's hand, walked out into the Kingdom of Ten Thousand Flowers.

ACKNOWLEDGMENTS

The following people have braved desert demons, fought mythological monsters, taken down evil empires, and discovered the wonders of Demon Gods with me in the journey that was this series:

Krista Marino, eternally fearless and sharp and brilliant, who wielded the mighty blade That Which Cuts Slow Pacing and conjured the Seal of Next-Level Character Arcs to bring this book to the next realm of mastery in all aspects. Thank you for always guiding these stories to their best form—I could not be luckier to have found you and your wild stories about foam parties, real housewives, and trips gone wrong.

Peter Knapp, the Nameless Master of Agents, who remains one of my fiercest advocates. Thank you for always having my back, for ensuring everything works so smoothly and seamlessly, and for being one of the best partners in this business.

Lydia Gregovic, wondrous assistant editor and soon-to-be fellow disciple of the Temple of Publishing! Thank you for overseeing the Legendary Pokémon to their finale. I am so grateful for your keen editorial eye and all our chats about the work-write balance.

The Masters of Delacorte Press: Grandmaster Beverly Horowitz and Master of Publicity, Mary McCue—thank you for the wonderful leadership and support for my stories. A tremendous thank you to Colleen Fellingham and Candice Gianetti, who wield the ancient, mysterious, and infallible magic of the Copyedits; Sija Hong, for another stunningly radiant illustration; and Angela Carlino and Alison Impey, for the beautiful final cover.

Stuti Telidevara, Andrea Mai, Emily Sweet, Kathryn Toolan, and the team at Park & Fine—thank you for the support for my books over the years, and for expanding the reach of my stories across borders and oceans. I am so grateful to be working with the best in this industry.

My friends, who have supported and inspired me over the years and shown so much excitement and enthusiasm over my publishing career—just as it takes time to cultivate the arts of practitioning, it takes time to learn the truths and the depths of friendship. I remain grateful for each and every one of you in my life.

Mom and Dad Sin, Ryan, and Sherry: thank you for all the holidays together as a family, for the wonderful, sun-filled days in Redlands, Empire of Her Majesty Olive. I am the luckiest girl to have joined your wonderful family.

Clement, my person I would choose in this world and the next, and ten thousand more. I'm sorry I almost forgot to add you in here, but I guess that's true love. Please stop eating all my food if I'm going to be with you forever.

Arielle, my sister and best friend, fellow teller of tales since we were little, weird children in the Northern Capital—your love for *Song* meant the world to me. Life without you would be unimaginable, the "looks like would kill you, is a cinnamon roll" to my "looks like a cinnamon roll, would kill you," the ENFP to my ESTJ. The Brothers will continue to guard our ever-expiring empire, and Toga will continue to fold socks.

妈妈爸爸：感谢你们一直以来支持我的写作，给我讲述历史与文化，带我游玩全国各地，寻找《山海经》里的怪兽（哈哈！）。希望我们一直，一直可以一起"闯江湖"。

我亲爱的姥姥、奶奶、姥爷、爷爷：希望你们在天堂幸福安详，保佑我们平安。我非常想念你们。

ABOUT THE AUTHOR

Amélie Wen Zhao was born in Paris and grew up in Beijing, where she spent her days reenacting tales of legendary heroes, ancient kingdoms, and lost magic at her grandmother's courtyard house. She attended college in the United States and now resides in New York City, working as a finance professional by day and a fantasy author by night. In her spare time, she loves to travel and spend time with her family in China, where she's determined to walk the rivers and lakes of old just like the practitioners in her novels do. Amélie is the author of the Blood Heir trilogy—*Blood Heir*, *Red Tigress*, and *Crimson Reign*—as well as the *New York Times* bestseller *Song of Silver, Flame Like Night* and its sequel, *Dark Star Burning, Ash Falls White*.

ameliezhao.com